Quicksand: A Family Foundation

Book One

VICTORIA THOMAS

AuthorHouse™ LLC
1663 Liberty Drive
Bloomington, IN 47403
www.authorhouse.com
Phone: 1-800-839-8640

Published by AuthorHouse 03/18/2014

ISBN: 978-1-4918-3416-9 (sc)
ISBN: 978-1-4918-3415-2 (hc)
ISBN: 978-1-4918-3414-5 (e)

Library of Congress Control Number: 2013919866

With love to:

Joseph and Emma
Diana
Elizabeth and Victoria

Contents

Acknowledgments

THIS TRUE-LIFE NOVEL IS THE first of a trilogy that spans three centuries.

It is the story of the paternal side of my family. The real people in the books have lived in my heart and mind since the age of five, when my grandmother first began telling me about the family background. I was inquisitive and bombarded her with questions every time she stayed with us. I listened to her for hours on end telling tales of our heritage. The tangled web intrigued me, and I fell in love with my ancestors.

When I was an adult, I learned it was all lies. It was then I understood turbulence, instability, and flaws were deeply seeded in the family lineage.

I couldn't have written the book without the encouragement from my family on both sides of the Atlantic Ocean, especially my children, who pushed me forward when I wanted to give up.

The research my cousin Jayne Phillips did on my behalf in Wales proved invaluable. She explored graveyards, searched church and civil records, and insisted on having access to medical records that went back to the 1800s. Thank you, Jayne, for spending your time, money, and energy on my projects.

I lovingly thank my sister Diana, who helped fill in some of the gaps. When others thought I was crazy to "dig up bones," Di urged me on.

I appreciate unwavering reinforcement from Judy and Larry, who not only believed in me, but also provided their houseboat as a sanctuary where I lived and wrote for a summer.

Gary, my staunchest supporter, thank you for constant reminders that I could do this no matter how many "real-life" problems tried to derail me.

Prologue

Coming to America

I HAVE BEEN DEPRESSED AND low for days on end. Everything is such a jumble. I keep trying to make sense out of the last few years, but I can't see anything with clarity. I think the fog has lifted, and then it descends again like a gray curtain.

I am back in the school district administration building at a retirees' reception, where I am one of half a dozen honorees. It is a pretty lame excuse for a reception after twenty-two years dedicated to one district in Texas. There's a large cake in the school colors of green, white, and gold, plus the yearly punch concoction of limeade, ginger ale, and sherbet ice cream. Then like a wedding reception, there are a couple bowls of nuts and mints. We each have a corsage or boutonniere to wear, of course in the school colors. The ritual lasts from three o'clock to five o'clock in the afternoon; school district employees, board members, friends, and family drift in and out, making small talk and offering congratulations. My husband arrives a little after four o'clock; my daughter Tina is already there. I have been going from group to group. I smile at the same comments and questions. How great it will be not to have to get up, I can travel, what will I do with all my free time, and on and on.

I really don't know what I am going to do, as my whole life has been scheduled by the ringing of bells at forty-five- to fifty-minute intervals. It started at age five, when I began school, and ended on the day of retirement. No matter how tired, how sick, how hungover I was, I pulled myself out of bed because that bell was going to ring for the beginning of the day, school couldn't function without me, and I could drag through until the last bell rang at the end of the school day.

I loved school from the first day of kindergarten in Mrs. Chew's class in Ocean City, New Jersey. Most of the kids were crying, which I couldn't figure out; I was happy to be there in my little desk in its neat little row. I had even ridden the school bus that stopped at the corner by my house. The driver was a big happy man, who reminded me of Santa Claus with his bushy eyebrows and straggly gray beard and a huge grin. His name was Lukey, and he drove me back and forth from school all the way through fourth grade. Mrs. Chew later told my mother that thankfully I got all the kids to quit crying by pulling off my sock and shoe to proudly display my six toes. Well, not really six, just a birth defect that caused my baby toe to be double its size, with two nails on it. Needless to say, my classmates thought it was amazing. That was the last time I voluntarily showed off this anomaly. It became a source of dreaded embarrassment in junior high and high school. Thank God by ninth grade we had moved to a suburb of Chicago and no one knew the secret lurking in one sock and one shoe.

A child's mind oftentimes is the breeding ground for lifelong insecurities. When I was born at 6 Herbert Avenue in Risca, the attending doctor, old Dr. Hull, explained to my mother that I had a defective toe. Since the bone in the toe was like a fork in the road, I would need an operation to remove one branch with one toenail. My mother's response was simply, "Oh, if that's the only thing wrong with her, leave it alone." My mother was not in the best state of mind to make any decisions regarding what was in my best interest. She suffered extreme postpartum depression, which of course in those days was not even a diagnosable ailment. The great medical minds thought she had a nervous breakdown from a difficult delivery. So I was handed off to mother's cousin Gwen for the first few months of my life. Obviously, no extra toe removal for me.

Experts theorize a baby bonds with its mother in the early weeks and months after birth. Moms have a recognizable smell their babies are drawn to, like a moth to a candle. I was just a moth fluttering around searching for my candle. Maybe this unusual start was the beginning of the shifting foundation I endured on a subconscious level throughout my entire life until a monumental experience enabled me to grasp the real me decades later.

My earliest memory is poignant, to put it mildly. I was standing on top of a wooden railing with my father grasping me tightly around the waist. I was three years old. The railing was on the third-class deck on the Cunard Whitestar ship *Mauritania*. We had just crossed the Atlantic Ocean in rough winter seas. My mother, my two sisters, my father, and I were emigrating from Wales. I was wearing a gray wool coat with a maroon velvet collar and velvet buttons and matching leggings. Even sporting my Sunday finery, I couldn't shake the dank cold of the drizzling rain and overcast clouds. The ship was ferried into New York Harbor at Ellis Island. Through the mist and drizzle, I saw a huge carved statue of a woman holding a lamp above her head. She had some kind of crown encircling her head, which reminded me of the crown of thorns I saw on Christ's head at our church in Risca. I wondered if Christ had a sister. The whole sight was a mosaic of small watercrafts, tugs, cheering people on deck, the statue, tall buildings in the distance, and my father. I looked down at him as he clutched me tightly, somber. There was no sound, no movement, only tears streaming down his beautiful face. I couldn't read his thoughts. It troubled me to see him crying, especially since I had no idea why he cried, but I learned many years later.

Disembarking at Ellis Island was an extraordinary event. The ship was divided into three passenger classes: first-class for the wealthy, second-class for the middle class, and third-class for the poorer travelers, better known as steerage. First- and second-class left the ship before third-class; we got onto shore last. The ordeal of going through immigration and customs was grueling for a three-year-old who wanted to be home in the safety of Nannie and Grampie's house, playing in the garden, eating fresh-baked bread dripping in butter, drinking a hot cup of tea, and warming in front of the kitchen fire. The cold, bleak New York day in mid-December was uninviting and lacked promise.

My sisters appeared to feel the same gloom I was experiencing. Diana, at age twelve, was moody, haughty, and quietly disgusted by the rank body odor of the milling crowds, the slang of low-class British dialects, and the so-called physical examinations by health inspectors. She breathed a huge sigh of relief when none of the Morris family had to be deloused or whisked into quarantine for tuberculosis or other communicable diseases. Susan, on the other hand, was shaky and afraid, and clung to my mother's coattails. She was eleven years old. My mother emerged from her postpartum depression with a stronger will than when she suffered the breakdown. Anyone with an ounce of sense could see she was in command of the family, not my father. After endless hours of being prodded, directed, categorized, labeled, and finally released, we collected our three suitcases and one steamer trunk, ready to hail a cab and find our new home.

Our family of five was allowed into America with a total of one hundred dollars, which was not much money even in postwar 1950. Our New York City apartment was a small flat on Eightieth Street in Brooklyn. My father secured it when he brought Diana to the States in 1949 for a medical consultation. My dad's sister, Peggy, and her husband, John, already resided in the United States in Brooklyn. My uncle John worked for Cunard Whitestar as a merchant ship captain. He had an excellent job, allowing him to support my aunt and my cousin Rod, two years my senior, in the American dream lifestyle. But chasing the dream was not why our family came to the States.

I don't remember my sister's groundbreaking innovative surgery. Diana was born with one leg three-quarters of an inch shorter than the other. It doesn't sound like a lot, but in actuality it was painful, which made walking difficult. She had a horrible limp and her balance was impaired. In England the only solution that medical science offered was a built-up shoe, dubbed a clubfoot. This was not a very viable solution, especially when the cruelty of children was factored into the equation. She was taunted and teased unmercifully. Her problem became the brunt of jokes at school. Today this type of treatment is bullying, and it has proven to be fatal for some kids, who opt to take their own lives to escape the constant ridicule by others. The result for Diana was an inferiority complex, isolation, and cynicism. These traits affected her entire life. Back at our home in Wales, Diana's childhood was fixated on her defective leg. While the other children in the avenue ran, played hide-and-seek, skipped, and played hopscotch, she sat on the sidelines alone. And as if the torment of the day wasn't bad enough, at night she screamed in pain from enduring her crooked stance. Our parents desperately sought help from the doctors in Wales and England, but every promising lead ended up a dead end and Diana was disappointed over and over. Her despair was palpable.

Right after New Year's Day 1949, Uncle John in New York City wrote my father a letter that would change all of our lives forever. Uncle John had been researching procedures attempted in the United States to correct the affliction Diana suffered. Much to his astonishment, there was a young surgeon in New York City conducting medical experiments in his field of orthopedics. Dr. Nino had performed one operation on a girl of sixteen, but it didn't work. His procedure consisted of operating on the longer leg. He inserted six pins in the growth plate at the knee, three pins on either side of the kneecap. The objective was to stop the growth of the "good" leg, and the shorter leg would catch up as the child grew. It failed on the sixteen-year-old girl because she had finished growing. Diana at age twelve still hadn't reached her full height.

The surgery was scheduled for spring 1951. One stumbling block was the cost. My parents didn't have insurance since they were British citizens and in the United Kingdom, socialized medicine took the place of private insurance. The whole American insurance industry was a new challenge for them. At first, my father felt defeated and inadequate because he didn't have the money to pay for Di's operation. He swallowed his proverbial pride and spelled out the situation to Dr. Nino. The surgeon was so anxious to test his new technique he promised to forgo his fees and he convinced the anesthesiologist to follow suit. The barrier remaining on this side of the Atlantic was the hospital cost and care. A plan was devised through the hospital administration that created a payment schedule to reimburse all costs. The span of the loan was three years. The next roadblock was moving the family from England to America.

Leaving one's life across three thousand miles of ocean had ramifications no one could have anticipated at the time. The drastic departure from an ingrained, familiar culture to the new one adversely affected each of the five family members for life. I have always believed the only thing in common between the Brits and the Americans is the language. Everything else is very different. Adjusting to relocation to New York City depressed each of us in profoundly different ways.

Our family did not emigrate to escape religious persecution or to avoid racial intolerance or to chase the American dream. We came for one reason only, to get medical attention for Diana, period. The family could not stay in Wales, as Di needed complicated checkups every three months. Nor could my father adhere to a binding contract with the hospital if he resided in the United Kingdom. Obstacles, obstacles, not insurmountable, just completely life-changing for each one of us, but our shaky family foundation was established long before we five ever set foot on American soil.

Chapter 1

Lillian Catherine

ON JULY 8, 1894, LILLIAN Catherine was born in Newport, Wales, to Edward Albert Watkins, a steelworker, and Jayne Watkins, a housewife. There were three older siblings already occupying the tiny house on Corporation Road. Lillian wasn't the last baby either; four more arrived, each within a year of one another. Although the house was spotless, it was small and cramped. There were two bedrooms, one for her parents and the newest baby and one for the boys; the three girls slept in an alcove on the settee in the combination kitchen and parlor. From the very beginning, Lillian felt she was better than her brothers and sisters and much classier than her working-class parents. Growing up, she hated her duties of helping with the babies, washing nappies, giving baths, and feeding them bottles. She knew she was above the mundane drudgery of living on Corporation Road.

She was an avid reader and was spellbound by the books in the library. Lillian lost herself for hours engrossed in the romantic novels she read and the nonfiction books about different cities and countries outside of Newport. Jayne, her mother, had no patience when it came to her daughter's fantasies, haughty attitude, and aloof interaction with the family. In fact, she discouraged Lillian from having expectations outside her station in life. She wanted her daughter to marry, have children, and live quietly in her hometown forever. Lillian secretly tucked her aspirations away in her mind until the right opportunity presented itself, and she was certain it would.

As she grew and matured, her beauty was breathtaking. When she, her mother, and the children who were old enough went to town market, the stares from both women and men alarmed Jayne. She didn't want Lillian to realize her stunning good looks and become conceited and manipulative. It infuriated Jayne when the young boys and men who should know better whistled and made lewd remarks. Lillian acted properly indignant, but instinctively she put their actions into her private place that held her secret ambition.

Lillian's wit and charm were characteristics that mostly came naturally, but she honed all aspects of these qualities for future use. She went to school until age thirteen, did the chores she was assigned around the house, and studied all she could from the books in the library. On the outside she was beautiful, with milky skin, long brunette hair that brushed the top of her slim waist, and penetrating blue eyes that riveted anyone who talked to her. Her body was feminine and seductive. Although on her father's meager wages she could not afford fashionable clothes, she was clever enough to take old dresses from her younger sisters, cut them up, and remake them into modern attire popular in the early 1900s. What she didn't realize was she could have worn tattered rags; women would still be jealous and men would still desire her.

On the inside, there was an insecurity she fought throughout her life. Whether it was caused by poverty, fear of failure, class distinction, or something else, no one ever knew. To cover the insecurities, Lillian put on airs of upper-class royalty, but the quest for true happiness was elusive.

By 1910 at the age of 16, Lillian wanted out—out of the house, out of her lifestyle, out of her obligations and into the world. The *Star of Gwent*, the Newport newspaper, was delivered every morning to the next-door neighbors, and even though it galled Lillian to stoop to digging in their trash bin, she did it nightly to retrieve the paper and scour the classified advertisements for work. After three weeks of rummaging through disgusting trash, she found the opportunity she was seeking. The ad read:

> *Hostess needed, The Chambois Restaurant. Inquiries to J. D. Head, 15 Chepstow Road, Newport, Wales.*

Lillian was ecstatic; her opportunity for escape had arrived! The next day, she borrowed writing paper from a school chum who still attended the local school. Without her parents' knowledge, she answered the advertisement with precision and convincing sincerity. Her response stated:

> *Dear Mr. Head, I am the perfect young lady for the hostess position advertised in the Newport paper 1 November 1910. I am well-educated, excellent with people, kind, but most importantly intelligent. I have been told I have a sweet smile that makes people happy. I would appreciate an interview at your convenience. Thank you in advance for the opportunity to meet with you. Sincerely, Lillian Catherine Watkins, 28 Corporation Road, Newport, Wales.*

When Joseph Head's secretary of business affairs opened the letter from a woman in the Pill district of Newport, he almost tossed it in the trash bin, but he read it again and thought what a pretentious response. He put it on the stack of replies that poured in and promptly forgot about it. He would give Mr. Head the pile the following day when the entrepreneur had a quiet moment to review the inquiries. Certainly Jacques's employer was a busy man with all of his business holdings in the United Kingdom and abroad. He felt extremely lucky Mr. Head brought him from France to attend to his daily business procedures in England. He assisted Mr. Head by meeting with him each morning and receiving his assignments, which included setting appointments, returning correspondence, screening persons who appeared unannounced, and any other task deemed appropriate by his boss. It sometimes irked Jacques that he wasn't given more leeway in mundane decisions like hiring a hostess for the Chambois, but Joseph Head controlled his businesses and personnel with a firm grip. He would never employ anyone, whether a dishwasher, dustman, chimney sweep, chef, maître d', even prominent investors, without personally interviewing him or her. He prided himself on his knack for summing up a person's character through an interview. His intuition was almost flawless. Rarely did someone slip through who was dishonest or unreliable. If someone in his business holdings proved disloyal or inadequate, he immediately sacked him or her without discussion.

Jacques began the dreary November day with his employer performing their daily routine. Joseph occupied a plush office suite above the restaurant where he conducted his affairs for his United Kingdom businesses. The two men were served coffee and biscuits by one of the waitresses from the Chambois. She brought the morning coffee at nine o'clock sharp each weekday. If Joseph needed anything else from the restaurant, he rang a bell that echoed into the kitchen through a dumbwaiter-type contraption hidden in the wall. The first thing on the list that particular day was the vacant hostess position for the restaurant. Jacques sat across the mahogany table from Joseph with a stack of applications in front of him.

"Mr. Head, there are several very viable candidates for the position who would meet our needs nicely," Jacques stated. He continued, "I have put them in order from my best judgment, best first, least impressive last."

"All right," Joseph replied. "Hopefully we can set interviews and get the position filled. It's been tedious since Sally walked out last month when her morning sickness became evening sickness. You think at the age of twenty-five she would have been careful not to get in that predicament. Well, it's done. I am moving forward with the Chambois as first priority."

"Understood, sir." Jacques was confused. What did that statement mean? He had to move forward; was it his child? Sally wasn't married, and his employer had a reputation as a lady's man in both England and France, especially France, where he was extremely well-known. Well, he'd dig around and find out about that situation once he had a free moment. Jacques pushed the stack over to Joseph while he quietly drank his rich imported coffee and munched on an array of delicious biscuits as his employer perused the job inquiries.

Joseph was shuffling through the stack rather quickly. Several inquiries looked very promising. He set two aside. He reached the last one from a Lillian Catherine Watkins. As he read her letter, he burst out laughing.

"This Miss Watkins is very presumptuous, thanking me in advance for the interview. Well, I will interview her out of pure curiosity." Jacques was instructed to respond to Lillian Watkins and set the appointments up for the last week of November. Joseph had to make a quick trip to France to attend to a problem at the European toy manufacturer's business he and his brother Henry owned. He had a dual purpose in crossing the channel, business and pleasure. He wanted to spend time in female company. An appreciative French woman was much more enticing than a hundred British prudes. Crossing the channel was also a plus. The sea air, although cold and wet this time of year, helped him relax, which he rarely did what with his businesses and after-hours entertainment. He literally loved being in the company of women; he just didn't want to marry one. He was named after his father, and in many ways, he was like him. His father remained a bachelor well into his thirties. Joseph was thiry-two. A frown crossed Joseph's forehead; was he truly like his father?

Chapter 2

A Clandestine Meeting

JOSEPH'S PARENTS MARRIED IN 1877 in England. His father was a British officer in the navy, and his mother, Emma, was a French girl who worked as a designer in a toy manufacturing business. It was extremely unusual for a woman to hold such a position in the 1800s, but her talent outweighed general protocol of the day. She took her drawings to the company owner, and he was so impressed he offered her employment instantly. She met Joseph by a total fluke. Emma's sister, Claudine, cajoled her older sister into another night out at the local dance hall. Emma accompanied Claudine for several weeks just to get out of the house after her two-year self-imposed sequestration. Emma really didn't want to go, because she had to work the following day and she put in long hours to make sure her position was solid. But to appease Claudine, she agreed to go for a couple hours only. The girls made their way through the city and arrived at La Mansion at eight o'clock. Claudine scanned the crowd to see if she could spot George, the man who currently caught her fancy. He was chatting with some other young men close to the bar. Claudine was making her way over to the group of young men when Emma lost sight of her in the crowd.

Why did she come? She had no interest in the blaring music from an awful band, and she certainly didn't want to indulge in drinking spirits on a weeknight. She felt awkward. She didn't fit in at all. There were a few seats unoccupied on the mezzanine level; she decided to sit down, put in her two hours, tell Claudine she was leaving, and then get home. Emma sat down uncomfortably and concentrated on a couple whirling and spinning on the dance floor. Behind the dancing couple, the far door opened and a group of seamen sauntered inside. The movement distracted Emma from the young couple, and she saw the blue uniforms clustered in a group. *Oh dear God*, she thought; *now I will endure a bunch of rowdy seamen flailing around the hall.* Basically coming to the dance hall made her more miserable. When young men asked her to dance, she refused so the regulars stopped asking. Most certainly she wouldn't accept a dance request from lascivious seamen.

She sat staring at her hands and twisting her linen handkerchief around and around in her lap. Emma had this same habit with her hair at home. The crowd was increasing and the dance floor was packed with groping couples. She wanted to go home more than ever, and that's exactly what she decided to do. She walked down the balcony stairs and was squeezing a path through the crowd when she felt a light tap on her shoulder. *Thank God, Claudine.* She turned around to stare directly into the most beautiful blue eyes she had ever seen. The man looked dazzling in his dark uniform adorned with medals and ribbons. His eyes and the uniform complemented each other like they were designed distinctly for that purpose.

"Bonsoir, mademoiselle, my name is Joseph Head, pronounced heed, like heed my warning." What a stupid introduction, Joseph rebuked himself; this captivating woman is going to think I am barbaric, a seaman with no brain. I finally have an opportunity to speak to the woman I have observed the past month, and I say something ridiculous.

He smiled and Emma melted like butter on a hot day. "Bonsoir, monsieur, I didn't quite hear what you said, as the band is so loud and the crowd so noisy."

Joseph mentally breathed a sigh of relief. He bent toward the gorgeous girl and said, "Sorry, I was introducing myself, I am . . ." The pulsing of the band drowned out his words.

Emma leaned in and said loudly, "I am sorry, sir. I cannot hear you with this ruckus, and I am leaving." She took a step and Joseph cupped her elbow and began moving her toward the large doors in the front of La Mansion. Emma's heart pounded and she felt light-headed just from his touch to her elbow.

When they reached the double doors, Joseph released her elbow and pushed the doors open. Emma walked out with him slightly behind her. The night was bright, with a full moon and thousands of stars twinkling in the sky. The spring air was quite warm for a change. It was quiet. The sounds from the dance hall were muffled almost completely.

He smiled. "Now for a proper introduction, my name is Joseph Head, and yours, mademoiselle?"

Emma felt like goo was oozing out of her pores as she stared at Joseph. He was one of the most handsome men she had ever seen. She managed to get out, "Oh, monsieur, my name is Emma Bouron." *I am a complete idiot, stumbling over my words and looking totally out of place.*

Joseph smiled. Then he casually asked, "May I walk you to your carriage?"

Emma replied, "We didn't secure a carriage; my sister and I walked. Oh, no, my sister, I didn't tell her I was leaving."

Joseph laughed a deep throaty laugh that sent chills up and down Emma's spine, and then she radiated with heat.

"Let's go back inside the hall, find your sister, and tell her your plan to make your way home."

"It is so crowded; it will take me ages to find her."

"Please, Mademoiselle Bouron, I will help you. What is her name?"

"Claudine," Emma said quietly.

Once again, Joseph cupped her elbow and gently moved her back through the doors and into the bustling hall. They checked the mezzanine; no sight of Claudine. They circled the dance floor; no Claudine. They were working their way to the bar when Joseph bent down and whispered to her, "Wait right here. I have an idea."

Before Emma could respond, he was blending into the crowd. *Maybe this was a good way for him to get rid of me. How could someone like him be interested in me?* Emma had one serious relationship when she was seventeen. She fell in love with a salesman from the toy company where she still worked. They courted with a chaperone, which was proper etiquette for her age and position in French society. They became engaged after a six-month courtship, and Emma began planning their wedding. Then without warning, he left the company and left her. She had absolutely no idea why. Her low self-esteem and the self-doubt that haunted her from childhood escalated. So Joseph disappearing after their brief encounter wasn't surprising. She had observed his uniform and knew he wasn't an ordinary seaman, but an officer with officer stripes, medals, and pips on his uniform. Well, he was gone. She felt a deep disappointment. She told herself, *You are being silly, you don't even know him*, but silently she began to berate herself. The band stopped blaring, and a vaguely familiar voice boomed, "Claudine Bouron, I am informing you that your sister is going home."

Emma was stunned. She was riveted to the spot where she stood, and in an instant, the band blared from where they left off, and he was by her side.

He laughed that deep, throaty laugh, and Emma broke into laughter too. "Now she knows you are going home." His eyes bore holes right through her head and she felt that weakness again. "Come, Emma, let me escort you home." He spoke her name naturally, as if he had known her for a long time.

As Joseph and Emma walked once again to the exit, insecurity seeped into her bones. Maybe she should nip this in the bud and thank him for his kindness, then escape into the night. It was over two years since her severed love affair ended so abruptly, but the reality of it still stung. She didn't allow herself to be in the social company of men since the breakup. Being alone with a gentleman had not happened, although different men had made overtures. No one even interested her. Now as this navy officer escorted her out of the doors of the dance hall, her doubts slightly dwindled. Once through the doors, he smiled, and any shred of resistance Emma felt vanished into the starlit night.

"I will hail a carriage; just wait a moment."

"No, monsieur, I would rather walk; it's not too far and it is such a beautiful night." God, she couldn't believe she had accepted his offer to accompany her home. A quick thought flashed through her mind; she actually didn't trust herself to be in the confines of a carriage with him. Safer to walk. The lamplights were lit along the city streets. The moon and stars were bright. His intoxicating persona could be kept in check this way.

"Certainly, Emma, a walk will be welcomed after the crowded dance hall. Follow your usual path; I will enjoy walking with you." *Good*, Joseph mused; *walking will give me extra time with her and an opportunity to get to know her. I am surprised she agreed to my escorting her; she appeared aloof at La Mansion.* He knew she only recently began to frequent the dance hall, and she always sat alone. Possibly, she arranged a liaison with a young man that did not materialize tonight? Joseph was quiet as he tried to decipher why such a beautiful young woman would be sitting alone, ignoring any man who requested a dance. His questions were answered immediately, as if she read his mind.

Joseph walked so close to her their arms brushed against one another's. Just that slight touch electrified her. She needed to make conversation. "I haven't been coming to La Mansion for a couple of years except for the past month. I only went tonight because my sister begged me to accompany her. The crowds, the awful bands, the thick smoke, and the inability to converse do not appeal to me." *Oh, God, I sound like a complete bore. This will be my first and last walk with Officer Joseph Head.*

Joseph raised his left eyebrow in surprise, his questions partly answered. "Well, what a coincidence. I do not frequent the halls either for many of the same reasons. I went tonight to accompany several of my men after a particularly difficult assignment." He didn't add that previously on his visits to the hall, he was watching her. "The only bright spot was meeting you, quite a bonus." He laughed.

Emma could not believe she was strolling home with this incredibly handsome, charming man, and he thought she was the bonus. Her destroyed confidence suddenly made her anxious and uncomfortable. She didn't know what to say. She was hopeless at making hollow conversation.

Joseph noticed Emma suddenly clasping and unclasping her slender hands. Instinctively he reached out for her right hand. She was shaking. "Emma, have I said something to upset you?" Joseph didn't engage in conversation with innocent girls; consequently he was quite baffled by her reactions.

"No, no, I am unaccustomed to receiving a gentleman's compliment." Her hand in his felt like a burning coal in a fire; the shaking was involuntary. Joseph dropped her hand and put a hand on each shoulder and slowly turned her toward him. Her lack of sophistication thrilled him. He now knew this was the trait that drew him in when he spotted her at La Mansion. Yes, she was beautiful, but it was illuminated by her purity.

She slowly looked up at him, her eyes brimming with tears ready to spill onto her lovely face; he felt a ripple of protectiveness. Yes, he dallied with plenty of women, but none that he loved or wanted to protect. He rarely returned to a woman after about the third tryst. He lost interest and each was disposable. He never courted a young woman or visited her home. He was detached. Sexual fulfillment was the only motivation to keep company with a woman. At the age of 35 he was a career naval officer and confirmed bachelor. He never longed for the family life. His career required an amazing amount of traveling. Joseph inevitably volunteered for overseas duty because he had no ties to a wife and children. He was in France for a naval assignment. But looking in Emma's eyes stirred new feelings. "Emma, I know we just met, but I feel I have known you for a long time. I want to really get to know you." Would his boldness scare her away?

Emma lowered her head so she was no longer staring into those blue pools that made her heart flutter and her palms slick. She wanted to be truthful. What did she have to lose? He could walk away and she could go back to her sterile life that she guarded until tonight. "Joseph, I have had one serious suitor. I mistakenly assumed he shared my feelings and we would marry and have children. Without explanation, he left his job and me. I was devastated by the betrayal and have protected myself ever since. I have thrown myself into my career and avoided being involved with any man. I am nineteen years old and my only confidence is in my job. I am a designer for a toy manufacturer, work long hours, and dedicate myself to excellence. This endeavor takes all of my energy and has healed my heart." Emma cleared her throat.

"I cannot say the same of my self-assurance and confidence, which I didn't have in the first place. I have dissected my past relationship to find what I possibly did to cause him to break our engagement and leave his job and home." Emma paused, then continued. She looked directly into Joseph's eyes. "And until tonight I felt nothing, but you, in a very short time, brought feelings to the surface that I have buried within for a long time. I am afraid I don't have what a gentleman like you requires."

Her youthful honesty moved him. "Do you have any idea what I require?" Joseph asked softly.

"I know by your medals and ribbons you are an officer of high rank in the British Navy. I know you must choose a partner with self-confidence and finesse. I do not possess those qualities." She talked so candidly and so quickly she didn't realize his hands were still on her shoulders.

Joseph pulled her into the shadows and encircled her waist. He decided to take a huge chance. He looked deeply into her eyes, his face inches from hers. She could feel his breath on her cheeks. He caressed her lips with his fingertips. Emma trembled. Slowly, gently, he brushed her lips with his. She felt her knees go weak; her defenses were shattered. Emma put her arms around Joseph's neck, and this time he kissed her with unabashed passion. His tongue was in her mouth exploring every inch, touching his tongue with hers. She pressed her body against his with a newly ignited fervor. Joseph's body was lean and firm. Emma pressed her breasts into his chest and her nipples were hard against him. He curled his fingers around her chignon and released her hair. He caressed her face, hair, and neck. Her knees weakened more, and she felt a pulsing between her legs. Her fiancé had kissed her properly as a gentleman was expected to do until marriage, and she responded accordingly, with expected etiquette and decorum. This consuming fire sprung up without warning and it was propelling her into uncharted waters. She could feel his hardness against her; she pressed into it. Her head swam.

Joseph was having a difficult time containing himself; he wanted her so desperately. He lifted her deeper into the shadows of the alleyway, where the passage was deserted and the streetlamps didn't shine. Emma did not resist. She could not think, only feel. Joseph breathed in her ear and whispered, "You are beautiful; you have everything I want, require, and desire." He slipped his wet tongue in her ear and probed lightly. It drove Emma crazy. What was happening to her? She didn't know, she didn't care, and she wanted Joseph. Wanted him how or to do what, she didn't know.

He couldn't help himself; he drew up her dress and petticoat and put his hand between her legs over her pantaloons. No one had touched Emma there before, but she couldn't stop the pulsing, the throbbing of raw desire. Joseph kept kissing her lips and whispering in her ear. He knew she was untouched. No other man had explored her body, he was certain. Her uncontrolled desire spoke volumes. Joseph was very experienced with women, and he knew how to bring Emma to a point that would catapult her into ecstasy. He whispered again, "Emma, you feel delicious and I want you. I don't want anyone else to make you feel how you feel now. I want to be the one. Let me be the one, Emma." Joseph's lyrical words were magical.

Emma gasped as Joseph manipulated her aching body. She couldn't stop moving. Her breathing was rapid and she heard moaning in the distance, only Joseph knew it was her as she reached a crescendo. Her back arched, and she let out a long gasp as her body shook from her first real orgasm. Joseph gently kissed her softly, very softly, and told her over and over how beautiful she was and he wanted to be the man to touch her, caress her. *Damn, I must have lost touch with reality because I mean what I'm saying.*

Finally, Emma could think. Oh, God, what must Joseph think of her? She totally gave herself to him after a brief evening of being together. Joseph would never come back. He probably thought she was a whore, cheap and nasty. A woman who strolls with a man and ends up in a passageway doing God knows what with him must be a despicable person. She turned her face away as tears cascaded down her blushed cheeks. Joseph sensed her thoughts. He took her chin in his hand and turned her head toward him. She avoided his eyes, but he raised her head and looked in her eyes.

"Emma, darling, I meant what I said; I don't want anyone to have you. I know this is the first time you have experienced passion and given in to desire. Knowing I am the first makes me want you totally. When I first saw you at La Mansion, which by the way was at least four weeks ago, there was a connection I could not explain. I have been waiting for the perfect opportunity to introduce myself. If you had not agreed for me to see you home, I would have followed you. Believe me, we are connected." *Lord, the reassuring words keep tumbling out of my mouth.*

"But, Joseph, I don't know what came over me. I have never ever felt that way before. I don't understand."

"Sweet Emma, it is desire, and you acted naturally."

"But what must you think of me? We have just met and I . . ."

Joseph put his finger to her lips.

"Shush, I think you are wonderful, beautiful, and I am going to take you places you have never been. This was only the beginning. You will feel desire you have never felt; you will burn with it, and I will quench it and fulfill you." He spoke truth. He actually didn't want another man's hands on her. He stared into her glazed green eyes. Contentment stared back at him. *Dear Lord, the thought of having an unscathed woman is exhilarating.* Joseph wanted all of her.

"Joseph . . ."

"Pin your hair back up. I have made a mess of it, and I will walk you home." He laughed that deep, throaty laugh, and Emma felt a twinge of desire rekindle. She wrapped her waist-length brunette hair around her fingers and pinned it at the base of her neck. Wild curling tendrils framed her heart-shaped face. She smiled as he watched her put the pins in her hair. The dimples in her face made her appear even younger.

As they emerged from the shadows of the passageway, she felt light-headed and exhausted. Joseph put his arm around her waist possessively as they began the trek to their original destination, Emma's parents' home. The conversation was natural and authentic. They talked about Joseph's naval career, his home in England, and his assignment in France. He would be stationed in Calais for three more months. It was an easy deployment. His task was to train his men in diplomatic relations with the French naval lieutenants. Commodore Joseph Head was the commanding officer, with highest rank in the troop. He and his men worked at the British Embassy, where the training was in progress. He worked easy hours, most days, from nine to six.

His officer's lodgings were located on Rue de Lyon at the Chateau Philippe, a small but tastefully appointed hotel. His men had single rooms, whereas Joseph was housed in an entire suite, as his position warranted. Breakfast was served to him either in his suite or in the dining room, whichever he preferred. Most mornings he ate with the other British seamen to discuss the agenda for the day. When he retired to his suite in the evening, the hotel maître d' provided a bottle and snifter of brandy he placed on the table in the front parlor area; usually several varieties of cheeses and bread were on a silver plate next to the brandy. The furnishings in the parlor were magnificent pieces of French craftsmanship from the Louis XIV era. An emerald green and red brocade settee was arranged in the center of the room, with fine oak tables at each end. The heavy silver lanterns on the two tables illuminated the room. The hotel concierge made sure a roaring fire was blazing in the stone fireplace across from the settee to chase the chill of the evenings away. A woven oriental rug in muted shades of brown and beige that complemented the settee covered the floor. A small sitting table with two cozy Queen Anne chairs was positioned by the beveled windows. The room had warmth about it that appealed to Joseph's tastes. It was uncluttered, elegant.

The adjoining bedchamber was more ornate, with the centerpiece being a massive bed, headboard up against the far wall away from the windows. The duvet cover was silk, in hues of red and gold, with a matching canopy above the bed. The wardrobe spanned the length of the back wall. It was embellished with master carvings in the wood and three full-length mirrored sections. On the opposite wall were two windows that overlooked the Rue de Lyon. Directly underneath those windows, Joseph had a writing desk he used in the evenings to catch up on papers or correspondence. A crystal chandelier hung over the center of the room, and when lit, sparkled like twirling diamonds. In the left corner of the room, a wooden silk screen hid the area used for personal functions. A washstand with a decorative bowl and a pitcher of water was also behind the screen. The bath and toilet were in a separate small room. The entire sleeping area could be closed off from the parlor by French doors. It was a comfortable arrangement and conveniently located near the British Embassy. Joseph could walk from the hotel to the embassy in approximately ten minutes, or if needed, he secured the embassy carriage. He enjoyed his time in France. Battles, blood, and death were far away.

Yes, Joseph mused, his few weeks in France were relaxing and totally uncomplicated until now. This innocent gorgeous girl standing in front of him, quietly pinning her hair back in a chignon, put a chink in his armor. He barely knew her, but just minutes earlier, he was telling her they shared a predestined connection. Did her uncharted desire and abandonment urge her forward so her resistance would evaporate and he could possess her? His worldly experience was the test of her virginity. She was so young and vulnerable. He was absolutely sure she was untouched until tonight. He meant what he said; he did not want another man touching her intimately. He was determined to make love to her first. Joseph was quiet for several minutes, and Emma looked up at him awkwardly. Her hair was perfectly back in place, her gown smoothed down; only her pink glow remained from her passion. He smiled his brilliant smile and pulled her close.

Emma's confidence was vanishing with every step that brought them closer to her parents' house. Self-doubt permeated her bones, and she shivered.

Joseph looked surprised, "Are you cold, Emma?"

"Yes," she lied, "the night air has become damp. The next house with the gas lantern lit in front of the entryway is where I live."

All the other lanterns in the house were snuffed and the wicks trimmed. Emma's parents had already turned in for the night. Mr. Bouron, an investment banker, arose early, dressed, read the newspaper, and ate breakfast prepared by the cook, then walked the two miles to the bank. His days were busy and stressful, especially since he advised wealthy businessmen how to invest their capital. Mrs. Bouron also was an early riser. Her days were filled with doing volunteer charity work for those organizations endorsed by her husband's bank and assisting her two daughters in whatever they needed. The housekeeper, chambermaids, and cook oversaw all the other chores of the household. The Bourons went to bed early, so it was not unusual for the house to be dark before eleven. When Joseph and Emma reached the house, it was some minutes after eleven.

Claudine was not home, Emma's parents were asleep, and the house was dark. It was a perfect scenario to say either good night or a good-bye to Joseph.

Joseph walked Emma up the front steps without saying a word. She pulled her front door key out of her evening purse and began fumbling with the key in the lock. The lighting was so dim in the entryway she was having difficulty. Finally the key slipped into the lock, the door opened, and she was able to take several steps into the foyer. She wished this whole night could be erased. She felt ashamed and ridiculous, and then she felt his breath on the back of her neck, his hands gently on her waist. His smell was intoxicating as he turned her body to face him.

"Kiss me good night, Emma, and tomorrow, I will call properly on your parents and request that I might become further acquainted with you and enjoy your company. With their permission, of course." *Damn,* Joseph thought, *at thirty-five, I am going to begin courting.* He wanted to laugh out loud, but instead he wanted to kiss her more.

Emma wanted to release a sigh of relief, but she held her breath as his mouth came closer and closer. His lips were on hers moving slowly. She felt that weakness again in her legs and the desire raging. Joseph moved her mouth open with his lips. She responded without thinking, only feeling a natural urge to explore his mouth. He leaned his back against the foyer wall. Again she pressed her body into his and she felt the hardness. She desperately wanted to grab his hand and push it between her legs. Her breathing was rapid and hot. He knew he could bring her to a quick climax, but he wanted to make her wait. He wanted her to desire him so much that there would be no turning back. He wanted to devour her and feel her naked body all over. Joseph pulled back gently. He held her and nuzzled her neck as her breathing returned to normal. Years of practice made him able to control his desire.

"Darling, that was quite a good-night kiss," Joseph laughed, "but I have much more for you; be patient. I should be here at half past six tomorrow evening, and with any luck, your parents will allow you to dine with me in the city. Until then, beautiful Emma, sleep well."

With that, he turned, walked down the steps, and was gone. Emma's head was pounding. She could not believe what had happened to her in the course of one evening. Was she a fool or the luckiest girl alive? She quietly went up to her second-floor bedroom. She managed to get undressed down to her pantaloons and bodice, then slipped into bed. The room was dark, which made her feelings more tolerable. Emma's analytical side told her she was unrealistic to even consider that a decorated officer in the British Royal Navy would be interested in her on a permanent basis. She couldn't even keep a toy salesman, who possessed none of the worldly qualities of Joseph Head. He was sophisticated, confident, and handsome. His deep laugh was charming and alluring. Why did he pick her out of the crowd at the dance hall? Did she look available because she sat alone? Did she seem easy when she walked out with him immediately, not even knowing him? She blushed in the dark when she thought about how he aroused her in a way she never ever knew existed, and she actually submitted to her desire. She cringed. She doubted he would call on her tomorrow evening. Emma knew from the way he touched her she certainly wasn't the first. Then it hit her; Joseph must have women all over the world. This thought made her head hurt more. She covered her face with the sheet, and the tears rolled down her face.

Suddenly the door swung open and Claudine bounced in. "Emma, Emma, who was that officer who announced you were going home?" Emma pretended to be asleep, but Claudine shook her by the shoulders. Emma wiped her tears as she pulled down the sheet.

Claudine rattled on, "He was so handsome and his voice deep and so manly. Tell me, tell me!"

"Oh, he was someone I met through a friend. I was simply ready to leave and I couldn't find you. He was bold enough to make that announcement. I was taken aback and very embarrassed. Sorry if it upset you, Claudine." Emma could lie easily in the darkened room.

"Upset me? I thought it was romantic. Did you talk more? Did he bring you home? Are you going to see him again?"

"No, Claud, I am sure I won't see him again. He's probably shipping out soon."

"Emma, didn't you ask? How are you ever going to be courted if you make no effort? You are hopeless ever since that worthless salesman jumped ship on you . . . sorry the pun."

Emma yawned convincingly. "I am tired, Claudine, and I have to work tomorrow, so good night."

"Honestly, Emma, what am I going to do with you?" Claudine kissed her sister on the forehead and went to her own room.

Emma slept fitfully on and off all night. When she did sleep, dreams of Joseph swirled around her. Once, she awoke in tears, mortified at her wanton behavior. By the time she got out of bed, she was convinced she would never see Joseph again. Well, she would immerse herself in her work and will him out of her mind.

Work was Emma's refuge; developing her new toy design completely consumed her thoughts and actually made the day pass quickly. At a little after six, her employer reminded Emma it was time to stop for the day and go home. She trudged through the streets exhausted from no sleep, a wicked headache brewing as well as a miserable empty feeling.

When Emma opened the front door of her house, Claudine flew down the staircase squealing, "He came to the house, he came to the house, presented his card, and spoke to Papa."

"What, who, what are you talking about, Claudine? You're not making any sense at all."

"The officer, the officer, he was here. Oh, he's gorgeous and so polite to Mama and Papa. He smiled at me too."

At that point in Claudine's rambling, their father came into the foyer. "Emma, a word with you. Let's go into the parlor and your mother can join us." Claudine was not going to miss this; she led the way into the parlor and quietly sat down so she could hear everything about her sister's possible suitor.

Emma was baffled and unnerved. Did Joseph really come to speak to her father about courting her? The color drained from her face. Did he come to say she was lewd and acted like a paramour and no upstanding banker should allow his daughter to act in that fashion?

Her mother interrupted her thoughts, "Why my dearest, you look ill. Are you all right?"

"Yes, Mama, just a difficult day at work."

"Your father and I received an interesting visitor today." Mrs. Bouron let a sly smile creep across her face. "Actually, a British officer in the Royal Navy presented himself with his official card and requested a word with your father and me. It seems, young lady, you have not shared meeting such a proper gentleman."

Emma began to interrupt, but her mother held up her hand to stop her daughter. "He explained that a mutual friend introduced you over coffee at the toy shop. Apparently Commodore Head is quite enamored with you and respectfully requested that Papa and I allow him to call on you."

Emma fought to keep her mouth from dropping open. Joseph created a story to make it look like they were properly introduced and knew each other for a time. He must want to see me. He told the truth, kept his word. Emma was ecstatic. She smiled broadly without even realizing it.

"I can see from your expression, Emma, this prospect pleases you immensely. I haven't seen you light up like this for a very long time." Mr. Bouron was pleased. He worried about his young daughter. She had possessed little confidence since she was a small child. She was distraught after the brief engagement and then the breakup. Edgar Bouron actually contemplated she might be a spinster since she ventured out so rarely. In fact, he was quite surprised she accompanied Claudine to La Mansion Dance Hall a few times during the month and again the previous night. Usually she drowned herself in her work and left little time for pleasure. She was an enigma to her father. His daughter was very intelligent, with a career, possessed a sweet nature, but most of all she was a beauty. Men and women admired her petite frame, porcelain complexion, thick brunette hair, and sparkling green eyes. Edgar was proud of her, but didn't understand her.

At age nineteen, Emma was too old for a chaperone, but not too old for restrictions imposed by her parents since she still resided at home. Mr. Bouron knew proper etiquette and would require it. He wasn't thrilled his daughter would be courted by an Englishman, but the man was a decorated officer, with a definite position in proper society. If the courtship led to marriage, Commodore Head would be acceptable in French society. Mr. Bouron's banking clients would be impressed with such a high-ranking officer marrying the daughter of their investor. Emma's father rolled out the restrictions. "My dear, Commodore Head is welcome to call on you as long as your mama and I approve in advance. You may dine, dance, and attend the theater, opera, ballet, and other suitable outings for a young woman of your background. You may not visit his lodgings unaccompanied. You must come home at a prescribed hour depending on the social event. Of course, any display of affection in the public eye is scandalous."

Emma blushed, responding quietly, "Papa, I understand."

"Most important to me," Mr. Bouron continued, "is the answer to one question."

Emma waited.

"Do you, mon enfant, wish to have Commodore Head court you?"

By now Emma blushed crimson, and Claudine beamed at her from across the parlor. "Papa, I would very much enjoy the company of Commodore Head."

Claudine could not control herself one more minute. She jumped across the parlor, grasped her sister, whirled her around, and then laughingly hugged her tight. "I told you he was handsome and dashing."

Emma blushed deeper and smiled. If they only knew she first laid eyes on him the night before and practically gave herself to him in an alleyway, they might think twice about etiquette, society, and restrictions.

"Emma."

"Yes, Papa."

"The commodore will be here at about half past six to escort you to dinner in the town center."

Emma gawked at her father. "What?"

"Commodore Head asked permission to dine with you in the city this evening. Now that we have things settled, I imagine you would like to change dresses before he arrives." Mr. Bouron laughed with delight.

Both of Emma's parents swooshed her up the stairs. Claudine followed in close pursuit to get more details from her sister.

"Aren't you the coy one, Emma? I asked you about him last night and you were very elusive. Why didn't you tell me more details when you met him at work? You acted like you just met him at La Mansion. You didn't act interested at all when I asked you. So, dear sister, tell me everything!"

"Claudine, you know me so well. I was embarrassed to say anything about Joseph because I didn't think he was interested in me." Emma's lie was a half-truth. She was afraid he didn't want to pursue her, but she didn't mind letting Claudine think they met earlier.

"Oh, Emma, you are so beautiful and don't even know it. That rotten fiancé of yours shook your fragile confidence to the core. You were at least carefree and happy before he deserted you for no good reason. You blame yourself for some invisible flaw that caused the breakup. Don't you know he was the one flawed? He left his beautiful fiancée, his job, and his home. He did you a favor. He cannot compare to Commodore Head by any measure."

"Sweet sweet sister, you know how to make me feel better about myself, and I love you very much."

"Tonight, Emma, I expect you to tell me everything! What he said, what you said, did he hold your hand, and did he try to kiss you, everything!"

"You're impossible, Claudine." Then Emma laughed like she hadn't for a very long time.

Chapter 3

The Courtship

EMMA DRESSED CAREFULLY IN A light green silk gown that accentuated her small waist and green eyes. She pulled her hair back in a loose bun, with curling tendrils framing her face. She wore her sheerest undergarments and didn't consciously know why. Delicate lace pantaloons and matching corset fit her body perfectly. Emma didn't use much face makeup. She patted on a little pink rouge on her cheeks and shiny balm on her lips. She was beautiful, but oblivious to her looks.

Emma heard the door ringer sound, and her heart fluttered. Of course Claudine was off the settee, bouncing down the stairs to greet Commodore Head. Their voices drifted up the stairway. She heard Claudine babbling about him calling her name last night and how pleased she was to meet him. Emma smiled at her sister's apparent infatuation. Then she heard Joseph. "So nice to meet you, Mademoiselle Bouron." His power over her was poignant. Her knees felt weak, and she was light-headed. Like in a fog, she heard Papa and Joseph exchange greetings, and then Mama asked Joseph to join them in the lounge for an aperitif. She couldn't hear their footsteps on the carpet, but their voices dimmed, which meant they had moved into the lounge. Emma took a deep breath, one last look in the mirror, then started down the stairs, knowing somehow she would never be the same after this night.

Joseph smelled her coming into the Bouron's lounge before he saw her. Emma's delicate scent was unique. It wasn't heavy and pungent, like worldly women slathered on, but light and clean, accentuating her innocence. Joseph placed the aperitif glass on a mahogany table, turned, and there she was. To say she looked captivating was an understatement. Emma's gown complemented her slender frame; the silk fabric gave the illusion that she floated as she moved across the lounge to greet him.

Shyly Emma extended her hand. "Good evening, Commodore Head."

Joseph bent over, brushed his lips over her gloved hand, smiled, and said, "Bonsoir, mademoiselle. I was enjoying the company of your parents and sister. I am honored your father agreed to allow me to take you to dine in the city and then attend a comedy at the theater."

"Commodore, I entrust my daughter to you and kindly request you escort her home before midnight." Mr. Bouron felt this was reasonable for their evening. By the time the carriage delivered them to the restaurant, it would be at least half past seven. If they finished three to four courses by nine, they would make the performance at the theater. The comedy shows usually ended by eleven o'clock at the earliest, depending on the length of intermission, so his daughter should be delivered home before midnight. He smiled to himself, thinking how clever he was to calculate the time of the events of the evening. Although Emma was nineteen, she was his firstborn daughter and he was protective. True, many French young women had married and had children by Emma's age, but that did not mean caution could be thrown to the wind in her case. Proper etiquette was essential for a girl of a prominent family in Calais. The Bourons were respected citizens in society, and maintaining respectability was paramount. Edgar Bouron was comfortable with the arrangement. Commodore Head presented himself as an English gentleman following convention in courting his daughter. The medals adorning the commodore's uniform also impressed Edgar. It was obvious he fought for England bravely. His uniform was covered in medals, most notably the Distinguished Cross and the Medal of Valor, along with an array of other medals and ribbons that were unfamiliar to Edgar. With the amount of decorations the commodore had on his uniform, Edgar wondered his age. Of course such a question would be barbaric. His good looks and perfect social graces made his courtship with Emma quite appealing, and it was obvious his daughter was smitten with the gentleman. All of these thoughts flew through his head while Joseph answered him.

". . . and may I add I have the greatest regard for your daughter's safety and well-being. I give you my word she will be home by midnight."

Joseph offered Emma his arm and they departed. Once outside and tucked in the British Embassy carriage, they both burst into gales of laughter. Joseph covered their laps with the carriage blanket and then spoke first. "Your parents are such lovely people. I am not usually deceitful, but I couldn't help myself because I wanted to spend time with you."

Emma laughed. "I even have my sister fooled; I followed your lead about us meeting over coffee at the toy shop. By the way, that was quite a reasonable explanation; my parents thought it plausible, and they are difficult to deceive, my father especially."

"I honestly am sorry I lied to your parents, but I suspect if they thought we met last evening, their consent would be impossible, and I couldn't have that, now could I?" Joseph's eyes twinkled. He took Emma's hand in his. "I am consumed with the thought of you. All day when I should have concentrated on the men and their training, you seeped into my mind." He couldn't see Emma biting her lower lip.

On the contrary, her day differed; she embroiled herself into her design plan; she chased thoughts of Joseph away because she feared his opinion of her. Emma's sudden quietness perplexed him.

"Has this whole ruse turned you against me?" His voice expressed his worry. The frown furrowed his brow again, an unusual expression for him.

Emma was embarrassed to tell Joseph the truth. She twirled her hair round and round. Finally she said, "No." Her voice dropped several octaves. "I wondered if you actually would call on my father and if you thought me forward and crass after what transpired between us last night." The words tumbled over one another, which made it difficult for Joseph to understand what she was saying and he certainly did not know why she seemed ashamed. Then it hit him; he was accustomed to being blasé about women. They pursued him, he used them, and it was over; but this was totally new for him. He squeezed her hand gently.

"Dearest Emma, I am going to reveal my deepest feelings. I have never been in love, but last night changed me. I have perplexing feelings about you. The mere thought of you excites me. I want to protect you, and I am absolutely certain I never want another man's hands on you. I realize this is sudden and unexpected. We have only known each other twenty-four hours, but all of my resolve regarding being a bachelor career officer traveling the world fulfilling my oath to my country receded into the background. I have a decisive nature, and once I make my mind up, it is difficult to dissuade me. We have so much to learn about each other, but at the moment, details are not important to me. Your virtue drew me in immediately. I have never wanted anyone or anything as much as I want you."

His honesty penetrated Emma's heart. Had the love she yearned for finally arrived? It wasn't that she didn't trust him, although she had known him so briefly, but it was fear, fear of abandonment, fear of desertion, fear of that icy emptiness infiltrating her soul that held her back. Would this man be the one to complete her or break her?

"Say something, Emma. Your look says I may have spoken too soon or last night was a mere fleeting interlude I misjudged."

"Oh no, no, Joseph. It is I; I am afraid." Emma twirled a lock of her hair round and round her finger.

"Afraid of me?" He was astonished. He went too far last night; he must have injured her physically. Was he so accustomed to experienced women he treated a lady, a girl, without regard?

"No, you are perfect in every way." She took her hand from his and clasped hers together. "I am afraid you will tire of me. I am afraid I can't live up to your expectations. I am afraid in every practical way. But my heart wants to burst with joy you might eventually love me."

Her honest revelations touched him deeply. Joseph tapped on the carriage window that separated the driver from the passengers. "Monsieur, change directions please and take us to Chateau Philipe on the Rue de Leon. It is not far from here, close to the Embassy."

"Oui, Commodore, I shall have you there within ten minutes."

Emma was surprised, but didn't say anything to Joseph. He smoothed back one of the tendrils from her hair and softly kissed her cheek. He took her hand in his and kissed her gloved fingertips. She shivered.

"We will dine in my suite so we can talk privately without interruption, and I will have a chance to reassure you what I feel for you is real."

Briefly Emma thought, *there goes restriction number one from Papa; I am about to go to Joseph's lodging.* But she didn't protest; on the contrary, she wanted to be alone with him. The carriage pulled up to the front canopy of the hotel. The driver jumped from his perch, opened the door for Emma, and helped her down while Joseph opened the carriage door from the other side and got out. He looked at his timepiece; it was half past seven. "Sir, come back around about eleven, please. We will wait here under the canopy." Joseph's usual driver, Percy, was not on duty tonight, so Joseph used a French driver.

"Right, Commodore, I will be prompt."

Joseph cupped Emma's elbow as he had the night before, which seemed ages ago to her. He led her to the door of the hotel. He twisted the brass doorknob and pushed the heavy door inward, and before she could have second thoughts, they were inside and going up the staircase. A girl would enter his private suite; a woman would depart.

Emma twirled the tendrils of her hair, her nervous habit since childhood. She walked around his parlor commenting on the furniture, the carpet, and the bright fire, anything to cover her anticipation.

The concierge lit a warm fire and the maître d' had left the brandy and snifter on the table. Joseph retrieved another snifter from a small sideboard. He poured two glasses of brandy and handed a glass to Emma. He watched her take a small sip of the golden liquid. He wanted to laugh when she swallowed the strong liqueur. Brandy is a rich strong drink he doubted Emma had tasted before. Proper French ladies sipped champagne or wine; they never indulged in drinking strong liquor, at least not in public. Such behavior breached the etiquette embedded in ladies of culture. He kept quiet as she took another sip. "Come and sit by me on the settee. Shall I order a meal for us? I did invite you to dinner after all." He laughed that deep throaty laugh.

Her back stiffened involuntarily.

"I'm not hungry at the moment, are you?" *That was an understatement*, Emma thought.

"My hunger has nothing to do with food." He laughed again, then reached for her. He took the glass from her hand, placed it on the table next to his, and with the other hand pulled off her gloves. Joseph kissed her fingertips lightly. The light-headed feeling was already upon her. He leaned into her and kissed her in a way to instantly arouse her. Just like the night before, she didn't resist him. Joseph knew tonight he would take her into a place that would seal them together, and he wanted it. He wanted her, all of her.

As he kissed her tenderly, his one hand loosened her hair, and with the other he caressed her breast on top of the material of her gown. Emma felt the pulsing sensation between her legs. Joseph adeptly lifted her from the settee like she was a feather, never stopping kissing her mouth, ears, and neck. He took her into the bedchamber and laid her on the bed. She was flushed. The glow from the fire in the parlor made it appear she was bathed in moonlight. Joseph took off his uniform jacket, then his shirt; he was naked from the waist up. Emma had never seen a naked man in the flesh; of course, she had seen paintings and sculptures. Joseph's shoulders were broad and his upper body muscular; it reminded her of the chiseled sculptures at the art museum. He lay next to her on the bed, turned her head to face him, and kissed her with a passion even greater than the night before, when she willingly yielded to his touch. He maneuvered his body so his bare chest touched her breasts. Slowly he unbuttoned the bodice of her gown and took it off; then he unlaced her corset, pulled it off, and lifted her chemise over her head. They were both nude from the waist up. He wrapped his arms around her and pressed her into his bare chest. He caressed her breasts. Emma's body betrayed her. The fire in her brazenly pushed her to move against him. Her breath came rapidly. Joseph needed to pull back. He slowed down, kissing her tenderly. He whispered, "You are beautiful, your body is perfect, it feels luscious." Emma pushed against him hard. He reached down, threw off her evening slippers, pulled down her undergarments, then stroked her calves and thighs. He moved down and licked her nipples until they throbbed.

Emma wanted him so badly at that moment she couldn't have cared less about being a lady. Quickly, Joseph pulled off her undergarments. He whispered in her ear, "Give yourself to me, Emma; don't hold back." He felt her, kissed her mouth, and moved his hand up and down where she needed it most.

Emma panted and her hands were all over his body. Emboldened by the heat of her passion, she felt Joseph's hardness and rubbed it even though he still wore his trousers. "Joseph, Joseph, I can't stop; I don't want you to stop."

"Don't stop, darling; your body needs mine. Trust me, let go, let go."

Then like the crest of a wave crashing onshore, she exploded and the pleasure was uncontrollable. Emma was satiated. She lay still on the down pillow, her heart pounding.

Joseph was only getting started.

He whispered in her ear, "You are everything I want, darling Emma. Your passion floods me with desire. When I see you flushed and glowing, your beauty is unmatched." He flicked his tongue in and out of her ear. She was still but her breathing was uneven, and Joseph knew how to make her want him all over again. He lightly brushed his tongue over her nipples and stroked her back. She was lying facing him on the bed, and in this position he could work his magic to get her aroused. He wove his hand in her long damp brunette hair; he pulled her face close to him and covered her mouth with his. When his kiss probed, she began to feel a fluttering of desire. Emma couldn't think properly. How could she want him again? Hadn't he just taken her to completion? But his body was next to her, and the feel of him made her head swim. Joseph turned her on her back and kissed her neck, her breasts, her lips, and her stomach. She was beginning to squirm under his touch. He wanted to ravish her naked body; he wanted inside her.

"Emma, baby, I want to touch your magnificent body like you have never imagined. Trust me, love; let me make love to you completely." He kept whispering and touching and kissing. Emma felt the desire rise up higher. She closed her eyes and breathed in his manly scent; it was intoxicating. Joseph kissed her stomach. She felt him going lower and lower. How was she supposed to know if this were right or wrong when it felt so right? Before she could think about anything else, he was kissing her thighs. She was moving and her hands were entangled in his hair. Then she felt an unbelievable erotic sensation. "Joseph," she moaned, "it feels so good, but is it wrong?"

"Nothing we do is wrong because our feelings are right." He unbuttoned his trousers and pulled them off. Emma wasn't sure what to do, but her instincts told her to touch him. Joseph showed her how to pleasure him. Then he stopped her hands and moved down again. He let his tongue make every nerve ending tingle. She tasted sweet and salty and wet. She was ready. He slowly, carefully penetrated her virginity. He went easy. He didn't want to hurt her, but her appetite for him overrode the brief sharp pain she experienced. She pulled him in deeper and their rhythm synchronized. Joseph was breathing hard. Did this innocent girl know what to expect? He hesitated.

"Don't stop, Joseph, don't stop." Her next words were muffled as she buried her lips in his neck. He thrust in and out. The sensation drove Emma further into the whirlpool of desire. With total abandonment she erupted, and while she was lost in the explosion, Joseph lurched and pushed hard inside her. He shuddered over and over until there was nothing left in his body.

Emma was overwhelmed with a feeling of total oneness. She had never felt so close to another human being. They lay still. She was smiling up at him with the innocence of a child. Her gorgeous body glistened with beads of sweat from both of them. Joseph thought she was the most sensual woman he had ever seen. He held her in his arms and waited until her breathing slowed. He stroked her hair with a tenderness she didn't know existed. Her sigh affirmed her contentment.

Joseph had had sex with many women all over the world, but he wasn't emotionally attached. Their race, color, or creed was insignificant. He fulfilled a physical need. Always the gentleman, he treated the women he bedded with kindness, but not true affection, only lust. His conquests were older than Emma and much more experienced. They gave into him because they hoped to land a husband and youth faded rapidly. He didn't make false promises; charm and good looks got him the results wanted. Often he shipped out without as much as a good-bye. He was married to the sea and his beloved country; permanency with a woman was foreign to him. Yet an innocent young girl mesmerized him. The hunger he felt for her was something new. She drifted off to sleep. Joseph studied her face. Complete relaxation. He noticed she wore no face powder or rouge. She didn't need it, as her face bore no blemishes or marks, and her cheeks were pink from her passion. When she smiled, dimples accentuated her pretty face. He wished this moment could last forever. He owned her virginity and the power was irrevocable. Emma stirred slightly, then bolted upright on the bed.

"What time is it? If I am late, my father will never let me see you again." Panic crept into her voice. Joseph was so accustomed to leaving a woman in her bed before night's end, the time had not fazed him until now.

Calmly he got up and retrieved his pocket watch out of his uniform jacket. He walked into the parlor where the lanterns were still burning and looked at his watch. He chuckled. "My dear, we are in luck; it is half past ten, plenty of time to sort ourselves out, get to the carriage, and deliver you home before midnight."

Emma was so relieved. Suddenly she noticed her nakedness. She quickly drew her knees up to her chest and wrapped her arms around her legs to cover herself. Joseph was amused; it endeared her to him more.

How was he going to explain what he meant by sort themselves out? He would bet a thousand francs she had no idea what had just happened to her. Losing one's virginity left telltale signs, plus he had filled her up. The ridiculous custom of mothers not discussing sex with their daughters was the norm for eons. He doubted Mrs. Bouron had broached the subject with Emma. In a way, Joseph was aroused by the idea that in a few minutes, he would explain the results of human lovemaking. The time ticked away; he'd better wade in.

"Darling." He looked so serious Emma was puzzled. "Let me see, how should I start? . . . When a man and a woman make love, as we did, a man releases . . ." He paced, his voice trailing off. Oh, dear Lord, was he making any sense? He took another stab at it. "You have part of me still inside of you, and what goes up must come down, law of gravity." She looked totally confused. His explanation sounded ridiculous. He must continue; she couldn't go home in her present state.

"I am going to heat some water over the parlor fire, then pour it in the bowl behind the screen. You will find soap, a washing cloth, and a drying towel on the stand. There is not enough time to draw a proper bath. Once you have washed, get dressed, and I will see you home." Joseph was sweating profusely. Did he say it right; did she understand?

"I see." Her voice was a whisper. "Should I stand up now?"

Her complete lack of worldly experience and the conversation aroused him. "No, no, let me get the water first." He forced himself to pull on his trousers and heat the water. Once heated, he poured the warm water in the bowl. "It's ready, darling."

Emma stood up gingerly and walked behind the silk screen. She washed her most private parts carefully. She heard Joseph dressing. When she finished, she wrapped the towel around her body, then walked from behind the screen and back into the bedchamber. He looked even more handsome in his naval uniform because she knew what was beneath it. After this night, she possessed intimate knowledge of him, using his body to take her to unimaginable heights. Joseph's sexual expertise reduced her to begging for more.

She gathered her clothes, which were strewn all over the room, got dressed, found her slippers, put them on, then went into the parlor. Joseph sat on the settee sipping the forgotten brandy. She picked up her hairpins from the side table and redressed her hair in a loose bun. Emma felt his eyes watching her every move; it thrilled her.

"Do you know; you look absolutely radiant?" Joseph smiled broadly.

Emma didn't know how to act coy; the truth came spilling out. "You say that because you had your way with me." She laughed. "Do you really think so?"

Her total honesty brought a contented smile to his face. "Emma, lovemaking becomes you, and although I thought it impossible, you look more gorgeous than before. And unless you want me to pick you up and lay you back on the bed, we better meet the carriage, or I will have broken all your father's rules." Her musical laughter filled the room.

When the couple got to the canopy, the carriage had already arrived. The driver smiled and inquired if they enjoyed their dinner. "Delicious," remarked Commodore Head. Once they were inside and the doors were closed, they smiled at each other with the nuances of conspirators in a secret plot.

Emma and Joseph chatted easily as the carriage traveled through the city. She lounged in his arms drinking in his smell, his touch. At that very moment, she was sure she loved everything about him.

His voice interrupted these thoughts; she looked into his eyes. "As I was saying, Mademoiselle Bouron, I will place a chaste kiss on your cheek to safeguard us from starting something we can't finish." His eyes twinkled and his smile broadened. "Tonight, it will have to suffice as a good-night kiss."

Emma laughed, thinking about their good-night kiss last night in the darkness of the foyer. "Fine, Commodore, that will be quite acceptable."

The carriage pulled up to the walkway and stopped. Joseph leaned over to kiss her cheek; Emma swiveled around and her lips met his. She laughed, opened her mouth over his, and their tongues found each other; he halfheartedly tried to pull away, but she kissed him deeper.

"If I don't stop now, I will be tearing your clothes off right here in front of your father's house. I am going to open this carriage door, get out, and walk you to the front door." Joseph smiled and looked at her sideways. "Why, I think I have made you a wanton girl who knows what she wants."

They both laughed. As it was the night before, the outside gas lantern was lit, but the interior of the house was dark. Her parents were most probably asleep as was their usual habit, but she bet Claudine was awake waiting to hear the details of Emma's evening.

As propriety dictated and the nosy driver watched, Joseph bowed, kissed her gloved hand, and bid her good night. Emma turned toward the entryway, but the deep need for verification of Joseph's love caused her to whirl around and call him back. "Commodore, a word, please?"

"Yes, mademoiselle?"

"I have not discussed with you our meeting tomorrow regarding the manufacturing business." Emma said this loud enough for the driver's ears, but not loud enough to awaken her parents.

"Well, mademoiselle, let us look at time slots of availability for tomorrow."

"Sir, I have my appointment book in the drawer of the sideboard in the foyer. Let's plan a definite time agreeable to both our schedules." Joseph turned to the house; of course, the driver was listening to every word. Joseph walked back to the entryway and signaled the driver to wait while he checked his schedule with Emma's.

When Joseph reached the entry to the foyer of the home, Emma pulled him inside, where neither the driver nor anyone could see them. She pulled him into the shadows and whispered, "Joseph, kiss me now. I am already yours by shedding my blood upon you."

Joseph was startled but exhilarated that she wanted him so much.

He drew her to him. "My darling," he whispered, "I want to kiss you over and over."

"Joseph, I have never wanted anything or anybody as much as I want you."

Joseph's desire was sparked by her bold move. He pulled Emma next to him in the shadows of the foyer and kissed her with deep passion.

Her response at first was hungry, but then suddenly she pulled away.

Joseph read consternation in her lovely face instead of total peace. "Emma, what is it? I made sure no one heard us. Is that what worries you, darling?"

"No." Her head hung so low her chin practically touched her chest.

He had absolutely no idea why this look of dread had popped up. "What is it, Emma? Did I hurt you? Do you regret our lovemaking?"

Joseph was baffled by her reaction.

Quietly, Emma spoke. "I know women are supposed to be coy and not direct, but I must know."

"Know what, my beautiful girl?" Joseph was confused.

"How will you not judge me? I acted like a loose woman. Do you make love with other women in the foreign places you travel?"

Her sincerity endeared her more to Joseph. He revealed his feelings to ease her uncertainty. "No, I don't have a slew of women all over the globe. Emma Bouron, I have never made love to another woman like I have with you. I do not want another man to touch you, to know your secret places, what brings you to the heights of pleasure, to kiss your sweet lips; I want to be the only man you desire and love. I have had dalliances with women over the years. I am a thirty-five-year-old healthy man so that is very natural, but I never pursued a woman, went to her home, met a female's parents on a formal basis, or followed any of the social parameters of courtship." He smiled sweetly, his handsome face alight with truth and honesty. "I want you and only you in every way. We will need to work out the logistics of our courtship, many intricacies, but all of that will unfold in time. Right now, spending as much time as possible together is most important." Joseph winked.

"Now I am going to turn and walk out the foyer door, down the pathway, and into the cab before I take you in my arms again."

Emma's laughter showed she was reassured and happy.

Joseph bent down, kissed her on the cheek, and cupped her face. "Sweet dreams of all the things I did with you tonight and the pleasures that consumed you."

Emma watched from the window in the door as Joseph made his way to the cab. She heard him say to the cabbie, "Sorry it took so much time, but working out a woman's schedule is a daunting task!"

Emma muffled her laughter; Joseph had protected her reputation. She climbed the stairs carefully so as not to disturb her parents or wake her sister. As she passed Claudine's open door, she was startled when Claudine called her name.

"Shush, Claudine; you will awaken the entire household. What are you doing up anyway?"

"Oh sister, I heard some strange noises coming from the foyer. I thought possibly an intruder wandered inside." Claudine's attempt at sarcasm was lost on Emma.

Emma blushed and smoothed her hair. "No, nothing that exciting. Commodore Head accompanied me inside the foyer so that I could retrieve my appointment book. We were selecting a mutually compatible time to meet tomorrow." Claudine giggled, but before she asked any more questions, Emma said good night and headed for her room.

She undressed quickly, used the cold water in the pitcher to wash, slipped on a white lace nightdress, and slid into bed. Her entire body was exhausted, but her mind raced with thoughts of their lovemaking, the way he hypnotically crooned in her ear and neck. How easily he aroused desires that had laid dormant her whole life. In the past, she overheard her mother's friends talk of enduring their "duty," bemoaning how they must endure to procreate children. Emma pondered the fact she was different from those women as this was no duty; it was pure love, joy, and lust. She blushed in the dark when she thought how she begged for more. She thought about how Joseph moved in ways that made her writhe uncontrollably. She revisited the moments when her body burst into thousands of quivering nerve endings, with Joseph smiling and kissing and loving and touching her everywhere. Emma remembered exactly the look on Joseph's face when together they reached a synchronized climax. This new love was the most tantalizing experience of her life. She knew without a second thought she loved Joseph Head. Emma could not picture Joseph with anyone but her; even the thought made her ill. How could it be possible her entire life had changed in a matter of two days? She knew secrets about her body that both shocked and thrilled her. She thought she loved her fiancé, but she had been infatuated with the idea of a wedding, a home, and a family.

The pattern of girls in her station in life was predestined by rules of proper etiquette. She threw out every bit of her etiquette training the moment Joseph kissed her. She didn't care because her desire blotted out the confines of proper behavior. Emma was shocked by her actions, but not shocked enough to act properly. She couldn't wait to be with Joseph again, to feel his body, to explore her newfound sexuality. Fleetingly she thought about her staunch Catholic upbringing. She studied the Bible in her catechism classes and at school. The church taught that fornication and adultery were sins, but Emma also loved the Canticles, the Songs of Solomon, that were love poems about a maiden and her lover and how the maiden lost her virginity to her lover. It was pure and unblemished, totally innocent. Oh, it was all very confusing. Tonight she wanted to dwell on love, not sin. She snuggled under the duvet and fell into a satisfied, deep sleep.

Usually Emma was awake early, anticipating a day full of creating her toy designs, but this morning Claudine was shaking her. "Emma, you must have had a good time with the commodore last night. Look at the time."

Emma saw the sunlight streaming through her bedroom windows. "Oh, Claud, I have overslept."

"No kidding." Claudine laughed.

"It's not funny. I mustn't be late to work; those sharks would love to ease me out of my position with the company."

"You better dress quickly. You have no time for breakfast, but if you are lucky enough to flag a carriage, you should make it on time."

Emma threw on her chemise, pantaloons, and a green muslin day dress, smoothed her hair back into a loose bun, shoved on her shoes, grabbed her briefcase, and ran down the stairs.

Her mother was choosing some greeting cards from the foyer sideboard when Emma burst through the door. "Why dearest, I see you are running late. You must have enjoyed your evening immensely."

"Mother, I have no time to chat about last night. I will be late for my job."

"Dearest, I think you will arrive at the toy factory with time to spare." Mrs. Bouron smiled slyly.

Emma waved her off and pulled open the front door. To her complete astonishment, the Embassy carriage was pulled up directly in front of her walkway. Her mouth dropped and she stared. Her mother was behind her in the doorway. "Go along, Emma. Obviously a very kind suitor is making sure you are not late to work. Now do not tarry, or his kind gesture will be for naught."

Emma quickly made her way to the carriage.

"Morning, mademoiselle." The driver smiled. "The commodore instructed me to take you to your destination as promptly as possible." He jumped down from the driver's bench, opened the door for her, and helped her inside. She hadn't said a word. She smiled weakly, still in shock. "I know the directions, miss; the commodore gave them to me earlier."

Emma slid across the seat to the opposite window. She settled back, trying to take in how perceptive Joseph had been about her time issues. Then she spotted it. In the corner of the carriage seat was an envelope. In beautiful script it merely read, "Emma." She grabbed it and broke the seal.

She felt the blush rising from her neck to her cheeks as she read his message.

> *Darling Emma, I thought my personal carriage would be useful this morning to transport you to work since there is a possibility your legs are quite weak from last night, Joseph.*

Her thoughts raced. Was this a kindness or was he mocking her enthusiastic lovemaking? She didn't know which way to think; he said all the right things and reassured her so much that she gave herself completely. Oh, when she thought about the way she pushed herself into him, it made her cringe. She felt her face go crimson. She urged him to take her over and over. Last night was perfect, but in the light of day, she questioned her boldness, her desire. Her insecurities wrapped themselves around her like tentacles. How could she ever face him again, or would she? Did he have her virginity and would he now discard her? Could she even get through work today with these nagging thoughts plaguing her soul?

The driver interrupted her anguished thoughts. "Mademoiselle Bouron, we are here."

Emma hadn't even heard him open the door.

The British naval petty officer thought the lovely young woman looked ashen. He wondered if Commodore Head sent him to fetch her because she suffered some type of malady. It was unusual for young women to take a carriage on a lovely spring morning. As he helped her from the carriage, she appeared totally different from the girl he had picked up from her home. As she stepped down, she did not make eye contact with Percy, Joseph's personal driver. "Is everything all right, miss?" She merely nodded. She was twisting the envelope tucked in her dress pocket. Its message was a dagger in her heart.

Percy was totally confused by her as he watched her walk up the pathway to the entrance of the toy factory. He turned to leave, then remembered. "Ah, mademoiselle, the Commodore asked me to pick you up at six o'clock this evening to take you home. He will return at 7:00 to fetch you for an evening at the Calais Art Gallery for a showing of Monet's works and then a late supper. He will clear it with Monsieur Bouron first. If this is not acceptable to the lady, he will completely understand."

Her relief was palpable. She smiled that captivating smile. "Oui, monsieur, please tell Commodore Head I will be ready by seven o'clock." Emma was ecstatic. Her lithe walk confirmed her approval of the evening plans.

Women were too fickle for Percy's liking; one minute the girl was sulking, and now she was beaming. Moody, that's what they were. Needless to say this was why he and his superior had never married. Getting satisfaction was one thing; making a commitment was something else entirely. He wondered what Commodore Head's interest was in this French beauty. Percy shrugged his shoulders and got back on the carriage driver's bench.

The day dragged for Emma. She took the note out over and over, sometimes blushing, other times frowning. What to make of it she wasn't sure. The only thing she was sure of was that she would see Joseph that night. The anticipation was grueling. Promptly at six o'clock the carriage pulled up to her business. Emma was out the door in a second. Percy noticed she was quite happy. Must have had a good day at work. He didn't equate her happiness with seeing Joseph; that was too complicated for him to ponder.

When Emma got home, her father awaited her arrival in the lounge. Jenny, the girls' personal maid and Emma's closest confidante since childhood, met her at the foyer door. "Mademoiselle Bouron, your father wishes to speak to you in the lounge." She only spoke formally to the girls when in earshot of others. Usually her tone was motherly.

"Certainly, Jenny." Inside her mind, Emma was praying her father was not going to deny her the evening with Joseph.

"Good evening, Father." Emma walked over to her father and kissed him on the cheek. She smiled sweetly, silently praying he would allow the evening out.

"Dearest," Edgar began, "Commodore Head sent over an invitation for you to accompany him to the Monet showing and dinner following."

"Oui, Papa."

"Emma, this courtship is moving quickly in such a very short time. I do not want to see you get hurt again as happened in the past; although I believe Commodore Head to be a man of honor and integrity. Are you comfortable with this pace, child?"

"I am, Papa, with your approval, of course. Commodore Head is a gentleman, kind and considerate. I am getting to know him at a slower pace at these gatherings," Emma lied. She was getting to know him carnally at breakneck speed, but she didn't care; she wanted to be with him constantly.

"All right then, I give my consent." Edgar saw the worried frown lines disappear from his daughter's lovely brow. She must be very enamored with the Englishman.

"Thank you, Papa. I look forward to viewing the renowned paintings of Monet and enjoying dinner with some of the commodore's contemporaries."

"Go, mon amie, he will be arriving soon."

Emma turned and walked casually out of the lounge. Once out of her father's sight, she bounded up the stairs to dress. Thankfully Claudine was out with friends for an early supper, so her prying questions could be avoided. Emma searched her wardrobe; her indecisiveness was maddening, but finally she chose a silver dress with lace appliqués and matching silver slippers. It took her so long to pick out a gown that she only had fifteen minutes to dress. She had Jenny fill her bowl with hot lavender water. With such little time, Emma bathed quickly and Jenny helped her dress. Jenny also pinned Emma's hair into a French twist, which gave her a sophisticated air for the art gallery showing. A fragile multicolored dragonfly comb adorned the twist and held it securely in place. Of course, there was no taming the tendrils scattered around her face and neck. She was flushed with the thought of seeing Joseph.

Jenny smiled. "Oh, Emma, you look like a beautiful angel. I don't know what it is, but your face is glowing. I can hardly believe I was away collecting fabrics and yarn for your mother when a new suitor entered your life." Jenny smirked.

"Why, thank you, Jenny, I hope the gentleman feels the same." A blush covered her neck and face. Jenny had been with the Bouron family as long as Emma could remember. She was Emma's confidante and friend and she loved her. It was Jenny who comforted her when her fiancé left her, and it was Jenny who nursed her to health after the devastating humiliation. The maid knew Emma thought she was in love with her fiancé, but her reactions to him were absolutely diminished compared to her reactions to the commodore.

"My sweet, the carriage is back!"

"Do I look all right?" Emma's confidence continuously wavered.

"Yes, you are so beautiful he won't be able to concentrate on paintings!"

"Jenny, you are prejudiced!"

"Oh dearest, he is coming up the walkway. He looks so handsome." Jenny winked.

Emma glimpsed out of her window and smiled knowing how he looked without the uniform. She shivered.

Jenny inquired, "Do you require a night wrap?"

"Please, Jenny, the pink light wool will be perfect for the cool spring evening."

The wrap draped across her bare shoulders made Emma look even more alluring. "Well, off I go, Jenny. Wish me luck with the gentleman." They hugged, and Emma floated out of her bedroom and down the stairs.

Jenny thought to herself, *there is something so different about Emma; I just can't put my finger on it. Maybe she is falling for the British officer, which wouldn't be difficult with his good looks and winning smile. It could be what some people call love at first sight, as she certainly hadn't known the man well except for a few days.*

Joseph chatted with Emma's parents just inside the foyer door. He declined the offer of a drink this evening as the gallery exhibit was starting promptly at seven thirty. Just seeing him, Emma felt her stomach drop and her knees weaken.

"Good evening, Mademoiselle Bouron." He bowed and kissed the top of her bare hand. She didn't wear gloves this evening, as the dress needed no accessories. His lips were warm, but she involuntarily shivered again.

"Is that wrap warm enough?" Mrs. Bouron saw the slight shiver. A mother's eyes don't miss much.

"Yes, Mama, I am fine."

She turned back to Joseph. "Bonsoir, Monsieur, it is so kind of you to invite me to the art exhibit and dinner. I am a great fan of the arts, and I am anxious to actually see some of Monet's works."

"It is my honor you have agreed to accompany me." Joseph smiled broadly.

"You two better be off if you plan to be prompt." Edgar was a stickler for punctuality.

"Quite right, Monsieur Bouron." They shook hands and Joseph bowed to Mrs. Bouron. As was his custom, he cupped Emma's elbow and led her through the foyer to the exterior front door and down the steps. Joseph was enraptured by her appearance from head to toe; she was perfect. He knew this insecure girl with the looks of an angel was what he lacked his whole life. He thought his career, investments, frivolous flirtations, and sexual conquests were fulfilling until he met Emma. She was an aphrodisiac; he couldn't get enough. What made her even more intriguing was her pure innocence and her trust in the way she gave herself to him. They barely got into the carriage and away from the curb before he pulled her to him and kissed her eyelids, cheeks, neck, and finally her voluptuous lips. He wanted her immediately, and her response made it almost impossible for him to resist taking her. With his mouth covering hers, she opened her lips and kissed him deeply. It was exactly the way he taught her. She tasted sweet, and her scent of light lavender filled his nostrils. He pulled back. "Darling

Emma, I have wanted to kiss you all day." He whispered in her ear, "You taste wonderful and smell luscious."

She arched her back from his hot breath and reassuring words. She willed herself to remember, *I am dressed for the art gallery and dining, not grabbing his hands and putting them all over me. Control, control. Pull away.*

Emma reluctantly pushed Joseph away. With any other woman, Joseph would have yanked up her dress and taken her in the carriage. He was accustomed to having his sexual needs met when he wanted, where he wanted.

He was breathing hard. "Do you know I have no interest in going to the gallery or dining out? My mind is filled with making love to you until there is nothing left but ultimate satisfaction."

She pulled away again, but her back was still arched with her unabashed desire for him. "Do you know, Joseph, when I got your note I thought at first that you were mocking me and did not want me." Emma openly voiced her concerns.

"But," Joseph was so surprised, "I was teasing; it was our private joke."

Emma put her finger to his lips. "When your driver said he would be back at six and we were to go out, a sense of relief flooded me. You have crept into every inch of my body and mind."

"Emma, I wouldn't hurt you like that at all."

"I know, Joseph, I can feel it." She smiled a coy smile he hadn't seen before; he frowned. "Let's make an appearance at the exhibit, mingle with your colleagues briefly; I will feign a headache and then we'll go to your quarters." Joseph smiled and laughed his throaty laugh that made her want him. With that said, she kissed him with hot, unquenched passion.

Joseph knew he possessed Emma completely; it was a feeling of wholeness. He took her innocence, he took her virginity, and he taught her how to satisfy lust and passion. He drank in her beauty, knowing he could never let another man touch her. This feeling was brand-new. This oneness was overpowering.

"Lovemaking becomes you. Emma, you are still radiant from last night." She was so content and happy she kissed his lips again.

Within moments the carriage stopped and Percy was opening the door. Joseph winked at her, got out of the carriage, took her hand, and helped her out. She looked stunning. The glow on her face made Joseph catch his breath. He whispered, "Emma, you will be the dream of every man in the gallery and the envy of every woman. I have never seen a more lovely girl in my life, and my darling, you belong to me."

His words filled her heart with pure joy. He thought she was beautiful, and he said she was his! She couldn't help her desire for him. Simply, she couldn't get enough. It was like he unleashed some creature dwelling in her that needed fulfillment in every way. They had done things together she never heard spoken about. The thought of him aroused her. Emma wondered if she were normal. Did other women feel this way but not discuss it? What a mystery! Her urges rushed in without warning. Sometimes when she pushed herself into Joseph, she just could not help it. The sense of urgency obliterated her knowledge of right and wrong. The Bible said she was wrong; French societal mores said she was wrong; her father's rules said she was wrong. But Emma's heart and body said she was right.

Emma's thoughts were so deep she was oblivious to her surroundings. They were walking down a pillared colonnade. Joseph turned and whispered to her, "Emma, come back to this world; we must greet people."

"Oh, Joseph, I am so sorry; I was deep in thought."

"I can only hope with the look of rapture on your face it was about me!"

She blushed. "Yes, it was all about you and me."

"Darling, get your mind off our later plans, and meet some of my colleagues and friends."

Emma laughed and then smiled a wicked smile at Joseph. "Why I was thinking about no such thing, and I would enjoy meeting your friends." This time she winked at him.

All eyes were on Commodore Head and the lovely girl gliding down the colonnade, her arm linked with his. It was common knowledge in Calais that Joseph was a dashing naval officer, but not interested in settling down and getting married. Several of the women in town tried to entice him into a liaison but to no avail. One young widow in particular, Cassandra Ballou, had lost her husband to the summer sickness, the plague, and pursued Joseph constantly for the past year. He was polite and kind to her at society functions, but had no interest in a relationship. At one point she misunderstood his kindness as interest. When she blatantly threw herself at him and tried to kiss him, he rebuffed her advances. Her pride was crushed, as many attendees at a British Embassy function saw her brash flirtations and the commodore's reaction. She hadn't spoken to him since. He dismissed her childish ways.

Joseph spotted the British Ambassador sipping a brandy in the main gallery. Protocol dictated Joseph approach the diplomat for small talk and an introduction. Joseph cupped Emma's elbow and guided her toward the ambassador. "Good evening, sir, it is a pleasure to see you. I would like to introduce you to my guest, Mademoiselle Emma Bouron."

Emma put out her dainty hand for him to kiss. "Bonsoir, Monsieur Ambassador, it is an honor to meet you." Emma's smile and sincerity took Jonathan Cookson quite aback. *My Lord*, he mused, *she is perfection, French perfection. I wonder where Joseph met her.* She was not an ordinary girl; she had good breeding from her aura.

At that moment Jonathan's plump wife waddled up to the threesome. "Why good evening, Joseph, and where have you been hiding this captivating young lady?" Sally Cookson was good-natured and nosy, but sweet and kind.

"Sally Cookson, the lovely wife of Ambassador Cookson, I would like you to meet Emma Bouron." Joseph beamed.

As was customary, Emma curtsied to Mrs. Cookson. "Bonsoir, madame." She smiled radiantly.

"So, Joseph, how did you meet Miss Bouron?" Sally didn't hold back when she wanted to know something; she simply asked!

Emma took the lead. "Madame Cookson, I am a designer for a French toy manufacturer, the Toy Depot, at the Calais office and plant.

A mutual friend of mine and Joseph's introduced us over coffee some time ago."

Other eyes in the room were on the two couples conversing, but mainly all eyes were on the young girl on the commodore's arm. The handsome naval officer never attended a function with a female guest before. If he brought someone, usually it was another officer visiting France. The women in the room speculated the girl was French; the men didn't care—they were intrigued by her startling good looks.

"Yes, Sally, my good fortune, my friend has an interest in the toy business. He and Mademoiselle Bouron were having a coffee; since I was conducting business in that part of town, I stopped to visit." Joseph assumed he would be barraged with more questions; consequently, he decided to put out the information he chose and the rest could be left to speculation. "An added bonus for me in getting to know Emma is her father, Edgar Bouron, a French investment banker. We have mutual friends in France and England." Emma quietly gazed at Joseph and smiled as he rolled out the fabrication. He looked down at her lovingly. It was easy to see for anyone watching—and most all were—Commodore Head and the girl were more than friends. Their faces told the story.

"Now, if you will excuse us, I promised Mademoiselle Bouron for quite some time that I would learn more about French impressionism from her, and this Monet collection is the perfect opportunity." Joseph cupped Emma's elbow to steer her to the exhibit.

Before they moved away from the ambassador and his wife, Emma displayed correct French etiquette; again she gave her hand to Ambassador Cookson and curtsied to Sally. "Adieu, it was lovely meeting you both." Then she turned and Joseph steered her away.

By the time the couple reached an isolated area of the exhibits, the main salon buzzed with speculation regarding Joseph and Emma. They were finally alone and couldn't contain themselves any longer; they both burst into gales of laughter. "Emma, everyone drooled with envy when they saw you walk through the door on my arm."

"No, Joseph, it was pure curiosity, but some of the women look saddened we are together, the eligible bachelor in the company of a French wanton woman." Emma laughed.

Joseph encircled her waist with his arms and whispered in her ear, "Why darling, what would they say if they knew there was nothing under your gown and petticoat?" Emma roared with laughter.

"Just what makes you think that, sir?" Emma laughed again.

"My secret." Joseph twirled her around and around until she was giddy. "You are a naughty girl, Mademoiselle Bouron." Their laughter filled the small anteroom.

Cassandra couldn't hear what they were saying, but from where she was spying, she saw a couple in love. Her jealousy consumed her whole body. She felt cheated. She knew Joseph first, and he was interested in her. The whole kissing incident was overblown and a mistake. If she just had more time to seduce him, she would be on his arm, not this French girl. They started walking toward her hiding place so she held her breath and crouched in the alcove. They were so engrossed in one another they didn't see her.

Joseph and Emma chatted easily with other officers and their wives or guests. It was a successful evening for their first public appearance together. At nine o'clock, dinner was announced. Since the show was hosted by the ambassador and his wife, it was to them Joseph and Emma excused themselves. Brilliantly Emma explained that normally she would love to stay and enjoy the dinner and the company, but unfortunately she had an early morning meeting at work with two of the investors. The host and hostess embraced her explanation and told Joseph to please make plans as a foursome for dinner and the theater. He promised. Emma floated through the room saying good-bye and expressing her disappointment in having to depart. After they were gone, they were the topic of conversation at every table.

When the pair reached the end of the colonnade, Joseph signaled to Percy to bring the carriage around.

"Not staying for the dinner, sir?"

"Actually, Mademoiselle Bouron has a headache, and the boisterous party made her feel worse. We will dine in the quiet of Chateau Philipe. Thank you, Percy."

Once inside the solitude of the carriage, Emma poked Joseph in his side and said, "I think my story of early work was quite plausible." She giggled. "But do you think Percy believes the headache excuse?"

"It doesn't matter whether he believes it or not; he works for me, actually is a dear friend, and is very loyal. He would never speak of you coming to the hotel quarters. Now, mademoiselle, since our escape, I have not had one kiss."

Emma laughed, "Monsieur, do you require, need, or want a kiss?"

"Yes, mademoiselle, I believe I do." They both laughed and reached for one another. Percy had left the carriage lantern burning, but it was very dim and the night was now black, not a star in the sky; they were shrouded in a cloak of darkness. Emma put her hands around the back of Joseph's neck and pulled him to her; she covered his mouth and their tongues intertwined. Joseph pulled back. "Wait until we get to my quarters. You can wait, can't you, darling?" He chuckled.

She looked out of the carriage window. "Joseph, we are almost there." She sucked in a deep breath in anticipation.

Once at Chateau Philippe in Joseph's quarters, the chef was summoned to cook sea bass and make a Greek salad and fromage tray. Anticipating bringing Emma to his quarters, Joseph asked the maître d' to have chilled champagne delivered to his suite. Dinner ordered, Joseph poured each of them a glass of champagne. They sat on the settee and sipped the cold bubbly wine. Joseph was curious; Emma was reflective and immersed in deep thought. "Emma, what are you thinking about?" He knew she was completely forthright, so he was confident he would get an honest answer.

"I enjoyed myself so much at the gallery. Your friends and fellow officers were warm and welcoming. Do you think I fit in with them?"

"Of course." Joseph didn't know what to make of Emma's question.

"Do you think they liked me?"

"Absolutely, they were dazzled by your beauty and charm." Now Joseph was getting worried.

"Joseph, I would never do anything to jeopardize your career or embarrass you."

"Emma, what in the world brought this on?"

The tears streamed down her face. "I don't know; I want to be what is best for you."

Joseph recognized her insecurities forging their way to the surface. "Sit next to me, darling"

Emma moved close to Joseph.

"You must know how spectacular you looked tonight, and your etiquette was flawless." He wiped the tears from her cheeks and took her hand. "I was proud to be your escort. I was the envy of every gentleman there."

The waiter knocked on the door. Joseph rose to let him in.

"Bonsoir, monsieur and mademoiselle."

"Bonsoir, garcon."

The young man placed the tray on the table, Joseph tipped him two francs, and he left.

"Come, Emma, you will feel better once you have something to eat." They both sat at the Queen Anne table. Joseph served the fish and salad. Although Emma was miserable, she was still hungry. They ate in silence, and Joseph could not understand the shift in Emma's demeanor. Did someone say something unkind? He couldn't fathom such a thing. They finished the fish and the salad, then moved back to the settee to enjoy the cheese plate and another flute of champagne. Emma rarely drank spirits, and even with the food, she could feel the third glass of champagne. She nibbled on a piece of cheese. Joseph couldn't stand being iced out one minute longer.

"Emma, I don't understand what I have done to make you so unhappy. Whatever it was, I apologize for being inconsiderate."

She blanched; the tears filled her eyes again. "Joseph, I don't want to fail you in any way." She sighed. "I don't know what I did to cause Richard to break the engagement and walk away from his employment, but I must have done something." The pain covered her face.

Joseph knelt in front of her. "Darling, the man was young and immature; he did not understand you are a jewel. I will work to rebuild your confidence, and I will assure you every day of your importance to me. Emma, don't you already know how I feel?" Joseph smiled tenderly. He could see her heart was breaking for nonexistent inadequacies.

"I think so . . ." she stuttered. "You know me inside and out."

"Emma, our courtship has been a whirlwind, and if I moved too quickly I am sorry, but I have never felt this way before, and I certainly never wanted to possess any other woman. Look in my eyes; you know I am telling the truth. I am not an immature boy who gets involved in an engagement before thinking it through. I am a thirty-five-year-old man who has traveled the world and knows what I want and what I don't want. I want you." Joseph kissed her lips tenderly, then picked her up and laid her on the bed. "Sweetheart, I am in love with you." He kissed her again. "I have never said those words to another woman."

This time Emma's tears sprung from her overwhelming joy. Joseph loved her! She was important to him! How could she have doubted his feelings? The way he made love to her, denied his own satisfaction to pleasure her. He had been with her constantly since their first meeting. Yes, their courtship was a whirlwind, but she knew from the first minute he touched her elbow and whispered in her ear, she loved him. The way his laugh thrilled her and sent shivers up and down her spine. Their first kiss sealed her fate and she knew. Why did these insecurities torture her? Joseph was so right. Richard was an immature boy, not a worldly man. He never kissed her passionately. A chaste peck on the cheek was all he stole from her, and she never had that weak feeling in her knees or stomach. She never longed for Richard; she merely accepted his boyish good looks and felt special when he proposed to her. Joseph's voice brought her reverie back to the present.

"Darling, I will be by your side and in your life forever." Joseph meant every word. His father taught him and his brother that honesty equaled freedom. People who told spiteful, hurtful lies were trapped. He had fallen for this girl, so why shouldn't he be truthful and tell her? It was evident she had a self-confidence issue. Why not bolster her confidence with his declaration of love? She was young, but not immature. She didn't play coy little games. For God's sake, he didn't think she even knew how.

"I love you, Joseph, with all my soul, body, and mind." Emma pulled him next to her and kissed his lips with a tenderness born of pure love. She wanted to show him her love and devotion in every way. She started slow, kissing Joseph softly, with her hands holding his handsome face. She looked into his endless blue eyes, the eyes that entranced her the moment she saw him. Joseph softly kissed her back, then slowly Emma moved in close to his body and kissed him with passion and desire. Emma sat up, pulled off every article of clothing, removed the comb from her hair and shook it free. She stretched across the bed like a purebred cat. Joseph watched her every move. She was absolutely gorgeous, and he loved her like he never believed possible. He yanked off his dress shirt, threw his shoes across the room, and pulled off his trousers. Emma opened her arms and Joseph embraced her nude body. In the hours that followed, there was not one inch of Emma's body he did not explore. He showed her how to pleasure him in every way. Once he satisfied her until she was weak and trembling, he heated the water, poured it in the washbasin, and slowly washed and dried her body. He brought her cheese, bread, and wine in bed so she had the strength to get dressed. All the while he told her how he loved her, how he cherished her, and how much he wanted her forever. He whispered the most erotic and sensual words in her ear when arousing her, and the most tender, loving words when bringing her back to normal.

Emma didn't think she had ever been so spent, yet so fulfilled. She and Joseph walked hand in hand to the carriage. Percy was prompt as usual, but he glanced at Joseph and Miss Emma knowingly. He could read from their expressions that they had indulged in more than dinner. The couple was oblivious to what Percy did and did not know. Emma's dress still gave the illusion she was floating.

Percy thought what a lucky bloke the commodore was to snatch such a lovely French woman. In all the years the two men had been close friends, he never witnessed Joseph enamored with a woman. Joseph used women for sex, but there was no one special, not even in England when he first got his stripes from naval officer training and young women his age were participating in the cotillion circuit. Joseph's parents were wealthy aristocratic landowners with a place in upper society. They waited and waited for Joseph to marry and produce grandchildren, but eventually gave up.

Joseph walked Emma to the entryway to her home and stopped. He whispered as he bowed over her hand, "My Emma, I love you and am yours as you are mine." Then with swift precision he declared loudly, "Mademoiselle, tonight was a lovely evening. I am so very glad you enjoyed the Monets, but I am sorry you have a headache." He knew Percy was straining to hear their conversation.

"Thank you, monsieur, for attending to my needs." She winked at Joseph. "My dreadful headache is so much better since we were away from the noise and enjoyed a lovely dinner."

"Mademoiselle, it was my pleasure. I know you are working very hard, but I would like for you to accompany me to the Ambassador's Annual Ball Saturday night. I realize this is short notice, but I extend the invitation in hopes you will make quick arrangements to accompany me."

Under her breath Emma whispered, "Joseph, how in two days' notice will I have the appropriate gown, accessories, and jewels to honor your station?" Emma was ready to throw up from the thought of being announced with the type of dignitaries who would be attending.

"My darling, you could wear a sackcloth and every man would desire you, but you are mine."

"Joseph, you know I would do anything for you, anything in my life, but I want to make you proud of me and I do not think I have a gown befitting of your position and the evening. Go alone, love; I won't feel upset at all."

"Emma, my love, you will be ready on Saturday evening at eight o'clock when I will fetch you for the ball."

"Joseph, I don't . . ." and before she could finish her sentence, his mouth was covering hers in butterfly kisses. Her mouth involuntarily opened to his kiss. "Joseph . . ."

He stifled her fears with kisses and whisperings of love, not passionate, but reassuring and loving. "Emma, you will be the prettiest woman at the ball. Trust me."

She trusted him, but his breath and kisses made her want him again. It was crazy! The way he aroused her was unexplainable; was it her life of void and confusion? Was it lack of open affection? Was it abandonment of commitment? She could not fathom the answer, but at that moment, she wanted Joseph with her whole being.

She beckoned him to enter the foyer of her home.

"Darling, I must go."

"No, Joseph, just a few minutes, please."

Joseph sauntered down the walkway. "Percy, give me a few moments, please."

"No worries; I will be right here." Percy had his own thoughts as to why the commodore needed more time, but it was none of his business. By the time he finished his conjectures, Joseph was at the end of the walkway out of sight.

Joseph stepped into the foyer where Emma waited. She looked so small and fragile. He no sooner stepped into the foyer than she grabbed his coat lapels. "Joseph, I want to be the perfect woman for you in your circle of colleagues and dignitaries. What must I do?"

"Come here. Look into my eyes; you see my love for you, that's all we need." She was so vulnerable, so innocent, and so perfect for his world.

"Joseph, come to my room. My parents' quarters are totally away from Claudine's and mine. They would never hear us, and you could leave by the back passageway by the servants' quarters."

"What about Claudine?" Joseph asked. Emma continued to mystify him. They made love over and over, but she always wanted more. The thought was thrilling.

"She sleeps like the dead." Emma giggled.

Before he had a chance to resist, Emma was leading him up the stairs. They passed Claudine's room and it was quiet. Emma suppressed a laugh as she pulled Joseph into her pristine bedchamber. She closed the door quietly behind them and locked it. As his eyes became accustomed to the darkness of her room, he could see it was decorated in a way that portrayed just how young she really was. The curtains were white batiste lace, and the duvet matched them. There were framed sketches of ballerinas on the walls. Her carpet appeared to be pink flowers; it was too dark to see the exact pattern. There were figurines on her bureau, but he couldn't see exactly what they were. This was a young girl's room that reflected innocence, or because of him, former innocence.

"Joseph, what is it?" Emma whispered.

He turned her body to his. "I was just thinking what a charming room you have. It reminds me of your youth and innocence."

"Why, Commodore Head, haven't you been in a lady's bedchamber before?" Emma laughed into his shoulder.

"No, mademoiselle, never a lady's." He winked and smiled. "Since I am in a true lady's chamber, I want to experience making love to my lady." He pulled her body close. She tugged and pulled at her clothes until they lay in a heap at her feet. Emma pushed Joseph onto her chaste bed and took off every piece of his clothing. She manipulated the shaft of his penis, first with her hand, then her mouth. Joseph groaned and tried to pull away, but Emma sucked harder. "God, Emma, you've got to stop." Sweet agony laced his voice. It made her more determined, and she sucked with a fervent urgency. Joseph got completely lost. Devoid of thoughts other than the sensations consuming his body, he came in a rush, filling her mouth. Emma kissed his stomach, his chest, then his lips.

"Emma, Emma, your lovemaking is the most sensual I have ever had, ever."

"My darling, you bring out a part of me that I didn't know existed. Every part of you feels so natural to me, like we were always meant to be. I don't know, Joseph, how I am consumed by you and want every part of you, but I am."

He loved her total honesty. Her openness about her feelings, her body, her desires, made him love her more. There were no silly games played as in most courtships he had observed throughout his life. Emma was an open book to him. It made him crave her, not just making love, but in their conversations and in their easy companionship.

"Emma, tonight is not over. The darkness is a friend that allows us to be together. We have been satisfied in one way, but I want to fulfill you by another." They smiled at each other. She lay on top of him. He looked in her eyes. Her eyes were ink black with the feverish need for him. He was an expert lover and he worked her body into a burning inferno. He moved in a circular motion that ignited a throbbing need; her mind was gone, only emotions leading the way. Suddenly she let out a scream and released her passion. He felt her insides quivering, so he thrust in harder and harder until he gave her every ounce left in his body. They both lay there panting and gasping.

In the servants' quarters, Jenny abruptly awakened. She had heard Emma scream. *Oh dear God, what evil has befallen the child?* Jenny grabbed her robe from the hook on the back of her door, threw it on, and jumped into the narrow hallway. She ran from the servants' quarters down the hall to Emma's door. She turned the handle, but the door was locked. That was unusual, Jenny thought. In a low voice she called her name, "Emma, Emma, are you all right? I heard you scream."

Emma and Joseph froze. Emma gathered her thoughts quickly. "Yes, Jenny, I must have had a bad dream." *Oh dear Lord, what if I've awakened my parents?* Emma was in a panic; Joseph squeezed her hand.

"Why is your door locked?" Jenny questioned.

"Claudine has pestered me every evening when I come home from an outing with Commodore Head, and tonight I was too tired to bother with her nosy questions. I have a very busy schedule tomorrow, so I locked the door. So good night, Jenny; sorry I alarmed you." Emma and Joseph did not move.

Jenny frowned and thought it odd and unlike Emma not to get up and unlock the bedchamber door for her. She stood there for a moment, heard nothing more, then headed back down the hallway. Emma and Joseph could hear her shuffling along. Emma crawled out of bed and put her ear to the door. She strained to hear the servants' door close. What seemed like eons passed, but finally she heard the creaking of the door as it was opened and closed. Emma tiptoed back to bed.

"Darling, I feel like a schoolboy caught with his hand in the chocolate tin!"

"Joseph, don't joke; that could have been a disaster."

"Mademoiselle, if you insist on fulfilling your wanton lust, you must pay the price." Joseph covered his mouth with the pillow so his throaty laugh would be squelched.

"You, sir, are impossible." Emma pinched his arm lightly.

"Ouch! Is that the payment I get for taking you to paradise tonight?"

Now Emma grabbed the pillow so her laugh would not be heard.

"Seriously, my love, I better get dressed and sneak down the back staircase before a real disaster happens. I am sure Mr. Bouron would ban me from seeing you again if he found me naked in your bedchamber in the middle of the night." Joseph tickled her side.

"Oh God in heaven, Joseph, that would be the end of us. He would chain me to the house and report you to the ambassador."

"Before such a fate befalls us, I am going." Joseph finished dressing. He combed through his hair with his fingers, bent down and gave Emma a light kiss on the lips, and lifted her to a standing position. "Sweet dreams, my love. I better hurry; the dawn is beginning to break. Tell me my escape route."

"Go down the hallway past the servants' quarters, and you will see a door that opens onto an exterior stairway. It is the private entrance and exit for our servants. The door won't be locked, and you should have little trouble leaving."

Joseph whispered, "Are we in a scene from a Shakespearean play?" Emma pinched his arm.

She quietly opened her bedroom door and looked up and down the hallway; it was deserted, as she expected. She took Joseph's hand and pointed the way. He stealthily slipped down the hallway, found the unlocked door, stepped outside on the landing, and began his descent. His carriage was parked only a few steps away, around the house.

Jenny spent a few minutes trying to get back to sleep since the incident with Emma, but she was unable to settle back down. Dawn would break soon, so she got up and fixed a cup of tea. She sat by the window watching the sunrise. Jenny almost dropped her cup and saucer when she saw a figure descending the stairway. Her shock stifled a yell or call; she was speechless. Jenny knew it was a man from his size, clothing, and the way he carried himself. Her mouth dropped open when the man turned down the path; it was Commodore Head! Dear God, what was Emma doing? If anyone found out about her indiscretion, her reputation would be stained forever and she would be an outcast. How did this happen? Emma was trained in proper etiquette and social graces. It was outrageous a man was with her all night. Then Jenny shuddered; did Emma have an intimate liaison with the man? Dear Lord, that was unthinkable. She would be shunned by French society and her parents would suffer disgrace. Jenny felt a cold chill in her bones that if Emma were found out, Jenny could be dismissed because such behavior would surely affect Mr. Bouron's position at the bank. His wealthy clients with their better-than-thou mentality wouldn't do business with a man whose daughter was a slut. Jenny would be discreet, and carefully plan the way she would broach this subject with Emma. She wouldn't let Emma know her discovery until the opportune time presented itself. *Lord, the girl must be mad! The commodore obviously lost his mind to risk staying in Emma's bedchamber all night.*

From the moment Joseph left her room, Emma fell into a contented deep sleep. She was exhausted and satisfied. The combination was like a sleeping powder. She didn't sleep long; there was a sharp knock on her bedroom door. "Emma Bouron, unlock this door." Emma groaned; *Claudine.* She got out of bed, unlocked the door, and stared at her sister.

"What is it?"

"It is time to get ready for work for your information, and why in the world is your door locked?" Claudine demanded an answer.

"Nothing mysterious, Claud, I just needed a good night's sleep and didn't want to gossip last night." Emma put her arm around Claudine's waist. "Don't pout, sister, I will tell you about my whole wonderful excursion when I get home from work this evening." Emma smiled and Claudine thawed.

"All right, Emma, but I want to know everything."

Emma lovingly pushed her out of her bedroom. "Go on, I must get dressed for my day." Claudine was appeased, and once she was out of the room, Emma sighed with relief. She and Joseph had gotten away with their stolen rendezvous. She blushed when she thought of their lovemaking and her unbridled passion. Emma stuck her head out of the door and called for Jenny.

Jenny reluctantly started toward Emma's room. She hoped her face would not belie her secret knowledge. "Good morning, dearest. Did you fall back to sleep after your nightmare?"

"Yes, Jenny. I am so sorry I awakened you for naught. Forgive me." Emma looked totally innocent.

"Of course, it was not your fault. One doesn't have control of dreams." *My*, Jenny thought, *she's become an adroit liar in a very short time.*

"Will you draw me a quick bath, please, while I choose a day suit for work?"

Jenny smiled and turned toward the bathroom.

Emma scrubbed her body quickly, dressed in a light two-piece taffeta suit, and had Jenny pin her hair in a loose chignon. She leaned over and kissed Jenny on the cheek, "Thank you for always helping me."

Her feet almost missed each stair. She skipped into the parlor, hugged her mother, and bounced out the front door. Once again, as it was the day before, the Embassy carriage waited for her to alight. Emma blushed. "Bonjour, Percy."

"Good morning, mademoiselle. I have been instructed by the commodore to take you to work and fetch you at six o'clock."

"Why, sir, that is very kind of him." Emma blushed.

Percy saw her face glowed; after all, he was parked outside all night and made his own assumptions. He had barely delivered Commodore Head to Chateau Philipe and then was told to return to the Bourons'. He had never seen Joseph so buoyant nor had he previously offered such kindnesses to a woman. Percy helped Emma into the carriage, closed the door, and started on their way to the Toy Depot, her place of employment.

The envelope was peeking out of the opposite seat the same as yesterday, and the flowing script again read one word, "Emma." She tore it open.

> *I hope you slept well, mademoiselle. I will pick you up at eight o'clock Friday night for the Annual British Ambassador's Ball. I look forward to another evening together. I have meetings with Ambassador Cookson the next two nights that will keep me away from you. I don't know how I will cope." Even his note made Emma's heart race. It was signed, "Yours, Joseph."*

Frowning, she mentally pictured each evening gown in her wardrobe. She owned nothing suitable for such a prestigious affair. She told Joseph to go alone. Why didn't he listen? She brooded the rest of the way to work. The days that normally flew by were now at a crawl. Finally six o'clock arrived. Percy was waiting. She was quiet and sullen when he helped her into the carriage. He wondered if work was particularly difficult. The glow was definitely gone from her face.

The next two days crawled by; each hour seemed longer than the last. She mulled over what she could wear to the ball. She had tried on every evening gown in her wardrobe. She felt inadequate and dowdy in every one. Her misery was compounded by Joseph's military duties keeping him away.

She dragged herself home at six on Friday. When Emma opened the door to the foyer, a large box was sitting atop the bureau. It was beautifully wrapped in gold paper and tied with a crimson satin ribbon. Her heart lurched; a white embossed card with her name was on top of the package.

Claudine must have heard her open the entryway door; she burst into the foyer. "Emma, Emma, Mama said this gorgeous package was delivered today from a famous designer in Paris." Emma stared from the glittering box to her sister and back again. "Open it inside the house; we are all dying to see what's inside."

Still quite stunned, Emma picked up the box and followed Claudine into the lounge. Her mother and father were enjoying a glass of chardonnay.

Smiling weakly, Emma placed the box on the table. "Papa, may I open it?"

"Of course, child. Let's see what the gentleman sent you from Paris."

Emma's hands were shaking as she untied the satin ribbon and lifted the gold box lid. Wrapped in tissue paper was a stunning gold evening gown of the finest silk, with matching gold dance slippers.

The card inside the box read, *"Dear Mademoiselle Bouron, I will be honored if you wear this gown to the ambassador's ball this evening, with your father's permission. I hope you do not think me too presumptuous in choosing a gown for the occasion."* Signed, *"Yours, Commodore Joseph Head."* The color drained from her face as she handed the card to her father.

Edgar read the card, lifted his eyebrows, and said, "My dearest daughter, you have obviously made a great impression on the gentleman, and his generosity speaks volumes of the way he regards you. Do you want to accept the gift?"

Looking from under her long black lashes she quietly said, "I am very flattered and want to wear the gown and slippers to the ball with your permission." Edgar knew his daughter and saw she was both delighted and embarrassed by Joseph's generosity. Claudine, on the other hand, was twirling in circles babbling on about how much Joseph must be in love with her to have such a glamorous dress designed for her sister. Their mother shushed her.

"Take the gown out of the box, Emma, and let's have a look." Marie smiled approvingly at Emma.

A courier delivered the package earlier in the day. The gown was exquisite. The silk was of the best quality. The style was high fashion directly from Paris, 150 kilometers south of Calais. The bodice was cut with a décolletage, but not too revealing. It was fitted, and crimson threads shot through the gold silk vertically to accent Emma's tiny waist. The corset was built into the dress, something none of the women had seen before. The skirt of the gown was full to the floor. No under hoop was in the box, which meant the gown had a more flowing effect. The gold slippers fit perfectly, and each shoe had a crimson bow adorning the top of the slipper.

Claudine was jumping up and down. "Try it on, try it on," she urged, her excitement bubbling over.

Emma summoned Jenny to help her try the gown on. They stepped into Mrs. Bouron's dressing room to check the fit. Jenny gasped; it looked like Emma had attended a personal fitting. It was breathtaking. "Oh, Emma, it is the most exquisite gown I have ever seen, and it was made for you. The color, the fabric, the style are all superb." Then Jenny's mind confirmed what she already suspected: Commodore Head knew Emma's body very well to have such a perfect fit designed. The thought was truly unsettling. Emma gazed in the looking glass. She was not conceited—actually the opposite—but she thought the dress gave her a sophisticated, worldly air she liked very much.

"Jenny, help me out of the gown, please."

"Ma chérie, aren't you going to let your mother and sister have a look?"

"No, I will tell them it is an adequate fit, but I want to be fully ready when they see me wearing it." Emma giggled. "Oh, Jenny, I think he's made a wonderful choice." She blushed and her eyes sparkled.

"Yes, yes, it so becomes you." Emma thought Jenny sounded a little sarcastic in the way she remarked, but she shrugged her shoulders and let it go. They stepped out of the dressing room and back into the lounge.

Claudine squealed, "Oh no, it wasn't a fit. Can we take it in or out, or what was the problem?"

"In fact, dearest sister, it fit very nicely, but I want to be fully ready with my hair groomed before Mama, Papa, and you see me." Emma's eyes twinkled; she knew her sister would be outrageously impatient.

"Emma Bouron, that is not fair. Why, none of us have had a gown commissioned specifically for us. You could have at least given us a preview." Claudine sulked.

"Now, now, Claudine, be understanding, your sister wants to be complete before we see her in the lovely gown. I agree with her. Off you go, Emma. Have Jenny assist you in getting ready for the evening." Mrs. Bouron smiled broadly at her daughter. She loved both the girls very much, but she knew Emma had suffered rejection and humiliation at the hands of her ex-fiancé, Richard. Well, good riddance, he could not compare to the dashing British commodore. A well-to-do man of the world with disarming good looks and manners was much more appropriate for her Emma. A boorish schoolboy could not compete. Mrs. Bouron silently prayed Commodore Head's intentions were honorable and for a lifetime. A mother's instinct told her Emma's psyche could not stand another betrayal. The British gentleman must be smitten with her daughter. It wasn't every day a man had a gown designed for a woman and at what an expense! It must have cost a fortune.

Emma washed her hair first so that it would have time to dry, and then she stepped into lavender bathwater. She bathed carefully; the water was hot and soaking felt so good after her last two miserable days. Jenny wrapped her in a towel when she got out of the bath. Emma carefully chose her most expensive pair of pantaloons, and she did not wear a chemise since the gold and crimson gown had the built-in corset. She laughed: what an ingenious idea, so less cumbersome than a separate lace-up. Emma instructed Jenny to heat her curling rod in the embers of the fire. It was important to her that her hair complemented her face and the golden gown. Jenny had been attending to Emma's hair since she was a little girl, so she was skilled at coiffing it. Tonight Emma did not want a chignon, twist, or bun; she explained to Jenny she would like it in soft loose curls with the tendrils around her face. Jenny retrieved the iron from the fire and curled Emma's hair section by section.

When Emma looked in the mirror, an idea dawned on her. "Jenny, please get the satin ribbon that tied the box."

Jenny looked puzzled, but took the ribbon out of the box.

"Now, can you weave it through my hair just behind my ears? Leave the curls around my face."

"Ah, Emma, what a wonderful idea." Jenny carefully wove the ribbon through Emma's hair, then tied it underneath at the nape of her neck. Her hair reached almost to her waist and glistened against the dress. Then she carefully applied a shiny gloss to Emma's lips. It was the only makeup she applied. Jenny stepped back to look at the child she helped raise, and in her place saw an exquisite woman. She drew in her breath. "You look absolutely exquisite. There will not be a woman at the ball who even comes close to matching your elegance." Jenny's eyes filled with tears.

Emma kissed Jenny's cheek. "You are prejudiced." She laughed. She put on the slippers and was ready for the evening. It didn't seem possible she was wearing a designer gown and going to a ball with the man she loved. How fate totally turned her world around in one week! It seemed like she had always been part of Joseph. He calmed her fears of insecurity and inadequacy. She felt loved and desired. The feeling was completely satisfying. Jenny snapped her out of her reverie.

"Come, Emma, I know your mama and papa are anxious to see you, and by now Claudine has probably driven them insane!" Jenny opened the bedchamber door, and they stepped into the hallway together.

Jenny ran down the stairs in front of Emma and bounded into the lounge. "Monsieur and madame, I proudly present Mademoiselle Emma Bouron." She bowed like an announcer.

Edgar stared at his daughter as she entered the room. His thoughts ran together: she was a vision of loveliness, she was a woman, courted by an English gentleman who was a decorated officer, she was pure, and he was so proud of her. His wife frowned as she watched her husband's expressions change. He wasn't the sentimental sort, but for a moment she thought he might cry. Claudine was jumping up and down going on and on about how gorgeous Emma looked.

Confused, Emma stood just inside the room, wondering if after all she did not look pretty in the gown and she had made a mistake with her hair.

Her parents' silence was broken by Edgar's huge smile and applause. "My Emma, your commodore has chosen a gown fit for a queen, and tonight you are that queen. You will turn every head at the ball."

Emma choked back tears she was so relieved by her father's compliment. She constantly sought his approval and was so happy he thought she looked pretty. She smiled back at him.

"Dearest, the gown fits you perfectly; the gold with the crimson complements your hair and complexion. The woven satin ribbon in your hair ties the whole ensemble together. You need no other accessories except possibly a cape for the chilly evening. If you will be very careful, you may wear my cream cashmere evening cape."

"Oh, Mama, thank you so. It will be wonderful in case the evening gets chilly, as it usually does in the early springtime." Jenny fetched the cape from Maria's wardrobe.

A knock at the front door stopped the conversation. Claudine shrieked, "I'll answer it; I know it is the commodore, I want to see his expression when he sees my sister!"

"She's impossible," Emma laughed, "but I love her so much." Her laughter was silenced when Joseph entered the lounge. He had never looked more handsome. He was in full military dress uniform, decorated with all his medals, ribbons, and pips. The uniform jacket was scarlet, adorned with twelve gold buttons and gold lace-covered epaulettes. A crown, two stars, and an anchor were intricately woven into the epaulettes, denoting his rank. His sandy blond hair was combed back in a ponytail that touched the top of the collar on his uniform. His air was one of confidence and grandeur.

He bowed at the waist when greeting the Bourons, and he bowed and kissed Emma's shaking hand. He had properly greeted Claudine at the front door. When he spoke, Emma was mesmerized. "I am overjoyed you are wearing the gown I designed for you and so pleased it is a perfect fit; you look stunning, Emma. I am honored you agreed to accompany me to the ambassador's ball on such short notice. Taking that into consideration, I felt embarrassed I had not given you and your mother ample time to select a gown." He glanced at Mrs. Bouron. "Please forgive me. Fortunately, my mother has a designer in Paris she travels to see several times a year, and that designer was kind enough to create this gown specifically for Emma. Joseph turned back to Emma "May I be so bold as to say you are a vision of loveliness?"

Emma was electrified by what he said; she felt her cheeks burning. She forced herself to respond, "Joseph, I am extremely thankful, for your gesture was more than generous, and I am pleased that you like the gown on me. I am looking forward to the ball and spending it in your company." Emma slightly curtsied and smiled a radiant smile.

Edgar watched their exchange intently, and it crossed his mind that it was quite familiar. Then he dismissed it from his mind as vivid imagination. Emma was merely enchanted with the Parisian gown, the ball, and the company of the prestigious officer, which was only natural.

"With your permission, sir, I respectfully request your daughter may attend the entire ball, and I will deliver her safely to your door at the appointed hour."

"What time do the festivities finish, Commodore?"

"Actually, sir, since it begins late and the ambassador makes his grand entrance at ten o'clock, it usually ends at 1:00 a.m. By the time the carriage arrives back to your home, it will be close to 1:30 a.m. If you have an objection, I will completely understand and honor whatever you permit."

Edgar thought for a few moments. "I put my daughter's safety in your hands. I would hate for her to miss any of the party, dancing, and entertainment, especially in that lovely gown." He winked at his daughter.

The two men shook hands. "Monsieur, she will be well looked after, and I will have her here by 1:30 a.m. Thank you for allowing this extension to her time." Joseph smiled his reassuring smile, and Edgar felt comfortable he made the right decision. With that settled, Joseph turned, cupped Emma's elbow, and led her out of the lounge.

"Mon Dieu, Edgar, are you sure all those hours unchaperoned is wise?" Maria looked concerned.

"Dearest, she is a young woman being courted, and Joseph is the picture of decorum. Plus I know our daughter; she will follow all proper etiquette." Edgar grinned.

Mrs. Bouron felt a twinge of discomfort. She couldn't put her finger on it, but the way her daughter and the gentleman looked at one another was openly intimate.

Jenny shuddered. She was sure the couple knew each other carnally; the way the gown fit, the way they looked at each other, and of course his secret visit to her room all pointed to a yes. She had to broach the subject with Emma, but timing was of ultimate importance.

Chapter 4

The Ambassador's Spring Ball

As the handsome commodore and Mademoiselle Bouron walked to the carriage, Percy could see the couple holding hands and laughing like they were conspirators in a giant caper. It actually was good to see Commodore Head thoroughly enjoying himself. Percy fought under his leadership. Joseph battled gallantly in the Second Opium War, when the British and French joined forces against the Chinese. Joseph had been a young nineteen-year-old lieutenant. The Chinese dominated valuable trade routes that the European forces desired. The leader of the Qing Dynasty, Xianfeng, signed commercial treaties with the British and French in 1856, and then he was forced to retract the treaties because the policy was so unpopular with the Chinese government. The British-French armies reconvened in 1860, and under the British leader Lord Elgin and the French leader General Charles Cousin-Montauban they attacked China.

The invading fleet consisted of 173 ships. Joseph Head was in command of the seamen under the captains of two ships. The Chinese forts that were attacked fell on August 21, 1860. The Anglo-French armies began moving inward to Beijing. Xianfeng was terrified that the invaders would get into the capitol, so he called for peace talks once again, but a despicable incident interrupted the talks. The British envoy,

Harry Parkes, and his party were arrested, tortured, and killed by the Chinese. The enraged European leaders marched into Beijing, and Lord Elgin and Cousin-Montauban took the city on October 6, 1860. The foreign troops took their revenge by looting and burning the famous Old Summer Palace. Although young, then Lieutenant Head fought with valor and bravery. Percy was one of the sailors under his command. They were in the skirmish on the outskirts of Beijing when Joseph was wounded in hand-to-hand combat. A Chinese soldier pierced Joseph's side with his sword. Joseph continued fighting until the Chinese soldier was down.

Joseph lost so much blood, he collapsed. Percy ran to him, tore off his own shirt, and stuffed it in the wound to stop the gushing of the blood. When the battlefield cleared, with the Anglo-French troops victorious, the medics attended to the wounded; other sailors and soldiers buried the dead. Young Lieutenant Head was spared because the sword missed his vital organs, but he was weak and unconscious, and suffered from high fever. Percy and another seaman carried their officer back to Taku Fort, where he convalesced for almost a month. His valiant fighting earned him one of the esteemed medals on his uniform. The incident sealed the friendship between Percy and Joseph, and it instilled in Percy a protective loyalty. The two were not separated since the war ended sixteen years previous.

Percy did not aspire to move up the ranks in the British Navy. He was happy being Joseph's attendant. It wasn't a taxing job and he enjoyed Joseph's company as they traveled all over the world together. Seeing Joseph enthralled by a woman was a new experience for Percy to witness. It made him smile, as they had female conquests all over the continents, but not one put a look like this on Joseph's face. *He would either tire of her,* Percy mused, *or take her as a mistress*; marriage didn't cross Percy's mind. The thought caused Percy to wonder. How would it impact him? Engulfed in his thoughts, he was brought back to the present by the commodore shaking his arm. "Percy, Percy, are you all right?" Joseph appeared concerned.

"Ah, yes, sir, my mind was drifting to days gone by." Percy winked.

Joseph laughed. "Come on, mate, or the lady and I will be late for the ball, and that just would not do." They both jabbed each other and roared. They knew the old British ambassador was a stickler for Victorian protocol.

Percy opened the door. "Yes, sir, we'll be on our way." He smiled at Mademoiselle Bouron. It was easy to see why Joseph was so taken with the girl; she radiated beauty, mingled with a gentle kindness. In the Parisian gown Joseph designed for her in record speed, she was a vision.

Emma liked the way Joseph and Percy interacted with one another. It was another facet of Joseph's personality she admired. A person's station in life was of no consequence to him; his or her character was all that mattered. She could see they were true friends.

Once in the carriage Joseph spoke. "Emma, you are absolutely radiant. I just knew the gold and crimson would be amazing on you." He leaned over and kissed her lips lightly.

"My darling Joseph, I don't know how to thank you for this exquisite gown. I absolutely love it!" Emma blushed with enthusiasm.

"Sweetheart, it was my honor to have a gown designed for your scrumptious body." He winked and kissed her bare shoulder. "It was quite an undertaking." Joseph laughed. "I sent a message to Mother's designer it was imperative to complete the order within thirty-six hours. Percy said the tailor almost hyperventilated! The important thing is he adhered to my exact specifications." Joseph smiled. "You look perfect, and I knew the colors and fabric of the gown would accent your attributes." Joseph winked again.

"When did you commission the designer?"

Joseph cleared his throat. "As soon as I arrived at Chateau Philipe the morning I slinked away from your boudoir!" Joseph belly laughed like a schoolboy.

"Joseph Head, you are impossible! What made you so sure I would wear it for a ball I knew nothing about?"

"My lady, the way your body speaks to me, I was certain you would attend!"

"Ah, sir, how presumptuous of you." Emma laughed and tweaked his arm.

He grabbed her hand and kissed her fingertips. "Why darling, I knew you would not want me going alone with all those hungry women there."

He was right, Emma thought; he was the most handsome man in Calais. The thought of him dancing, holding close, whispering to another woman made her recoil.

Had he said the wrong thing? He feared her inferiorities might surface. Why did he say something so stupid? He put his hands on her shoulders and turned her to him. "You know, my love, I am only teasing. If you had not accompanied me, I would have done what I do every year, which is go to the ball so I would not insult the ambassador, dance with his plump wife and a few of my friends' wives to be polite. During the dinner and entertainment, I always sit with other officers who are solo, and then take my leave." Emma smiled. "But this year, I have the honor of escorting the most beautiful girl in the world, whom I am desperately in love with and I do believe she loves me back." Joseph pulled her close and kissed her lightly on the lips. "I would kiss you more deeply, but I fear one true kiss would cause me to pull off that lovely gown and ravage you right now." Joseph laughed, hoping to reassure her fragile ego.

Finally Emma laughed.

During the rest of the carriage ride, they talked easily and enjoyed one another's company. As the carriage got close to the Embassy, Joseph took her face in his hands, looked deeply in her eyes, and said, "I am going to kiss you now passionately to bring that rosy glow to your cheeks I love." His mouth covered Emma's with a torrid kiss. He pulled away, threw his head back, and laughed his throaty laugh.

The carriage pulled up to the Embassy. Percy jumped from the driver's bench, opened the door, and assisted Emma in stepping down. Emma gave him a warm smile. "Thank you, Percy, I appreciate your kindness."

Percy melted on the spot. "Ah, of course, mademoiselle." He was blushing from ear to ear. Joseph observed the whole interchange and stifled a laugh. Emma flustered Percy; it was hilarious to see his old buddy rattled.

As was customary, when Joseph and Emma stepped into the arched entrance to the Embassy, they were announced. "Commodore Joseph Head of the Royal British Navy and Mademoiselle Emma Bouron of Calais." All heads turned. The people who attended the Monet art show immediately recognized the French woman. Those who were not at the function were very surprised to see Joseph with a female guest.

She was absolutely gorgeous. Many people surmised she was very wealthy because the gown she wore was obviously from the finest designer and of the finest material. She was a golden vision. The gown emphasized her petite physique and alluring figure. As the couple walked into the ballroom, the attendees speculated about the lady. Joseph annually attended the ball, but he brought no female guests. He was always the gentleman, cordial, conversational, but detached.

Emma's heart raced; she wanted desperately to make a good impression on Joseph's friends and colleagues. Little did she know her dazzling appearance mesmerized the whole room, women and men. As they descended the stairs, one of Joseph's lieutenants stepped forward to greet him. "Good evening, Commodore. This is a special affair, and I am so honored we were included." Joseph smiled; he knew Breton just wanted to meet Emma so he could report to the others!

"Good evening, Breton, I would like you to meet Mademoiselle Bouron."

"Bonsoir, monsieur, it is my pleasure." Emma smiled.

Breton bowed and kissed her hand. "I have not seen you at British Embassy functions before. Is tonight a first?"

Joseph thought the lieutenant was crass and bold to say such a thing.

Emma smiled her fetching smile and replied, "Why, no, sir, Commodore Head and I attended the Monet showing, which was so very moving. I love the work of the French impressionists, don't you?"

That caught the lieutenant off guard, Joseph snorted under his breath.

"Uh, no, mademoiselle, I do not know much about art."

"Well, sir, I think you would love the beauty and depth of the impressionists. I highly recommend it to you." She smiled sweetly. Joseph could have swept her off her feet, twirled her around, and kissed her. She was up to any challenge. She baited Breton, and he took the bait. Poor Breton looked like a deflated balloon. He so wanted to impress his superior, but he ended up appearing foolish.

To rescue him from his silly chatter, Joseph said, "Lieutenant, would you mind getting the lady and me a champagne?"

"Why, why, I would be delighted." His face was as crimson as the ribbon in Emma's hair, but he had an escape route.

Breton was mortified at the way the whole conversation deteriorated at his expense. He chastised himself for being nosy and pompous. He walked up to the bar and asked for two flutes of champagne. He was an idiot. He hoped the commodore would not be too upset with him. He walked across the ballroom, and much to his chagrin, people surrounded the commodore and the lady. He nudged his way through. "Excuse me, excuse me."

Breton bowed. "Sir, a glass of champagne for you and the lady."

"Ah, Breton, thank you so very much; so kind of you." Joseph nodded.

Emma's radiant smile made the previous disaster disappear. The orchestra started to play. She whispered in Joseph's ear, out of hearing range of anyone else, "Darling, suggest Breton dance with me." Joseph looked at her puzzled. Emma smiled. "It will make him feel important and you accessible." My God, Joseph thought, she is not only beautiful, sweet, and sexy, but intuitive, which was an added attribute.

"Breton, we would be honored if you would dance with the lady." Joseph gestured toward Emma.

"Lieutenant, I would be flattered to dance with you." Emma's smile was reassuring.

"Commodore, with your permission . . ."

"Go, go, Breton, before the orchestra takes a break." All three laughed.

Emma handed Joseph her champagne, winked, and turned to Breton. "Sir, I think they are playing our waltz." Her smile melted him. He took her hand and led her to the dance floor. His waltz was not the most refined, but she was so light on her feet she followed him like a swan gliding on water.

Joseph was watching, thinking what a magnificent person she was. Her glistening coiffed hair seemed to move to the rhythm of the music. It looked enchanting with the crimson ribbon woven through it and the loose tendrils wild around her porcelain face. He saw she had Breton eating out of the palm of her hand. Joseph felt a hand on his shoulder; he turned and there was Cassandra Ballou beaming at him. *Oh God, why doesn't she realize I am not interested in her at all?* She was pretty in a way, but her pushy personality turned him off completely. He covered his dislike by bowing and smiling briefly. "Good evening, madame, how nice to see you again."

"Good evening, Commodore. Since your guest is dancing with one of your lieutenants, I thought it a perfect opportunity for us to dance."

"Madame, how thoughtful of you, but as you can see, I have a glass of champagne in each hand." Not a very convincing excuse, but Joseph had no desire to dance with her.

"Easily remedied." Cassandra beckoned one of the waiters circling the room with his silver tray in hand. He hurried over. "Garcon, would you mind taking the flutes from the gentleman as we would like to dance."

"Of course, madame."

Damn it, she was so forward. Joseph was annoyed, but stuck. He begrudgingly took her hand and stepped onto the dance floor. He held her loosely and at a distance. She tried to squeeze in closer, but he was firm in keeping her from holding him close. She chattered incessantly about nothing he was interested in, so he just kept nodding his head, trying not to show his disdain. Finally the waltz was over. The floor filled up with dancing couples; Joseph walked Cassandra through the crowd, thanked her, and walked away in search of Emma.

Cassandra felt deflated by his attitude toward her. He must be very enamored by Emma something. She decided to watch them closely throughout the evening to assess their situation from their body language. She prided herself in being able to read people. They certainly looked like lovers at the Monet event.

Joseph didn't give Cassandra a second thought. He spotted Emma in conversation with some of his colleagues she had met at the gallery.

They were drawn to her like magnets. He stood back and watched her laugh and visit with them all. She possessed a special quality of making the person talking to her feel like he or she was the only person who had her attention. He was pleased with the gown he had commissioned for her. She was by far the most attractive woman at the ball, and she was his. He couldn't suppress his broad smile. He walked to the group. "Emma, I see you have become reacquainted with my friends."

"Yes, Joseph, they have been sharing with me tales of England. It sounds like a lovely country, but it is very sad Queen Victoria is still in mourning for her late husband. His untimely death occurred many years ago, yet she still wears black clothing."

"Under Queen Victoria's rule, it is amazing how England has flourished in literature and all the arts actually. The whole country is quite priggish, though, not warm and liberated like your countrymen, the French." Joseph smiled a wicked little smile. Emma caught his innuendo, but kept her innocent countenance with a questioning smile on her face.

One of the young officers changed the subject. "Sir, we are honored tonight to have General Cousin-Montauban attending with a group of his men and their guests. I know you were highly decorated while in battle with the joint British-French armies and seamen at Beijing. Isn't that when you were awarded the Medal of Valor after you were wounded?"

Joseph looked annoyed. He consciously didn't discuss the battles and his participation, let alone his wounds, with Emma. He made light of it. "Conrad, you are too kind; it was nothing notable."

Emma had a chill climb up her spine at this exchange. She had not considered Joseph might be called away to war. Relations between England and France were cooperative, and they were at peace with the world. Emma didn't follow politics or worldly affairs. She was born in 1857 and only a baby when the French fought with the British against China.

She shuddered when she thought about the Franco-Prussian War from 1870 to 1871; the casualties in and around Paris were staggering. There were 24,000 dead and wounded, 146,000 French captured, and

47,000 civilian casualties. The fall of Paris ended the war on May 10, 1871. The French were not only devastated by the loss of human life, the wounded and the captured, but they signed the Treaty of Frankfurt, which gave Germany the provinces of Alsace and Lorraine. Emma heard her parents discuss it with fear and trepidation, which caused her and Claudine to be apprehensive, but they were little girls protected at home and life went on. Now she had fallen in love with Joseph; war, casualties, troops captured were all real and terrifying.

Joseph saw Emma's stricken look. He could choke Conrad for bringing up the battle. It was obvious she was distraught. Joseph moved to her. "Shall we enjoy some champagne and prawns, mademoiselle?" Before she could answer, Joseph cupped her elbow and led her to the buffet tables. He bent down and whispered, "Darling, don't be alarmed by the idle chatter of the young officers. They are always anxious to prove themselves on the battlefield, so they tend to glamorize something they know nothing about."

"The thought of you being in danger in a war is more than I can stand." Tears were beginning to brim in her eyes.

"Emma, I assure you I am going nowhere. Our world is at peace, and as I told you when we met, I am here for a minimum of three months with a very easy assignment. Please don't be so chagrined. You look dazzling, and tonight we are going to enjoy a marvelous evening." He smiled at her tenderly, and the color began to come back to her cheeks. "Let me get you a glass of champagne."

The group of officers watched the exchange between the couple. "Well, Conrad, it looks like you put your foot in your mouth and upset the lady." Breton laughed. "There must be something serious going on between our commodore and the lady. He doesn't normally bring a woman as a guest to a public function."

"He's never had that look either," Conrad said. "I should have kept my mouth shut about such a sensitive subject to women. They are so squeamish about these matters." Conrad glanced at Joseph and Emma. "Thank God, whatever he's said to her, she looks happy again. Maybe he won't chastise me too much!"

Emma was relieved. Joseph convinced her she was worrying about nothing. Once he assured her, the evening flew by. They danced, mingled, enjoyed the appetizers, and laughed at each other's private jokes. She imbibed several glasses of champagne, which helped her relax and enjoy the ball.

Once again the partygoers gossiped, speculated, guessed about their relationship. All agreed Emma was the most beautiful woman at the ball. The men found it difficult not watching her twirl and dance. Her gown was magnificent and her hair luminous. It was apparent Commodore Head had a special interest in her. Who could blame him? She was a prize.

The clock struck ten o'clock, and with a flourish Ambassador Cookson and Mrs. Cookson were announced. The room became quiet except for the applause. Once in the ballroom center, the ambassador and Mrs. Cookson greeted the quests as a whole, then pointed out certain dignitaries. "My wife and I are honored to welcome the Duke and Duchess of Suffolk, Generals Roberts and Stewart of the Royal British Army and their lovely wives, and my dear French friend General Charles Cousin-Montauban and his daughter, Annabelle. It is so kind of all of you to attend the British Ambassador's Ball, our yearly signature event."

Emma whispered to Joseph, "Who is the French general? I don't know much about the military, but he looks very distinguished, and his uniform bears many medals and ribbons."

"He was the general in charge of the French troops when I was a young lieutenant in the war with the Chinese."

"Oh, when you were wounded." Emma's voice was so quiet Joseph could barely hear her.

"Darling, that was a long time ago. In fact, it is rumored that Cousin-Montauban is close to retirement. He and the ambassador have been friends and colleagues for years. He usually comes to the ball if he is in Calais and brings a new batch of young officers with him to expose them to British culture." Joseph's eyes twinkled.

Emma laughed at his poke at culture since he knew the French considered themselves the most cultured country in Europe. Dinner was announced, which ended their conversation.

Joseph offered Emma his arm, and they found their place cards at the head table. They were seated with Ambassador Cookson and his wife, the Duke and Duchess of Suffolk, the British generals and their wives, and the French general and his daughter.

"Good friends, please enjoy your dinner, but first, a toast to my honored guests." Ambassador Cookson cleared his throat.

"Ladies and gentlemen, my wife and I celebrate the French-British alliance and are very pleased you have traveled to attend our annual ball. Indulge in the excellent French champagne and the delicious courses of fine British cuisine." Ambassador Cookson raised his glass, and all guests followed suit.

Emma was seated next to Joseph on her right and General Cousin-Montauban on her left. On the other side of Joseph was seated the wife of General Roberts. Emma was the youngest guest at the table. Her insecurities crept up her spine like a spider creeping along the silk of its web. She clasped her hands in her lap and looked down. She would stay quiet and not try to make idle conversation with these dignitaries and their worldly wives. Joseph was in conversation with his former commanding general and his wife. The French general was laughing with his daughter. Emma felt ridiculous. She picked up her glass and took another drink; at least it occupied her time and possibly helped her not look so out of place. It seemed like an eternity, but the first course of the banquet, mushroom soup, was served.

As Joseph thanked the waiter for his soup, he turned to Emma. "Do you fancy mushroom soup?"

"Yes, I like it fine."

"I think it is highly overrated." He laughed the throaty laugh she loved, but she didn't look at him. Instead, she stirred her soup around and around in the bowl without taking a bite.

"Emma, what is it? You are quiet as a mouse, and I can see you are unhappy."

She looked down. "No, no, everything is fine."

He didn't care who was looking. He took her chin and turned her face toward him and stared into her brimming eyes.

"What is it, darling? Has someone offended you, or have I said something wayward?"

She could see his sincerity in the blue pools staring at her. She mentally struggled with telling him her feelings or glazing over them with a shrug and a smile. She smiled. "Honestly, Joseph, everything is fine."

He knew she was not truthful, but now was not the time to challenge her about whatever was bothering her. He attributed it to her youth and sheltered upbringing.

Just at that moment the French general looked at Emma. "Mademoiselle, may I call you Emma as your place card denotes?"

Rescued. Emma breathed a sigh of relief. "Bonsoir, General, I have heard many tales this evening of your gallantry and bravery in battle. And of course I would be delighted if you called me Emma."

Joseph observed the general was charmed by her sincerity and manners. She was the brightest star in the ballroom. He was pleased with his choice of style, fabric, and fit of the gown. It was astonishing he met her and fell in love with her in such a short time. The fact she returned his love and gave herself completely to him was even more astounding. Emma and the general were chatting in French, and he didn't know the gist of the conversation. He rebuked himself: he was in France so much but hadn't learned the language.

General Cousin-Montauban put Emma at ease. He talked about how much he adored Calais and the different points of interest they both knew well. The general's daughter, Annabelle, joined in the conversation. She was a pretty girl. Joseph guessed her to be older than Emma, maybe twenty-five or so.

Emma relaxed. The general was kind, and speaking their native language was soothing for some reason. Annabelle was delightful. Emma learned from the conversation as dinner progressed that the general's wife died when Annabelle was fourteen from the sweating sickness, and his lovely daughter dedicated her life to caring for him. She was not married, and as she got older, the suitors dwindled and fell by the wayside. Emma thought it was such a shame, as Annabelle was sweet and loving. She would be a good wife and mother. Plus she had missed the passion and desire that consumed Emma, which she believed would deepen after marriage vows. She was so engrossed in the conversation that the aperitif was being served. Oh dear God, she had inadvertently ignored Joseph during the entire meal. She looked to her right, and Joseph smiled.

"Why, Emma, I thought you forgot I was here." Joseph laughed.

"Mon Dieu, I am so sorry. I didn't mean to slight you, Joseph, but I became so involved in conversation with the general and Annabelle, the time flew. Please, forgive my manners."

His blue eyes sparkled. "I am crestfallen, my love."

Emma tweaked his arm. "Joseph Head, you are impossible."

Their eyes locked and they both laughed.

General Roberts was watching the commodore and his gorgeous guest. He saw there was an unspoken bond between them. He speculated the girl was very young and wondered how long Joseph had been courting her. He looked at her hands and saw no rings, so they were not engaged. Paul Roberts presumed she was wealthy from her attire. The gown must have cost a fortune, and it fit her like a glove. Clearly, she was the most spectacular woman at the ball. They made a very handsome couple. He wondered if Joseph would marry after all. His wife patted his arm and his attention shifted.

Dinner was over and the orchestra resumed the dance music. General Cousin-Montauban leaned over and kissed Emma on the cheek. Emma stood, and as was custom, she and Annabelle kissed each other's cheeks. "Emma, Annabelle and I have thoroughly enjoyed passing the evening with you, and I hope you and Joseph will come to visit us when you are in Paris."

"Sir, you are so kind; I would love to visit."

"Commodore," he shook Joseph's hand, "you have a charming young lady."

"Thank you, General."

"Annabelle and I would welcome a visit from the two of you to our home in Paris. The young ladies enjoyed a brilliant time throughout dinner, and a budding friendship must be nurtured." He gave Joseph a sincere smile.

Annabelle and Emma were chatting about the stout women at the party and how silly they looked in frills and lace. Their gossip was fun and lighthearted. It gave General Cousin-Montauban an opportunity to be more serious and candid with Joseph, whom he liked very much. "Commodore, my daughter has dedicated her life to me since my wife's untimely death. Selflessly she denied herself friendships with other girls and rebuffed suitors. Tonight she opened up to your Emma, and it warms my heart to see her enjoy herself so much, especially since Emma is so open and honest. I am a good judge of character, Joseph, and I don't think your girl has a mean or deceitful bone in her body. Her innocence of the world makes her a good match for Annabelle, who also knows so little of life outside her self-imposed cocoon. Please don't get me wrong; I am not trying to push my child away, but I am getting on in years and she will need a dear friend and ally when something happens to me, and nature does take its course."

"General, I am honored by your faith in both Emma and me. Since we are being totally candid with one another, I must tell you, Emma is very young, not yet twenty years of age. Her father, Edgar Bouron, has shown me complete trust, but I sincerely doubt he would allow Emma to travel to Paris with me unaccompanied."

"Joseph, doesn't she have a nanny who became her chambermaid who helped raise her?"

"Ah, yes, she does. Monsieur Bouron may allow her a trip if Jenny were to chaperone."

"Why don't you let me help with this endeavor? I am known by most gentlemen of society by my reputation, which I might add is impeccable!"

Both men laughed. The girls turned to look at them with questioning stares.

"Nothing, ladies, just male bantering. You know, we find ourselves quite entertaining." Cousin-Montauban's eyes danced.

"Oh, Papa, you are impossible." Annabelle smiled lovingly, and then the girls returned to their own conversation and ignored the men's chatter.

"Joseph, I will call on you at the Embassy to coordinate our schedules so we can plan a trip."

"It will be an honor and privilege to visit you in Paris, and I would love to show Emma the city."

"Don't answer me, Joseph, but anyone with one eye open can see you are utterly taken with the girl."

"Well, I . . ."

"Come, come, my friend, no denials. They will only fall on deaf ears. Let me tell you this with all sincerity: young women like Emma or Annabelle do not come along often in life. Innocence, honesty, beauty, kindness, and loyalty are difficult qualities to find in one package. Guard what you have, Joseph, as it is just as obvious, the girl is totally in love with you, which makes you, sir, a very, very lucky man."

Joseph smiled broadly and laughed his throaty laugh. "Oh, I will guard my good fortune; I guarantee you that, General. From the first moment I saw her, I knew she was special."

"May I compliment you on your choice. It must be true: good things in life are worth waiting for, because you have waited a long time, Joseph."

The waiter offered both men a snifter of brandy. They clinked glasses, and each took a long pull on the golden liquid. Joseph's vibrant blue eyes stared directly into the general's eyes, and without wavering, Joseph confided. "General, I never considered marriage, children, and the family life. I am a career naval officer, with only aspirations of serving my country and traveling the world. All of that changed in an instant when I met Emma."

"Young man, I experienced that same powerful feeling when I first met my wife. There was nothing in this world I would not do for her. I would have traded my life for hers if she could have lived. I don't want to become melancholy tonight, but sometime I will tell you everything that happened to us as a family. Now, my advice to you is hold on to Emma with all you have. Enough of this talk; let us look forward to grand times in Paris." Cousin-Montauban touched his glass to Joseph's, and once again they took a long drink. "Let's join the two loveliest women at the ball." Joseph smiled.

Emma felt Joseph behind her before she saw him. She was engrossed in conversation with Annabelle about all of the wonderful attractions in Paris, but his nearness diverted her attention. Annabelle caught Emma's look and knew her gentleman was approaching. "Hello, monsieurs, I see you have decided to keep company with Emma and me again." The girls laughed. An outsider would have thought the two young women had been friends for a long time, their demeanor was so comfortable with one another. The orchestra began a waltz.

Joseph bowed. "Mademoiselle Bouron, may I have the pleasure of this dance?"

"Oui, monsieur, delighted I'm sure." Emma stretched out her arm and hand. Her laughter was contagious. Annabelle, the general, and Joseph all joined in.

When they reached the dance floor, Joseph encircled her waist possessively and whispered slowly in her ear, "Emma, darling, every man in this ballroom envies me at this very moment because you are in my arms and not theirs." His breath and words in her ear made the hairs stand up on the back of her neck. As he pressed her body in closer, she felt the shiver run up and down her spine. She closed her eyes and let Joseph and the music take her away. It was like she was hypnotized. When she opened her eyes, she saw Annabelle at the other end of the ballroom waltzing with a French soldier. His back was to Emma, but something about his movements seemed oddly familiar. She didn't remember seeing anyone from the French military she knew. Then Joseph interrupted her thoughts. Whispering once again, "Darling, the music is about to stop. Shall we bid our host and new friends adieu?"

"Is it time to go, Joseph?"

"My love, it is just past midnight . . ."

Emma put her finger to his lips. The mischief sparkled in her eyes. "Why, sir, do you wish to be alone with me?"

Joseph laughed his throaty laugh and nodded. "You have been the focal point of the evening; now let's give the other poor ladies a chance to shine." Her smile dazzled him. He fetched her cape and draped it across her shoulders, then cupped her elbow and led her to the ambassador and his wife.

Emma spoke first. "Monsieur and madame, I have never attended a more spectacular ball. Every aspect of the evening was absolutely perfect. Your hospitality is unmatched even by my own countrymen." Her next gesture overwhelmed them both. She reached in the pocket of her cape and handed each a small wrapped box.

"Why, my dear," sputtered Sally Cookson, "what's this?"

"Please open them. These are small tokens of my appreciation for allowing me to attend this special occasion."

Sally and her husband unwrapped the boxes, and inside were folded puppets dressed in bright clothes of the day, one girl and one boy. Sally looked confused.

"Commodore Head shared with me that you have two young grandchildren, a boy and a girl. I design toys, and these puppets are from my new line. I thought the children might enjoy them." Emma smiled, but reddened with embarrassment. Dear God, was this a faux pas? Had she made a brazen mistake?

Sally jumped up and embraced Emma. "This is so very kind of you. The children will adore them and get hours of pleasure playing." Emma blushed again, only this time with relief.

The ambassador, who was not a demonstrative man, also hugged Emma for her thoughtfulness. *What a genuinely kind girl*, he thought; it made her outward beauty intensify. *Joseph Head would be a fool if he let this prize slip through his fingers.*

Emma constantly amazed Joseph. What an incredible gesture, and she never mentioned a word about it to him. He thought he was going to explode with pride. He could not believe what a truly thoughtful person she was. This kind gesture showed excellent upbringing by her parents. At that moment, he loved her deeper than when they were in bed. Joseph bowed and kissed Sally's hand and shook hands with the ambassador. Emma smiled radiantly. "Please excuse us; we must say good night to our friends, the Cousin-Montaubans. Again, I enjoyed every moment of this evening."

Emma took Joseph's hand and scanned the room for Annabelle and the general. They were close to the entryway talking to some people Emma did not know.

"Annabelle, I am sorry to intrude, but Joseph must take me home so I do not break any of Papa's rules. You know how that is." The girls laughed.

"Promise me, Emma, you will come to Paris very soon to visit. We will have a grand time exploring the city."

"As soon as I can get it arranged, I promise." They kissed each other's cheeks and knew a deep friendship was beginning.

Joseph and the general were saying their good-byes. Cousin-Montauban kissed Emma's hand. "Until Paris, my dear."

Emma suddenly clasped Annabelle's hand and asked, "Who were you waltzing with the last waltz? I thought it might be someone I knew."

"Oh, just one of Papa's lieutenants. I think he orders them to dance with me at least once."

"Annabelle, you know that's not true."

The girls giggled.

"Good night to you both. Come, Emma, I must not get you home late." Joseph took her hand and they made their way through the archway.

Percy was lounging on the carriage driver's bench when he spotted a vision in gold gliding down the walkway. He knew it was Emma. Ah, once again they were leaving early. Percy jumped down and greeted Joseph and the lady. They looked like they were in some private dreamworld of their own, with no one else inside. "Hello, did you enjoy the ball?"

"Yes, Percy, it was enchanting, but not as enchanting as Mademoiselle Bouron." Joseph winked.

Emma laughed. "We had a lovely time. Thank you for inquiring, Percy."

Percy opened the carriage door and Joseph helped Emma inside. As Percy was pulling the door shut, he noticed Joseph lowering the flame of the carriage lamp to a muted glow.

As Percy was climbing up to the driver's bench, Joseph opened the carriage door and called, "Drive us around the park before we take Miss Emma home."

"Right, sir, just tap and let me know when to drive to the Bourons'." Percy smiled to himself; *I bet they are going to do more than enjoy a drive through the park.*

Joseph was bursting with pride and love and lust all at the same time. He could hardly contain his thoughts. He took Emma's face tenderly in his hands and kissed her lips gently. He stared into her eyes and thanked God she came into his life. Emma smiled that loving smile that was so innocent and endearing.

"I don't know what to say, Emma, but this was the best night of my life."

She couldn't believe what he was saying; it was pouring out like a waterfall.

"You were the most dazzlingly beautiful woman at the ball, with the kindest heart and the best manners. Your whole countenance is totally perfect, your gown, your hair, your smile, everything, perfect. You make me a better man, a whole man, a proud man."

"I am so happy I pleased you. I would do anything for you, Joseph."

"From the bottom of my heart to the depths of my soul, Emma, I love you, not just now but always." Joseph's eyes spoke volumes.

She had never felt so complete. This man who stumbled into her life without warning loved her. He loved her. She was trying to drink it in, but it was difficult to comprehend. Before she could say anything else or think any other thoughts, he pulled her to him and held her in his arms. He kissed her eyelids, her hair, her cheeks, her ears, and her nose. Joseph sat her on his lap and held her face. He stared into her eyes, and the emotion made her heart ache with a love felt in the pit of her stomach. He covered her lips with his in a tender kiss and looked deep into her eyes. Emma put her arms around his neck, closed her eyes, and opened her mouth under his lips. "Emma, my golden goddess." He kissed her passionately. "Tell me you love me, baby."

"I love you, Joseph, so much, so much."

"I meant what I said, Emma, I love you." Joseph's husky voice was raw with true emotion. He held her in his arms and kissed her hair. "I am so happy you and Annabelle Cousin-Montauban have such a connection. I admire both her and her father, and I believe she will be a good friend to you, darling."

"Oh, Joseph, she and I had such fun together. We really got along so well. I admire the way she takes care of her father; it shows what a loving person she is. She has virtually sacrificed her own happiness to care for her father."

"Yes, she is an honorable girl."

"Did you talk to her father about going to their home in Paris for a visit?"

"Oui, ma chère. The first order of business will be finding a common time that you and I can be away from our jobs. Most importantly, I must convince your papa to allow you to travel with me."

"Honestly, Joseph, I have never given him or Mama a reason to distrust me. Of course, if they knew what I have been doing these past days, I would be locked away in a dungeon!" Emma giggled. "I think if you ask him and say you want Jenny to accompany me, he will say yes."

"As soon as I go over my schedule, I will approach Monsieur Bouron about the trip. In the meantime, darling, tomorrow I am going to give you a rest from my boring company as I have neglected my paperwork and must get caught up, especially if we will be going to Paris."

Emma looked crestfallen. In a quiet voice she said, "I don't want to go a day without seeing you. Don't you know I will be miserable?"

"Sweet, sweet girl, I will be adrift without you, but I must not jeopardize my position here by not fulfilling my duties. That could be disastrous."

"What do you mean?"

"This assignment in France was coveted by several other officers, but I was awarded the commission and I must do a perfect job for my men, my commanding admiral, and the ambassador. You understand, don't you?"

"I don't pretend to comprehend military service, but I certainly know from my position at the Toy Depot I have to be on my toes so no one else usurps my position. It worries me all the time. Until I met you, I lived for the place." Emma gave Joseph a half smile. "I know we both have to be dedicated to our employers, but it is difficult when I think about you all day."

No coy double entendres, just truth. He would miss her company tomorrow, but he knew he must buckle down and get his work done. If against customary etiquette, Edgar were to allow her the Paris trip, it would be imperative she spend quality time with her family. "Emma, I think it is important for you to spend time at home with your family. If they have the remainder of the weekend with you, your father will be more likely to allow the trip."

"The remainder of the weekend . . ." Emma was disappointed.

"Darling, I am going to thoroughly immerse myself in my work; please understand."

"I do, Joseph, and I don't want to be a pouty child, but being without you is like being without air." Her eyes were brimming with tears, and then spilled over.

Her words cracked his resolve, but her tears melted his heart. He wiped her tears with his fingertips and kissed her softly on her quivering lips. "Please, Emma, when you are like this, I can't resist you . . ."

"Oh Joseph, I am so selfish." Emma felt immature and ashamed. "Of course you are right; I am being a spoiled child. Forgive me."

"There is absolutely nothing to forgive. I am the luckiest man alive that you desire my company so fervently." He meant it; he was lucky to have Emma love him. She didn't realize it, but she could have any man in Calais, but she loved him. The way she gave herself to him was both innocent and full of lust, a combination he had never experienced before with any of his dalliances with other women. They all wanted something. He wasn't interested enough to stick around. Now here he was in love with a young girl he had no intention of relinquishing. He hugged her close.

Emma responded and hugged Joseph hard. It was going to be all right. She knew he was being sensible. They had spent almost every evening together since they met at La Mansion, and she willingly gave herself to him over and over.

Emma trusted in Joseph's decisions. He was right. Spending time at home with her mother, father, and Claudine would hopefully predispose her father to agreeing to the Paris trip. She would spend the weekend as she had for the past two years, cooking and sewing with her mother, reading to her father, and gossiping with her sister. It would put things as they were before she fell in love.

"You are so quiet, Emma. What are you thinking?"

"I believe in your decisions. I know you are right, and I will put on a happy face at home and enjoy my family. When I am cooking with Mama, I will be thinking about kissing you." Emma's laughter resounded in the carriage. "When I am reading to Papa and he is sipping brandy, I will be thinking about being in bed with you without our clothes on." She laughed again. "When Claudine is gossiping and babbling about the boy she has a crush on, I will be thinking about sensations that make my whole body quake." She straightened her back and looked Joseph in the eye. "That's what will get me through the weekend until we are together again." Her laughter again filled the carriage.

Joseph tickled her waist. "You are a naughty girl, aren't you!" They both laughed. Then Emma kissed Joseph tenderly and whispered, "I love you with my whole heart."

Percy could hear their muffled laughter from his perch on the driver's bench. He was almost to the Bouron house. He wondered what his boss's intentions were toward the French girl. She certainly caught all eyes when she was in the room. It was obvious Joseph was enamored with her. Well, who wouldn't be? She was a looker, smart, and kind. Percy also imagined from the way they acted that Joseph knew her body. Percy didn't know to what extent, but from the way the gown fit, he was sure Joseph had felt every inch of her. Whether he knew her carnally was another matter. He would be surprised if Joseph had captured her maidenhead, although he spent a night at her home. Percy speculated she allowed Joseph to kiss and fondle her, but that would be the extent of it. Anyway, from past experience, if Joseph made love to her, he would already be tired of her. He pulled up to Emma's house and jumped down to open the door.

"Sir, we have arrived."

"Thank you, Percy. I will walk Miss Emma to her door. Be back in a few minutes." Joseph offered his hand to Emma, and she emerged from the carriage.

"Good night, Percy. Thank you for driving us. I had a lovely time." She smiled that winning smile and Percy melted.

"Yes, mademoiselle, of course, uh, glad you enjoyed the ball, uh . . ." Joseph chuckled at Percy's tongue-tied response. Emma caught him off guard with her sweet appreciation. He wasn't accustomed to women thanking him for doing his job.

"I'll be right back." Joseph laughed.

Emma didn't know what the joke was, but she smiled happily and held Joseph's hand. They walked hand in hand to the entryway. Percy watched and sincerely thought they made a picture-perfect couple. Then they blended into the darkness.

Joseph embraced Emma tenderly once out of Percy's sight. "My darling, I will miss you this weekend, but I promise to work diligently to get everything done so we can have a lovely visit with Annabelle and the general. Enjoy your family so they won't mind you being away for a few days. Dream of Paris—shopping with your new friend and being with me on special excursions."

"I will, Joseph, but I will truly miss you. I am also going to carve out some time to work on my latest project for work so I will be able to miss a few days." Emma kissed Joseph good night, and for the first time since they met, went into her home and closed the door. She knew if she tarried, her resolve would melt and she would beg to see him over the weekend.

On the carriage ride back to the hotel, Joseph thought about the way he felt about Emma. He knew he loved her and wanted to protect her. She was very young and terribly insecure about her own self-worth, but he believed in time, once their relationship became permanent, those insecurities would dissipate. He could still smell her light scent in the carriage. As he breathed it in, he drifted off to sleep.

When Emma ascended the staircase to her bedroom, she could see a dim light peeping out from underneath Claudine's door. She knocked quietly so as not to awaken anyone else in the household. "Claudine, may I come in?" Emma whispered through the door.

"Of course, you goose; the door is not locked." Claudine stayed awake specifically so her sister could tell her all the details of the British Ambassador's Ball.

When Emma entered through the doorway, Claudine studied her. She looked more beautiful than when she left for the evening. There was an air of happiness that she hadn't seen before in her sister, not even when she was engaged to Richard. Emma carried herself in a more dignified mature way now. What an effect the commodore had on her! Claudine's eyes narrowed. "Emma, I stayed up to hear all about the ball, but looking at you, I have another question."

"What is it? You sound so mysterious." Emma laughed.

"Are you in love with Commodore Head? Don't try to skirt around it; I am your sister and best friend."

Emma plopped on Claudine's bed. "Yes. I didn't mean to get swept off my feet, but Claud, he is everything I dreamed of and more. He is brilliant, handsome, kind, and a man of the world, mature. Can you believe he had this gorgeous gown designed just for me? It shows his kindness and generosity. He comes from an aristocratic British family, so his manners and decorum are impeccable. His friends and colleagues are extraordinary. I have to pinch myself to believe my good fortune is true."

"Emma Bouron, he is lucky to have my sister in love with him. You know, all the eligible men in Calais drool after you." Claudine smiled brightly at her sister.

"Oh, Claud, do you think so?"

"Of course. You have your head buried so deep at the toy manufacturer's you are oblivious to the effect you have on men and women, as a matter of fact."

"Thank you, Claud, for supporting me and giving me much-needed confidence."

"Always. Now, I want to know about the ball and how many times he kissed you and was it romantic? Most importantly, is he in love with you?" Claudine knew the answer before her sister confided in her. The commodore brought out qualities in Emma that were deeply buried.

"Dragging me to the dance hall was the start of a magical journey I hope has only just begun. I resisted going that night. I went only because you begged me." Emma took Claudine's hand. "You are responsible for me meeting the love of my life." Claudine's eyes opened wide. They had known each other such a short time, but apparently long enough for her sister to have fallen desperately in love.

"Really, Emma, you think he's the love of your life?"

"I do. I cannot imagine sharing my life with any other man. Joseph is the prince of my dreams."

"All right, all right, Em, I understand how you feel; now tell me how he showed you his love."

"Nosy, nosy!"

"Stop teasing. Tell me, tell me."

Emma's mind thought of their first night together when he pulled her into the shadows on the walk home. How he kissed her and awakened a dormant passion. How he touched her and made her reach the peak of desire. Then their intimacies erupted over and over. For the first time, she consciously realized she gave Joseph her virginity. She didn't think about it before, as it was all so perfectly natural. A chill rippled through her body. Had she trusted too much? It was too late; nineteenth-century social norms rigidly required a woman to be a virgin until she entered the marriage bed. The women who gave away their purity ended up marrying below them or turned into prostitutes or spinsters. Emma shuddered; she put her complete trust in Joseph, and it had to be right.

"Em, you are lost in reverie. All the color drained from your face. What in the world are you thinking?"

"I, I was trying to pinpoint the answers to your questions and got lost in my own questions." Emma shook off her doubts to appease Claudine.

"Emma Bouron, do not start sinking into thoughts of inadequacies. You made yourself miserable pining over that weasel Richard. He was not worthy enough to kiss your feet, yet you allowed him to reduce your sense of confidence to ashes. Don't repeat the past, sister."

"Darling Claudine, you know exactly what to say; you know me so well." The color returned to Emma's cheeks, and she grinned at Claudine. She would keep the extent of her sexual explorations quiet and tell her just enough to satisfy her curiosity. Thinking about Joseph holding her and kissing her and caressing her face and hair bubbled over as she chattered to her sister. She told Claudine how his manners were gallant and he kissed her hands and cheeks the first few evenings. Emma wove a tale of romantic kissing and hugging on the third outing. Claudine was wide-eyed and intoxicated by the story of her sister's courting. She was entranced by how the worldly commodore kissed and caressed her sister. Claudine threw her legs over the side of the bed, jumped up, grabbed Emma by the hands, and pulled her upright.

"I can't stand it one more minute! Why do you think he loves you?"

Emma twirled around and around. The golden gown cast a shadow on the bedroom wall. "Look at this gown. Look at these lovely golden dance slippers. If he didn't love me, why would he lavish me with this custom-made gown and slippers?" Her eyes sparkled in the dim lamplight glowing from the bureau in her sister's bedroom. "He introduced me to his esteemed colleagues and friends. He is attentive and kind, always a gentleman."

"But Em, did he say he loves you?" Claudine was getting frustrated; she wanted to know for sure if Commodore Head had declared his love.

Blushing, Emma bowed her head and whispered, "Yes."

The girls embraced and laughed and embraced again. Emma swore Claudine to secrecy. She totally trusted her sister not to breathe a word to their parents or anyone else for that matter. It was fun to share her feelings about Joseph, and Claudine was sweet and encouraging. She liked Joseph and thought he was perfect for Emma. She was thrilled for Emma because she loved her sister very much. She hated seeing her depressed and full of self-doubt when Richard abandoned her.

"Now, Claud, I must go to bed. I am worn out from the ball."

"Oh no, I want to know everything about it. I have never been to any event like that, and I want specifics."

"Dearest, I am ready to fall in my tracks. I will be home all weekend, and I promise, promise I will tell you everything." Emma kissed Claudine's cheek and squeezed her tight.

Claudine moaned. "How can you keep me waiting?" She really was miffed. Emma smoothed her feathers by promising more details about Joseph too. "Oh, all right, but after breakfast in the morning we are talking!"

"Promise; good night, Claudine." With that Emma swirled, opened the door quietly, and went to her room. She was exhausted from the whole experience. Getting ready for the evening, trying to make a good impression on Joseph's men and friends, dancing—all of it was draining, but satisfying. She slipped out of her gown and shoes, took the ribbon out of her hair, washed quickly, and got into bed. She was asleep before her prayers were finished.

Chapter 5

A Commodore's Career Concerns

Joseph arose early Saturday morning. His desk was piled with paperwork, plus he wanted to eat breakfast with his men. He needed to reconnect with them. He was so consumed with Emma, his duties weren't neglected, but his concentration was not as acute as usual. He was a detail man, organized and thorough. Joseph dressed quickly and went down to the dining room at Chateau Philipe for the meal. He was famished. The men were already seated around the dining table.

"Good morning, gentlemen. I hope you all enjoyed yourselves at the ambassador's ball."

All chimed in at once. "Jolly good." "Lovely evening." "Thank you for the invitation." Breton and Conrad both squirmed. Joseph chuckled inside. Both men were swept away by Emma.

"Today and tomorrow, gents, you may spend your time as you wish. I have much to do and will not be able to work with you on our projects. Don't get into any trouble, boys." Joseph laughed.

"Thank you, sir" was heard all around the table. The men deserved two days off. They usually had Sunday off, and pairing it with Saturday gave them a nice long weekend. The men were hard workers and dedicated to serving their country. This group was especially anxious to learn and advance their careers. Training them at sea was second nature to Joseph. He loved being a commodore, commanding ships at sea and training men to become excellent seamen, then recommending elevating the best to petty officer, chief petty officer, warrant officers, midshipman, and on up the ladder to sublieutenant, lieutenant, and up the higher ranks, lieutenant commander, captain, then like Joseph, commodore. The highest ranks were rear admiral, vice admiral, admiral, and the highest rank, admiral of the fleet. This officer commanded the entire Royal Navy. Joseph did not aspire to reaching the highest rank. Being in charge of the Royal Navy was all-consuming since the British Navy was the most powerful in the world.

Training the men in France was a bigger challenge to Joseph because it was more diplomacy than he enjoyed. He was most content at sea. Not that he wasn't capable; he received the commission because of his meticulous training regimen and attention to detail. The men under his tutelage received the most comprehensive training possible. When Joseph was finished with them, they were ready to tackle any obstacles. The men would be promoted quickly through the ranks. The stint in France put these men in position to assist in negotiations with the French military when British-French relations became strained, which was a pattern throughout the two countries' long history.

The British seamen agreed being commanded and taught by Commodore Head gave them a distinct advantage over other men in the navy. Their leader was tough but fair, and a more honorable man they didn't know. His valiant war record spoke for itself. He was a hero, wounded in battle, never leaving a man behind, navigating his ships to British advantage. Joseph was well-known for having fewer casualties than other high-ranking officers. All in all, the men felt blessed to be led by Commodore Head. Plus working at the Embassy was very light duty compared to work on a ship. Joseph was relaxed and spent time with each of his men, imparting years of his own diligent training and expertise.

France had entered the Belle Epoque (Beautiful Age), lasting from 1871 to 1914. After the horrific losses of the Franco-Prussian War, the fall of Paris, and losing Alsace and Lorraine Provinces to Germany, the French government had to rebuild the nation. The following thirty-five years saw rapid commercial, social, and cultural development, and mostly peace. Huge industrial development commenced, and mass consumerism ensued. The wealthy benefited the most, and Edgar Bouron fit into that category as an investment banker. The family personal wealth ballooned over the next decades, and Edgar made sure his own investments yielded high profits. Emma as a young adult and into adulthood reaped the good fortune of the period.

On the other hand, Joseph had flickers of concern regarding the ambitions of the British monarchy. Their prize was India, and protecting British domination in that country was paramount. Diplomatic rumblings suggested the Russians wanted to snatch India from British rule. There was nothing definite at the moment, but Joseph was keeping his ears attuned to discussions regarding problems with the Russians and other nations in that part of the world. Since Britain had the most powerful navy in the world, the government did not hesitate in declaring war on countries that attempted to usurp their authority.

Shielding Emma from matters involving his career was a necessity. Her reaction the night before showed that Conrad's reference to battles and Joseph's wounds upset her greatly. He didn't want her to fret and worry about his safety; after all, it was his career. Until she entered the picture, his life was dedicated to service in Her Majesty's Royal Navy.

After finishing a proper English breakfast of fried eggs, bacon, cooked mushrooms and tomatoes, and freshly baked bread, Joseph bid his men a good day and went back to his quarters to begin the tedious task of sorting out his paperwork. It was a daunting endeavor since he was with his men during the day and usually attended to his paperwork in the evenings, but since being with Emma, he had been lax.

Chapter 6

Maria's Suspicions

EMMA SLEPT LATE, AND CLAUDINE did not awaken her because she knew if Emma were in a bad mood from not enough rest, she would not get details of the ball and Joseph. Instead, she went downstairs for a lovely breakfast of fresh fruit, baked buns slathered in butter and jam, and a steaming cup of coffee. Her mother joined her at the table in the alcove off the kitchen. "Well, dearest, did you get all the news of the event of the season from your sister?"

"Oh, she told me a little, but she was so tired from the whole evening, before we could talk properly, she went to bed. She's still asleep." Claudine was certainly not going to betray her sister by telling her mother Emma's secrets. Surely that would come soon enough as fast as the courtship was moving. Claudine at eighteen years old was unlike Emma; she was more immature. Being the younger child, she was coddled by Edgar and Maria.

Maria conceived a third child after Claudine's birth, but miscarried the baby at about six months. It was a boy. She was inconsolable, especially when the doctor told her she could not carry another pregnancy to term. Complications from having two babies within a year of one another caused her uterus to tilt. When the unborn baby reached a certain size and weight, her body could not handle it. Depression clutched her soul.

Misery clasped her heart. She stayed in bed for weeks. Jenny took care of the little girls while Maria either slept or cried. She berated herself even though the doctor, Edgar, and her friends told her she held no blame. The house was shrouded in a sadness that was palpable. It was during this time that Jenny became the mother figure to Emma and Claudine. She fed them, bathed them, played with them, and put them to bed. When Edgar came home from work, he tended to his wife, which left only slivers of time for the girls. Jenny, Emma, and Claudine formed a bond for life. Jenny never left the Bourons to have a husband, children, and a home of her own. She was totally content to raise "her" girls.

Through cajoling, medication, and talking to her priest, Maria finally joined the family again, but the dynamic had changed. The girls went to Jenny for everything from scrapes to tummy aches; their mother could see the shift, but she didn't have the will to mend it. The children loved and respected their mother, but it was more natural to go to Jenny. Edgar wasn't in the picture much as he worked long hours and when he came home he spent his time with Maria. He adored Emma and Claudine, but Jenny cared for them; and he needed to give his full attention to his wife's recovery. Over time, Maria healed; she loved her girls, but left the mundane chores to Jenny. Since Claudine was the younger and the last child she would have, Maria tended to spoil her.

The miscarriage impacted the Bouron family for life. The girls were too little to understand much except Mama lost a baby, Papa didn't have time for them, and Jenny became the staple in their lives. Emma often wondered when she was older, shy, and awkward, if her father's inattentiveness bred the insecurities that swirled around her constantly. Claudine was a more precocious child and demanded attention. Her foundation was solid; Emma's ebbed and flowed. Claudine was a very pretty girl and at eighteen had an outgoing personality that made her the hit of any crowd. She had loads of friends, and presently was infatuated by George, the young man at La Mansion. She had gentlemen callers, but none of them sparked a flame in her so she kept looking for just the right suitor. Maybe it would be George. He came from a good family and was boyishly handsome.

"Claudine."

"Yes, Mama?"

"What exactly did you think about the gown Commodore Head designed for your sister?" The way Joseph and Emma looked at one another, the fit of the gown, and Joseph's whirlwind pursuit of Emma piqued Maria's curiosity. She wondered about his motive. He was sixteen years older than Emma and a man of the world. She did not want any indiscretions that would harm her daughter or besmirch the Bouron reputation. She experienced an unsettling feeling ever since the day they were all in the lounge before Emma and Joseph went out for the evening.

"Oh, I thought the colors and the fabric were absolutely stunning, and it fit her perfectly."

"How do you think he knew the exact size for your sister?"

Claudine felt uncomfortable, but was obliged to answer her mother; she hesitated a minute trying to get a rational thought in her head.

"Well, answer my question." It was obvious Mama was impatient.

Claudine thought, *here goes; let's see if I can trick Mother as usual.* "Mama, Commodore Head saw Emma in evening dresses for the theater, dinner, and the art gallery. Undoubtedly he consulted with his mother; plus those couture designers have drawings of ladies in gowns, and I am sure the gentleman picked one for the designer as an example." *Lord, did that sound plausible?* Claudine smiled a sweet innocent smile at her mother.

Maria tapped her finger on her lips. "Yes, that seems logical." She knew from having gowns commissioned in Calais that the drawings were part of the process. What was she thinking? Letting her mind run wild was ridiculous; Emma was a good, sensible girl.

Claudine decided to plunge in. "Mama, why do you ask about the gown fitting Emma?"

"Nothing, dear, I was simply admiring the commodore's excellent eye for fashion." Maria covered her queries up very well, she thought. "His mother must be a very kind lady to lend the commodore a hand with the designer and the gown. Has Emma mentioned anything about his parents?" Maria wondered about their station in life.

Mama is fishing. Claudine wasn't stupid. "I think you should ask her about that when she gets up because I don't know."

"Ask me what?" Emma smiled at her mother and sister. They didn't hear her come into the kitchen.

"Good morning, dearest. We want to ask about the ball and all the festivities."

Emma sat at the table, asked the chef for a cup of tea and a poached egg with toast. Then she turned to her mother and sister; she was glowing. Her words tumbled over one another as she described the Embassy ballroom, the lavish decorations, the appetizers, the champagne, the delicious dinner, the marvelous orchestra, and the dancing. She painted a picture of the entertainment while the guests ate seven courses of the delicious meal. She saved the best part for last. She turned and looked directly in her mother's eyes. "Mama, Commodore Head and I were seated at the head table with the ambassador and his wife, the Duke and Duchess of Suffolk, and two decorated British generals and their wives. Joseph was on my right, but on my left were seated General Charles Cousin-Montauban and his perfectly exquisite daughter, Annabelle. She is just a little older than me, but her mama died when she was fourteen and she has taken care of her father ever since. She has sacrificed her own happiness to dedicate herself to the general. She has the sweetest, kindest heart. We talked like we had known each other all of our lives. Her father is also a true gentleman. I spent the entire dinner in conversation with them! It went by so quickly I didn't realize I ignored my escort throughout dinner. I was so very embarrassed when I realized, but Joseph just laughed and said he was pleased I enjoyed them so much. We chatted in French all evening. Joseph does not speak much French. Do you think it was poor etiquette, Mama?"

"No, Emma, it is your native tongue and you were conversing with French people. Now, if you purposely spoke French when in conversation to keep British people who do not know French out of the discussion, then that would be rude. In a group setting, you speak the language of the host."

"Thank you; I would never do anything to embarrass you or Papa." Emma smiled at her mother. She hoped she had laid the groundwork for visiting her new friends. Emma's food was getting cold and she was hungry so she concentrated on eating. She must have appeased her mother, as Maria stood, kissed her girls on the cheeks, and excused herself.

Claudine whispered, "After you finish your breakfast, come up to my room so we can talk." Her expression was one of concern.

"Of course, Claud, is everything all right?" Emma didn't understand why her sister looked quite unsettled.

"No, it's not; Mama questioned me during my entire breakfast."

"About what?"

"Umm, let's see, the fit of the gown, how Joseph knew your size, his parents, on and on."

Emma felt deflated. Why was her mother barraging Claud with these types of questions? *Does she suspect an inappropriate relationship between Joseph and me?* The egg was stuck in the back of her throat. She couldn't swallow. She sipped her tea and the food went down. "I will be up in your room directly. Just let me finish so no one discusses the food I left on my plate." The sarcasm was unlike Emma, but she truly felt threatened for some unknown reason.

Bounding up the staircase Emma's mind was racing. Could anyone know about her liaison with Joseph? Had either of them been indiscreet in front of her parents, or other people at the gallery or the ball? Her heart began to pound. What if a family friend or one of Papa's clients saw her entering the Chateau Philipe on Joseph's arm? By the time she burst into Claudine's room, her palms were slick and her lips quivering.

"Sister, you are shaking. It's not that bad, but our mother, I think, has a sense that your courtship is like a runaway train. You must admit since we went to the dance hall, you and Joseph are inseparable except for work and sleeping."

"Exactly what did Mama ask?"

"Simple at first. Did you tell me all about the ambassador's ball, did you enjoy it? The usual. But then she asked if I liked the gown Joseph designed for you. I told her the fabric and color were beautiful. Then she pointedly asked, 'How do you think the commodore knew her exact size?' That threw me." Emma's face was colorless; he knew the exact size because he knew every inch of her body.

"What did you answer, Claud?" Her voice was a trace above a whisper.

"I gave a very logical response. I said his mother helped, and in the fine design houses they have drawings of gowns, and I suspected he chose one similar to your frame. I also mentioned he saw you in different evening attire. Mama said of course I was right, then she went on to ask about his parents. That's when you walked in the room."

"I wonder why she inquired about Joseph's parents."

"Dear sister, she probably wants to know what kind of family you will be marrying into!" Claudine howled with glee. Emma found the whole conversation strange and premature. She frowned at her sister.

"Don't be ridiculous; we just began courting. What if he doesn't ask me to marry him in the future?" *Why should he?* Emma mused; he possessed her virginity. She freely gave herself to him and even initiated the lovemaking. Was she a fool? He was going to be in Calais another couple months. That was the only certainty she had. Would he go back to England and resume his life as it was before they met? He said they were going to be together, but would they?

"What plans do you and Joseph have this weekend, Emma?"

"Actually, he has to work this weekend. Since we went out so many evenings, his paperwork has become monumental. Remember, I told you last night I would be home all weekend." Emma sounded defensive to Claudine; probably the talk of his family and marriage shook her sister's confidence, what little she possessed. She still could not understand why Emma was so insecure. She was beautiful, intelligent, from a good family; it made no sense.

Claudine knew her own limitations; she was pretty, fun, and lighthearted. She wanted a career like her sister's, but the opportunity hadn't presented itself yet. She didn't turn heads the way Emma did, but she was secure in herself. Even though her mother and father were removed from her daily upbringing, it did not shake her security because Jenny filled the void and Emma was a doting older sister, always protective. Plus, at eighteen, she didn't need a man to give her self-fulfillment or her father to make her grounded. Basically she was happy, had loads of friends, and several young men who caught her fancy. Right now Claudine was smitten with George Reneau. He was handsome, fun-loving, and very rich! She was hoping he would ask her father to court her. The closing of her bedroom door snapped her out of her reverie. Emma was gone. Damn it, she wanted to ask her about the ball and more about Joseph. She certainly wanted to inquire why she became so sensitive regarding Joseph guessing her dress size. Now she would have to wait because when Emma shut down, there was no getting in until she was ready.

Chapter 7

The Telegram

Joseph was at his desk wading through the mundane paperwork; it was moving along quickly. He forced himself to concentrate on last week's logs to help him develop the schedule for the next week that he would coordinate with the French liaison. Sunday he planned to arrange the training schedule for the week after so he and Emma could visit the Cousin-Montaubans in Paris.

Breton bounded up the stairs to the commodore's quarters with a telegram just delivered to the Chateau Philipe by a British naval courier. He was curious about the contents, but most of all, he felt this was a good way to get back in Joseph's good graces after his faux pas the night before. Breton knocked with authority. Joseph answered the door dressed in comfortable clothes and without his hair coiffed. "Yes, Breton, what is it?"

"Sorry to bother you, sir, but this telegram was just delivered for you."

"Thank you, Breton, much appreciated." Breton stood there gawking; Joseph closed the door. *Curiosity killed the cat*, Joseph chuckled to himself. He tore open the telegram. It read:

Unrest along the Afghan border stop. Sending small flotilla for observation stop. If situation escalates will recall you and seamen back to your ships full stop. Rear Admiral Smyth.

"Bloody hell," Joseph said to the empty room. This was not welcome news at all. In the recent past, a chance to return to sea commanding his ships, maneuvering his position to protect British interests, would make his heart race with excitement. He inhaled and almost smelled the salt air. But now Emma was in his life and he wanted to cultivate their relationship. She was young and unaccustomed to the life of a military wife. Well, there it was, Joseph admitted, wife, he thought of her as his wife. He made an immediate decision. Sharing this information with his men or Emma could cause unnecessary speculation; he would tell no one. He vowed if his seamen got wind of it, he would order them to be silent on the subject. He also made another decision. He would work into the night and finish up on Sunday morning, then surprise Emma by calling on her in the afternoon.

Chapter 8

Damaged Goods?

Emma sulked in her room after her conversation with Claudine. She plunged headfirst into a courtship that was unstable because he was British and she French. He could leave her anytime for his home or a deployment. Did he love her enough to commit his life to her? The nagging question made her shudder. She was damaged goods. She not only gave her heart, but her body. Losing her virginity was not a light matter. In her mind, it bound her to Joseph; and if he didn't want her, neither would another man. She gazed out of her bedroom window looking at the familiar lawn, garden, walkway, and street. The tears sprung from both a loss of innocence and a deep resolve. If she couldn't have Joseph, she wanted no one. Everything looked different to her through this new lens of knowledge. She knew she needed to go downstairs and tell her mother and Claudine about the ball, or they might suspect she was melancholy and then the questions would assault her. Emma sighed. She had become a liar, deceitful, and worse, an avid sexual partner.

Emma wiped her tears, pinched her cheeks for a little color, and went downstairs. Claudine and her mother were in the sewing room working on embroidery. She masked her sadness with a brilliant smile and hugged them both. "Sorry about this morning, Claud. Sometimes I react so stupidly to the silliest things."

"Were you girls bickering?" Maria looked surprised as they rarely said a cross word to one another.

"No, Mama, I was inconsiderate of Claudine." Emma dropped the subject quickly. "Now don't you want to know everything about the ball?" Her laughter filled the room.

Both chimed in, "Yes, yes, everything!"

"The whole evening was spectacular. When we arrived at the Embassy, the grand guards announced us. I felt like a princess. Joseph greeted friends and colleagues and introduced me to so many, many dignitaries." Emma giggled. "I hope I didn't appear too enthralled. Joseph and I danced to the music of a full orchestra, and I drank two flutes of champagne. The appetizers were scrumptious, canapés, shrimp, slices of exotic fruits, oh so much. At ten o'clock the ambassador and his wife were announced and made a grand entrance. He toasted the guests and we were seated at dinner. I haven't told you about the entertainment. An extremely talented vocalist sang throughout dinner. After the last course, jugglers performed. A magician did amazing tricks, and a dance troupe performed a graceful ballet. Once they were finished, the orchestra played more music. Honestly, my gown was the loveliest of all the gowns, and I so appreciate Joseph buying it for me." Emma blushed. "Joseph was the most handsome man at the ball."

"My sweet daughter, I think you are very taken with the commodore. I dare say he literally has swept you off your feet." Maria smiled approvingly at her older child.

Emma twisted a lock of her hair and smiled at her mother. She satisfied their curiosity and was ready to escape. "I am going to work on my designs for my puppet line."

"On the weekend?" Claudine chirped.

"Yes, we are in a crunch at the toy shop to get more produced as they have been so well-received. Children love them, and we are replenishing supplies to all the outlets that carry them. I am designing new puppet characters for the line." Emma changed the subject. "Where is Jenny?"

Maria frowned. She knew Emma was going to tell Jenny all the details of the ball and most probably more than she shared with her and her sister. "I believe she is upstairs ironing your dresses for the week," Maria said curtly.

"Thank you, Mama." Ignoring Maria's tone, she kissed her mother on the cheek and headed for Jenny's quarters.

Emma knocked on Jenny's door. "Jenny, it's me, Emma, may I come in?" Her voice cracked.

"Of course, mon enfant."

Jenny opened the door and Emma fell into her arms sobbing. "What in the world happened, my lovely girl?" She was completely perplexed. The evening before, Emma was giggling and swirling in her designer gown and slippers, a picture of happiness and joy. Something drastic happened for such a dramatic mood swing. "Come along, sit down, and I will make you a cup of tea. Here's a hanky; dry your eyes and we will sort out whatever caused this sadness." Jenny filled the kettle.

Emma slumped into an overstuffed chair upholstered in navy blue velvet. The chair was worn from many years of use. When the girls were little, they often perched on Jenny's lap in the big chair as she read storybooks to them or brushed their hair or simply cuddled them.

Jenny took the lace handkerchief from Emma, wiped away her tears, then handed her a steaming cup of strong India tea, freshly brewed on Jenny's small gas stove. "Now, sweet girl, what brought on this distress?"

Her eyes held a deep maudlin look that unnerved Jenny. She had seen the same look many times, and it was always caused by something hurtful, whether tangible or intangible.

Emma stumbled over her words. "It's my courtship."

"What do you mean? Are you not suited with the gentleman? Is he unkind or thoughtless? Oh, dear God, did he make intimate advances toward you?" Jenny bristled.

Emma interrupted the onslaught of questions. "No, no, he is everything I could ever want. Jenny, I know already I love Joseph and want to spend my life with him."

Jenny stared at her precious young lady in disbelief.

"Ma chérie, you have only known the commodore for a short while. How can you be sure? He is a worldly man who travels all over the earth, continent to continent. I am sure his charm is an aphrodisiac that sparked unfamiliar feelings." Jenny gave Emma a half smile.

"I have faith he feels the same." Emma looked at her surrogate mother with an urgency Jenny needed to unravel. Her mind, of course, conjured up the sight of Joseph descending the outside stairs at dawn.

"What gives you this assurance?" She didn't want to be too hard on her protégée. Emma's self-esteem shattered like glass as a child. Jenny was determined to probe in a subtle way until she found out exactly what the relationship entailed.

"Well, he told me he loves me, and never considered the married life before or a family." Emma gave a weak smile.

"Do you believe him to be honorable in his intentions?"

"Yes, I do, but I have . . ."

"What? Emma, you know your secrets will die with me. Whatever you tell me, I will not condemn you or rebuke you. I am here to help you, ma chérie."

"It is complicated." Emma cast her eyes to the floor. Should she blurt out that her virginity was gone? She trusted Jenny with her life, but would she be disgusted with her behavior? She had to take the chance so Jenny could advise her. She was miserable. "Please hear me out before you say anything. This is very difficult for me, but you are the only person in the world I trust with my secrets."

This must be serious, Jenny thought. There was nothing light about whatever Emma needed to share. Out of sheer love, she held her hand gently as Emma began her story.

"I lied about a mutual friend introducing Joseph and me. The evening I went to La Mansion with Claudine is the first time I ever laid eyes on him. He came up behind me and escorted me to the door, then asked if he could see me home. Oh, Jen, from the first minute I looked into his beautiful blue eyes, I felt butterflies. His laugh excited me. We talked so easily. It was as if I had known him forever. The very first night he kissed me; I was exhilarated. I knew I should be coy and shy, but you know I am no good at playing games with emotions. I kissed him back and I felt truly alive." Emma decided to keep the part about the alleyway to herself. "The whole courtship is magical. The places he takes me, the people I meet, all of it is so wonderful."

Jenny's heart pounded as she perceived the direction the conversation was going. "Well, then, sweet girl, what is the problem that brought on these floods of tears?"

Emma whispered, "I am no longer pure." There it was, the stark truth looming in the cozy room. "I gave Joseph my heart and body without reservation."

The skin all over Jenny's body chilled with goose bumps. She conjectured as much by the familiar way they looked at each other. The perfect fit of the gown. The flush in Emma's cheeks and the buoyancy in her steps. Commodore Head claimed her sweet innocent girl's virginity. Oh dear God, this secret must be hidden away in her soul. She decided to plunge in deeper to get the exact details of the disastrous event. "Ma chérie, when and where did this liaison happen?"

Emma decided not to give Jenny descriptions of their lovemaking and the number of times they made love. She wasn't lying, just eliminating graphic details. The look on Jenny's face was ashen already. "Well, I got a terrible headache the night of the theater outing, so we went to his quarters at Chateau Philipe for a quiet dinner."

"Mon Dieu," exclaimed Jenny. It slipped out before she held her tongue.

"Please, Jen, I need you to listen, and you can judge me later."

"Oui, oui."

"It was all so natural, and I must tell you in all sincerity, the gentleman did not push me or influence me at all; I wanted it as much as he did. He even asked me if I was sure. He is so loving, and he taught me what love between a man and a woman really means. Even in his deep embarrassment, he explained what to do after lovemaking." Emma blushed and lowered her eyes to the floor.

Jenny's mind raced. Emma's purity vanished in the spring air. Unless she were betrothed and married to the commodore, she most probably would end up a spinster. The gentlemen of France wanted the women they married to be untouched. It was condoned by society that men dabbled in salacious dalliances, but such behavior was absolutely prohibited for females. A wife was subservient to her husband. The man was the head of the household, who worked away from the home, but the woman ran the house, directed the servants, produced children, and fulfilled her husband's every need. Most upper-class marriages were not love matches. Many were for the melding of landowning families, escalating social status, and solidifying aristocratic bloodlines. The upper-middle class, like the Bourons, obtained more wealth generated from the birth of bustling businesses and investments. But they tended to pattern themselves after the upper class, and expectations for their offspring were similar. Strict etiquette was paramount. Had Emma tossed away her future? In a split second Jenny made a decision; she grasped Emma's shoulders.

"Look at me, ma chérie. You are not to breathe one word of this to anyone, especially Claudine. We must keep these secrets between us. Do not tell Commodore Head you shared this news." Jenny's eyes narrowed.

"I wouldn't tell Claudine under any circumstance, Jen. I told her I love Joseph and he loves me, but that is all. Why should I keep our talk from Joseph? He knows I am closer to you than my own mother."

The last words softened Jenny; she would protect Emma with her life, she loved her so deeply. "Emma, I suspected you were closer to the gentleman than anyone knew."

"Why?"

"The night you screamed from a nightmare and I came running to your room, the door was locked, which was unusual. I went back to my quarters, but couldn't sleep so I made a cup of tea and watched the dawn break. I saw him descending the outside staircase."

"You said nothing to me, Jen." Emma was shocked.

"My dear, it would be a lie to say I was not deeply concerned, but I knew you would tell me the circumstances when you were ready."

Jenny could hardly breathe Emma hugged her so hard. "You have stood by me my whole life and you understand me completely. What am I to do now?" She was crestfallen and miserable.

"Ma chérie, it seems like a precarious situation, but we will work it out between us. What makes you think the commodore is wavering in his love for you?"

Emma squirmed in the chair and twisted her hair over and over. "I don't know. What if I am just a diversion while he is in Calais?"

"Have his actions suggested such after, uh, after . . ."

"No, but we are not seeing each other this weekend so he can catch up with paperwork he put aside to entertain me each evening. Do you think it means he doesn't want to be with me?" There was desperation in Emma's voice.

Jenny felt Emma's anxiety. "Think logically, my dear. Isn't it plausible Commodore Head has massive amounts of work to do since he is the highest-ranking naval officer in Calais with a prestigious demanding job? Think: he put everything aside to court you this whole week." Jenny gave Emma a little squeeze of affection.

A week, is that all it's been? Emma felt she had been a part of Joseph's life much, much longer. She shuddered; his French life—she knew nothing of his life in England. This realization made her feel worse. Flashes of their lovemaking like a moving picture crossed her mind. She shuddered again.

She shrugged. "I guess you're right, Jenny."

Jenny knew she didn't mean what she said. Her voice and body language oozed self-doubt. *Beautiful Emma, never sure of herself.* This entire week she blossomed with confidence and joy, but she reverted to her underlying flaw. By the time the weekend was over, Jenny speculated, she would convince herself the commodore didn't mean anything he said; she would be lost once again. Never mind that; the problem still hung like a shroud: her virginity was gone.

Emma interrupted Jenny's thoughts. "I love you, Jen. Thanks for your confidence. Moping around your quarters won't change a thing. I am going to concentrate on my puppet line. At least the puppets can't commit mortal sins." Then out the door she went.

Chapter 9

A Decisive Man

No wonder Joseph's stomach grumbled; he looked at his watch and it was ten o'clock. He was so immersed in his work the time vanished and night had fallen. He stretched his legs, then threw on a casual jacket and went down to the hotel restaurant. It was empty except for a few late diners. The maître d' seated him at a table and handed him a menu. Joseph was famished. He ordered a carafe of Bordeaux, a fromage board, fresh bread, and slices of rare beef. He didn't want to sup on a heavy dinner this late. He poured a glass of wine. It was delicious. The French knew how to ferment wine to perfection.

He completed the tasks he outlined for himself. The only thing left was to coordinate schedules with the French liaison in the morning, and then he could call on Emma. It surprised Joseph how void his life felt without her. Their courtship was only a week old, yet he knew he couldn't let her go. He smiled to himself. At thirty-five years old, he planned to marry. His parents would be ecstatic. The Head legacy would live on through their older son when he bore children. The lands and manor house that were in his family for centuries would pass on to him and subsequently his firstborn son. If he produced daughters, they would go to the eldest. Dear God, the Afghan border was in peril, and he, Commodore Joseph Head, was daydreaming about marriage and his lineage. If anyone told him a week earlier this would be the case, he would have thought that person was cracked! The waiter arrived with his dinner. He devoured every morsel as if he'd been deprived of food for weeks.

When Joseph returned to his rooms, he retrieved his sea maps from his trunk and studied all the passageways to India. If the border of Afghanistan with Russia were broached, the Russians had a clear land route to India. Protecting the British territory by sea was another matter, his matter. He loved his ships, and he felt protective of the men he commanded. Being prepared was of utmost importance to Joseph. Joseph's naval persona took over, and he studied and sketched, studied and sketched. At one o'clock he was satisfied with his proposal for Rear Admiral Smyth if the situation escalated. His naval plan was completed before he retired for the night.

He was tired, but slept fitfully. A dream of Emma made him restless and left him wanting her. The next dream, he was on the deck of his ship, watching smoke from the canons wafting in front of his eyes. He smelled the acrid gunpowder and his eyes burned from the smoke residue. He finally fell into a deep sleep in the early morning hours. Images of Emma's naked body and the sea snaked through his brain.

Joseph roused himself later than usual, nine o'clock. He lit a fire, heated his water, then washed thoroughly and dressed in his day uniform. He went down to the dining room for coffee and some light pastry. As soon as he finished, he awakened Percy, who by the look of him was out late the night before; he was disheveled and still in his clothes. Joseph laughed. "Good morning, Percy, aren't you chipper this day."

"Ah, sir, me and the fellas went into Calais central last night, went to the dance hall, and then closed down the tavern."

"You boys didn't get into any trouble, did you?"

"No, but I did see Miss Emma's younger sister at the dance, and Cassandra Ballou. In fact, she was chatting with Miss Bouron. She's a nosy one and pushy. She's sniffed around you since becoming a widow." Percy snickered.

Joseph wondered what in the world would a woman like Cassandra be doing at La Mansion and why would she talk to Claudine. It briefly concerned him, but he was too busy to waste time thinking about her nighttime activity and dismissed his thoughts.

"Well, my friend, clean up, get some coffee, and I will meet you in an hour in front of the hotel. I have a meeting with our French liaison for the week's preparations, and then I would like to go to the Bourons." Joseph smiled.

Nicholas, the French liaison, waited for Joseph at the port. They met in Nic's office and went over the upcoming week's schedule. Joseph added a set of seamen shore drills. Nic acted surprised and questioned his British colleague, "Do you actually want to run through shore drills with your young officers?"

"Yes, Nic, can't have them getting complacent." Joseph chuckled.

Nic's eyes narrowed. "Joseph, I know you well over many years; you always do something for a reason. What is it?"

"Honestly, friend, my men have enjoyed quite an easy time over the past several weeks, and I really do want them in tip-top shape."

Nic didn't buy it, but dropped it. He had something else on his mind. "Another oddity, Joseph, occurred at your ambassador's ball."

"What's that?"

"When and where did you meet the lovely lady in the golden gown?" Nic grinned from ear to ear; he knew his question embarrassed Joseph.

"I met her through mutual friends, and I know her father." Joseph concentrated on sounding casual, but Nic saw a light in his friend's eyes he'd not seen before.

"Since she is only an acquaintance, I would like to meet her and escort her out." Nic was toying with Joseph. It worked; his friend looked appalled. He concentrated on keeping a straight face. "She is a national French treasure; she needs a French man." Nic burst out laughing at Joseph's look of dismay.

"Forget it, mate. I am officially courting her." Joseph smiled and winked at Nic.

"Anyone with eyes could see how you felt the way you looked at her. She's absolutely beautiful, poised, and full of class. You are a lucky man, Joseph."

Joseph knew Emma was a jewel inside and out. What made him feel really possessive was the way she made love to him. Pure abandonment, nothing held back; he would not lose that. He decided to tell Nic about his plan to take her to Paris. Nic knew General Cousin-Montauban well; he had served under him. He knew Annabelle as well. "Nic, I want to take a few days at the end of the week to take Emma to Paris to visit with Charles and Annabelle Cousin-Montauban."

"Oh, that is why we have the whole week mapped out, and that's probably why you are putting the men through their drills." Nic roared with laughter and lightly punched Joseph on his arm. "No problem, my friend; I will take care of everything."

"Thanks, Nic, I really appreciate it."

"You owe me, buddy!" They both laughed.

Chapter 10

High Tea

It was three o'clock Sunday afternoon, a perfect time to stop by the Bourons' home to see Emma. They should have finished their midday meal but would not be quite ready for tea. Joseph didn't want to impose since he was arriving unannounced. He could not go the entire weekend without seeing Emma. Being in her company made him happier than he had ever been, even when away at sea and commanding his ships. A woman hadn't been a top priority for him, so at thirty-five years old, this experience was new. There was an emptiness surrounding him because he hadn't seen her. Joseph asked Percy to stop at a flower vendor's stall along the Calais trading district. He chose two bouquets, pink roses for Mrs. Bouron and white lilies for Emma. He wished sunflowers were in season. They were his favorites, but he chose his second best.

The Bouron family returned from Mass at about eleven o'clock, and as was their custom, the chef prepared a cooked dinner for noon. Today he prepared roast pork, stewed apples, boiled potatoes, and cauliflower florets. A light honey mustard glaze flavored the meat, and the boiled potatoes were rubbed with fresh-churned butter and parsley. Edgar, Maria, and the girls supped in the formal dining room on Sundays and when they entertained guests. The custom helped teach Claudine and Emma proper dining etiquette, which silver utensils were used with which dish, and which course came in what order. They engaged the girls in polite conversation, making sure they were abreast of the important topics in France and abroad. When a light sponge cake was served with clotted cream, the conversation turned to the ambassador's ball. Edgar purposely steered the conversation in that direction, as Emma seemed preoccupied and aloof during the meal. "Your mother tells me, Emma, that the ball was spectacular, with an accomplished orchestra, dancing, entertainment during and after dining, and prime seating for you and Commodore Head."

"Yes, Papa, the whole affair was lovely, but most of all I found an instant friend in Annabelle Cousin-Montauban. Her father is a highly decorated general in the French Army. They came to Calais for the ball, but their primary residence is in Paris."

Edgar sat taller in his wing-backed chair. "Why, of course, I am familiar with the feats of General Cousin-Montauban. He is renowned for his courage, bravery, and finesse in battle. What an honor you have become acquainted." Edgar smiled.

Emma's mood brightened considerably. It was obvious her father was extremely impressed with her new friends. This certainly worked to her advantage to gain approval for a trip to the Cousin-Montaubans' home in Paris if Joseph still wanted to make the trip. She smiled brightly at her father and stretched the truth to set the trap. "Papa, I overheard Joseph and the General talking about your banking business. Something about investment possibilities, but I didn't listen closely as Annabelle and I were more interested in discussing the fashions at the party."

Edgar was ready to burst. Becoming financial advisor to the commodore and the general would be a staggering accomplishment. His regular clients would be impressed and feel deeper confidence in his recommendations. This was welcome news, to say the least. Emma's courtship might reap many rewards. He tried not to sound overly impressed. "How kind of the gentlemen to recognize my financial expertise. I am flattered." Edgar smiled casually at his elder daughter, but underneath his heart pounded.

As the maid cleared the table, the girls excused themselves. Claudine went to the sewing room to continue work on hand lace, while Emma went up to her room to finish up two new puppet characters she created over the weekend. The drawings showed much promise as she worked and reworked the little toys. The time flew by, and before she knew it, the hall clock struck two. She wondered what Joseph was doing. Had he completed his work? Did he think of her, even miss her company? She put her drawings into her attaché case as the clouds lowered over her mood. She stretched out across her bed and closed her eyes. Visions of Joseph fluttered through her mind. Thinking of his passionate kisses, she drifted off to sleep.

The clatter of horses' hoofs awakened her from a light sleep. Emma jumped up and looked out of her bedroom window. It was the British Embassy carriage, with Percy driving. He pulled up to the walkway and stopped, and Joseph alighted from within. Her heart skipped a beat. What was he doing here? She ran over to the looking glass, smoothed down her Sunday dress, quickly combed her loose hair, pinched her cheeks, and dabbed on a trace of lip balm. She took several deep breaths and waited, not knowing what she was waiting for exactly. Her door was closed, but she heard the bell ringing. Jenny was downstairs, and she answered the door.

"Good afternoon, monsieur."

"Good afternoon, madame." Joseph smiled and bowed. "I do hope I am not intruding, but I ventured over to see if Mademoiselle Bouron had plans for tea." Jenny stared at Joseph as if he'd just committed a crime. She knew what he had done to her darling Emma. Damaged goods, that's what she was now. Joseph waited for a response while Jenny looked at him with real disdain. He tried again. "Madame, is mademoiselle accepting company?" The question brought Jenny's thoughts back to the present.

"I will check with Monsieur Bouron." Her voice was like ice, and Joseph wondered what he had done to turn the woman against him. He needed her for the Paris trip. She left him standing in the foyer holding two bouquets. He was totally baffled by her behavior.

Edgar came trotting out of the parlor. "My apologies, Joseph. I do not know what got into the girl to leave you standing here." He would strangle Jenny if her rudeness offended the commodore. The thoughts of conducting business with him and his friend Cousin-Montauban were of great importance to him.

"Please, monsieur," Joseph started.

"Call me Edgar; we know each other well enough now." He smiled broadly.

"Please, Edgar, don't blame the girl. I arrived without a proper outing planned and," he laughed, "without an invitation. I finished my work early and thought if Emma was not too busy, she might enjoy Sunday high tea."

"Come in, come in, Joseph. Let me send Jenny to get Emma from her room. She has been immersed in work this weekend."

Edgar sent Jenny up to Emma's room with a look of reprimand. Jenny noticed immediately, of course, and even though she knew she had been rude, she couldn't help herself. If the gentleman did not intend to marry her precious Emma, then life was going to become very complicated. Jenny barely turned the handle on the bedroom door when Emma yanked it open. "Child, you almost pulled my arm from its socket."

"Well, I have been straining against this door to hear what's happening, but all the words are muffled. What is Joseph doing here?" Jenny shrugged. "I mean it, Jen, what is going on?" Naturally she thought the worst. He came to tell Papa he could no longer court her. He was going back to England. That's why Jenny looked so distraught!

"He wants to take you to high tea this afternoon." Jenny smirked.

"What?"

"He wants to take you to tea." She sneered.

Emma shook Jenny by the shoulders. "I shouldn't have confided in you. I can see the ire and disdain in your face. How can you act this way? You know I love him." The hot tears of anger streamed down her face. All the fear of abandonment and betrayal bubbled to the surface like molten lava. Jenny was the mother she trusted and loved unconditionally. Emma slumped on her bed. The outburst jolted Jenny.

"Oh, Emma, I'm a fool. I was so worried about our confidence, I ignored what you must be feeling." Jenny wrapped her arms around Emma. "Forgive me, dearest girl. I love you so much and will stand by you for life, as I always have." Jenny kissed her forehead. "Please, I will not judge your Joseph, I promise. I have become old and jaded and forget the pull of young love. Let me dry your tears so you will be lovely when the commodore sees you."

"Please, Jenny; I need you to be supportive and not judgmental. Please." The desperation in Emma's voice was all Jenny needed to make a promise.

"Forgive me, Emma. I promise I will keep your secrets no matter what happens with you and Joseph or anything else in your life."

Edgar could not understand what was taking so long. It was an easy task to fetch Emma from her room. He planned to have a stern talk with Jenny regarding her behavior, although he knew it was to no avail because even in his mind, she was a member of the family, not a servant. If not for Jenny, Edgar couldn't have coped when Maria had her breakdown.

His impatience got the best of him. He excused himself, stood at the landing of the stairs, and called up to summon the women. Emma's door opened immediately. The two looked like conspirators, but never mind; he could not keep Joseph waiting any longer. "What on earth took you so long?" His look was meant to reprimand Jenny.

"Papa, I was napping when Jenny told me Joseph was here. I freshened up as quickly as possible."

"Come, come, the gentleman is patiently waiting in the parlor. Emma, he has invited you to Sunday high tea with my permission, which sounds like a perfect gesture."

"I haven't been to a British high tea and would love to go. Are you going to approve, Papa?"

"Yes, yes, harmless afternoon invitation." Jenny rolled her eyes behind their backs. *Harmless indeed! Who knew when he would seduce Emma again.* She didn't let them see her expression. When Edgar, Emma, and Jenny went into the parlor, Joseph was chatting with Maria. Emma's mother was holding a lovely bouquet of pink roses. Emma smiled; *ah, Joseph was reeling in her mother.* The maid brought in a porcelain vase for the flowers.

Joseph turned toward Emma, a broad smile covering his face. "Bonjour, mademoiselle. I hope I haven't made a nuisance of myself by turning up at your doorstep to request your company for Sunday tea." He bent over and kissed Emma's hand and winked, which was for her eyes only. She couldn't help but giggle.

"As a matter of fact, sir, I have had a very productive weekend and was taking a rest when Jenny let me know you were here. With my father's permission, I would enjoy tea with you." Emma turned to Edgar.

"Commodore, I think Emma will enjoy the experience of a British tea. We French have not mastered the art." Both men laughed.

Joseph turned his attention to Emma. "I hope you like lilies." He handed her the bouquet, all the while gazing deeply into her eyes. His blue pools mesmerized Emma. She couldn't help but stammer a thank you and sent Jenny to place them in a vase, then put them on her bedroom bureau. Emma kissed her parents on the cheek, then linked her arm with Joseph's. They were out the door without a time limit imposed by Edgar.

Once outside, Joseph whispered to Emma that he worked late into the night and all day to get his business in order so he would finish in time to see her. "I could not wait until Monday evening to see you. It has taken every bit of concentration to focus on my work because you kept invading my mind."

Emma tweaked his arm and laughed. She was thrilled to see him. He looked comfortable and relaxed in his civilian day clothes. Every time before that she was with Joseph, he wore one of his uniforms. His sandy blond hair was pulled back loosely in a ponytail. He looked much younger than thirty-five. "Honestly, Joseph, you never crossed my mind since the ball." Emma threw her head back and laughed. He squeezed her hand. He knew she was teasing him by the look in her eyes.

They had an enjoyable carriage ride to the Chateau Philippe. Percy heard their laughter from his perch on the driver's bench. He was surprised when his boss said he was going to the Bourons' because Joseph hadn't told him to be ready in advance, very out of character. Joseph meticulously prepared his schedule week by week, day by day, and this was not on the calendar. He was more taken with the French girl than Percy originally perceived.

Joseph and Emma went into the dining room for Sunday tea. The spread was lovely: cucumber finger sandwiches, a variety of pastries, and delicious black tea from India. Emma put sugar and cream in her cup of tea. Joseph watched her every move. She was dainty and poised. The other people at tea couldn't help snatching glances at her. Emma's hair was loose to her waist; it was thick, brunette, with auburn highlights and a relaxed natural curl. It struck Joseph how young she looked in her Sunday church dress and her hair loose. Many of the women he bedded plastered on face makeup to look younger or more attractive. Emma wore nothing and looked perfect.

"Joseph, what are you thinking about? I have been in a one-way conversation." Her laughter bounced around the room, and other diners smiled.

"I am sorry, sweetheart; I was drinking in your loveliness instead of my tea and listening to conversation." Emma tweaked his arm and giggled.

"You, sir, are incorrigible." Her confidence caused Joseph to smile with relief. Possibly he was succeeding in reassuring her of his feelings. He had been tender, attentive, and loving—uncharted water for him. The sea had been his love for sixteen years, but now a new love rocked his world. One week changed his life forever. He was a decisive man, and from the first night he knew he wanted Emma permanently. After the ambassador's ball, he realized permanently meant marriage, children, and a home. Dear God, in his wildest dreams he never considered having a wife, let alone children. He smiled to himself. The thought of children with Emma was totally different. His parents would be ecstatic, especially his mother, who had tried to marry him off to every eligible girl in all of England!

"Joseph, your mind is wandering again," she giggled. "Are you bored with my company?" Emma was teasing him.

He playfully jabbed back. "No, not at all. This reminds me of my dinner conversation with you at the ball."

"Oh, you are wicked, aren't you?" Her laughter rang out again. She loved being so at ease with Joseph. Her trust in him had become deep in a short period. Every time she had questioned him in her mind, he had proved her wrong. The way he treated her and guarded her feelings made her feel safe. How could she, Emma Bouron, be so fortunate? She loved everything about him: his looks, his personality, his character, and his bravery as an officer. There was not one thing she would change. When he made love to her, she gave all of herself because she trusted him. Even a slight touch from him electrified her in a way that she had never imagined possible.

Emma's mood swings from self-doubt and fear to trust and conviction boomeranged through her mind.

"If you are finished, Emma, shall we retire to my salon to make plans for the Paris trip?"

Luckily the stairs to the private quarters were separate from the dining room. No one would see the couple ascending to the second level from the vantage point of the dining area. Joseph was cognizant of protecting Emma's reputation. Once inside his private parlor, he took her in his arms and kissed her tenderly. "Darling, I could not go an entire weekend without being with you." Their eyes locked and an unspoken affirmation passed between them. Emma's arms were around Joseph's neck and she squeezed him close.

"I, as well, missed you terribly. Crazy thoughts tumbled through my mind."

"What thoughts?"

"Oh, that you were tired of me since we had no plans for the weekend." Joseph began to protest. Emma put her finger to his lips. "I know those thoughts are ridiculous, and you coming to my home to see me made me realize how silly I was being. Thank you, Joseph, for bringing me to tea."

Her sincerity and honesty were like a refreshing breeze. He totally disliked the parameters of courtship, the man and the woman circling each other like prey. The woman acted coy when it was obvious to onlookers that an ulterior motive provoked the sparring. Joseph thought that's why he had avoided it like the plague. Having brief interludes without strings was most attractive to his tastes. But now, he had fallen for a girl who didn't play games. It was most appealing to him. In fact, it was the one dimension he didn't think he would ever find in a woman. Yes, she was insecure and riddled with self-doubt, but he was certain once they were betrothed and married, that would change completely. He knew the previous brief engagement had rattled her, but there was something deeper in her foundation as a person that caused the lack of self-esteem. Joseph felt assured that in time he would unlock the secrets of her being.

"I would like to travel to Paris on Thursday and return on Sunday. That way both of us will only miss two days of work, and it will give us all day Friday and Saturday to enjoy the city, one another, and the Cousin-Montaubans. Plus, I will have Monday and Tuesday of this week to convince your father the trip is harmless and Jenny should accompany us on the journey. What do you think, Emma?"

She flinched when he mentioned Jenny traveling with them, but realized there was no possible way her father would allow her to go without a proper chaperone. She must have another talk with Jenny to smooth the way for a pleasant trip.

"I think that's a splendid idea." They were sitting on the settee in front of the fire. Emma slid over and perched on Joseph's lap. "Now, Commodore Head, how are you going to persuade Papa to let me go?"

Joseph hugged her. "You leave that to me, mademoiselle. I can be very convincing." They both laughed. Then Joseph nuzzled her neck, entwined his fingers in her thick hair, and kissed her. Emma's response was instant. She maneuvered her body so she pressed against his chest. He could feel her breath coming quickly. He had to pull away before he lifted her in his arms and took her into the bedchamber. Lord, he wanted to make love to her, but getting her home early would show Mr. Bouron respect for his daughter. He knew no time limit was imposed; consequently, arriving early should make a positive impression. He lightly pushed her away.

Emma looked crestfallen, like a disappointed child.

"Darling, listen to me. I want to get you home early so your mother and father see I respect you and them. I know Edgar did not tell me a time to have you home. Maybe he is testing me. Let's tread lightly so that Paris is in our grasp." Joseph smiled broadly.

"You are so wise, Joseph, and of course, you are so right. Papa will definitely see the admiration you have for him by taking good care of me." Emma whispered in his ear, "I shouldn't have looked dejected, but when you kiss me like that, I want all of you."

"Oh God, Emma, stop, or all my resolve will be shattered." He was hard beneath her lap. She could feel him. She jumped up and pulled him to his feet. Smiling, she gazed into his blue pools, then closed her eyes and kissed him passionately once again.

She threw her head back and laughed. "Joseph, I love what I can do to you. But I agree, we must go."

"This is torture." Joseph's throaty laugh filled the stairway as they went down the stairs.

Edgar heard a carriage pull up to the house. He looked out the foyer-door window; to his surprise, the carriage had the British Embassy emblem on the door, which meant Emma was home. He frowned as Joseph and Emma walked up the pathway. They had only been gone for a couple of hours. He wondered if they had a squabble, but observing them, they looked perfectly happy. He opened the front door. "How was the high tea?" He smiled broadly.

"Papa, it was lovely. We were served sandwiches, pastries, bread and butter, plus the most delicious tea I have ever tasted." Emma smiled sweetly at her father.

"Sir, thank you for allowing Emma to accompany me. It made my Sunday afternoon delightful." Joseph spoke in the most respectful manner. "I hope you and your family have a pleasant evening. Emma, I look forward to seeing you soon." He bowed, kissed her hand, and gave her a private wink. Smiling, he shook Edgar's hand, then turned down the pathway and hopped into the carriage.

The short outing piqued Edgar's curiosity. Asking Emma some probing yet carefully worded questions would satisfy his speculations. He put his arm around his daughter's tiny waist and steered her toward the interior of the house. "Ma chérie, do you enjoy the commodore's company?"

Emma blushed. "Yes, Papa, I think he is the kindest and most honorable man I have had the pleasure of knowing, except for my own father."

"Ah, sweet girl, you are the one who is kind. How did you like the British tradition of high tea? It's something we French do not have."

"I did. The table was laid splendidly and the food scrumptious."

"You are home quite early." Edgar thought if he made it a casual statement, Emma might readily embellish more information regarding her relationship with the commodore.

"Papa, that is part of what I mean about Joseph being honorable. He felt quite awkward interrupting our Sunday afternoon. He thought I would be pleased to go to tea, which was very kind. We went for a long walk, and I chattered on and on about my new friend Annabelle Cousin-Montauban. I don't have many fast friends. My sister is my closest friend and confidante, but Annabelle and I bonded immediately. She is such a lovely person. I was telling Joseph how many things we have in common. She loves art, music, museums, the interests I have." Emma was carefully laying the groundwork without her father having any idea of her motives. "Joseph and her father are very close, as they fought side by side in foreign wars." Emma smiled sweetly at her father. "You know, I am not well versed on the military or politics, so it is a delightful combination that the men can discuss their interests and Annabelle and I can chat about fashion, my work, art, and our love of architecture."

Conversation regarding the Cousin-Montaubans piqued Edgar's interest. It would be a coup if he became their financier, which could lead to other notable individuals investing through him. "Dearest, I share your opinion of Joseph. Of course, I do not know the Cousin-Montaubans personally, by reputation only, but I am pleased you have forged a new friendship with Mademoiselle Cousin-Montauban. She must be a wonderful girl, because you are not easily impressed. I encourage you to develop the friendship. We need faithful friends in life, Emma. Remember that bit of wisdom from your old papa."

Emma smiled at her father. She felt overjoyed she had successfully set the wheels in motion for the Paris visit.

Chapter 11

Through Fate Stars Align

WHEN EMMA ARRIVED AT WORK Monday morning, she shared her sketches that she developed over the weekend. The other designers and her employer loved the new puppets she created, along with the clothing option. The female puppet was a princess and the male a prince. Little girls played for hours pretending they were living in a castle with a handsome prince, courtiers, and ladies-in-waiting. Emma explained a new concept of making the clothing removable so other ensembles could be purchased separately for the same puppets. Emma clarified how parents would have the opportunity to buy several outfits without having to purchase more puppets. Profits potentially would escalate. Manufacturing interchangeable clothing would prove less expensive than producing puppets wearing one set of clothing. Different puppets would each have a line of clothing, so if the family were of means, they could indulge their children with more than one set of the marionettes; if not, they could purchase different ensembles. Emma sketched different gowns and suits for the prince and princess.

The company manager in Calais was more than impressed by the idea. His instincts told him it would be a winner for him and for his designer, Mademoiselle Bouron. He praised Emma for her innovative presentation, then went into his office. He calculated a cost analysis and was highly impressed by the results. It could mean a promotion for him and the designer. The best avenue to take was to present the concept and drawings to the owner at the Paris headquarters; of course, Mademoiselle Bouron definitely would make the presentation.

Late in the afternoon, Manager Ferra summoned Emma to his office. "Mademoiselle, I commend you. I worked most all day on an in in-depth cost analysis of the concept you presented at our Monday morning meeting. I strongly believe your idea is brilliant and extremely profitable for the company. My projections show a much larger profit margin than we are now experiencing. Emma, I dare say this could mean a promotion and advancement for us both." Emma blushed with pride.

She was excited at the thought of a huge successful step forward in her career. Plain and simple, she loved her work, because it gave her confidence, an inner satisfaction human relationships denied her. Dealing with concepts and inanimate characters protected her from the heartache and disappointment she felt in people. A concept, character, or toy did not possess the power to hurt her or make her feel unworthy. Only people had that power.

Ferra continued, "Our next move is gearing up the production line to make what we will call the *Royal Marionettes,* plus four or five interchangeable ensembles. If I call the team together today, we should be ready by Friday to present the line to top management in Paris."

Emma could not believe her ears. Was this really happening? A business meeting in Paris fell in her lap? No circumstances would keep her father from approving, especially if Joseph escorted her and General Cousin-Montauban offered lodging! She knew Edgar had grown to trust Joseph in a very short time, which she attributed to Joseph's age and station in life. Plus, bringing Jenny along would make a denial impossible.

"Say something, Emma. Does this not please you?" Ferra questioned his lovely designer.

"Yes, monsieur, I am overwhelmed with your endorsement and generosity." Emma was very truthful. Next to Joseph, her career was of utmost importance. "As you know, Monsieur Ferra, I am not of age." Emma looked downcast.

"I forget. You are a pioneer in this field, and your age eludes me." Ferra laughed. "What you have designed surpasses creations of craftsmen much older than you."

"Because I haven't reached the age of majority, which when I last checked was twenty-one," Emma laughed, "I must be chaperoned on an out-of-town trip." Ferra started to interrupt, but Emma stopped him. "The gentleman I am courting was planning to visit a colleague in Paris at the end of the week. If I can persuade him to leave Friday instead of Thursday, I am sure my father would agree, plus my chambermaid would accompany me."

Ferra sighed with relief. "Perfect, Emma, perfect. I will make all the arrangements regarding the home headquarters. Right now, time is of the essence. I want you to go to each department and order what you need for the ensembles. Tomorrow morning the team will meet to get the development rolling." He smiled a huge toothy smile. "You may have just bolted to the top of our field. I trust you to clear the way for the trip with your father."

"I will have his answer for you first thing in the morning." Emma had turned to exit Ferra's office when he stopped her.

"I do not want to seem intrusive, Emma, but I wasn't aware you were officially courting. Who is the lucky gentleman?" Ferra hoped his inquisitiveness would not offend her. He had known since she first came to work in toy design that her future was bright. She was extremely intelligent and beautiful, but what Ferra admired most was her unassuming nature. He heard the gossip in the shop that the young lad who worked in sales a couple years previously broke their engagement and disappeared. He witnessed how she immersed herself in work and never complained, but the look on her face was desolate for months. It dawned on him that the past week she literally glowed.

Emma blushed and twisted a lock of her hair around and around. "Monsieur Ferra, I am courting a British naval officer, Commodore Joseph Head."

"Why, Emma, aren't you the coy miss?" Ferra laughed.

"No, no, it is just we have only been courting a short time."

"I trust Monsieur Bouron has blessed this courtship," Ferra said.

"Yes, Joseph made a formal request and my father approved. He and Joseph have a mutual admiration for one another." Emma giggled. "My mother is completely besotted with his charm and kindness. He brought her roses yesterday."

Ferra saw Emma was completely enamored herself. He was interested in meeting the commodore. He must be special to have gained Emma's trust and love. Well, soon enough; they would be off to Paris on Friday. Ferra returned to his office, satisfied life was about to change because of his young designer's pioneering in the toy industry.

By the time Emma arrived home, her exhilaration turned to concern. She conjured up fantastical reasons her father would refuse. Ridiculous, she would tell herself, then back to apprehension. She needed to choose the exact right time to approach Edgar. As previously agreed on Sunday, Joseph stayed away, so she had the evening to pick the right moment.

After freshening up, Emma went downstairs to the parlor. Her parents were conversing over a glass of Bordeaux before the evening meal. "Bonsoir, Mama, Papa." *Great timing*, Emma thought. They were relaxed, enjoying a glass of wine, and chatting. The perfect opportunity for her announcement and request presented itself. She beamed at Maria and Edgar.

"Dear girl, you are aglow." Edgar wondered what had transpired to make his daughter so elated.

"What is it, Emma?" Maria questioned.

Their daughter bubbled over. "I have the most phenomenal news. When I arrived at work this morning, I presented my concepts I developed this weekend. The manager, Monsieur Ferra, was so impressed he studied the ideas, compiled a cost analysis, and then called me to his office. He believes my designs will be endorsed by the owner and we will both get promotions!" Edgar and Maria enthusiastically congratulated their daughter. They were both so proud of her and told her so. Emma continued calmly, "One part that Monsieur Ferra thinks is vital to launch the line is a presentation to the owner and top managers at headquarters in Paris."

"Paris?" Marie was confused.

"Mama, the company headquarters are in Paris; the Calais plant is a subsidiary of the main office, and the owner makes all decisions on new products. My design and concept is brand-new and will be a risk and substantial investment for the owner. Monsieur Ferra wants me to make the presentation." Emma smiled innocently.

"But, Emma, it is inappropriate for a girl of your age to travel with a gentleman even for business purposes. I have already scheduled appointments for this week, and your father must be at the bank available to those whose finances he manages. Neither of us can get away on such short notice." Maria's strict adherence to etiquette usurped her desire for Emma to advance her career.

"Please listen. I have a solution, if you both will agree." Emma smiled sweetly. "Joseph planned to visit the Cousin-Montaubans at the end of the week at their residence in Paris. He invited me, but I hesitated to ask Papa. I was afraid it might cross the lines of etiquette, and I was reluctant to put you in a difficult position.

"Now it is most important I have the opportunity to see my design come to fruition. I want the chance to further my career, but also assist parents. This toy line will help children explore their beautiful imaginations and be affordable for parents." Emma looked at her father directly, imploring him with her eyes.

"My girl, although this is very unusual, I have tremendous trust and faith in Commodore Head. So far, he is a model suitor, whose decorum is impeccable. Through reputation I know General Cousin-Montauban, and he will be a superior host. You deserve the chance to make a professional presentation and achieve a promotion. I am going to give my permission for you to go on this trip, with Jenny chaperoning of course."

Emma threw her arms around Edgar's neck and kissed his cheek. "Papa, you have made me so happy; thank you for your understanding and kindness." Maria was staring at the two, disbelieving the whole situation that had just unfolded. She never imagined Edgar would agree to the trip. It was highly irregular for a girl of Emma's age to travel with a suitor; business or chaperone didn't matter when social etiquette could come into question.

Maria Bouron went from living with her parents straight to living with her husband. As a girl growing up in the early 1800s, she never aspired to cultivating a career. Her job was to be a good wife, mother, and household manager. Very few girls of her class worked outside the home; consequently, she simply did not comprehend her elder daughter's ambition and drive. She understood at a surface level that Emma designed toys, but she didn't inquire about what the job entailed. Yes, she was pleased that Emma was advancing, but she would much rather Emma marry and start a family. The changing values of the mid-nineteenth century, with women pursuing careers, eluded Maria's perception of the world order. Women should marry, reproduce, and be content with running the household. It was the man's obligation to earn a living and provide for the family. Edgar was very successful in the banking business, which made Maria proud plus it secured their societal position. Claudine and Emma understood their mother's expectations, but it didn't mean they would follow in her footsteps.

Emma began drawing and sketching characters from her imaginary world when she was very little. It gave her an outlet from the cloud of darkness that covered the Bouron household after the death of her infant brother. She was a self-taught designer and started her portfolio at a very young age, eight or nine. When Maria climbed out of her deep depression, she showed little interest in her daughters' hobbies. She never dreamed Emma's childish drawings would develop and someday land her a job in designing. It wasn't that Maria didn't love Emma and Claudine, but she didn't understand them, especially Emma. Her ambition for success in the business world baffled Maria. A young lady of her background should be married and a homemaker.

"Maria, I will discuss the arrangements with the commodore and delineate the guidelines for the trip. Stop frowning. You should be happy our daughter is so clever her efforts are being recognized."

"I am happy for her, but traveling to Paris with a gentleman who is not her husband is quite audacious and possibly construed as a breach of etiquette."

"Darling, adjusting etiquette is not a crime; women today are much more modern than when we grew up. It is acceptable for a woman to have a career outside the home. In fact, a woman of 1876 can have employment and be a wife and mother. Maria, times are changing."

I don't care what they talk about, Emma mused, *because Papa gave his permission, which was all I need.* She sat quietly thinking about getting word to Joseph regarding the newly hatched plan and, of course, her career news. Plus, she must be casual when telling Jenny about the trip. She certainly didn't want her getting all puffed up about going to Paris with Joseph. Emma smiled to herself. She would seal the proposition with the promise of a shopping trip. Jenny loved to shop, even though she rarely socialized except at church activities.

Listening to her parents banter back and forth wasn't accomplishing anything. She knew her father's decision was final. She decided to write Joseph a quick note, hail a carriage, and have the note delivered to his quarters. "Mama, Papa, the evening is still warm. I think I will take a stroll before dinner." With that said, she left the parlor, rushed up to her room to retrieve writing paper, jotted the note, then bounced back downstairs and out the front door to hail a carriage.

Chapter 12

Paris Invitation

Joseph was lounging on the settee when a messenger arrived. He smiled broadly after reading Emma's note. Postponing the departure until Friday was not a problem; in fact, it was better in case they decided to stay an extra day since she had to work. Joseph sat at his desk and penned a letter to the general giving him the definite dates. He requested a reply. He jogged to the embassy and sent a courier with the letter to Paris. He should have an answer by midmorning Tuesday. He would go to the bank and speak to Edgar as soon as he received Cousin-Montauban's response.

Once back at Chateau Philippe, Joseph lounged on the settee and smoked a cigar. He wished his mother would be in Paris so she could help Emma shop. His mother had exquisite taste in clothing, and fashion came naturally to her. He decided at that moment to send her a telegram inviting her to Paris the following Monday. She could meet Emma and shop with her. The Heads owned a building in Paris in the fourth arrondissement. It was situated on Île St. Louis in a residential neighborhood overlooking the River Seine. His parents frequented Paris often, and it was more convenient to have their own apartment than stay in a hotel. He didn't suggest he and Emma stay there because they were not married and tongues would wag.

He didn't remember if he told Emma about the apartment. He thought she would thoroughly enjoy the area. Paris began in the fourth arrondissement or district, and the other nineteen districts spiraled out from the heart of Paris in a clockwise expansion. The River Seine cuts an arc through Paris flowing from the southeast to the southwest. The north side of the river is le Rive Droite or Right Bank. The south side, le Rive Gauche, is the Left Bank. At the widest part of the river, a footbridge connects two islands. The small island, Île St. Louis, is mostly residential neighborhoods, whereas the larger island, Île de la Cité, is a mixture of private dwellings and businesses.

Paris was a vibrant, beautiful city in the nineteenth century. One of the most famous buildings in the world was located in the fourth arrondissement, the Cathedral of Notre Dame. Joseph was anxious to show Emma the cathedral, as she was a strong Catholic. His knowledge of the architecture of the building would captivate her interest. Also, he believed it would be a spiritual experience for them to share, even though he belonged to the Church of England. Notre Dame moved even the coldest of hearts.

Joseph received the formal invitation from General Charles Cousin-Montauban early Tuesday afternoon. The general expressed delight that Joseph and Emma would be paying a visit. They were expected to arrive on Friday. Annabelle was already planning their outings in the city. She was thrilled to have her new friend visiting.

Cousin-Montauban gave directions to his home, located in the third arrondissement on Rue de Sevigne. Joseph was familiar with the area, as his parents took him to the famous Carnavalet Museum when he was a boy. The two old hotels made into a museum were under construction. The city purchased the buildings in 1866, and the renovation as far as Joseph knew was still in progress. Cousin-Montauban must have done well for himself; some of the wealthiest Parisians lived in the mansions along Rue de Sevigne and Rue des Francs Bourgeois that accessed the museum from the courtyard.

Emma hardly concentrated on her presentation Tuesday. She was so anxious to hear from Joseph. Her mind was flooded with scenarios of Joseph not getting an invitation, Papa refusing when Joseph paid him a visit at the bank, or headquarters of the toy company deciding this was not a good time to launch a new product. She twisted her handkerchief so much it was almost in shreds. All her fears were for naught. Ferra received confirmation from Paris that he and his designer were expected the following Monday. Percy delivered a note to her from Joseph that said he received the invitation from the general, and his visit to the bank was a success. Also at Edgar's invitation, he would dine with the Bourons for Tuesday evening dinner. Emma basked in her perfect world. Promotion, Paris, Joseph—it was astounding.

The chef prepared a rich four-course meal, but Emma hardly ate a bite. She listened quietly to the conversation at the table. Joseph and her father discussed something about India. Maria rattled on about the magnificent design houses in Paris, Claudine hung on every word, and Emma smiled and nodded like she was enthralled by the whole conversation. Actually she couldn't wait for dessert to be over so she could have a few minutes alone with Joseph. Finally, her father suggested they enjoy a brandy in the lounge. That ritual lasted another half hour. Emma suppressed her desire to yank Joseph out of the lounge. At last, Joseph stood.

"The meal was delightful, madame. I am afraid I indulged myself to the point I may burst." Maria smiled at Joseph's compliment. It was obvious Maria reveled in the attention. "I have also enjoyed the brandy, Edgar, but if I am to prepare for the trip on Friday, I must get back to my quarters. On a more serious note, I am honored you have entrusted your daughter to my care, and I can promise you she will be safe and looked after. The Cousin-Montaubans are highly regarded upstanding citizens."

"Thank you, Commodore. My wife and I want Emma to have this opportunity of advancement and to enjoy some sights in Paris." Edgar smiled.

"I think this will put you at ease as well. My mother will be in Paris while we are there and can chaperone evening activities." He turned to Emma. "I want you to meet her and get to know her." He smiled broadly. This news signaled to Edgar that the commodore was indeed very serious about Emma. He literally beamed at Joseph.

"Monsieur, you have thought of every detail. I will be relaxed and confident while Emma is away. Thank you so very much." Edgar shook Joseph's hand.

"It is I who thank you for allowing me to accompany her to Paris." Joseph gave Edgar a winning smile.

Emma couldn't stand one more minute of this banter. "Joseph, shall I walk you to the entryway?" The news about his mother drained every iota of color from her face. She needed details of the travel arrangements and activities.

"Of course." He bowed to Maria and Claudine and shook Edgar's hand again. Emma snatched his arm and practically shoved him out of the lounge. Joseph was thoroughly amused but kept it to himself.

Once out of earshot, she pinched his arm. "What do you mean your mother will be in Paris and chaperoning?"

Joseph restrained his laughter, but he couldn't help smiling. "Darling, I asked Mother to come to Paris to meet you."

They stepped into the foyer. There were daggers in her voice. "When were you going to give me this news, and why right now when I am ill-prepared, have work, and want to be with Annabelle?"

His throaty laugh got the better of him. "Emma, I asked Mother to come so she can take you and Annabelle shopping, not to chaperone. But what I said about wanting her to meet you is very true." She tweaked his arm and felt the tension release from her stiff shoulders. "She'll be staying at the apartment, not with us at the Cousin-Montaubans."

Her shoulders stiffened again. "What apartment?"

"The family has owned living quarters in Paris since the 1700s. The building is in the fourth arrondissement on Place des Vosges on the Île St. Louis. The Cousin-Montauban home is in the third arrondissement by the Carnavalet Museum. Not particularly in close proximity to one another." Joseph laughed. "My mother and father come over at least four times a year for shopping, different festivities, and to visit friends, which is what Mother will be doing when we are out in the evenings."

"Joseph, how could you do this to me when you know the trip is not just for pleasure but also for my work?" Her insecurities bubbled to the surface from the cave within. How could she possibly impress Joseph's mother, trek around with Annabelle, and produce a viable presentation? He saw her shriveling before his eyes.

"Dear God, Emma, this was not to cause a stressful situation. My mother is a sweet, unassuming woman. She will adore you, and you will likewise adore her. If this is too much, I will send word for her not to come."

"You can't do that now; it will look like I don't want to meet her." The misery in her voice cut through his heart. Joseph held her face and kissed her lightly on her lips.

"My sweet, sweet girl, if I thought for one minute this presented a problem, I never would have mentioned it to her. I thought you would enjoy shopping, and I felt it was insurance if your father balked at me taking you."

> *Emma lowered her eyes. What is wrong with me? He wants me to meet his mother, go shopping. Any other girl would be thrilled. I must be mad. Plus he put a safeguard in place if Papa refused. Where is my unconditional trust?*

Emma swallowed, then looked up at Joseph. The tears were trickling down her cheeks. "Can you forgive me? I am being stupid. It's just that I was caught by surprise. Do you think she will like me?"

Joseph took out his handkerchief and wiped her tears. Even crying, she was beautiful. "There is nothing to forgive." He kissed both cheeks, caressed her hair, and held her for a moment. He whispered in her ear, "Trust me. I guarantee you will have an extraordinary trip and return to Calais happier by far than when you left." She desperately wanted to trust him completely, but before the departure date she would conjure up a thousand reasons why Joseph's mother wouldn't approve.

"Now, darling, I must go. We have much to do before we leave on Friday. I think it wise if I do not see you until Thursday evening. You will have a chance to pack and prepare for the trip. But on Thursday, we'll go to town for a light meal, be sure we have everything in order, and enjoy an after-dinner drink at the Chateau." He winked.

Emma finally smiled. "I would like that, sir."

"One kiss and I bid you good night." Joseph pulled her to him and kissed her passionately. Emma was breathless. "Thursday, my love," he whispered. She watched him stride to the carriage. *Dear God, he is everything to me.*

Claudine was listening from the landing. She heard them squabbling, but about what? She knew by Emma's tone of voice she was angry, then the voices dimmed and the front door closed. Well, not too serious. How lucky that Emma was going to Paris, shopping with Joseph's mother, and showcasing her new designs! Claudine loved her sister, and to her this was all good news. She felt so sad for Emma when Richard walked out. Her sister barely functioned emotionally for the first six months after the breakup. She put on a good front at work because her job was a lifeline. Once away from the toy factory, she shut down completely. Even Claudine couldn't reach her. Through a slow process, Emma came back to normal at home, but she didn't have any friends or companions except for Claudine. Both girls were strong Catholics and believed God had a plan for their lives. Understanding what the plan was caused the anxiety. Emma never questioned her faith during the two years after Richard broke their engagement, but she questioned herself. She was convinced she must have an innate character flaw. Seeing Emma this happy thrilled Claudine; hopefully the self-doubt had been chased away by Joseph's love and God's plan was in action.

The next few days flew by as both Joseph and Emma were working and getting ready to leave on Friday. Everything fell into place. Joseph met with Nic again to change dates and finalize training for his men. Emma, under the direction and support of Ferra, had the puppets and the ensembles ready for reveal in Paris. The whole team participated in finishing the products. Emma cajoled Jenny into accepting her chaperone role with anticipation. The promise of shopping definitely helped the situation.

Joseph arrived at the Bouron residence promptly at seven o'clock in the evening. He prearranged with Edgar that he and Emma would go into town center for a short evening. It would give them an opportunity to review the travel arrangements. Edgar agreed willingly. Actually, Edgar's ulterior motive was paving the way for collaboration with Joseph and the general in financial matters. He viewed his daughter's trip as a business venture for him. He knew Maria didn't understand why he agreed to the journey, but his wife didn't know how gaining such prominent gentlemen as clients could change their lives in a dynamic way. The thought of much more money rolling into Edgar's coffers seduced him completely. It might mean a second residence for his family in Paris, which would catapult them into a whole different social class. Doors would open for each of them, but especially Claudine. Her range of suitors would expand automatically. He smiled to himself. Joseph was a huge asset, especially if he became Edgar's son-in-law.

Joseph and Emma spent a quiet evening at the Chateau. Joseph ordered a cold meal delivered to his suite and a bottle of the best French chardonnay. They shored up all the arrangements and agreed to depart from Calais early Friday morning, which without incident should put them in Paris by early evening. They would take the direct railway link into Paris and then hire a brougham carriage to take them to the Cousin-Montaubans. Emma's manager, Ferra, was traveling independently and not arriving until Sunday night. Joseph's mother planned to also arrive in Paris Friday evening, but wouldn't visit with Joseph until Saturday.

"Our plans are set, darling, I promise to make this a memorable few days, and I have complete confidence your new toy line will be enthusiastically received by the owner." Joseph saw the excitement rippling through Emma's body. She was animated, giggling, and full of joy. Her countenance charmed him, and he smiled.

"Since we have everything in order, have supped, and drank a glass of delicious white wine, I would like dessert." Emma looked shyly at Joseph from under her dark lashes.

"I am totally remiss, Emma. I didn't request any pastry or cakes," Joseph answered seriously.

She jumped on his lap and wrapped her arms around his neck. "Why, sir, I think you are sweeter than a pastry. Let me taste." Emma kissed Joseph teasingly. He responded by sensually probing her mouth with his tongue. He anticipated the response and was not disappointed. Emma kissed him back with desire.

Whispering in her ear, Joseph confided he didn't think they would have private time in Paris. Kissing her throat and the hollow in her neck, he felt her getting aroused. "I want you now, Emma. It may be our last chance until the end of next week." She answered by taking his hand and leading him into the bedchamber.

Chapter 13

Rue de Sevigne

EDGAR AND MARIA BROUGHT THE girls to Paris after Maria's slow recovery from the loss of their unborn son. The city was much more magical than Emma remembered from her childhood. They arrived in the evening, and the streets were bustling with activity. All the streetlamps blazed. As the brougham carriage wound its way through the haphazardly laid-out streets and boulevards, the activity of the fourth arrondissement receded into the background as the residential area became more prominent. General Cousin-Montauban and Annabelle lived on a quiet street lined with huge old family mansions farther from the vibrancy in the heart of the city. The carriage pulled up to a huge house on Rue de Sevigne and stopped. "All right, ladies, Emma, Jenny, we have arrived at our destination. I'll get one of the servants to help us with the luggage. Wait here a moment."

Joseph reached for the fox-head brass knocker, but before he grasped it, the oak door swung wide. Annabelle grinned from ear to ear. "Joseph, welcome, you must all be tired after traveling all day. I am so anxious to see Emma. Father and I have wonderful plans for the weekend. Oh, I am rambling; come in come in."

"Would you mind asking your manservant to help me with the luggage?"

"Where are my manners? Of course. Father is waiting in the library; Gerard will show you in and have the luggage fetched. I am going to get Emma."

Annabelle secured the help, then ran to the carriage. She and Emma embraced. Emma introduced Jenny, and then the two girls began to chatter. Once inside the massive foyer, a butler greeted Emma and showed Jenny to her suite in the servants' quarters. It consisted of a small sitting area, a dressing room, and a shared bathroom.

"Emma, you must be so exhausted after such a journey, crossing the channel, the train, then the carriage, are you all right?" Annabelle asked.

"I am so thrilled to be here; I am not one bit tired." Emma gazed at the lavishly decorated foyer. The ceilings were at least sixteen feet high, with ornate carvings in the expensive wood. The massive staircase, covered in claret-colored carpet, led to the second floor. Emma couldn't wait to see the whole mansion.

Annabelle showed Emma to her suite of rooms so she could freshen up before dinner. The three rooms were exquisite. Her clothing had been placed in the wardrobe and her toiletries in the bathroom. The chandeliers cast a soft light in the bedchamber. The four-poster bed had blue velvet curtains that at the moment were pulled back. The whole room was feminine and expensively decorated. Annabelle smiled about her new friend; it was obvious Emma was impressed with the home. Annabelle had lived here permanently since birth. There were short respites at their other residences in Calais and London, but this was her home—the place where she was raised, the place her mother died, the place she cared for her father, the place she loved the best. She shook herself from the reverie just as Emma came out of the bathroom. "Are you ready?"

Emma beamed. "Yes, I am, and starved." The girls laughed.

The men were in deep discussion in the library enjoying a whiskey and cigar. Charles hugged Emma sincerely. A maid dressed in a stiffly pressed white uniform summoned them to the formal dining room. The dining room was huge. A banquet table stretched at least twenty feet in length. Six ornate silver candelabras served as centerpieces. A lovely white lace tablecloth made in Calais draped over the expanse of the table. Since this evening only the four were dining, the place settings were clustered around the far end of the dining room table.

The five courses of the meal were superb. Emma thought they were more sumptuous than she had ever tasted, and her appetite was ravenous. The trip was long, and they hadn't eaten much since the early morning when they departed from Calais. Plus, Emma didn't like to eat heavy meals when traveling. It just didn't sit well with her, so to say she was hungry was an understatement. Joseph was amused at how uninhibited she was with the Cousin-Montaubans. Most French women were taught that proper etiquette called for a lady to pick at her food. Emma couldn't care less. She enjoyed every bite of the meal.

The foursome decided on the activities for Saturday, with the highlights of the day being a visit to Notre Dame and a shopping trip with Joseph's mother. They would have the evening meal at the Heads' apartment. Annabelle and Emma chattered easily while Charles and Joseph discussed the military, some situation in Afghanistan, and the Franco-British War they fought in together. Emma only heard snippets of their conversation. She was much more interested in gossiping with Annabelle about Joseph. She was intrigued when Annabelle confided she was interested in one of her father's young lieutenants who had visited at the house and taken them both to a play at the theater. The evening flew by, and it was midnight before they knew it.

"Ladies, if we are going to gad about the city tomorrow and enjoy the duchess's dinner plans, then we had better retire." Charles laughed. He was a charming figure, not tall like Joseph, but still distinguished-looking, with a shock of gray hair and long sideburns and a handlebar mustache. He had a paunch, but still looked aristocratic. His military career had been long and immensely successful. In fact, he was Minister of War under Napoleon III, and then lost the battle at Sedan, which caused the emperor to be ousted. Charles went into exile in Belgium at that time, then came back into favor in 1871 and returned to France. Because of the general's high profile, many rumors swirled around him. It was speculated that his great wealth came from the looting and plundering of the Peking Summer Palace in China. This was never substantiated.

The two men and women ascended the stairs together. Joseph kissed Emma on the cheek, and then Charles showed him to his suite. Annabelle's suite was in the family wing, but to be close to Emma, she was staying in the suite next to Emma's. The girls hugged good night and went to their separate quarters. Jenny was waiting for Emma. She helped her undress, drew the curtains around the bed, then retired to a small bedroom adjacent to the main bedchamber. She didn't go to the rooms that were provided for her. No way would Joseph be able to slip into her girl's quarters for a secret tryst. Emma climbed into bed and snuggled beneath the down coverlet. One thought danced through her mind before she was fully asleep. *Didn't the general say, "duchess"? Was Joseph's family British peerage?* She was too tired to contemplate the whole thing.

Chapter 14

British Peerage

A HIERARCHY CONFERRING TITLE AND land, British peerage is an aristocratic system still in existence today; it was developed through the King of England, Edward III, in approximately 1337. A peerage consisted of a hereditary title with land attached to it that passed down from father to eldest son. Five degrees of peerage exist in England, the highest title being duke, which Edward created when he bestowed the title and land on first the Duke of Cornwall and then the Duke of Lancaster. The next title was marquis, which Richard II dubbed Robert de Vere in 1385. He became the Earl of Oxford and the Marquis of Dublin for life. Next in descending order was earl, created during the Saxon conquest. Next was viscount, introduced by Henry VI in 1400. Baron was the fifth title in the peerage system and was actually created in 1264. A barony is lands passed through a hereditary system; the title and land confer nobility on the person. Not only the land and title hold prestige, but the chief privilege is being a member of the House of Lords in Parliament.

The Head family barony encompassed an area called Whitfield in the county of Kent, which had been held in early feudal times by the Cadman Barony, but died out when the last Duke Cadman produced no heirs. The barony passed to Cadman's firstborn male cousin in the Head family.

The manor house was north of the town center of Dover, quite a strategic location for exporting and importing because of the harbor so close at hand. The small village of Whitfield sprouted up in the tenth century as a hub for the serfs who worked agriculture on the land for the duke. The major attraction in the village was the beautiful church, St. Peter's, built during the Saxon period sometime before 1066, when the Normans under William the Conqueror came to power. The huge bell dated from the thirteenth century. Although much damage occurred throughout the centuries, two original stained glass windows remain from the original structure. The church was enlarged and restored in 1894. So for now, much work needed to be done, but church services were still conducted there every Sunday. Joseph's mother, Catherine Sutton Head, and his father, David, attended each week when in residence.

Catherine Head was a good mother to her sons, Joseph and Charles, and good wife to her husband, David. She was a stately figure, tall and slim, with creamy porcelain skin that glowed when she became animated. Living in the manor house at Whitfield suited her perfectly. Catherine adored the country lifestyle. It was the perfect place to raise her two sons. Being a member of the aristocracy came to her naturally, and she put on no grandiose airs; this most certainly accounted for her popularity with the other members of the nobility. Her generosity and kindness to the people working the estate made Catherine a beloved duchess. She made sure all the needs of "her" people were met.

Her major indulgence was Paris. Catherine treasured the Head's apartment in the fourth arrondissement, the center of city life. She thoroughly enjoyed the nightlife in Place Royale, the museums, the culture, and especially the shopping. It thrilled her to choose the rich textiles, fabrics, buttons, and appliqués. Accessories and shoes complemented the clothes she commissioned. She was well-known in the couture houses along the Champs-Élysées and the traditional French food shops on Rue Mouffetard. She enjoyed cooking French dishes even though a chef traveled with her. Catherine never tired of wandering for hours visiting and revisiting the Arc de Triomphe, Castles of Versailles, the Louvre, and Eiffel Tower and walking along the banks of the Seine River and the Pont Neuf, the oldest bridge in Paris. Today she would experience her favorite haunt, Notre Dame, with her elder son and the young French girl, Emma. A mother's instinct led her to believe this was not a passing fancy for Joseph. It was the first young lady he showed a serious interest in. Having a ball gown designed and made for her indicated this was serious, but bringing her to Paris made Catherine think a permanent commitment would be forthcoming. The ultimate indication of her son's intentions was introducing Emma to her. She only wished David had been able to make the trip, but business kept him in England.

Chapter 15

Excursions in Paris

It seemed like Emma had just laid her head on the pillow when Jenny opened the bed-curtains. The sun streamed through the huge windows. She smiled; it was going to be a gorgeous spring day and she was in Paris!

"Come along, dearest, you have slept like the dead, and I must help you bathe and dress for today's outings."

"Jenny, you're a dream. Did you sleep well?"

"Yes, comfy bed, close to you."

"Good, I am glad you rested well after the trip. What would I do without you?" Emma kissed Jenny's cheek.

"I have drawn you a hot bath laced with lavender water and chosen a day dress for you to wear. It's one of your best, of course, to meet your future mother-in-law!"

Emma tweaked Jenny's arm and laughed happily. By the time Emma was ready for breakfast, she looked beautiful. She wore a light green taffeta dress and a small dignified matching hat with a purple plume. Her long brunette hair was twisted in a loose bun at the nape of her neck, and the wild tendrils framed her face. "Do you know if Annabelle is up and dressed?"

"Yes, she knocked on the door right before I awakened you. Her chambermaid will take us downstairs to the courtyard for breakfast.

Oh, Emma, the weather is so lovely we are to have our meal outdoors." Jenny's excitement was contagious. They danced in circles together, laughing and twirling.

Joseph was on his way down the grand staircase when he heard the laughter echoing from Emma's guest suite. He couldn't help smiling. Just her laughter brought joy to his life. He was anxious to show her the sights, especially Notre Dame, and then Mother would meet them at a small café for a light luncheon. He had no reservations about introducing Emma to his mother. He wanted Emma for his wife. After lunch the women could shop along the Champs-Élysées. He and the general would spend the afternoon at the gentlemen's club where Charles had belonged for decades. A fine cigar, a glass of port, and conversation would suffice for a quiet afternoon respite.

The foursome plus Jenny took the omnibus to Notre Dame. Emma's excitement was contagious. Joseph held her hand as they traveled through the streets of Paris alive with activity. Even on a Saturday, businessmen scurried down the avenues at a quick pace to get to their workplace. Street vendors barked out what wares they were selling. Fashionably dressed ladies strolled from shop to shop. The whole experience fascinated Emma. Every time she saw a beautiful structure or landmark, she squeezed Joseph's hand. Annabelle pointed out several small fine boutiques where she shopped. Charles noted the crowded cafés, where people were eating their breakfast at outside tables. The scene was quite picturesque, like a postcard of a boulevard only this was not a postcard but a thriving city. When the bus pulled up to the cathedral, the group became quiet. The building's architecture was stunning and a marvel to behold. Emma's thoughts were interrupted when Joseph quickly walked toward a striking lady in her mid-fifties. He kissed her warmly on each cheek. She smiled sweetly, her eyes twinkling with delight.

"Mother, I thought we were going to meet at the café for lunch."

"My dear boy, you know how I love Notre Dame, so I hoped you wouldn't mind if I joined you and your friends."

"Oh, it's your curiosity that motivated your change of plans." Joseph winked at his mother; she tried to give an innocent look, but Joseph saw right through her. "Come on then. I have someone special I would like you to meet, plus dear friends." Emma couldn't hear what transpired between them, but her heart raced. She so wanted to make a good impression on Mrs. Head. Her mind began the old tricks; fear crept in, warning her Joseph could never love a woman his mother didn't like. She looked down and tried to cast the fears away. Annabelle was whispering in her ear.

"Emma, dear friend, I think you are about to meet your future mother-in-law." She laced her fingers through Emma's and held her hand. It was apparent Emma's nerves were getting the better of her. "Smile, Emma, you have nothing to worry about. I loved you instantly and so will she." Annabelle's words calmed her. She took a deep breath as Joseph and his mother approached. The introductions went smoothly, and outwardly Emma appeared confident. Joseph put his arm around her protectively because he knew she needed his reassurance.

Catherine's mother's intuition kicked in; she knew she was meeting the young woman her son would marry. Joseph never looked at another human being the way he looked at this very young girl. He seemed to drink in every single inch. It was easy for Catherine to see why. The girl was beautiful, with an innocence about her that drew you in. The lovely green dress and hat she wore complemented her creamy skin, her hair was a shimmering brunette, but it was her eyes that had endless depth. Yes, Shakespeare was right when he wrote the eyes were the windows to the soul. Catherine was certain this young woman had substance. She liked her immediately. She wanted to get to know her in the short time they would spend together.

She smiled at Emma. "Joseph tells me this trip is not only pleasure but business for you also, Emma. May I call you Emma? And you, dear, must call me Catherine. Tell me about your work. It is rather unusual for a lady to have a career. Well, now that's not completely true. It is becoming more and more common for ladies to have a job outside the home." Emma was sweating; did Joseph's mother think it crass for her to have a career? Joseph hadn't dropped his arm from her waist. He gave her a small squeeze.

About work she was confident; speaking about her job flowed easily. She described the toy company, some of the toys they produced, and how she was a designer. Catherine seemed fascinated that this young girl had such a prestigious position, one usually held by men. That Emma was in Paris to introduce a new project intrigued her. Joseph had chosen someone not just for looks but brains too. Maybe this was the combination that eluded him in the past and kept him a bachelor. She never really knew why her son had not married; enough girls in Kent flung themselves at him. It amused him, but he never took any of it seriously, even when the mothers invited him to tea or dinner trying to pawn off a daughter. Joseph might go, but he rarely invited anyone out. On the occasions he did escort a woman, it was because couples were expected to attend. *Yes, in England,* Catherine mused, *society had its unspoken rules of etiquette as much as the French.*

Catherine thought about her sons. Joseph loved the sea even as a little boy. She and David took him and his brother to Dover often so Joseph could play on the beach and swim, but what he enjoyed most was watching the ships come in and out of the harbor. He watched for hours without a peep, whereas Charles would get bored and whine. The look on her older son's face as a child spoke of his love for the sea. Catherine and David were not surprised at all when Joseph decided to embark on a naval career. They would have preferred him to work the family business on the manor since he would inherit it once they were gone, but he left it up to Charles to be groomed for the country life and the business. The fine wool from their sheep was exported around the world. This is how they amassed a huge fortune. A barony may have a title and land, but money didn't automatically come with it. Those who farmed their property lived comfortably, but the money was in wool exports, not purely agriculture. The nineteenth century changed the way the world had operated in the past. Booming industries sprang up all over Europe, and as transportation and communication vastly improved, so did business. David Head was a shrewd businessman who converted an agricultural property into a wool-producing entity. They still grew crops, mainly for those families who lived on their lands for generations and for food for the barony's household. It was self-sufficient, but farming was secondary. Raising sheep came first and occupied most of the acreage.

Joseph broke into her thoughts. "Mother, we are about to enter the cathedral. Come back to earth." She laughed and walked close to Emma.

"Notre Dame is my most favorite architectural marvel in Paris, Emma. When I look at the craftsmanship in the windows, the portals, the statues, and the wood carvings, it moves me greatly. To think that the building was constructed in the 1200s is another facet that is difficult to comprehend. Mostly I come here when I am in Paris because I feel the presence of God in this hallowed cathedral. You know our family is Church of England, but that doesn't matter to me; I feel God in a Catholic church. I don't think he is stuck on a certain religion." Catherine laughed. "I presume you are a Roman Catholic, as most French are."

"Mother, how rude," Joseph admonished her with a frown.

"No, Joseph, I don't mind at all. Yes, madame, my family is Catholic, and I have been raised in the church." Emma smiled. She felt strongly about her faith and didn't really know much about Protestant religions. She knew Henry VIII of England formed the Anglican Church so he could divorce Catherine of Aragon, but the order of service, Mass, stayed very close to its Catholic roots. Emma hadn't studied other branches of Christianity.

The group wandered into the cathedral through the west entrance by the portals. The portals depict scenes from the life of the Virgin Mary, Christ on his throne judging the living and the dead, and the portal of Saint Anne. Emma shivered looking at the Virgin Mary. She was so pure, and Emma had given herself to Joseph totally. Guilt cascaded through her body. Here she was in one of the holiest churches in Europe, looking at the Virgin and not being one herself. The color drained from her face. Joseph felt the tension emanating from Emma. He could choke his mother for discussing religion. He hadn't thought about the difference in their churches. He didn't care what her religion was; he loved her no matter what. Annabelle was tugging on Emma's hand.

"Come with me," Annabelle whispered, "I want to show you the most amazing stained glass windows in the cathedral." Emma gladly followed and tried to flush away the thoughts of her lost virginity.

Annabelle showed her the North Rose Window, which was the oldest glass in the building, completed in 1250. It represents the Old Testament. The South Rose Window, completed ten years later, represents the New Testament. The last stained glass the girls viewed was the West Rose Window, dedicated to the Virgin Mary in 1270. Once again, seeing the Virgin made Emma feel unworthy. General Cousin-Montauban quietly appeared and explained to Emma a restoration of the cathedral was started in 1845 and finished in 1868. It was restored to its original beauty. Hundreds of Parisians and tourists from all over France and the world visit Notre Dame every day of the year.

Joseph sauntered up with his mother and smiled widely. "Have you ladies enjoyed what you've seen so far?" Both Emma and Annabelle nodded. "I have one more area I would like to show you, Emma. I know it is not new to mother, the general, and Annabelle. I think you will find the sculpture unmatched in France." He guided Emma across the church, with the others following. "This, darling, is the Gallery of Kings. Each of the twenty-eight statues is one of the kings of Judah." Joseph watched as Emma studied and admired each king. She looked perfect. He saw how the cathedral moved her. What he didn't see was the deep-seated guilt over her lost virginity.

Catherine watched her son and Emma walk down the gallery. Their body language spoke volumes. She saw the way Joseph looked at her and how he easily took her hand and draped his arm around her waist. Emma looked at him like he was the only person in the enormous building. Catherine wondered how long Joseph would wait before proposing to her. He was a decisive man like his father, so she didn't think it would be too far in the future or a long engagement.

When she was alone with her son, he told her to help Emma choose as many dresses and accessories as she pleased. She saw the look in Joseph's eyes when he told her to put all the items on a bill for him; price was no object. He also requested that Catherine help her select a suit for her presentation on Monday. He wanted her to feel confident for her special day. After his instructions, Catherine chuckled. "Why, Joseph, I do believe you are totally love-struck with this girl." Joseph smiled and returned to Emma's side.

After a delicious lunch, the women headed to the Champs-Élysées to shop. In every shop, Catherine was received warmly. It was obvious to Emma that Catherine was well-liked and respected. Emma saw it was not just because of the money she spent, but the kindness she showed to each person in the shop, from the tailor measuring and fitting to the designer creating sketches. Joseph must have learned from his mother to treat all people equally no matter what their station in life. His close friend and confidant Percy was a testament to the way Joseph believed in equality of all people.

The shopping spree was magic. Catherine chose silks, satins, taffeta, and linen. Emma tried to protest the extravagance. She certainly did not want Catherine to think her greedy, or worse a gold digger. Every time she expressed it was too much, Catherine reassured her it was by Joseph's orders. Annabelle was tended to like a princess as well. Her father allowed her to purchase whatever she desired. The general knew the sacrifices his daughter made for him, and it was the least he could do for her. He was proud because she never took it for granted or expected her father to spoil her. These qualities made him treasure Annabelle even more. Catherine observed both girls. She could see why they were such fast friends, each demure, sweet, and kind.

As they continued to shop, Catherine watched Emma from the corner of her eye. A special bond existed between her and her chambermaid, Jenny. She wondered what lay behind the tender relationship. Emma picked out dresses for Jenny. They giggled, laughed, and whispered, more like a mother-daughter friendship. Poor Jenny blushed continuously! The afternoon flew by. Emma was overwhelmed with the generosity Joseph's mother exuded. Each time Emma protested, Catherine jokingly admonished her. It made Emma blush and twist her hair incessantly. She had difficulty absorbing the depth of kindness shown to her.

Finally the four women called it a day. The afternoon was a huge success for each one. Annabelle chose four gowns for evening, plus matching slippers. Emma picked three day dresses for Jenny and a lovely church dress made of soft cloth and a matching bonnet. Joseph's mother had numerous sketches of evening gowns and day dresses presented to Emma. She carefully picked three gowns out of the seven presented. Catherine suggested a ready-made business suit from the rack for Monday's meeting with the Toy Depot owner and upper-echelon managers. It fit Emma like a glove. As they left the last shop, Catherine kissed the girls good-bye and went on her way to the apartment to prepare for the evening. After spending the afternoon with Emma, it was easy to see why her son had fallen so deeply for her. She didn't take anything for granted and genuinely showed appreciation. The way she included her chambermaid warmed Catherine's heart. It was the important quality she taught her boys. All people deserved respect regardless of their circumstances in life.

The minute Emma, Jenny, and Annabelle were seated in the carriage, they instantly fell asleep. It was a very full day. Joseph met the carriage when it pulled up to the Cousin-Montauban mansion. He laughed and laughed when he opened the door and all three women were in a deep sleep. "Come on, ladies, you are home; and if you hurry, you can finish napping in your suites before we leave for Mother's."

"Joseph, I can't believe what a day this has been. I have to tell you every moment when I get up, but I must have a rest so your mother won't be able to resist me tonight." Emma tweaked his arm and laughed.

"Darling, I think you already have her conquered, but go on and get a rest. I will send up the chambermaid to awaken you and the others in about an hour. I'll have her bring each of you a cup of tea and biscuits." Emma kissed Joseph quickly on the lips. *He is so thoughtful. He thinks of everything. I am the luckiest girl in the world to have this perfect man in my life.*

Emma and Jenny jumped in the big bed together, pulled the curtains, and were asleep right away. When the chambermaid arrived with tea and biscuits, it seemed they had just got into bed. Once they drank their tea, both were refreshed. Jenny wasn't going to Catherine's only the foursome, Emma, Joseph, Annabelle and the general would spend the evening at the Head's apartment. Jenny would sup with the staff at the mansion and go to bed early and read. Jenny taught herself to read when she was much younger and became a fluent reader so she could read to Claudine and Emma when their mother was incapacitated after the death of the newborn baby boy. Jenny developed a lifelong love of reading from then on. She looked forward to a quiet night. The day was exhilarating, what with the spiritual visit to Notre Dame, a fancy lunch, and her beloved Emma selecting and buying her new dresses; she was now ready for some solitude. Her heart was joyful because she observed Emma and Annabelle form a wonderful friendship. Both girls were alike in temperament and personality.

The Head family apartment was located in the very fashionable Place des Vosges on the right bank of the Seine River. Many of the palatial homes of medieval times were converted into luxurious apartments. Catherine decorated the rooms with expensive French furnishings and draperies. The floor coverings were elaborate oriental rugs imported from China; in fact, several of them Joseph had sent to his mother during the time he spent in China in the early 1860s. Large tapestries depicting early life in Paris adorned the walls. Crystal chandeliers illuminated the public rooms in a soft warm glow.

Joseph's and Catherine's fondness for one another was apparent in their easy conversation and mutual respect. Their interaction put Emma at ease. The nervous apprehension she felt during the carriage ride dissipated once she was welcomed by Catherine. The whole evening went splendidly. Conversation was steady, with no uneasy silences, the meal was delicious, and Emma felt completely comfortable with Joseph's mother. After a relaxed dinner, the group visited in the lounge. Joseph and Emma sat close together on one of the settees. Catherine watched her son and Emma engage in a social situation. It was clear to her by their actions, their feelings were deep and they were well-suited to each other. She did realize Emma was quite a bit younger than Joseph by her youthful looks and demeanor, but she was mature beyond her years. Actually her age was a positive, because she was in the prime of childbearing years. She could give Catherine and David the grandchildren they longed for. She made a mental note to ask Joseph Emma's age.

When the evening ended, Catherine hugged Emma and kissed each cheek. "My dear, I look forward to seeing you again soon. You must have Joseph bring you to Whitfield." Catherine laughed. "I know it is difficult to tear him away from the navy, but I think you are just the one to accomplish that feat." She winked at Joseph.

"Mother, I assure you, as soon as I get a break from duty, I will bring Emma home if Mr. Bouron agrees." Joseph laughed. "And, of course, if Emma wants to come to Whitfield."

Emma tweaked his arm. "Joseph, you know I would love to see your home and where you grew up." They both laughed, as if it were a private joke.

Throughout the evening Catherine absorbed all the banter between her son and Emma. It was quite obvious to Catherine that Joseph had fallen deeply for this lovely young girl. She hadn't seen him in love with another woman. It was as if he hung on her every word, laugh, look. The way he looked at Emma was a little unnerving because the look of intimacy was deep. Something made her fear Joseph knew her carnally. Such a relationship would totally taint Emma's reputation and social standing. In fact, it could ruin her and her family. She prayed Joseph had exercised restraint.

Catherine was worldly enough to know her son was not a virgin; for God's sake he was thirty-five years old and traveled extensively. She felt sure he hadn't dallied with street prostitutes; their cleanliness was quite questionable. It would surprise her if Joseph paid for sex since women fell all over themselves to get his attention; so realistically she was certain he got what he wanted free of charge. Catherine made a decision at that moment; she wouldn't speculate about his relationship with Emma. She liked the girl, and her dream would be fulfilled if the heir to the barony produced children, especially a son. It was a charming evening, with not only Joseph and Emma but also Annabelle and Charles, but after a day of sightseeing, shopping, and entertaining, she was ready to retire.

Once back at the Cousin-Montauban residence, Emma wanted a few minutes alone with Joseph even though she was completely exhausted. She whispered to Annabelle, "Is there a way I can speak to Joseph privately?" She giggled. "I want to ask him if he thinks his mother liked me."

"I would be dying to know too. Go up to your room. I will send Jenny to the scullery to make you a cup of tea. I'll make an excuse that my chambermaid is drawing me a bath. It will take about fifteen minutes for her to fetch the tea and be back to your suite. When I bid Joseph good night, I will tell him to meet you in your room for ten minutes." Annabelle smiled; she would want Joseph's assessment of the way his mother reacted to Emma if he were her beau. The girls hugged and went up the grand staircase.

Jenny left to make the tea, and shortly Emma heard the light tap on her door. She opened the door wide enough for Joseph to slip through. By the time he entered the suite, Emma was awash with insecurities. Did Catherine like her? Was she an interesting conversationalist? Would she fit into Catherine's world? The tears brimmed to the surface.

Joseph was surprised to see her in tears. "Emma, darling, what is it?"

The words rushed out, "Oh, Joseph, do you think your mother liked me? Did she think I was interesting? Do you think she thought me bold or greedy when shopping? Does she think I am suited for you?"

"Hold on, Emma, hold on, you're going so fast."

"Well, what do you think?" There was desperation in Emma's voice and eyes.

Joseph's heart was filled with love and compassion for her. She was so fragile. To anyone other than Emma, it was quite apparent his mother warmed to her immediately and enjoyed her company. Emma's lack of confidence allowed her to negate the positive ways his mother interacted with her. Joseph had only a short time to comfort and reassure her.

"Darling, my mother adored you immediately. I saw the glint of happiness in her eyes, as she knows me so well and she knew exactly how I feel about you. She told me she thought you beautiful, engaging, and intelligent. Stop worrying and come here." Joseph held her in his arms and whispered, "My Dearest, I have missed holding you, kissing you, and making love to you. It seems like ages since we were entwined in each other's arms." He breathed in her ear and kissed her neck. He felt her stir in his arms. He pulled away. He could see in the glow of the lamplights she was flushed. "I am going before Jenny finds me here with you."

"Don't go; sit on the settee with me, and we'll tell her you came to share tomorrow's plans." Her eyes implored him. "I feel so much better now, and I want your company for a few minutes longer." Joseph nodded affirmatively. No sooner had they sat down than Jenny came in with the tea trolley. She didn't see Joseph at first. "Sweet Jesus, that elevator contraption was quite shaky." Jenny looked up from the trolley and stopped. "Why, Commodore Head, I didn't expect to see you in the suite." She sounded very indignant. Joseph was amused.

"Ah, Jenny, I didn't mean to upset you. I came to tell you both about plans for tomorrow. I thought you were in the suite and I could catch you both before retiring." His voice was like butter; he sounded convincing.

"Yes, sir." Jenny offered a weak smile. She looked at Emma and all seemed innocent. She relaxed. "Sorry, Commodore Head, I was taken aback to see you." Emma flashed daggers at her.

"Well, Joseph, please tell us the plans so we will know what to wear and when to be ready." Emma motioned for Jenny to serve the tea. Joseph declined as he knew there were only two cups, and he wanted Jenny to have hers as it might soothe her displeasure.

"Jenny, please sit down." Joseph motioned to a comfortable chair across from the settee. Joseph became animated. "Tomorrow, ladies, we will go to church just down from the mansion on Rue de Sevigne, which is within walking distance. Then we'll have a stroll to the Carnavalet Museum. I am very excited about this excursion, as the museum has been closed to the public since 1866, when it was purchased by the city. It won't reopen until 1880. Because of the general's reputation and connections to the mayor of Paris, our group will be allowed to explore the completed portions of the building."

The ladies were absolutely thrilled. To think that they would have access to a museum built in 1548 and only their group allowed inside was very exciting.

"After we have enjoyed the museum, we'll have luncheon here on the terrace. The remainder of the day I set aside for Emma to prepare for Monday's important meeting." Joseph's thoughtfulness gave Emma a real boost. It was true she needed time to refine her presentation, but she wouldn't seek it out herself and Joseph anticipated her needs. The love she felt was boundless. How lucky could one person be? He was everything she wanted in a life partner. All of her fears vanished. She smiled at him with devotion. She wanted to be alone with him to show her feelings. Waiting for several more days was going to be difficult. Yet there was the excitement of Paris and her growing friendship with Annabelle. Emma sighed.

"Finish your tea, ladies; I am off to bed." Joseph kissed Jenny's hand and Emma's cheek. Jenny was still blushing as Joseph went out the door.

Sunday was another perfect day. The church Annabelle belonged to was another architectural marvel, and the priest delivered a moving homily. Emma felt spiritually fulfilled when she exited the sanctuary with Joseph. The guilt that permeated her soul at Notre Dame with the Virgin Mary rebuking her at every turn hadn't bubbled to the surface today.

They made their way down Rue des Francs Bourgeois to enter Carnavalet Museum from the courtyard. Emma adored the statue of Louis XIV sculpted by Antoine Coysevoux in 1689. Behind the statue were the bas-relief sculptures of Jean Goujon; represented were the four seasons, marked by signs of the zodiac. Gerard VanObstal created bas-reliefs of the four winds and the four elements. Emma glided through the areas of the museum opened for their enjoyment. She appreciated fine art. Joseph watched expressions of appreciation and wonder cross her lovely face. He carefully studied her profile. Her fine bone structure could be sculpted or painted by any renowned artist. Her heart heart-shaped face had high cheekbones, and when she smiled her dimples showed. She had an aristocratic look about her, but her nature didn't have one shred of arrogance. He admired her sincere kindness. Emma broke into his thoughts. "Joseph, you have a faraway look. What is it?"

"I was thinking how absolutely lovely you are, both inside and out. I love you, Emma Bouron."

Emma pulled him behind one of the bas-reliefs and kissed his lips. "I feel the same. You have a handsome face and wonderful, kind spirit. I am the luckiest girl on earth."

The remainder of the time in the museum was magical. When it was time to return to the residence, Annabelle and Emma had to be coaxed by Joseph and Charles. The girls reveled in the exhibits that displayed the history of Paris.

"Father, what are the plans for this evening? Remember, Emma needs an early night because of her important meeting tomorrow," Annabelle said.

"Once home, Emma will have a chance to review her presentation and rest. We will dine at half past seven. Oh, and by the way, I invited several guests, including the young lieutenant." Charles gave a wicked little smile under his bushy mustache. Annabelle blushed but didn't say anything.

"Joseph, I did ask your mother, but unfortunately she is going back to England in the morning."

"Very kind of you, General. I knew it was a short visit for Mother." Joseph winked at Emma.

The afternoon flew by for Emma. She was completely ready to introduce the new puppet line to management. She forced herself to lie down for a rest. It was important to her to look her best for the evening and to shine for Joseph. His approval was vital for her self-esteem.

After her nap, Jenny helped her get ready. Emma relaxed in a bath. The gown she chose was a brilliant red silk, no bustle, no bows, plain and alluring. She loved silk because it flowed and gave an illusion of floating. Jenny dressed her hair in a loose twist with pea-sized crystals pinned randomly throughout. The crystals gave a dazzling effect as the light gave off different colors that danced in her thick brunette hair. A matching crystal choker necklace further accessorized the silk gown. The look was not ostentatious, but subtle. Emma was pleased with her image in the full-length beveled mirror. She worried so much about her appearance critiquing herself was difficult. It crossed her mind the hair adornments might be too much, but it was too late to change now. She chased perfection in every aspect of her life.

She saw Joseph, Annabelle, and the general waiting for her at the bottom of the grand staircase. Joseph looked up, and his breath was taken away. Charles saw Joseph's gaze and looked up also. *My, my,* he thought, *Joseph captured the heart of a beauty.* Plus the girl was kind, with a loving nature. He instinctively knew for some reason she had cracks in her self-confidence, but he couldn't fathom why. He was pleased his precious Annabelle found a true friend. He also hoped a romance might blossom for Annabelle with the young lieutenant whose company she had been keeping and who was coming to dine. The evening appeared promising.

Emma kissed all three—her lover, her new friend, and the general. The girls cooed and complimented each other on their gowns and appearance. Both men laughed. The butler, Gerard, accompanied them into the formal drawing room, where the other guests would be received. The gaiety between Annabelle and Emma was infectious. A lively conversation ensued. Champagne and caviar were served by one of the servants. Gerard entered and announced the first guests. "General Cousin-Montauban, I present Monsieur and Madame Blaize." Introductions were made all around. These friends were neighbors and frequent visitors to the mansion. Charles welcomed his guests and shared that they were awaiting three more friends and dinner would be served shortly after they arrived. Gerard returned, stating, "General Cousin-Montauban, I present Colonel and Madame Cologne." The colonel served under the general for years and they were dear friends. He was instrumental in helping Charles and Annabelle when Charles's wife passed away. The party was lively.

Joseph thoroughly enjoyed watching Emma interact with the newly introduced guests. He knew she would be an asset as his wife and fit into all social situations he would have in his official capacity as a high-ranking officer. All of that was a bonus to the way he felt about her. The way she gave herself to him in complete innocence the first time and the way she learned to explore her sexuality thrilled him. Knowing he was the only man who ever touched her triggered a newly ignited possessiveness. These thoughts rushed through his mind as he watched her make polite conversation with the general's guests. Gerard entered the drawing room with a young lieutenant following. Joseph speculated he might be a future suitor for Annabelle. He remembered the girls gossiping about a young man Annabelle wanted to court.

"General Cousin-Montauban, I present Lieutenant Richard DeBarge." A tall, good-looking man sauntered into the room, his eyes on Annabelle. A winning smile covered his face. Suddenly the sound of glass shattering on the marble floor drew all eyes to Emma. Her face was devoid of color; her hands trembled. She tried to take a breath and talk. "Oh, I am so very sorry." She bent down to pick up the glass. A shard cut through her hand.

Joseph picked her up by the shoulders. He saw the fear in her eyes. He surmised it was from embarrassment and perception of social blunder. "Darling, you've cut your hand." The blood was dripping on the floor. It blended with the color of her gown.

Charles rushed forward, as did Annabelle. "Emma, dear, sit down. Let me see how bad it is. Not too deep. Annabelle, take Emma upstairs and have your chambermaid clean and dress the cut."

"I'll go with you. I want to make sure no glass remains in the cut." Joseph truly looked worried.

Emma stammered, "Please, it's nothing, it's nothing." Still no color in her face. *It's like she's seen a ghost*, Joseph thought. By this time, Gerard had grabbed a linen cocktail napkin and placed it over the slice in Emma's hand. A maid was wiping up the spots on the floor. "Please, Annabelle, you stay with your guests; Joseph can take me, please."

"No, I am going upstairs with you. We will only be gone a few minutes. Father is very capable of entertaining." She smiled caringly and insistently.

The three left the drawing room. Emma's mind was reeling. Oh dear God, the lieutenant Annabelle was falling in love with was Richard! How had this happened? The irony of the situation covered her like a veil. How could she hide from Annabelle that Richard had been her fiancé, deceived her and left without a word? She had to tell Joseph, but how should she reveal the news? Her knees buckled on the staircase. Joseph caught her before she could fall and picked her up. Tears were streaming down her ashen face.

"Annabelle, tell her it was an accident, and no one will judge such a minor mistake. She is embarrassed to tears. She is sensitive and wanted to make a good impression on your friends."

"Oh, Em, don't cry. No one cares about a dropped glass. Come on, we'll get a bandage on your hand, get your face washed, and rejoin the party." She wiped Emma's tears with Joseph's handkerchief. Emma said nothing.

Joseph didn't allow the chambermaid to dress the cut. He wanted to see how bad it was and if any glass remained. It wasn't deep and no glass was in it. He washed it thoroughly. Annabelle handed Joseph some antiseptic salve and a small bandage. Emma still said nothing. Joseph instructed the chambermaid to fetch a bottle of brandy and a small snifter. "Darling, I want you to drink some brandy to dull any discomfort you feel. The cut is not deep and should heal quickly, but a slice between the thumb and forefinger is in an awkward place and tender." Joseph touched her cheek and smiled. He poured two fingers of brandy in the snifter. He told her to sip it slowly and try to relax. Joseph sat her on the bed, and Annabelle sat next to her, holding her uninjured hand. She lovingly reassured her friend a splendid evening still lay ahead, with a delicious dinner and entertainment by a well-known pianist, and Emma would so enjoy hearing Mozart and Bach. They shared a love of classical music, and hopefully this would entice her to cheer up and rejoin the party.

Emma swallowed, looked at her friend, and quietly told her, "Annabelle, I am so sorry. I feel I have spoiled your dinner party by my stupidity." She rambled on, "I don't know how the flute slipped through my fingers. I should have been paying more attention." Tears began to brim again. Annabelle squeezed her friend's hand.

"Nonsense, Em, you are not stupid or clumsy. Those flutes are narrow and flimsy. No one will think a thing of it except wonder about your welfare, so come on, drink a little more, and we'll go back down."

"Annabelle, would you mind if Joseph sat with me while I finish the brandy so you can go back to your guests?"

Annabelle began to protest.

"Really, it would make me feel so much better if you rejoined the group and Joseph stayed with me. I will freshen up and be down shortly."

"Of course, if that's what you would like." She stood up and smiled kindly at her friend. "I promise, Em, you will still have a lovely time." Annabelle left the couple alone. She totally understood why Emma wanted to be with Joseph. It was confusing why the incident upset Emma so much, but the more she got to know Emma, the more sensitive she realized her friend was, but it was an endearing characteristic. She was sure after some time with Joseph, Emma would happily rejoin the soiree. Now that she knew her friend was not hurt too badly, she was anxious to get back down to the party to be in the company of Richard. He was the first man who sparked a true interest in her for a very long time. Her father's encouragement in her responding to the lieutenant's advances both pleased and amused her.

She had dedicated herself to Charles's care for so many years, at times it slipped from his mind that Annabelle should be courting, marrying, and having children. Just recently he realized her youth was diminishing and he was getting on in years. He liked Lieutenant DeBarge, which made things pleasant and extremely promising. Annabelle hurried down the staircase.

"Take another sip of brandy. Good girl. Now, Emma, I know you, darling. Dropping a glass and cutting your hand embarrassed you, but there is something deeper." Joseph spoke gently. "You know we have no secrets between us. You must trust me unconditionally. What is it?"

Her soft crying was the only sound in the suite. She knew she had to tell Joseph that Richard was downstairs, ready to court her friend, and he was not trustworthy. Of all the men in the world, why did it have to be a totally unreliable person like Richard that wanted to worm his way into Annabelle's life?

"Joseph, when the butler announced the last guest . . ."

"Yes, the general's lieutenant."

"I heard the name and could not believe my ears. Richard DeBarge. My astonishment was verified when I looked up and saw my former fiancé standing in front of us. I couldn't help it. I became weak and the glass slipped from my hand."

"Quite ironic, but what does your past affiliation have to do with us?" Joseph was confused.

"Nothing, nothing at all, but I am afraid for Annabelle. She is completely enamored with him, and he is not of good character. Remember, I told you he walked out on me and his job without a word or glance back. What if dear Annabelle is going to get the same treatment? I couldn't bear it, and she doesn't deserve it after the way she has cared for the general, sacrificing her own joy."

"Oh, I see. This is a wretched turn of events. If you tell her, she will be terribly hurt; and if you keep it from her, it is a betrayal."

"What am I to do, Joseph?" By now Emma was pacing up and down the room, torn between doing the right thing and ignoring the truth.

Joseph wondered if this were the full extent of Emma's reaction. Did she still have feelings for the man? As if Emma read his mind, she stopped pacing and looked Joseph in the eye. "I love you, Joseph; don't ever doubt me. I promise my concern is Annabelle and her happiness. What if he captures her heart and then abandons her like he did me?" A cold shiver ran up and down Emma's spine. "Oh, my God, what if he is after her wealth? Everyone knows the Cousin-Montaubans are rich and Annabelle the only heir. If he marries her, when Charles dies, he will inherit his fortune according to French law." The little color that had returned to Emma's face drained again.

"Emma, you are jumping to conclusions that may never come to pass. First, darling, let's address the situation at hand. How do you tell Annabelle of your former involvement with the man and his despicable treatment of you? Would you like me to talk to her?"

Emma thought for a moment. "No, it will be better coming from me, and I can answer any questions she will most likely have."

"All right, but for now, we must get through this evening without incident. How's the hand?"

"It's fine. I feel ridiculous."

"You are not ridiculous. We better get back to the group before they think we have eloped." He had finally eked a giggle out of her, and she seemed to relax. "Kiss me, Emma, and show me I am the only man you desire now." She threw her arms around his neck. "Show me." Emma reached up and put her lips on his. She started tenderly, then opened her mouth. Her hands rubbed his back, and she pressed into him. Joseph responded passionately. Emma felt the weakness in her knees. Joseph touched her breasts. The feel of the expensive silk aroused him, and he knew she felt it. "God, Emma, I have missed making love to you."

"I have missed every inch of you, Joseph." Her breath was coming quickly.

His mind told him to release her, but she felt so good, smelled so good. He must be mad to think he could take her right now, but he wanted it and she knew it. He let his hands caress her all over.

Emma moaned, "If you don't stop, I will not be able to stop."

Joseph started toward the door to lock it, and just then it opened.

Joseph recovered instantly. "Annabelle, we were just coming down."

"I got worried, as we thought you would be down sooner." She moved to Emma. "You look much better. The color has returned to your cheeks."

"I drank the brandy, which definitely helped me feel no pain." The girls giggled.

Joseph was relieved. A moment later, he and Emma would have been making love. Being discovered would have had horrendous ramifications. He shuddered to think of his host's reaction and the reaction of Mr. Bouron if he found out. Annabelle would have been devastated if the door were locked. She wasn't stupid; surmising the obvious was a short jump. It would have ruined her friendship with Emma.

Joseph flashed his winning smile. "Girls, let's join the party. I believe dinner will be served shortly."

Annabelle frowned, "Are you sure you feel ready to come down, Em?"

"Of course. I am sorry I reacted so badly, but I was so distressed I might have embarrassed you and myself. Plus, my hand really hurt, and I hate the sight of blood, especially my own." Emma laughed and Annabelle joined in. The threesome headed downstairs.

"There you are, Emma. How's the cut, dearest?" The general was truly concerned. He didn't care at all about the priceless crystal flute, but he didn't want Emma to be hurt.

Emma smiled. "Charles, thank you for your kindness. I am fine." She faced the other guests, turned on her greatest charm, and said, "I feel so foolish and apologize. It was a stupid accident." She winked at Charles. "I hope the flute was not too expensive." Her lovely laughter filled the room, and the other guests laughed as well. Joseph was observing Richard. He was a nice-looking chap, blond, muscular, and tall. His eyes were riveted on Emma in sheer disbelief. Joseph couldn't read the man's thoughts, but the way he stared made Joseph uncomfortable.

"Dearest, you and Joseph did not meet our guest who arrived when the accident occurred." Charles turned to Richard. "Lieutenant, let me introduce you to our dear friends, Mademoiselle Emma Bouron and Commodore Joseph Head." Emma curtsied, and Richard took her hand and kissed it. Joseph shook his hand. Richard had a quizzical look. He wondered how long his ex-fiancée had been involved with Commodore Head. He turned his thoughts to Emma. In two years she had blossomed into an absolutely gorgeous woman. The butler interrupted his appraisal of her by announcing dinner.

The sumptuous meal was regally presented. The fine bone china was imported from England. The pattern was gold and blue from the Royal Albert collection. The dinner service was ornate silver, with the Cousin-Montauban crest etched into each handle; the glassware also displayed the crest. The maids and head butler of the kitchen impeccably served each course. The seating arrangement, unlike the dinner, had much to be desired.

When Emma saw the seating placards, she felt ill. She was seated between Richard and Colonel Cologne. Annabelle was next to Richard on his other side. Joseph was across the dining table from her. She consciously immersed herself in conversation with the colonel and subconsciously pushed the food around the plate without taking a bite. When the conversation expanded to include the whole group, Emma tuned it out. She was abruptly brought back to the present. "Emma, tell our guests about your exciting business here in Paris," Charles prompted with a smile.

"Pardon," Emma stammered.

"Don't be shy, Em. I am very impressed with your career, and I think our other guests will be intrigued. You have such a unique job." Annabelle beamed at her friend. It was clear she was proud and wanted the guests to know how clever her friend was.

"Really, it's not that glamorous." Emma attempted a weak laugh.

Richard turned to her and looked directly in her eyes. "Mademoiselle, I am sure it is fascinating since career women are not that prevalent in France as far as I know." His voice and look revolted her, but she knew if she ignored him, the others would think her rude and gauche.

She couldn't curb the curtness in her answer. "Well, sir, I am a designer for a toy manufacturing company called the Toy Depot."

"What does that entail?"

Emma felt mockery in his voice. She wanted to scream at him. You should know, you were a salesman for the company; you knew what I did on a daily basis. You left. You are a coward. Instead, she smiled so her friend wouldn't detect a problem. "I design new toys. I have collaborated with my manager at the Calais office, and we have a new puppet line to present to our company president here in Paris."

This piqued the interest of both Madame Cologne and Blaize, who both had children and young grandchildren. The conversation centered on toys for a good fifteen minutes. Finally the group began discussing the theater. Emma breathed more easily. She felt Richard's hand grasp hers under the table. Instinctively she drew back. He leaned in. "Emma, you look so different from the last time I saw you. Gorgeous, I might add." He smiled and winked.

"Why are you here?" she hissed under her breath.

"Well, my dear, since I departed Calais," he cleared his throat, "I joined the army, where I had a chance of career advancement, plus I quite like the military life. The toy job was a dead end. Fortunately for me, I was assigned to serve under General Cousin-Montauban and ascended the ranks under his command. A real plus was meeting his lovely daughter, who I think has taken quite a liking to me." His smirk made Emma sick. He knew Annabelle was attracted to him. It was obvious. The boyish young man she was engaged to two years prior was gone.

How had she misjudged him so completely? She had pined for him, became reclusive, and questioned her own self-worth. Now he was telling her he needed a more lucrative career. Why hadn't he confided in her, and they could have met the challenge together? It was crystal clear. Her family had social standing and prominence, but not massive wealth. Dear Lord, how will I ever tell Annabelle of his cunning deceit? She felt wretched; her head hurt. He never loved her. The whole courting ritual and engagement was a sham. Emma looked across at Joseph. He was staring at her with those endless blue pools. It was like he was reading her thoughts and commiserating with her. She bowed her head and silently thanked God for Joseph.

Richard broke into her thoughts again. "So, Emma, how long has Commodore Head been courting you?"

"Don't be ridiculous. I am certainly not going to discuss my relationship with Joseph." Emma was incensed. Just who did he think he was?

Her venomous tone didn't surprise Richard. He was sure his departure affected her deeply, as she had showed unabashed devotion to him. Emma took people at their word. He knew she didn't suspect his proposal was backed by an ulterior motive. Old Edgar Bouron had a very respectable job, lived in a very nice house, and had servants, social standing, and some wealth. Richard's parents did not have the same type of resources. They were average middle-class people. Early on in his life, Richard was aware that his good looks and precocious personality could take him far. His formal schooling ended with the last level of secondary school, and there was no money for university. He landed the toy salesman job by a fluke. That's where he met Emma, and she could have worked out well but the sales job had no future. Edgar didn't take him under his wing for a banking position, and being stuck with a wife and mediocre money simply lost its appeal. He left and never looked back.

The military presented an excellent avenue for Richard. The continual unrest in Europe meant an active-duty army was necessary at all times. He dedicated himself to going above and beyond the call of duty to get recognition from his superiors. Being assigned to one of Cousin-Montauban's regiments was a stroke of good fortune. He exceeded in his duties, which caught the eyes of upper-echelon officers, and promotions came rapidly.

His commanding major, a good friend of Cousin-Montauban's, took a liking to Richard's work ethic and devotion. He introduced him to the general during a routine inspection of the troops. Richard turned his charm on the old man, and the next thing he knew he was transferred to Cousin-Montauban's personal entourage. He was ecstatic, but his real excitement came when he discovered the general had a pretty unmarried daughter. From the other men in the guard, Richard learned her name was Annabelle, she was unattached, and she doted on her father. It didn't prove difficult to get an invitation to the mansion for a dinner party. Richard began to lay the groundwork to inch himself into Annabelle's world. He played it perfectly, not too overly attentive, just enough to gain her trust and admiration. Richard knew she found him attractive, and he used it to his advantage, as he always had in the past. He was getting closer and closer to her. In fact, he planned on finding an opportunity tonight to kiss her for the first time. Emma being here threw a possible obstacle in his way. He would not, could not, let that happen. He actually hadn't given Emma a second thought since he left Calais other than to feel relief at shedding the responsibility. No twinge of conscience crossed his mind. Now he needed to make sure she didn't ruin his plans to woo Annabelle Cousin-Montauban right down the aisle. Charles was old, and although he looked in good health, he couldn't live forever. It was crucial Richard was married to Annabelle before the general died. French law stipulated such a condition to inherit the estate.

He turned his attention to Annabelle. "Mademoiselle, after the aperitif, I would enjoy seeing your lovely courtyard. Would you mind showing me?" This time he grasped her hand under the table and gave it a light squeeze.

Annabelle's heart fluttered. "I would like that very much. The terraces are lovely in the twilight." She blushed.

Emma overheard the exchange between them. How could she stop Annabelle succumbing to his charms? She looked at Joseph imploringly. He responded with a slight shrug. He observed Richard flirting with Annabelle, and she was flattered. He knew Richard's look from years of using the same tactics to get women in his bed. He realized Emma faced a dilemma: should she or shouldn't she warn Annabelle about the cad?

Emma twisted her serviette around and around her fingers. She suddenly felt Richard's eyes upon her. "Before I stroll with Miss Annabelle in the gardens, I must talk to you, Emma. Meet me at the bottom of the grand staircase while the other guests are assembling for the entertainment." His voice dripped with honey.

"I certainly will not, sir. I have nothing at all to discuss with you."

"Well then, possibly the commodore will find interest in what I have to say." All sweetness disappeared.

A cold wind blew through Emma's bones. His tone was pleasant on the surface, but an underlying threat hung in the air between them. She had no choice but to meet with him. "I will speak with you briefly, then return to the party." Her voice quivered even though she fought to control it. Why would he want a private meeting with her? They had nothing to say to one another. When he left two years before, it was over; nothing was left but her broken spirit and shattered self-esteem.

Dessert was a delicious chocolate mousse. Emma took one small bite and watched the other guests devour every morsel. Gerard announced the entertainment would begin in the drawing room in fifteen minutes. The guests began to mill around the dining room.

Emma whispered to Joseph, "Darling, please excuse me while I freshen up."

Joseph smiled and nodded at his socially correct lady. He thought it silly that women didn't say, "I am going to the toilet," but polite society would be appalled. He laughed; he knew her so well. "Of course, I will see you in the drawing room. I am going to indulge in a cigar and a brandy." He kissed her lightly on the cheek and turned to the library. Emma watched him walk away. She loved the way he carried himself.

She loved everything about him. Her thoughts were interrupted by a hand on her waist at the small of her back. She whirled around. Richard was standing directly behind her.

"May I walk you to the ladies' powder room?"

"Why yes, sir. Where is Annabelle?"

"She is helping her father organize the guests for the classical piano concerto."

They walked through the archway toward the grand staircase. Richard grabbed Emma's hand; she pulled away, but he didn't let go. "What do you want? You left two years ago, and why must I tolerate your return now? I have rebuilt my life and found stability. You show up at my friend's house, ready to court her."

"I am not ready to court her; I am going to court her. I will ask her father very soon. I must ensure you will not get in the way of my happiness."

"You talk of happiness as if I should welcome your relationship with Annabelle after the horrible way you treated me. Well, sir, I won't stand by and see you hurt her."

"Let me tell you exactly what you will do." Richard's eyes narrowed, and his face was inches from hers. "You will encourage our courtship and be supportive of her relationship with me."

"And what makes you think I would do that when I know you are not trustworthy or dependable?" Emma was indignant.

"I see you are in love with Commodore Head, Emma." Richard smirked knowingly.

"What business is that of yours?"

"To secure my place in Annabelle's life, I am making it my business. If you do anything to jeopardize my courtship and ultimate marriage to Annabelle, I promise you I will tell your commodore we consummated our engagement." His face was dead serious.

Emma couldn't control her outrage. Her face contorted into a dark scowl. "You are despicable. You know our courtship and engagement followed strict lines of etiquette. A chaste kiss is the most passion we shared."

Richard bellowed with laughter. "I may be despicable, Emma, but you will do exactly what I say and act happy about it. And I daresay, from the way you and Joseph look at each other, he knows much more of your body than I ever did."

"What are you two laughing about?" Annabelle bounced into the hallway.

"Oh, I was telling your friend Emma you promised to show me the manicured terraces by moonlight. We were laughing about getting lost in the dark." Emma immediately picked up the double entendre of his remark. Richard turned every speck of attention on Annabelle. It was clear she was excited to be his focus. "Will you excuse us, Mademoiselle Bouron?" He smiled so sweetly, his eyes sparkled, and he gave Annabelle a longing look. He put his arm around her waist and headed for the doorway leading to the courtyard. Annabelle looked over her shoulder and winked at Emma. A weak smile and wave were all Emma could muster. She made her way to the drawing room for the entertainment she had so anticipated, but which now paled in comparison to the web of deceit Richard wove so maliciously.

Emma sat down next to Joseph by the pianist. The musician was ready to begin his repertoire. Joseph took her hand. "Darling, are you unwell? You're like a ghost."

"I am fine, just a little tired," she lied.

Charles leaned close to Emma. "Dearest, I think your close friend, my precious daughter, may be enamored with the handsome lieutenant." He smiled broadly. Emma responded with a nod and smile.

"Don't you approve, my dear?" Charles seemed baffled. Emma had a serious beau; surely she wanted his daughter to find love.

"Oh, Charles, I am very happy for Annabelle if Lieutenant DeBarge is her choice. She is a prize for any man. I only want her to be completely happy, as I am with Joseph."

"Yes, dear, I know you want the best for her. I apologize for questioning you, but you appeared uncertain. I was mistaken. I am old and can't read women as I could as a young man." They both laughed. Emma kissed his cheek as affirmation that she was in favor of the courtship, although it was still not official.

Outdoors in the terraced gardens, Richard and Annabelle sauntered through the latticed pathways arm in arm, both oblivious to the conversations inside the mansion. Leaving Emma, the Toy Depot, and Calais behind was the best decision Richard had made until now. He was attracted to Annabelle. She was pretty, intelligent, and loyal, as demonstrated by her unselfish dedication to her widower father. He was even more attracted to her opulent wealth and social status. He felt confident he could have it all. Keeping Emma at arm's length until he married Annabelle was paramount, especially if Emma's resolve faltered and she revealed their history together. It would ruin all his plans. Getting Annabelle to fall in love with him was his first goal, and he didn't think that would be difficult. He merely turned on the charm.

"Sweet Annabelle, tell me the history of the mansion and the gardens. The house and the grounds are so very beautiful. Shall we sit on this stone bench while you enlighten me about your home?" His interest sparked delight in her heart. She loved her home and the property where it was situated in Paris. It gave her comfort and security when her mother died. She spent many happy years on Rue de Sevigne even after her mother's death.

"This house was built in the 1600s by the same architect who designed and built the Carnavalet Museum just down the street. My father purchased it when my mother was a new bride in the early nineteenth century. She worked diligently to commission remodeling, decorating, and landscaping. Papa was often away on military service, which gave Mama time to refurbish the mansion and make it a true home. They were very happy here, as I have always been as well." Richard could see a wistful gaze on her face. This was an opportune time to make his move.

"I have pried, Annabelle. I am so sorry. I never meant to bring up hurtful memories of losing your mother at such a young age. Forgive me." He put his arms around her and kissed her gently on the lips. Annabelle felt butterflies in her stomach. She didn't resist, which gave Richard a signal to be bolder. He pulled her closer and held her in his strong, powerful arms. He covered her mouth with his and tenderly put his tongue in her mouth. She tasted sweet, like fresh lemons doused in sugar. By God, the girl aroused him. It made him even more forward. He cupped her face with his hand and whispered, "Annabelle, you know from the minute I saw you, I couldn't take my eyes off your lovely face. I have done all I can to be in your company as often as possible. I will be honored if you allow me to court you. Is my dream possible?" Annabelle's heart still raced from the kiss and his declaration of intention. She closed her eyes, afraid if she looked he would disappear, a mere aberration. Her stillness gave Richard the chance to steal another kiss. He brushed his lips over her ear and then her neck, ending with their lips together. He stroked her face. He gauged her response correctly. It was the first time she was led by desire and not intellect. Richard aroused her by kissing her with urgency, then pulled away, leaving her breathless. "If you do not intend to court me, please, precious Annabelle, tell me now so my hopes are not crushed like the blown flower pedals beneath my feet."

His words were melodic poetry dancing in her ears. She followed decorum and didn't give in to her feelings of desire. She willed herself to stand up. Richard feared rejection from her abrupt reaction, but his fear was short-lived.

"Lieutenant DeBarge, courting you will be a pleasure and an honor, for I know you are a true gentleman. My father is an excellent judge of character, and he likes you very much." Annabelle blushed from ear to ear.

Richard jumped up and hugged her tight. "Mademoiselle Cousin-Montauban, you have made me the happiest man in all of France. I beg one more kiss before I approach the general." He didn't wait for an answer. He held her in his arms and pressed his body into hers. This time the kiss was sincere, not calculated. She accepted him! He felt a stirring in his loins as he kissed her with expertise. Annabelle opened her mouth to Richard. She felt an aching that was unfamiliar yet sensual. She might be twenty-five years old, but her experience with men was limited at best. These emotions were new. His kisses were new.

Richard lightly pushed her away by her shoulders. "Darling Annabelle, the purest girl in Paris and in my heart, I must contain myself, or I will ravish you right here." His laughter filled the night air. "Tonight, my love, I will ask your father for permission to court you and call on you as often as you will allow before you get tired of me." He pulled her close once more and held her in his arms. The silk of her gown and her scent were erotic. He needed to leave her with a lasting desire. "Annabelle, darling, my body betrays my good sense when you are in my arms. Forgive me, but I cannot bear to release you without showing you the depth of my feelings one more time." He caressed the small of her back with one hand and daringly felt her breast with the other. She did not, could not, resist. Annabelle's heart pounded as Richard covered her neck and ears with seductive kisses. The feelings made her head swim. His lips were on hers. His blatant desire captured her heart. "I will dream of your sweet love tonight if I sleep at all," he crooned.

"I will dream of you when the black night hides the smile on my face and the joy in my heart," Annabelle said breathlessly. She was weak in his arms, wanting him to kiss her again and again. The rush of desire filled her completely, but Richard pulled away.

"Come, the entertainment should be about finished, and I will have a word with your father when the other guests depart." Hand in hand, Richard and Annabelle walked back to the house.

The guests applauded the magnificent performance of the classical pianist. He surpassed Emma's expectations enough that she forgot the wretched situation at hand and the time flew by. She gazed around the room. Were Richard and Annabelle still gone? He must be charming her friend with his boyish good looks and perfect physique. Joseph's voice brought her back to reality. He spoke softly. "Emma, the lieutenant and Annabelle have been absent during the entire performance. Have you decided what to do? Are you going to tell Annabelle?"

When she looked in Joseph's eyes, he saw a sadness that was not there before tonight. He wondered what gravity of despair she felt. "Yes, I have reached a final decision, although it pains me to be less than open. I won't tell Annabelle about my past with Richard. It was two years ago, and we were both very immature. Since Richard left Calais, he has obviously grown, carved out a career, and found his niche in the military. I am not to sit in judgment of his prior acts, but respect that he has become a man. Just because I did not fulfill his hopes for the future doesn't mean his sincerity isn't real with Annabelle. If he and Annabelle are happy, then who am I to ruin their relationship? She's experienced only slivers of joy since her mother's death, and I will not stand in the way of her finding true happiness. As her friend, I must respect what she wants in life. She is still young enough for a husband and children. I was remiss in concluding he was interested in her wealth and social standing. When her father dies, she surely will want a husband and children to share in her inheritance. Wandering around in this gigantic house would be terribly lonely for her. I want her to be as happy as we are, Joseph." She laced her fingers through his and smiled radiantly. The sadness left her eyes as quickly as it had appeared, and only her love for him shone through.

What an enigma, Joseph mused. *One minute she's terrified her friend will end up with a gold digger; the next she's giving her blessing. Women, confusing and mystifying.* He wished Annabelle happiness, but it was her business. Emma's past with the DeBarge fellow was not important to him. He knew with confidence the lieutenant never captured Emma's heart or her body, so whatever happened with Annabelle and him was insignificant. He was glad Emma had reached a decision that gave her peace. "Darling, you settled on a wise course of action. I am proud of you. But, now, off to bed, as tomorrow is your big day at the firm. Let's wish everyone good night, and I will escort you to your suite."

Emma wished the guests and her host and hostess a good night and apologized once again about the ruckus with her hand. As she and Joseph left the drawing room, she glanced at Richard, and he winked at her. His audacity was annoying. At least Annabelle was happy. It was written all over her face.

Chapter 16

Presentation Day

JENNY WAS HELPING EMMA PUT her new ensemble on for the business meeting. Emma was excited and nervous all at the same time. She kept moving about as Jenny tried to get all the buttons done up. "Finally, I have you in that suit, Emma, I swear it was like trussing a live turkey." Emma giggled. "Now look, my girl, you stay still while I dress your hair or it will come tumbling down right in the middle of your talk." They both giggled. Above their laughter, Jenny heard a knock at the door. "Who is it?"

"Annabelle. May I come in?"

Jenny opened the door. "Come in, mademoiselle, I am wrestling with a wiggly worm. Trying to get her dressed and hair done is a daunting task, I can tell you." All three women laughed.

"Oh Em, don't be nervous. I am sure you will be wonderful and the company president will endorse your concept for the new puppet line." Annabelle laughed as she bobbed around the room.

"You are in a stupendous mood, dear Annabelle." Emma tried not to look suspicious. "I am guessing you have some news to share." She could tell by her friend's demeanor things must have progressed last night with Richard.

Annabelle plopped on the bed and giggled. Finally she confided, "Last night, when all the guests departed and you retired, Richard asked Papa if they could share a snifter of brandy and have a visit. Papa obliged, of course, and that's when it happened."

"What happened?" Jenny and Emma said in unison.

"Lieutenant Richard DeBarge formally asked Papa permission to court me. Papa said yes, of course. You know how much he likes Richard and thinks he has a brilliant military career ahead of him. Tonight, we will dine together and go to the opera. Isn't it exciting? Emma, the four of us will be fast friends for life." Annabelle's enthusiasm bubbled over. All the while, Jenny stared in total disbelief. She looked from Emma to Annabelle and back again. Emma gave her a searing look to keep her from blurting something out about Richard. Emma wanted to get Annabelle out of the room before Jenny said something revealing.

"Dearest friend, I am so happy for you. I want to hear every detail, but right now I must take the carriage to the Toy Depot headquarters for the introduction of my new designs." Emma kissed Annabelle on both cheeks and hugged her tight.

"I am so inconsiderate. Of course, it is your big day. Away with you now, and we will gossip when you get home." With that she turned and bounced from the suite.

Jenny looked like a frozen statue. She snapped to once the door closed. "Emma Bouron, what in the world has transpired? Has that rogue somehow found your dear friend and stolen her heart?" Emma told her the whole story while Jenny finished pinning her hair. Jenny made one comment. "Oh, what a dark, dark day that he is back in our lives; Lord have mercy."

Emma gave her a firm warning. "Do not acknowledge you have ever met him or know anything about him. If Annabelle learns of my past with Richard, there may be dire consequences for her, for him, and especially for Joseph and me. The past is dead and buried. Its resurrection will doom my future." She held Jenny by the shoulders, her voice inadvertently raised. "Do you understand me?" Jenny nodded slowly, then crumpled into the closest chair.

Her thoughts were on Emma. The healing process after Richard's desertion was arduous and lengthy. Jenny knew that even though Emma had sacrificed her virtue to Joseph, she was happier and more secure than she was since early childhood. In fact, she blossomed. Now reappearing was one of the sources of her demolished self-esteem. She must encourage Emma in every way possible so the insecurities would remain at bay. She straightened her back and stood facing her beloved child.

"Put all of this unpleasantness out of your mind. I will never give an inkling he is familiar to me. Now, dearest, a light breakfast awaits on the terrace before the carriage fetches you. I dare say the dashing commodore awaits also." Jenny hugged Emma with a mother's touch. It gave Emma confidence and reassurance. "Here, take your attaché case."

"You think of everything." Emma smiled lovingly.

It was after four o'clock, and Joseph paced up and down the hall in front of the grand staircase and the main entry to the mansion. He expected Emma to return much earlier in the afternoon. She left Rue de Sevigne at nine that morning. The presentation shouldn't have taken all day. He thought how professional she looked in her dark blue ensemble. She projected an air of confidence that always emerged where business was concerned. When she left the mansion, her excitement was tangible. He prayed management gave her a fair opportunity to show her new puppet line. He was keenly aware men were just beginning to accept women in the work world. If things went poorly, her fragile ego would sink to a new low. It was bad enough that DeBarge resurfaced to remind Emma of a failed relationship, but a slight at work would be debilitating.

He was alone most of the day. After he and Charles took a walk through the neighborhood of palatial private homes, the general excused himself to attend a meeting with his superior. Annabelle stayed in her suite all day; primping for the evening was Joseph's guess. Charles confided he gave his approval for DeBarge to court his daughter. In fact, he was very pleased. He admired the man's dedication to excelling in the French army. Although he had only been enlisted for two years, he had proved himself a talented soldier. The moment Charles met him, he was interested in his charismatic personality and knowledge of the

French military, plus he was a quick study. These qualities swayed the general to transfer him to his personal entourage. The young man's interest in his beloved Annabelle was an unexpected development. He shared most of the information with Joseph during their trek around the neighborhood. Joseph mainly listened, smiled, and nodded. He was certainly not going to be the one to burst Charles's bubble and reveal DeBarge's past.

After the general went out, Joseph read the Paris newspapers in the library while he sipped another cup of excellently brewed coffee. He ate a cold lunch on the terrace, then took a nap. He bathed and dressed in his evening clothes, thinking Emma would arrive within the hour.

So here he was pacing, worrying and sweating in his perfectly pressed evening attire. He chose not to wear a dress uniform for dinner and the theater. Instead, he wore a black evening suit with a white silk shirt and white satin tie. His boots were of exquisite leather, designed and crafted by a Parisian shoemaker. To say he looked handsome was an understatement. His hair was combed back and held by a loose black silk ribbon. He kept his face close-shaven. This showed his aristocratic bone structure, high cheekbones, and a cleft in his chin, topped off by arched eyebrows and those intoxicating blue eyes. Joseph didn't choose the style to show off his good looks, but from preference. Whiskers drove him crazy, and he didn't have the patience to shape and groom a mustache or beard. His mind was certainly not on his wardrobe or looks, but on Emma still not home. He started toward the library to have a whiskey before dinner and to calm his nerves. The front door opened. Joseph whirled around and Emma stood in the entryway. She was glowing.

She literally skipped toward him. "Joseph, I cannot believe what happened today. We were treated superbly. The president and management had zero qualms about me being a female. I was treated without deference because I am a woman. Both my manager and I handled the presentation. I introduced the characters and described the clothing interchange. Monsieur Ferra presented the cost analysis and company profit. He closed with how the streamlined manufacturing of the puppets with the clothing would substantially increase earnings with little overhead." Joseph smiled. Her words were running into each other with her unbridled excitement. She grabbed his hands and danced him in circles. He tossed his head back and laughed his deep throaty laugh.

Emma jumped in his arms. "Do you know what this means? I am being promoted to senior design executive. I will be allotted at least two designers under me, plus a sales crew for our products. Not to mention a substantial salary increase. Joseph, I am overwhelmed!"

"Darling, this is wonderful news, but I didn't question your success. You are clever, innovative, and a pioneer in the toy business. I am so pleased for you. I hope this chases away all the unpleasantness of last evening." Her look became pensive. "What is it, Emma?"

"I really meant what I said last night. I can't stand in the way of Annabelle's happiness. I must believe Richard gained integrity through maturity. I will give him the benefit of the doubt and not interfere." She kissed Joseph with determined spirit. She rationalized that even though Richard threatened her with a concocted lie, she would keep quiet for Annabelle's sake.

Joseph respected her decision they had discussed the night before. He felt certain she had Annabelle's best interest at heart. He didn't particularly like DeBarge, and not because he was Emma's previous beau but because he was transparent. The way he fawned over Annabelle was obvious to him, but must not be to the general. Well, it wasn't his concern; his focus was Emma and her brilliant career advancement.

Her new position served a double purpose. It bolstered her confidence, and it would keep her extremely busy when he was deployed. The situation in Afghanistan was worsening, and he projected he would have about three weeks before he and his men shipped out. A telegram was forwarded to him from Breton this very afternoon. He couldn't spoil Emma's triumph with his news. He would wait until the orders from the admiral were served. He wished they had more time in Paris in one way, but in another, he wanted to get back to Calais. He was aching to make love to her again. The front door opened; Charles came in the foyer. Emma was running up the stairs to tell Annabelle about her promotion. Joseph laughed. What a strange day all around.

Annabelle squealed with joy over Emma's news. Emma noticed Annabelle looked lovely. She spent the afternoon getting ready for the evening with the help of her chambermaid, Nora. It was odd really; both Emma and Annabelle had chambermaids who were more mothers than servants. Nora loved and protected Annabelle as Jenny did Emma. When Annabelle's mother died, Nora committed herself to stepping into those shoes, as it was doubtful Charles would remarry. He was dedicated to his wife, and losing her was devastating. He clung to his daughter; she was all he had left.

"My, my Annabelle," Emma chuckled, "don't you look alluring in your green silk gown? It matches your eyes and accentuates all of your assets." She giggled again. Annabelle blushed crimson.

"Emma, you are impossible. But I adore you and am so happy we are such fast friends." The girls hugged each other.

"Now, don't you have some tales to tell of your moonlight stroll last night?" Emma asked.

Nora put her apron to her mouth, giggling into it to muffle the sound. "I see you have confided in Nora. Now tell me every detail."

Laughter filled the room. "Well, let me see, we walked arm in arm through the latticed pathways, the moon was glowing, and the breeze just perfect." Emma tweaked Annabelle's arm.

"Real details, Annabelle." Emma tried to look serious. But both girls laughed harder.

"Em, it was very romantic. We talked about all sorts of private things." Emma flinched slightly. "We stopped at the stone bench at the bottom of the flower garden. When we sat down, he asked if I would court him, and we kissed several times. All at once it was like magic. I felt butterflies in my stomach and fluttering in my heart. I could hardly think straight." Annabelle's cheeks were bright red. Emma knew the feeling and so much more. She blushed, thinking about making love to Joseph.

"You girls have cheeks like red apples." Nora giggled. "I think you both know the pangs of desire."

They pretended to ignore her, only snorting with laughter didn't help. "Emma, hurry and get dressed so we can go down and celebrate for you and me."

"All right, I won't be long, quick bath and into my evening gown, and I'll be ready."

"The most expensive French champagne will be chilled and waiting." Annabelle's true friendship evoked a profound love from Emma.

When the ladies joined the men in the drawing room, Richard had already arrived. The three men were smoking cigars and sipping whiskey. Charles broke from the conversation. "If it isn't the two most charming women in Paris. I see Nora ordered vintage champagne from the wine cellar that is chilled. May I entice you?"

Charles poured champagne all around. "I have a toast to make. Raise your glasses. First, to my beloved daughter, may you find happiness and joy in your courtship." Annabelle felt the color rising up her neck; she smiled sweetly and lowered her eyes. Richard's adoring gaze spoke volumes. They all clinked glasses and took a sip. "Secondly, to our dearest Emma, congratulations on your well-deserved promotion." Now it was Emma's turn for embarrassment, and once again everyone drank to the toast. If Richard were envious of Emma's advancement in the career he abandoned, he didn't show it. He was relieved the general accepted his courtship proposal. The next proposal was marriage. Richard smiled brilliantly at the group.

It turned out to be a wonderful evening in Paris. Fine dining in the city, box seats at the opera, and camaraderie in the group. Emma was bone-tired when they got in the carriage to return to the Cousin-Montauban mansion. It had been a long day filled with many emotions up and down the spectrum. She couldn't wait to fall into bed.

Chapter 17

Adieu to Paris

In the morning it was time for Joseph, Emma, and Jenny to make their way back to Calais. Emma felt a little blue leaving Annabelle, but she was anxious to get home and share her promotion news with her family. This would definitely please her father and hopefully gain his respect for her accomplishments. She wanted to get back to Calais most of all so she and Joseph could resume the intimate side of their relationship. She missed his tender lovemaking, but she deeply missed the erotic sensations and fulfillment her body was racked with after he adeptly brought her to total ecstasy. There were many times in Paris his look, his laugh, or his light kiss made her feel giddy. Last night in his formal evening wear, he looked handsome and sexy. The way he carried himself exuded sex appeal. At the opera, during intermission, she noticed women milling around admiring him. Some even approached him with silly remarks. He simply laughed. Back in their box seats right before the lights dimmed, he looked deep in her eyes, and without words they communicated their thirst for each other.

Charles noticed the raw emotion, but Annabelle and DeBarge were oblivious. They were locked in a world of their own chattering. Charles was pleased he had given Lieutenant DeBarge permission to court his daughter. Father Time was marching on, and he felt out of sorts lately, although he hid it from Annabelle. He didn't want to die without her having a husband. She needed her own happiness and family.

The carriage rambled into the muddy streets of Calais. It had been raining all day, and the trip from Paris was long and arduous. Emma and Jenny were ready to stretch and get to bed. Joseph, on the other hand, would go to see Nicolas to get information on the Afghan situation. When they arrived at the Bouron residence, Joseph opened the door of the carriage and assisted both women out of the vehicle. "The driver and I will bring your luggage to the foyer. I know you are both exhausted from the journey."

After delivering the luggage to the house, Joseph kissed Emma good night. He was tired too, but had much on his mind and needed to be brought up–to-date on the rumblings of discord between the British and the Russians. He assumed the Russians were trying to pluck Britain's jewel, India, from the British Empire. Afghanistan was an overland passageway to India and must remain in British hands. "Darling, thank your father for allowing me to accompany you to Paris. I will visit with him in the next day or two, but I am too tired for conversation tonight and ready to bathe and drop into bed."

"I agree one hundred percent. Look, Jenny has already taken leave of us." They both laughed. Jenny was terrific on the trip, a perfect chaperone, but she was drained from the rainy, bumpy carriage ride home. "Sweet dreams," Emma said.

In a whisper, Joseph replied, "Emma I wish I was laying next to you while you dream."

She giggled and pushed him toward the door. He looked over his shoulder and left.

It was late and the house quiet. Emma was able to quickly bathe and sink into her own bed. She was asleep immediately. The next thing she knew, Claudine was shaking her shoulders. "Wake up, Emma, none of us can wait another minute to hear about Paris. Mama and Papa are waiting in the breakfast room."

"What time is it?" Emma rubbed her eyes and saw the light shining through the curtains.

"Since you have the day off and so does Papa, on purpose may I add, we have let you sleep, but it is almost ten o'clock. Rise and shine. I'll have fresh coffee waiting for you downstairs."

"Let me splash some water on my face and slip on my dressing gown. Tell Mama and Papa I'll be right down."

"Hurry up; we want to know all about it."

Emma was still a little tired, but anxious to give the news. She received hugs from her parents, and both said how much they missed her. She went through the whole trip day-by-day, explaining all of the wonderful places they visited, the gourmet meals, the interesting people she met, the Cousin-Montauban mansion, shopping, meeting Joseph's mother, but she saved the best for last. "My greatest part of the trip was meeting with management at headquarters."

"I was wondering when you would get to that," Edgar joked.

His daughter explained all the details of the meeting and the most stunning outcome. Her line had been accepted with enthusiasm; she received an impressive promotion, and an even more impressive raise in salary. Maria and Edgar were ecstatic. A woman advancing so high within a company and at such a young age was unheard of in Calais. Yes, it was becoming more and more common in Paris, London, and other large European cities, but Calais moved at a slower pace. Then she looked at her sister to propose what she had contemplated ever since she was informed she could create own team.

"Claudine, I will have my own team at Toy Depot. You are cleaver, sketch much better than me, and I think you would be an asset to the company." She smiled broadly. Deep inside, Emma thought Claudine needed to channel her enthusiasm in a career. Her sister looked dumbfounded. Her mouth opened in surprise. "Let me finish. If you accept my offer, I will arrange for you to stay with the Cousin-Montaubans and be trained at the head office. After completion of the course work, come home and take my old position. You are always fiddling with my discarded drawings, and I think you will be very successful." Emma laughed. "Of course, I will be your boss!" Emma saw the appreciation in Claudine's eyes.

"I don't know what to say. I didn't know you took notice of my sketching and watching you while you worked at home." Claudine was a little breathless, then she started to quietly cry. "Emma, thank you for having such faith in me. I am at a loss for words."

"Don't cry, dear sister, I was younger than you when I began at the Depot, and I believe you will be the inspiration I need on my team and surpass what I have done. Well, what do you think?" Emma smiled a dazzling smile at her beloved sister.

Claudine almost knocked over the chair when she jumped up and into Emma's arms. "I will never let you down, I promise. I will work so hard and make you proud." Emma kissed her wet cheeks.

"Girls, I am overjoyed at having both of you at such a reputable firm. Why, the Bouron sisters will be the talk of Calais." Edgar hugged them both. "Emma, this is very generous of you."

"No, Papa, it is not generosity that made my decision, but true belief in Claudine's talent and work ethic. When she sews lace with Mama, she is meticulous almost to a fault. I dare say, a perfectionist. Her success with me is a guarantee."

Maria was quiet as she observed the interchange between sisters and then their father. Emma had a maturity about her that was new and more stable. She never understood why the girl was bound tight in so many insecurities or why she clung to Jenny for emotional validation. She wondered where Commodore Head fit into this puzzle. Once he entered their lives, Maria saw a change in Emma. Her imagination ran wild at times thinking her daughter lost her virginity to the man, but then at other times, she saw Emma's innocence. Too complicated. She was pleased Claudine would have a future without dependence on a man or an inheritance. Spirits lifted, she embraced both girls and showed her delight. "It is a mother's dream that her children find happiness and fulfillment. Having the both of you working together gives me tremendous joy."

Chapter 18

Nineteenth-Century World Order

WHILE THE BOURONS WERE CELEBRATING Emma's news, Joseph was regrouping after his discussions with Nicholas, which lasted late into the night. His intuition proved right. The Russians were clamoring to infiltrate Afghanistan to clear a passage to India for a takeover. India was part of the British Empire and lucrative in the importing and exporting global business. The nineteenth century saw the world change dramatically with the collapse of the Spanish, Portuguese, Chinese, Roman, and Mogul Empires. These collapses paved the way for the growing influence of the German Empire and Empire of Japan, but most significantly the British Empire.

The Pax Britannica (British Peace) was a period of calm and relative peace in Europe from 1814 through 1914. Some skirmishes naturally flared up, but their longevity was brief. The Crimean War between Britain and Russia from 1854 to 1856 was the only global war during this time frame. The Russians suffered a resounding defeat. Overseas British expansion was the focal point of imperialism. Britain managed such huge success because the country controlled most of the key maritime sea routes and possessed unchallenged sea dominance. The British Navy was at its pinnacle of world renown.

The most brilliant shifting of power came from the French building of the Suez Canal during the reign of Napoleon III. It linked the Mediterranean Sea with the Indian Ocean. The French engineer Ferdinand de Lesseps dredged the canal from the delta of the Nile to the northern tip of the Red Sea at Suez. The Suez Canal was ninety miles long and connected the East with the West. Travel, mail, imports, and exports previously took up to a year to reach their destination through overland routes or sea routes around Capetown, South Africa. With the opening of the Suez Canal in 1869, business was conducted in three months and travelers enjoyed shortened trips. Originally the waterway was controlled by France and Egypt, but in 1875 the British conservative government under Benjamin Disraeli bought Egypt's 44 percent ownership. England wanted total control but that did not happen; consequently France and Britain both used the strategic waterway. The canal was the British lifeline to reaching India, part of its empire.

Queen Victoria became Victoria Regina et Imperatrix, meaning Queen and Empress of India in 1877, a year hence. Amazingly, once Victoria ascended the throne as empress, Britain controlled 20 percent of all global territory. Victoria's accomplishments during her sixty-three years as monarch were monumental. First, she restored respect for the monarchy by eliminating the tremendous self- serving excesses of the Hanover House of kings, who ruled Britain from George I through George IV. His heir William IV was on the throne from 1830 to 1837. He tried to restore restraint, but his reign was not long enough to accomplish his goal. He clung to life long enough to ensure Victoria reached eighteen before he died. This meant she wasn't required to engage a politically motivated regent to rule for her. William realized she was young, but he had great faith in her education, independent nature, and love of the people.

Victoria was a queen of will, intellect, and emotion. She married Prince Albert from the House of Saxe-Coburg and Gotha. Although it was an arranged marriage, the couple fell deeply in love and eventually produced nine children, all of whom lived, which was highly unusual in the nineteenth century. When Victoria ascended the throne, she leaned heavily on her prime minister, Lord Melbourne, but once she and Prince Albert forged an unbreakable bond, he became her partner in every aspect of her life, especially government.

When Albert died at the age of forty-two in 1861, the Queen was distraught. For a period of almost ten years, she withdrew from public life, during which time she wrote two best-selling books. The first was published in 1868, *Leaves from the Journal of Our Life in the Highlands 1848-1861*, which chronicled the couple's time together in Scotland at Balmoral Castle. She would publish another in 1883, *More Leaves 1862-1863*. The subject was the same, her life with Albert before typhoid claimed him.

Victoria was forced out of seclusion when the British people demanded her to rule and attend to her public duties. She ruled for more than thirty years after her deep mourning. She was a symbol of power and stability, as depicted through the Pax Britannica, a hundred years of peace. Another monumental accomplishment occurred during her reign, the invention of the compound steam engine, which reduced the cost of shipping, shortened the route to India, and contributed to the enlargement of the British naval fleet of battleships.

Joseph didn't discuss with Emma such subjects as British politics, expansionism, colonialism, and the role the British Navy played in these areas, not because he thought she wouldn't understand it. On the contrary, he feared she would worry about how he fit into the overall picture. In Paris, she became aware of his family's position in the aristocracy, but he didn't know if she realized their duty to God and country. She expressed her concern about his career, but also accepted he would at times be assigned for periods to other parts of the world.

Joseph learned from Nic that Admiral Smyth would send deployment orders for him and his top four lieutenants. Both Joseph and Nic speculated the assignment would be the Suez Canal. The British brass wanted a show of presence in the area and backup if needed for the soldiers on the ground. The documents should arrive in about ten days.

The sea ran through Joseph's veins, and on the one hand, he was anxious to see his swallow-tailed pennant with the Saint George Cross flying high above his battleship denoting the commodore was in command. Yet on the other hand, he was torn leaving Emma behind. Her personal view of herself was bolstered by the crowning success she achieved in Paris, but was that enough to keep her doubts in check? Time would tell.

He felt it imperative to schedule a trip to Whitfield for the purpose of discussing with his parents his future with Emma. He wanted his father, David, to bless the union. He felt assured his mother already approved after her visit with Emma in Paris.

Once back at his quarters at Chateau Philipe, he was exhausted. It was well after midnight, so he would only have a few hours' sleep. He bathed quickly and got into bed. Sleep eluded him. His mind was jumbled with the thoughts of his duty and his thoughts of Emma. Finally after tossing and turning for hours, he made a decision. Although it was quick, he was going to ask Edgar Bouron for Emma's hand in marriage. With Edgar's permission, when he returned from the first leg of his tour, they would wed. He planned to squeeze in a quick trip home to England to tell his parents, and with the railroads up and running, it shouldn't take long and the trip across the channel was very fast. He hoped Edgar would allow Emma to accompany him once again. With his decisions made, he slept like the dead.

In the morning Joseph awakened and felt refreshed from sleep and resolved in his decisions. He would send Percy, whom he trusted implicitly, to Paris to choose a ring for Emma. He rang for coffee and toast, then sat down at his desk to rough sketch an engagement ring. He knew Harrods would have exactly what he wanted. He didn't personally buy much jewelry there, but tagged along with his father and grandfather when they purchased gifts for special occasions like anniversaries, birthdays, and often Christmas. When he finished his sketch, he was pleased with the design. The ring would suit Emma perfectly. She had long slim fingers like his mother. He guessed her size as the same. If it were too large or small, he would have it adjusted after he presented her the ring. He sat back and sipped his second cup of coffee, marveling at how his life had radically changed in a few weeks.

Percy arrived promptly. Joseph smiled broadly when he opened the door for his devoted friend and confidant. Joseph shared his plans, and

Percy was not in the least surprised. He saw a look in his friend's eye that had never been there before. Well, he would lose his carousing mate, but he was happy for Joseph. A wife and an heir would be a superb addition to the Kent barony.

First, Joseph met with his officers and explained the unrest along the Afghan border and what he learned from Nicholas the previous night. The Russians were threatening the Turks as well. They were maneuvering to attack Constantinople and seize the capital city of the Ottoman Empire. The ancient city was the center of interactions between the Eastern and Western worlds for six centuries. The Russians were flexing their proverbial muscles on two fronts; consequently, the British army and navy would divide to protect both foreign interests. India as part of the British Empire required diligent monitoring on all fronts at any cost.

Joseph rallied the young lieutenants' patriotism by ensuring them the British Navy dominated the world and was indestructible. He explained he was ordered to recommend four men for his battleship, and the rest of the men would be assigned to other commodores for the time being. He emphasized the importance of secrecy so the element of surprise would shake the Russians on either front. Commodore Head smiled and shook hands with each man and expressed his pride in their loyalty to Britain. He explained departure would occur in approximately ten days hence. Joseph wondered if Admiral Smyth would send him to the Suez Canal, the safer of the two deployments, or to the port at Constantinople. He dismissed the thought. It was the sea; that's all that mattered.

Chapter 19

Impending Deployment

Emma arrived at the Toy Depot to congratulations from her colleagues. The day was exhilarating. She met privately with Monsieur Ferra, and they chose together who would be on Emma's team for design and production. He also approved her selection of her sister for an internship and then a position. The day flew by. It was after six o'clock when Emma began her walk home. She didn't want a carriage. The day was lovely, and she wanted to drink in the scents of the flowers and trees plus trek along with others in the bustling port town. She loved Calais. It was beautiful in every way. The harbor and the sea, the cobbled streets, the neat row houses that gave way to the larger homes, the city center with museums, galleries, restaurants, small cafés, two theaters, and shops of every sort. It had been her home her entire life and she loved it. She passed La Mansion Dance Hall where she met Joseph. It seemed eons ago. She still blushed thinking about their passion in the alleyway. Joseph meant everything to her. She wondered if she would see him tonight, as she hadn't received a note from him and Percy was nowhere to be seen. He was most likely totally engrossed in his work after being in Paris. Thinking of Paris reminded her she must get a note off to Annabelle to ask if Claudine could stay with her and Charles during her training period. She ambled along, her mind jumping from one thing to another. Emma was completely enjoying herself. The stroll refreshed her. As she walked the pathway to the front door of her house, the door burst open and Jenny came running to her.

"What has happened, Jen? Is it Papa, Mama, Claudine?" Panic tinged her voice.

"No, no, nothing like that, but Joseph asked to speak to your father! And he is coming to take you out to dine and the theater. I heard what I could, but a lot of it was like mumbling."

"You were eavesdropping?" Emma was astounded. It was so unlike Jenny to be so forward.

"Yes, I admit I was. No one else was about, and I couldn't help myself. I mean, we just returned from Paris and he's already come 'round. He has it bad for you, Emma Bouron!"

"Jenny, you are a sneak." They both laughed and skipped down the path together.

Edgar called from the lounge. "Emma, I heard you come in. May I see you, please?"

"Of course, Papa, what is it?" She sat down on a beige velvet Louis XI chair. He got up, went to the trolley, and poured Emma a glass of chardonnay.

"Here you are, dear girl. Bonne nuit."

"Bonne nuit, Papa." *This is strange.* Emma looked at her father. Why, he looked like he'd swallowed a butterfly. He flitted around the room with a gleam in his eye. She dare not ask why Joseph came because she didn't want Jenny reprimanded for listening.

"Daughter, your gentleman came calling today." He grinned like a Cheshire cat.

"Oh, I didn't know he was planning a visit." Emma spoke the truth.

"Yes, he and I conducted some business regarding the bank." Emma looked surprised. *Why didn't Joseph see Papa at work?*

"He also made an unusual request." Emma looked confused. "He invited you, and Jenny, of course, to go to his family estate in England."

"What? He never mentioned it to me." Now Emma was mystified. Why in the world did Joseph want her to travel to England? She just got back to the Toy Depot, and with the new line she was piled with work. She stared at her father.

"He will discuss it with you tonight over dinner." Her father looked particularly amused.

Emma stood up. "Papa, have you agreed to this trip?"

"At first I was hesitant, but the commodore was quite convincing so I gave my approval." His eyes lit up like a Christmas tree.

Emma was stupefied. Did her mother know and agree? How would she get off from work again? This was extraordinary. "Am I permitted to go to the city with Joseph tonight?"

"Yes, yes, dearest; then you can plan your little excursion." Emma gulped down her wine. Edgar chuckled. "Be careful or the wine will make you giddy."

Emma felt emboldened. "Pour me another glass, please, Papa, and I will sip it in my room as I get ready."

Edgar poured the wine and handed it to his daughter. Let her be a little giddy. He was, and it certainly wasn't from the wine or brandy he'd drunk with Joseph. He was aglow because his elder daughter would be engaged to a respected British officer. Edgar was ecstatic, and so was Maria. She hadn't joined them in fear she might give it away. She promised herself to get accustomed to the idea before seeing Emma. In her wildest dreams, she never envisioned her daughter marrying a decorated British naval officer. Fate was miraculous!

Jenny helped Emma ready herself for the evening. Tonight she chose a blush pink gown with cinched waist, tight bodice, and lace sleeves. The hemline of the gown was adorned with matching lace. Emma pulled her hair back in a long ringlet tied with a pink satin ribbon that matched her dress. She wore her silver slippers. The ensemble showed off her youth. She applied no makeup, but dusted silver sparkles across her shoulders, cleavage, and neck. The whole appearance was ethereal. At the last moment, she put a light pink gloss on her lips.

"Emma, I swear you look like an angel," Jenny gushed.

Emma smiled sweetly and hugged Jenny lightly. She didn't want the sparkles to rub off. They had heard the carriage arrive a few minutes earlier. Joseph was downstairs chatting with her mother and father.

Claudine was dining out with a group of friends. She was still bouncing on air in anticipation of training in Paris, staying at the Cousin-Montauban mansion, and stepping into a wonderful career.

When Emma entered the parlor, Maria inadvertently gasped. *My dear Lord, she looks like she's arrived from heaven.* Maria smiled; *what a perfect bride she will make.* She got up and kissed Emma on the cheek. *She has brought honor to the Bouron family.*

"Dearest, you look so captivating, you took my breath away." Maria smiled and squeezed her hand.

"Thank you, Mama." She curtsied to her father. "Good evening, Papa."

"Bonne nuit, mon enfant."

She turned to Joseph, who smiled at her from across the room. Emma looked deeply into his eyes; a charming smile spread across her face. Those blue pools were drowning her on the spot. She felt the fluttering in her stomach.

Joseph strode across the room, bowed over her hand, kissed it, and stood up straight. "Why, Mademoiselle Bouron, you are lovely as always."

"Thank you, monsieur." She looked at her parents; each of them, for some reason, exuded an air of secrecy. It made her nervous. "Papa, may I have a glass of the wine we shared earlier this evening? I left my other glass upstairs." Yes, she left the glass, but drank every drop of the wine. Something was afoot.

Edgar seemed confused. He'd thought they would leave right away, but he couldn't refuse her now. He poured the chardonnay and handed the glass to her. Joseph was still sipping on a whiskey, as was Edgar. Maria was half finished with her wine.

Joseph scrutinized the woman he loved. He felt her curiosity, but vowed not to say a word until Percy returned from Paris with the ring. Edgar was very receptive when Joseph asked for Emma's hand in marriage. He explained to Edgar he would be deployed and didn't know as yet for how long. He wanted to commit to Emma before he left. Edgar approved, which was a relief to Joseph, and the bonus was he agreed to the trip to England.

The wine was making Emma a little light-headed. She put the half-empty glass on a table and suggested they go for dinner. Handshakes, kisses, smiles all around. *Weird*, she mused. *Well, I don't give a care what they are hiding; I want to be alone with Joseph.* They walked down the path hand in hand.

Emma looked at the carriage. "Where's Percy?"

Joseph chuckled. "Why, I didn't know you were so interested in Percy."

Emma tweaked his arm. "You rogue, I simply wondered, as he is usually your companion and driver."

"Darling, he worked very hard while we were away, and he has the night off. I guarantee he will roust about with the other boys at the dance hall or club." Joseph laughed his deep throaty laugh. Emma shuddered involuntarily. He looked amazing. He wore tights and green velvet knickers that were the fashion. He had on a white silk shirt and white ermine cape. He looked like a prince from a storybook.

"What thoughts are going through your pretty little head?"

"I was admiring how handsome you look, Joseph."

He smiled and opened the door to the carriage. "May I help you in, Mademoiselle Bouron?"

"Why yes, monsieur, that would be dashing." She burst into laughter.

"Driver, Chateau Philipe, merci beaucoup.

"Are we dining in, Joseph?"

"Yes, my love, we are doing just that. I thought it would give us a good chance to talk alone, which was sparse during our trip. Other than a few stolen moments, we were in someone else's company for days."

"So I see, talking is your motive. I thought possibly you might have something else in mind." Emma dripped with sarcasm, but couldn't stop herself from giggling.

Joseph pulled her to him. "Close your eyes," he whispered in her ear. Emma closed her eyes and felt his mouth cover hers. She responded immediately. The kiss aroused them both. He pulled back. "Emma, I must take a breath. I want to wait until we are in my quarters before I completely ravish every inch of you." He noticed in the dimming light she was flushed from his one kiss. It thrilled him he possessed such power over her.

Once in Joseph's private quarters, he gently undressed Emma one garment at a time, never taking his gaze from her eyes. Then he quietly disrobed. Both naked, he lifted her from the center of the parlor. Entranced, Emma couldn't stop looking into his deep blue eyes. Her heart beat faster and faster; her breath came quickly. Joseph's body was magnificent, strong, and firm. He held her with a possessive grasp that thrilled her inside and out. He laid her on the bed softly, still staring in her eyes. Joseph drank in the scent of her hair. He twisted his fingers in her luscious brunette curls. His face was inches from hers. Neither of them had spoken a word. Their looks spoke volumes of love, lust, and desire. Joseph rubbed her back, then traced the curve of her hips with his fingers. Emma trembled. He awakened her cravings, which were kept in check while in Paris. She wrapped her legs around him and pushed her body into his. They made love passionately, totally relinquishing themselves to each other, then lovingly with slow exploration and fulfillment. When Joseph and Emma were both quenched, they slept in each other's arms. Joseph told the maitre d' to send dinner to the room at nine o'clock. When the knock came at the door, Joseph bolted out of bed and grabbed a pair of trousers and shirt. He called out, "Un moment, s'il vous plait."

Emma stirred and stretched. She felt weak and a little disoriented. Looking around, she realized she was in Joseph's bed, her body weak from their passion. The bed was empty. She heard Joseph speaking to someone, but the doors were closed and their voices muffled. She smiled in the dark, as the lamps hadn't been lit. Her mind danced with the images of their bodies entwined and the sensations that invaded her.

Joseph opened the doors, and the flames from the parlor fire outlined his body in orange light. "Darling, slip on my dressing gown; the waiter brought up our dinner. I am ravenous." Joseph laughed. "We have poached salmon, roasted potatoes, brussels sprouts, and fresh bread with butter. Plus a strong pot of tea to wipe the sleep from your face." Joseph laughed again.

"Joseph Head, you are impossible. You expect me to be fully awake with less than an hour of sleep after what you put my body through! But I am starved, and I am sure I will be replenished by food and hot tea." Emma pretended to be indignant, but laughter engulfed her. Her infectious mirth sent Joseph into gales of laughter too.

Joseph watched Emma as she ate with a robust appetite. The enthusiasm she had for her food confirmed that any shred of ladylike pretenses melted away. He saw she was completely at ease with him. He hated to put a damper on such a perfect evening by discussing his impending deployment, but hoped talk of visiting the Head estate in Kent might soften the blow. He waited until she ate, until her plate was clean.

"Emma, do you want some cheese and grapes? The fromage plate is on the sideboard."

"Not another bite! Look at my dinner plate—not a trace of food!"

"Then let's enjoy a brandy in front of the fire."

"You know I drank two glasses of chardonnay before we left my house. I was quite giddy, but my, um, exercise and food brought me back to normal. So, yes, I will have a small snifter." She purposely didn't mention she had indulged in the quantity of wine she drank because her father had revealed Joseph's plans of a trip to England. She wanted him to tell her.

Joseph looked serious. It sent a cold chill through Emma and shook her calm countenance. He handed her a brandy. She didn't say a word while he explained the world's upheavals and how it affected their lives. History intrigued Emma when she was at school, but she didn't follow politics or read newspaper editorials. When Joseph finished his explanations and their consequences, Emma felt ill. He would leave her, and for how long no one knew. He minimized the dangers, but she didn't believe he would be completely out of harm's way. Joseph could almost see her thought process. He definitely saw the rosy color drained from her face and the fear in her eyes.

"My darling Emma, I know this news upsets you deeply, but as a career officer there will be times throughout our lives that I will be called away from you. I want you to remember that serving my country is what I was born to do; it is nonnegotiable, but Emma, it doesn't have to be a negative factor. You will become accustomed to military ways."

He forged ahead. "I do have a wonderful surprise." Emma stared at him. "I spoke to your father today about the Russian situation and explained with a deployment imminent, I wanted to take you to Whitfield to meet my whole family. He was very kind and understanding and gave his approval. Edgar is very generous. If you agree, darling, you and I and Jenny will go to England next week. What do you think?" He was enthusiastic. Emma could see he craved her understanding and agreement. It was difficult, but she loved him so much she smiled and lied.

"Thank you for planning a trip for us. I will be honored to meet the rest of your family. I hope they like me. I am French, you know." She managed a weak smile.

Joseph laughed. Inside, he was flooded by relief.

"They will adore you, Emma. You are perfect in every way." He meant every word. She was perfect, beautiful, kind, sensual, and most importantly, he knew she loved him without reserve. She had shown him for two phenomenal hours.

The week flew by for both Emma and Joseph. She was covered with work, and Joseph was busy with his maritime charts and communications.

Emma heard from Annabelle. She and Charles graciously agreed to have Claudine stay at the Cousin-Montauban mansion during her internship in Paris. In fact, Annabelle was excited about getting to know Claudine and introducing her to Parisian society. Her courtship with Richard was progressing also.

Claudine was still processing the life-changing events graciously bestowed upon her by her dear sister. The thought of living in Paris with the Cousin-Montaubans as part of it was beyond her wildest dreams. She knew Emma was giving her a tremendous opportunity. She swore to God she wouldn't disappoint Emma or her parents. She lost interest in George and stopped going to La Mansion. She filled her days sketching clothing for the marionettes. Claudine experienced blind ambition for the first time in her life.

Chapter 20

Whitfield

Joseph, Emma, and Jenny set out from Calais to Dover the following Wednesday. The trip was quite pleasant. The spring weather and calm sea made the Channel crossing speedy and uneventful. The train from Dover to Whitfield had two club cars. The private train quarters thrilled Jenny. She had never been in a club car that had a personal porter who served luncheon on a table covered with a white linen cloth. The threesome enjoyed chicken quiche, cheese, fruit, and a trifle for dessert. After the midday meal, each rested for the remainder of the trip. Before they reached Whitfield, the women had a chance to freshen up. Emma wore a lavender day dress with a matching cloak. Her hair was pulled back and arranged in swirling curls at the base of her neck, with tiny silk purple flowers nestled in each curl. Joseph admired her ensemble. Many others eyed her on the ship and the train. He imagined the look on his father's and brother's faces when they met the woman he adored. What pleased Joseph immensely was that they would see how her inner beauty matched her striking outer appearance.

The conductor shouted, "Next stop: Whitfield. Whitfield, next stop."

After disembarking from the train, Emma spotted an ornate landau carriage with a crest embossed on the side panel. She recognized the crest. Joseph had the exact same one on a topcoat he had worn in Paris. Her heart began to flutter, and her hands felt slick in her pink leather gloves. She tried to imagine exactly what Joseph's ancestral home would be like. She knew it dated back centuries, but was it modernized? Her imagination was running amuck when Joseph's hands gently shook her. "Darling, are you all right? Your face is quite devoid of color. Was the train journey after the meal uncomfortable?"

"No, no, I am nervous about meeting your father and brother."

"Emma, you will come to love them both. Charles is a carbon copy of my father. He loves the land with a passion as I love the sea. They are both easygoing gents with no pompous airs. In fact, the dirtier Charles gets, the happier he is." Joseph smiled at the thought of his father and brother. "I assure you, my darling, you will take their breath away as you have mine."

Blushing, Emma looked up at Joseph through her thick black lashes. "I am taking you at your word, sir." She relaxed and smiled.

"That's my girl." Joseph gestured to Jenny, and the three climbed into the open landau. The day was glorious. The sun was still shining through the trees in the late afternoon. Whitfield Manor was a short distance from the train station. The road to the manor house was hilly but well-graded, so the bumps were kept to a minimum. The land was green and lush, with beautiful trees and wildflowers growing in clusters. Emma remarked how splendid it was. Joseph smiled, promising that the manicured grounds around the main house were even lovelier. He hoped she would indulge Charles. His brother was sure to show off the neat rows of crops and the pastures of grazing sheep. He didn't think she would be ready to explore the slaughterhouse or the stalls where the sheep were sheared. This visit he wanted her to enjoy the beauty of Kent.

As the carriage traversed over the crest of the last hill, the whole countryside underwent a metamorphosis. Thick green grass spread like a blanket up to terraces of flowers of all varieties and colors. They served as a bright contrast to the gray stone walls of the massive structure that was the house. Inadvertently both Emma and Jenny caught their breath. It was more, much more than Emma ever imagined. She was beginning to understand exactly what position her Joseph held in British society.

It was easy to acknowledge while in the surroundings of Calais or even at the Cousin-Montauban mansion on Rue de Sevigne that he was a nobleman, but she hadn't grasped the enormity of it until now. What he called a house was a castle. Yes, a castle! Joseph watched as different emotions danced across Emma's face. He anticipated she would be surprised by his family's position, but he hoped it didn't trigger her own insecurity and self-doubt. He was determined to reassure her every time those feelings surfaced.

He patted his jacket pocket. He rubbed the small box snuggly nestled inside the inner pocket. Percy arrived back from Paris Tuesday evening with the ring. It was perfect. Harrods didn't let him down, although his bank account was considerably reduced. They had a ring in the shop very similar to his sketch; only minor alterations were made. With the expertise of their goldsmith and precious gem expert, and the price consideration, the manager made sure the ring was ready.

It was unique, as was Emma. The bezel of the ring was platinum with 18 karat yellow gold prongs holding the center stone, which was a magnificent square emerald of the finest cut, weighing 7 karats. The band that held the deep green gem was thick lustrous platinum. The wedding band Joseph planned to lock in the safe in his room was platinum-encrusted, with perfect diamonds all around. Worn as a set or separately, the rings were stunning, a masterpiece of fine jewels fit for a duchess. Joseph hoped his mother wouldn't be hurt he didn't choose one of the many heirlooms, but he wanted to create something for Emma he personally designed. She would inherit many of the Kent jewels in the future anyway. His mother held a soft spot in her heart for her older son, and he was sure he could win her over once he explained why he chose to get a ring outside of the Kent collection.

As the carriage pulled up to the main entrance, the colossal door swung wide open. Joseph's parents watched for their son's arrival in the adjacent morning room, which looked out over the flowered terraces. Catherine Head was quite anxious for David to meet the sweet French girl Joseph had fallen in love with. Her mother's sixth sense told her this was not purely a social visit. It was so soon after the Parisian trip, something else was up. Catherine watched her husband's reaction as

Emma alighted from the landau. She knew David so well his reaction was an open book to Catherine, plus he was a miserable liar. She observed immediately that Emma's astounding good looks captivated David, but it was her youth that astonished him. When she returned to England from France, of course, she gave details of the woman who finally captured Joseph's heart, but she purposely didn't mention Emma's exact age. Only Catherine caught David's surprise. His face regained complete composure immediately, and his charming demeanor took over.

Two servants magically appeared to take the luggage from the back rack of the carriage. Joseph stepped forward to warmly greet his mother and father, then immediately turned to Emma, smiled, winked, and took her hand. "Father, it is my great honor to present to you Mademoiselle Emma Bouron."

David kissed her free hand. "Welcome to Whitfield, Emma. I hope you will enjoy the lazy country lifestyle compared to the busy city life of Calais." She blushed crimson. Then Catherine stepped in.

"Emma, it is so lovely to see you again." The women kissed each other's cheeks.

Joseph introduced Jenny to David as Emma's companion. Now it was Jenny's turn to blush. She bowed and curtsied. "So pleasant to meet you."

They moved inside the great hall. Jenny gawked wide-eyed at the portraits of dukes and duchesses from several centuries. They lined the walls of the great hall. A pretty girl about Emma's age appeared from a room off the hall. Catherine took her hand.

"Jenny, this is my personal assistant, Phoebe. She will show you to your rooms and make you afternoon tea. Your luggage is in the bedchamber, so if you would like to freshen up after the long journey, Phoebe will have one of the maids draw you a hot bath and you can rest before dinner."

Emma turned to Jenny. "You've had an even longer day than I. You rose before daylight and readied our belongings for the trip. Please, go with Phoebe and refresh yourself." Emma smiled and caressed her shoulders. The gesture was not lost on Catherine. She saw once again the special bond between the two women. Jenny's relief was apparent.

The preparations and the trip itself had tired her. Phoebe led her up to her rooms, which had been prepared for her in the servants' quarters.

Catherine smiled at Emma. "Would you like to rest now? I didn't mean to be rude, but we were so looking forward to your arrival."

"Actually, I feel wonderful from the lovely open carriage ride and the fresh air." Emma smiled broadly. She squeezed Joseph's arm.

David noticed his son beamed. He had never seen Joseph look at a woman in this way. He would admit; she certainly wasn't hard to look at. She was lovely, with fine bone structure, peaches and cream complexion, luscious thick brunette hair, a petite perfectly proportioned figure, and an innocence that belied her youth. He must ask Joseph her exact age. Catherine was bustling them along to the family parlor. The remainder of the afternoon was entrenched in pleasant conversation. It gave the Heads an opportunity to visit with Emma on a casual basis. They sipped sherry, typically British, and nibbled at buttery scones. David was very impressed; the girl had a progressive career in a man's world. As Emma explained her love of toy design and her position, the parlor door burst open, and a tall, handsome man in dirty clothing and boots stomped into the room.

He took the room in three strides and threw his arms around his brother. "Joseph, I am so happy you are home." He didn't see Emma sitting in the petit-point chair. Joseph ruffled his brother's crop of thick blond hair.

"Charles, you rogue, you will get me filthy and smelling of sheep. Plus, you are incorrigible, as you ignored my special guest." Joseph laughed his throaty laugh and bear-hugged his brother. Charles scanned the room. He spotted Emma sitting quietly. He looked like a deflated balloon. He turned to Emma, bowed at the waist, and tried to apologize for his gauche behavior. Joseph laughed harder.

Lucky for Charles, his mother interceded. "Oh, Joseph, stop teasing your brother. He meant no harm."

Emma stood up, walked toward Charles, and extended her hand. "I am sure, monsieur, your brother exaggerates. I have looked forward to meeting you. Joseph told me such wonderful things about you. I am anxious to explore the estate with you to see the crops and sheep Joseph brags about. He says no one in all of Kent can manage the land and the livestock like his own brother."

Charles was mesmerized by her every word, even though he was embarrassed. Why, Joseph wasn't even seriously interested in a female relationship, yet he brought home the perfect woman. Charles tried to apologize, but stumbled over his words. He couldn't concentrate with those penetrating green eyes looking at him and her winning smile so sincere. He quickly excused himself, mumbling he'd join them for dinner. He practically ran from the room.

Joseph was still chortling. "Darling Emma, you made my brother blush and left him speechless."

"Oh, Joseph, he didn't know I was here and you embarrassed him. You owe him an apology."

"As usual, you are right, darling. I capitalized on his discomfort. I will tell him I am sorry at dinner."

David almost gasped. *She's got a lot of spunk. I like her chastising Joseph for embarrassing Charles.* The boys were so very different, Joseph in love with the sea and Charles in love with the land. Joseph so self-assured and worldly, Charles dignified yet more jagged around the edges. Both boys experienced superior schooling and superb etiquette training. Both were of good character, honest, loyal, and trustworthy, but their interests were different. None of that diminished their love of one another. The brothers were fiercely protective of each other. No one dare criticize the other, but between each other, they joked, cajoled, and teased.

Joseph and Charles hadn't discussed the future after their parents were deceased. It was a given that Joseph would inherit the land as the peerage law dictated, but he knew in his heart the land should belong to Charles. It was a paradox he didn't like to think about. But his father was in his late sixties, so the topic wasn't too far away. He didn't want to dwell on that now, as tonight he planned to discuss his marriage proposal with his parents. If they gave their blessing, tomorrow would be the day.

Emma was shown to her rooms in the West Wing, which housed rooms for guests. She had no idea how many rooms the sprawling castle contained. The wing she was in seemed to stretch on forever. As it was at Annabelle's, Jenny's rooms were adjacent to Emma's, only bigger and even more lavishly decorated for servants' quarters. The rooms Emma occupied were opulent. The wardrobe was one of the most ornate she had ever seen. She opened the first set of doors, and the clothes she packed were hanging neatly according to color. She opened the middle door, and behind it was a set of pullout drawers. Her sleeping gowns and undergarments were neatly put away. Her shoes were lined up on the bottom shelf under the last drawer. Everything was put away, but she was curious to see the inside of the last set of doors.

Emma was amazed and humbled. Hanging on the rod were the gowns commissioned in Paris, and not just the few she chose, but every single one she admired. It took her breath away. Joseph was the most generous man she had ever known. She took the emerald green gown from the wardrobe. It was perfection. She closed the ornate door and looked in the full-length mirror. She held the dress up to her body. Other than her gold ball gown, it was the most stunning dress imaginable, and it was hers. Once again, Joseph's thoughtfulness overwhelmed her. She wasn't sure how formal evening dinner would be, so she decided to put the emerald dress away until the proper occasion presented itself. Emma pulled out a light blue dress that was not too formal, but appropriate for a semiformal evening.

One of the servants showed Emma to the family dining room. She later learned the family dined in this room when only a few guests attended. The formal dining room was utilized for large numbers of guests. The room was decorated in light pastels, with twinkling chandeliers that made the silk fabric on the furniture shimmer in the semi-dim lighting. Joseph immediately went to Emma's side. He kissed her cheek, then whispered, "You look perfect, sweetheart." Emma smiled and stared into his eyes. He could feel her thoughts of appreciation for the gown mingled with her love for him.

Joseph put his arm around her waist and led her to the group chatting by the fire. "Emma, you met my dapper brother." Joseph chuckled. Charles shot him a dark look. He took Emma's hand and kissed it. He smiled a sparkling smile.

"Good evening, Charles. I don't know when you look most handsome, in your sheep britches or proper evening attire." Emma smiled and squeezed his hand.

Charles laughed. "I think she'll be a match for you, Joseph." David and Catherine laughed along with Emma. Joseph shook his head.

Another young lady was led into the dining room. She walked straight to Charles and looped her arm through his possessively. Emma noticed the laughter abated and Catherine stiffened slightly.

Charles broke the uneasy silence. "Constance, I would like you to meet Joseph's special friend, Emma Bouron."

Emma smiled sweetly at the young lady, although she wasn't quite sure of her position with the Heads. Was she Charles's intended?

"Good evening, Constance. I am very pleased to make your acquaintance."

"Oh, from your accent, I gather you are French." Her smile was insincere.

Joseph interjected, "Hello, Constance. Yes, you have adroit ears. Emma is from Calais, France, a beautiful city across from the Straits of Dover."

She giggled. "Joseph Head, you know I am acquainted with Calais." Her smiles and voice dripped with sarcasm. She turned to Catherine and David. Her whole persona changed. "I am so pleased to be dining with you this evening. It is special for Charles to include me." She looked at Charles and smiled her disingenuous smile.

Emma was confused the whole evening. It was apparent Joseph did not care for Constance. She wasn't sure, but she got the same inclinations from his parents. Charles seemed quite neutral, neither interested nor disinterested. Emma didn't play games, not only because it wasn't her nature; she didn't know how to go about it. All in all, the evening was uncomfortable. Maybe English girls were just different. She didn't care. She could only be true to herself. She definitely caught a scathing look from Constance when Catherine mentioned Emma's dress.

"Emma, my dear, I see our purchases reached your wardrobe on time." Catherine smiled brightly. "The blue looks lovely. The fabric was a perfect choice. Of course, nothing matches French couture."

"I absolutely love it, Catherine, and the other ones. Thank you for your expertise and perfect taste."

"Yes, Mother, I think you girls enjoyed a very successful shopping trip in Paris. I am more than pleased." Joseph got in his dig.

Constance looked like she swallowed a chicken bone from the coq au vin. Charles was oblivious to the whole conversation. David didn't have a clue what the women were bantering about. He beckoned the waiter who poured him another sauvignon blanc. He knew from Catherine's rod-straight posture she was annoyed at something. After a light dessert, Catherine brought the evening to a close. She mentioned it was a long day for Joseph and Emma traveling from Calais and an early night would be in order.

Emma sensed Catherine was anxious for the evening to conclude quickly. She responded to her cue. "How kind of you, Catherine. What with the early departure, the boat, the train, and then the carriage, it was quite tiring. I enjoyed the delicious meal, but I bid you all a good night so I will be refreshed for an adventure tomorrow." She hugged David, kissed Catherine on both cheeks, and shook hands with both Charles and Constance.

"Mother, please send Phoebe to take Jenny to Emma's suite," Joseph said.

"Of course, sleep well, dear." Catherine gave Emma an appreciative grin.

As soon as they were in the great hall, Joseph confided in Emma how much he loathed Constance. He told Emma she was a gold digger and social climber, but Charles was too naïve and too kind to see it.

Emma nodded. Suddenly she actually was exhausted. When they reached her suite, Joseph kissed her tenderly. He looked deep in her eyes. "Darling, I love you so very much. Rest well, and I will see you in the morning."

"I love you, Joseph. I'm sorry; I really have become so tired."

"Get some rest, my love. We have a big day tomorrow."

Chapter 21

Formal Approval

Joseph went directly to the family dining room. His mother and father were alone, each drinking a brandy. Charles was taking Constance to her parents' estate since she sent her carriage home, a convenient way for her to cinch time alone with Charles.

Catherine declared to her husband and son, "I absolutely cannot tolerate Constance. I don't know why Charles can't see through her. But I dare not say anything; I don't want to push him toward her. On the other hand, Joseph, you know I will speak my mind with you. Emma is an absolute delight. She is not only beautiful, but also gracious and kind. It would take a blind man not to see how much she adores you."

Joseph finished pouring himself a snifter of brandy. "Father, Mother, it must appear odd I brought Emma to Whitfield since, Mother, you saw us two weeks ago."

"I knew there was a reason for this impromptu trip. Call it mother's intuition." Catherine's happy demeanor returned.

"I know you see I have fallen in love with Emma, and I want to make her my wife."

"Joseph, I only met her today. She is a charming girl and fits well with the family, but son, how old is she?" David asked the question he'd wondered about since Emma's arrival.

"Father, I thought you would ask that question." Joseph laughed. "I saw your surprise when she stepped down from the landau." Joseph took a sip of brandy. "She is nineteen. She is very mature for her age, an enigma really, so innocent on one hand and so worldly on the other. It is one of the qualities that attracted me to her." Joseph cleared his throat. "I want to propose to her tomorrow. I have spoken with her father, a well-respected banker, Edgar Bouron. He gave his blessing. I realize this is sudden and we have only been courting a little over a month, but I tell you truly, I knew she was the one the first night I met her."

"Son, I was in her company only a few times, but I think she is perfect for you." Catherine took her son's hand and smiled.

Joseph chuckled. "I see right through you, Mother; you want those grandchildren." Catherine tried to look incensed.

"Before you give your answer, Father, there is something else. I told Emma I have an impending deployment, but I didn't tell her the exact assignment yet. I am about to be deployed to either the Suez or the port of Constantinople. The Russians are trying to shake India out of Britain's grasp. We can't let that happen. I will know my destination within ten days. I don't want to leave Emma without her being betrothed to me. I know she loves me and wants to spend her life with me. When I am at sea, planning our wedding plus her job will keep her busy and happy." Catherine looked stricken; she hated it when Joseph was deployed in harm's way.

"Joseph, this is much to digest. Pour me another brandy, son." David mulled over all he had just learned from his elder son and the next Duke of Kent. Joseph was thirty-five years old and knew his mind, plus David liked the girl immediately. He also was certain Joseph wouldn't change his mind. "Joseph, I give you my blessing and permission."

Joseph didn't know why, but tears clouded his vision. "Thank you, Father. You make me so very happy."

Catherine jumped up and threw her arms around her husband and son.

Joseph gave her a quick squeeze, then pulled back. "Now, Mother, I have something to tell you that I hope isn't a disappointment." Catherine looked confused. Joseph reached inside his dinner jacket to the secret pocket in the lining and took out the Harrods box. "The ring set was crafted by Harrods. Please understand, it is not because the Kent jewels are not exquisite beyond compare, but I wanted to have rings made for Emma that were personally designed by me. Please understand."

Catherine laughed, not what her son expected. "Joseph Head, who would guess after all these years you are a hopeless romantic? I think it's a lovely gesture. Now open that box and let your father and me see."

Joseph revealed the rings wedged into black velvet slits in the blue box. His mother gasped.

"This emerald is perfection, Joseph." It was one of the most perfect emeralds Catherine had ever seen, and she knew gems.

"Yes, Mother, exactly like the woman who will wear it."

Chapter 22

The Proposal

PHOEBE AWAKENED EMMA AND JENNY. She announced breakfast would be served in the morning room, and Emma should wear a dress appropriate for riding. Once Phoebe left the room, Jenny rattled on about only having an hour to get Emma ready, what dress should she wear, would she be safe on horseback. Emma burst out laughing. "Jenny, you are a worrywart. I brought a dress specifically for riding and the proper shoes. I know I'm not an accomplished horsewoman, but Joseph will take perfect care of me and teach me how to ride. Now, let's draw a bath and get me prepared for my day in the country." It was Jenny's turn to laugh.

After a delightful breakfast with Joseph and his mother, father, and brother, Emma anticipated introduction to life on the manor. Charles would guide Emma and Joseph since the land was his pride and joy. Charles chose a docile mare for Emma to ride. Her proficiency was quite natural, a surprise to both men.

The day was sunny but brisk. It was perfect. Emma jogged along the rolling green countryside and garnered an appreciation for the land. Whitfield was picturesque. She loved seeing the green fields and pastures of sheep, especially the mothers with the baby lambs. Watching them frolic brought a smile to her lips, and she didn't know why, but tears welled in her eyes. Charles showed off his fields of crops and explained the planting and harvesting process. They rode through the village and stopped for a mug of beer and a sandwich at the local pub. *The Fox and Hounds* was a gathering place for villagers, especially on the weekends. Several of the men and a few of their wives sat around the fire enjoying a day of camaraderie with fellow workers and neighbors. It wasn't lost on Joseph or Charles that the blokes stared when they saw Emma bounce in smiling and joking with the Head boys. They whispered when they heard her lilting French accent with its musical intonation. The men winked and punched one another. The wives were more inquisitive and guessed she was with Joseph, since it was common knowledge Charles was keeping company with Constance, whom they all disliked. She acted superior and haughty. No one fathomed what a kind man such as Charles saw in her.

Charles shook hands or spoke to most of the men who worked on the manor, as had their fathers and their fathers' fathers before them. Joseph bid them hello, and the dainty jewel who was with him curtsied slightly and gave a sincere dazzling smile. The villagers were instantly drawn to Emma's sweet smile and kind eyes.

When the threesome arrived back at the manor house, Emma was exhilarated, but tired. It was close to three o'clock. They were gone most of the day. Joseph suggested an afternoon rest before the evening festivities. He explained to Emma his parents were having a small dinner soiree so she could meet friends from close surrounding manors and some friends from Dover. Catherine's dinner parties were infamous, and the Heads' friends would often cancel other plans to enjoy an evening at Whitfield. Joseph kissed Emma lightly on the lips. "Get some rest, darling, and I'll be back to escort you at six o'clock." He began to walk down the hall. Emma watched as he left. Suddenly he turned and said, "Wear the emerald green gown from Paris. It will be perfect for tonight." He winked and sauntered off down the hallway. Emma felt the weakness in her stomach. His look, his touch, and his kiss made her giddy. She was excited he wanted her to wear the emerald gown. She loved it, and even though she didn't have a conceited bone in her body, she thought she looked attractive in it; the color accentuated her eyes and hair. She sighed with happiness; tonight would be special.

Jenny opened the bedroom door for Joseph. The emerald gown highlighted all of Emma's many assets. Joseph mused. She was a vision of perfection. He loved the way Jenny dressed Emma's hair. It hung almost to her waist in loose curls. The front was held back with tiny diamond hairpins, but the wayward tendrils escaped and gave her a sexy aura that was innocent, an unusual combination. Her face glowed from the day in the sun. Her long dark eyelashes and big green eyes were naturally beautiful. She had glazed her lips with a light rose balm. Seeing her so lovely and knowing she belonged to him made Joseph desire her. The rise in his velvet knickers attested to his manly urges. He tried to concentrate on the damn tapestries hanging along the west wing walls. Under control, breathing steadily, he stopped and turned her toward him. "Emma, I thought you and I might have a quiet few moments together before I surrender you to family friends who will clamor to meet you. Let's go to one of the small family drawing rooms and have a glass of champagne together."

She smiled up at him so sweetly. "Joseph, that sounds tres bon. Are you sure your parents won't be offended?"

"Of course not. Most of the guests won't arrive for at least another hour, so we can have a few stolen minutes alone." Catherine had already helped Joseph get the drawing room ready. Vases of pink roses were placed around the room. A fire burned in the marble fireplace, and a bottle of hundred-year-old champagne was chilling in an ornate silver ice container that had belonged to David's grandmother. Two crystal flutes from Catherine and David's wedding service were on the matching silver tray beside the champagne. The drawing room was at the far end of the north wing. It wasn't used except for intimate family functions or small private gatherings. Joseph wanted to be far away from the arriving guests. The servants were told not to go into the room until the following day. Catherine and David were the only ones who knew Joseph was going to propose before the party. Joseph wanted to tell Charles, but he disappeared after the day's ride.

"We are going down the north wing, sweetheart. The way the manor house was built centuries ago was quite common architecture. The main rooms for the public are in the center of the building on the first floor. The second floor has all the turrets and carved-out cannon stations that, of course, haven't been used for several hundred years. Charles and I used to play up there when we were children until Mother caught us and hauled us back down to our playroom. The west wing houses servants' quarters, the scullery, kitchen, rooms for arms, ancient weapons, and a couple of family rooms, like the morning room that faces the terraces. Those rooms have large windows so the occupants can enjoy the grounds. On the second floor are the guest suites, with rooms for their servants. The north wing is a conglomeration of family rooms, some public rooms, special servants' quarters like for Phoebe, Father's manservant Bernie, and others of that status. The upper floor of the north wing belongs totally to family members. My parents' rooms, Charles's rooms, my rooms, quarters for our grandparents, a schoolroom in the nursery—and naturally the nursery is quite large, with a kitchen for the children to dine—several bedrooms, and Nanny's rooms, as she would be considered a member of the family, are all in the north wing. I will show you the whole manor house tomorrow, even my secret places as a child." Joseph's eyes glinted.

"Joseph, it is overwhelming, and I don't mean that in an unkind way. The manor is like something out of a fairy tale. What a magical place for you and Charles to grow up. I look forward to seeing all of it, especially those secret hideouts." Emma tweaked his arm and giggled.

They reached the end of the hall of the lower floor of the north wing. Joseph opened a beautifully carved oak door. Emma quickly glanced around the drawing room. It had an intimacy about it that drew her in. Lovely roses from the garden were in crystal and porcelain vases on several tables. The fire was low and glowing in a pinkish marble fireplace, the mantel crafted from the same marble with vases of roses on each end. A glass table under the center floor-to-ceiling window held a bottle of chilling champagne and two crystal flutes. She shuddered when she thought about dropping the expensive flute at Annabelle's. Then she smiled thinking how Joseph cared for the cut in her hand, his tenderness true and loving. She turned around. Joseph was watching her with a distinct intensity. She was puzzled. What was he thinking?

He poured them each a glass of champagne. "Emma, sit on the settee next to me." Joseph didn't realize he looked nervous; his palms sweated, and his heart raced. He took a gulp of the wine.

"Are you all right? You have a peculiar look on your face. Have I done something to upset you, Joseph?"

It hit him he was gawking at her like a tongue-tied schoolboy. He laughed. "Here, let me take your glass." He put both glasses on the table in front of the settee. "Come to the window with me, Emma. The chandelier gives off subtle light and the glow from the fire makes the room cozy, but the natural light of the sun setting will let me see so deep within your eyes I will see your heart."

His words were lyrical. He took both her hands and led her to the window. She was confused. One minute he seemed dazed; the next he was saying the most romantic words, pure poetry. He held her shoulders like the first night on the streets of Calais. His gaze was so intent she believed he actually could see her heart. "Emma, I have loved you from the first moment I saw you at La Mansion. My love has grown stronger and deeper every single day."

Her heart began to sink; he was preparing her for the worst. *I have loved you, but now realize it will not work because of our age difference, my career, and your career. I love the sea most.* She began to shake. Her stricken look pierced his heart. Emma turned from him. It was barely a whisper. "Joseph, if you have realized I don't fit into your world, tell me now. I will try to understand."

Oh dear God, from what he said, she thought he was ending the relationship. He whirled her around, dropped to his knees, and kissed the palms of her hands. "I love you, Emma Bouron. Will you do me the honor of being my wife?"

Emma was wide-eyed. She had misunderstood everything he said. What was wrong with her? She fell to her knees and threw her arms around his neck. "Yes, yes, yes." She kissed his lips and opened her mouth so he could feel her tongue. Joseph kissed her back, sweetly at first, then with probing desire. He forced himself to pull away. He lifted her to her feet. Never taking his eyes away from hers, he pulled the ring from his pocket and slid it on her left-hand ring finger. "Then it's official." Joseph winked. Emma looked at her hand. She was absolutely stunned. The center stone danced and sparkled in the dwindling light from the window.

"Mon Dieu, Joseph, this is the most gorgeous ring I have ever seen in my life. I don't know what to say. Is it . . . ?"

"Yes, darling, it is a 7 karat emerald specifically designed by me for my future wife. The surrounding stones are diamonds, and the metal is platinum and 18 karat yellow gold. Your wedding band matches the betrothal ring and is locked away in my safe."

Tears flowed down Emma's face. She couldn't comprehend that her dreams for happiness were really coming true. The man she loved from the depth of her being moments ago proposed and placed a ring fit for a princess on her finger. The whole thing seemed surreal. She stared at the ring. He took great pains to design exactly what portrayed their love, an intertwining of heart, body, and soul. She had never been happier. He dried her tears with his handkerchief. He laughed. "You did say yes, didn't you?" Emma held him so tightly Joseph thought she might meld right into his body. "Come, darling, sit down and have a glass of champagne with your fiancé." They sat on the settee. "A toast to my beautiful bride. To Emma, the girl who stole my crusty sailor's heart." Emma finally laughed.

"To Joseph, the man of my dreams and the love of my life." They clinked glasses and sipped the delicious champagne, then shared a tender kiss.

Emma sat up rod-straight. "Joseph, my father." Pure dread shook her.

"My darling Emma, I asked your father for your hand in marriage before we departed Calais. Both he and your mother gave their blessing." Emma was shocked. "I wanted to come to Whitfield because it is part of our English custom that the father of the sons or daughters must approve. I wanted Father to meet you and get his approval."

Emma burst out laughing in relief. "Why, Commodore Head, you have been adhering to strict etiquette and all behind my back." She imitated a mocking laugh. "I never knew English sons needed parental approval." Joseph seemed somewhat uncomfortable. Then it dawned on Emma. He was required to get approval because he was aristocracy, next in line for Duke of Kent. Emma felt needles in her stomach. As Joseph's wife, she would be the Duchess of Kent. The enormity of it caused her to tremble. Joseph read her thoughts.

"Emma, do not be disturbed by our responsibilities far in the future. By the time you and I inherit the title, we'll be very gray and long in the tooth! Mother will have years to teach you how to perform your duties, and you in turn will teach our children." Joseph laughed. "We are getting much too ahead of ourselves. We have to get married first. Let's take one thing at a time." Joseph stood up and pulled Emma to her feet. "Now, may your future husband have a chaste kiss?"

Emma circled her arms around his neck. "Chaste, sir, we shall see." Her kiss spoke volumes of love, trust, honor, and lust. Joseph was instantly aroused. This kiss sealed their betrothal. She pulled away, walked quickly to the oak door and pulled the latch across, then skipped back into his waiting arms. She kissed him deeply. He subconsciously noticed the light from the windows disappeared. He pulled her into him. She whispered in his ear, "Joseph, lift up my gown and feel me. Please, just for a minute." There was no earthly way he could resist her. He knew he should resist, but he couldn't think straight. Emma stared in his blue eyes and guided his hand. She pushed against him once, then harder. All of her inhibition disintegrated; she took control. Logic didn't exist, only the burning fire throughout her whole body. "Open the flap on your knickers, Joseph." She didn't take her eyes away from his. He quickly opened the buttons. She felt his hardness, kissed his lips, maneuvered her tongue in his mouth. "Sit down on the settee." He moved backward and Emma moved with him. She put her hands on his chest and pushed him down. Joseph was breathing hard. Emma lifted her emerald gown; she pulled her silky pantaloons down to the floor and stepped out of them. She stared into his eyes and whispered, almost crooning, "Joseph, take me now, now." Emma straddled his lap; his penis slipped into her easily. She stared at Joseph as they moved in unison. The raw desire in her eyes drove Joseph crazy. She was his, only his. No man would ever have this passion from her. He panted with lust and the need to let himself go. He buried his lips in her neck to muffle his cry as he gave her every ounce in his body. He was shaking and spent, and in his own quest for completion, he ignored her need. It didn't matter. Emma pushed and pushed until she fulfilled her aching body. She let out a low moan and couldn't control her quivering. They didn't speak, waiting for their breathing to slow and their bodies to relax.

Joseph stroked her back. "I think that ring made an emerald vixen out of you."

Emma couldn't contain her laughter. "You are so right, my love." Emma put her pantaloons back on, rearranged her clothing, took a sip of champagne, then stared at her ring finger. She was certain this was the most perfect ring in all of England and France. "Joseph, you make me so very, very happy. I will strive to be the best wife and worthy of your love." They kissed softly, and then Emma kissed her ring.

"Darling, Father is going to announce our betrothal tonight. Both Mother and Father are so happy to marry me off, and may I say, to gain the most wonderful daughter-in-law in the entire world." Joseph laughed.

Tears of joy brimmed in Emma's eyes. All of her dreams, hopes, and plans for the future were coming true. She shuddered to think that if fate and God had not intervened, she would have married Richard and never known true fulfillment, or worse, ended up a spinster living with her parents.

Joseph watched his future wife carefully. He didn't know exactly what she was thinking, but he could see by her introspective look it was of importance. He took her hand. "Emma, you have such a faraway look."

His tenderness released the tears and they trickled down her beautiful face. "Joseph, you have made me the happiest woman in the world. God blessed me with a man I love more than I knew possible. I promise, I will devote my life to making you happy and proud."

He squeezed her hand and brushed her tears away. "Having you as my wife will complete my life." He smiled that gorgeous smile. "Now, my love, freshen up in the ladies' powder room next door and get ready for our grand announcement." Emma bounded to the door, her recent tears erased.

The heir to Whitfield and his young companion entered the formal dining room to see many of the guests had already arrived, about twenty in all. Constance was hanging on Charles's every word. Emma thought her fawning over Charles was so obvious, but Charles was oblivious to her motives. He laughed and talked about the manor. "Joseph, did you tell Charles of your proposal?" Emma asked.

"No, I wanted to, but I couldn't get him alone. I tried to find him when you were napping, but he was out in the fields and I wasn't able to catch up with him."

"I think you should tell him now, as it wouldn't be fair for him to learn at the same time as the guests. Please, Joseph." Emma smiled.

"Of course, let me peel Constance from his arm and tell him privately." Joseph's throaty laugh caused people to turn. Emma felt like a bug under a microscope. All the guests were openly staring at her. She prayed she looked appropriate for the occasion. Catherine strode across the room and embraced her.

"Why Emma, dearest, you look lovely in the emerald gown. It matches your eyes."

Emma whispered, "And a perfect match for my perfect ring." The two women looked like conspirators in a secret plot.

Constance observed the whole encounter, as Joseph had taken Charles aside for some odd reason. She disliked Emma. The French were a strange lot, plus Joseph displayed open affection for her, a threat to her plans of being the only daughter-in-law of the Duke and Duchess of Kent. All the local people concluded Joseph wouldn't marry. It was her children who should rightfully inherit Whitfield. She didn't particularly love Charles but could pretend her affection was real to get what she wanted. He was handsome, but consumed with his land and crops and sheep. It bored her. Stimulating conversation to him always centered on the manor. She liked kissing him. He never failed to arouse her, but she set her mind on not going too far with him. She wanted him to believe that she was chaste and pure.

Her virginity was tossed away on a persuasive rogue. The fellow came down from London for business dealings with her father and stayed at their house. Their attraction to each other was instant. The third night of the stay, he quietly slipped into her bedroom. She acted surprised and alarmed, even though earlier she made sure he knew which room was hers.

The fellow knew she was acting coy, so he took his time seducing her until she begged him to take her. Constance saw his dark handsome face and chiseled body. Goose bumps covered her body. She ached for him with his cavalier whispers and hands caressing her in secret places. They made love all night long until her body was exhausted. She was sure they were through, but he satiated her one more time with his tongue. It was the most sensual sensation she ever experienced. Close to dawn, he left her quarters as quietly as he arrived. She drifted off into the most contented sleep.

He wasn't at dinner that night. She casually inquired about him, and her father reported their business had concluded, so he returned to London earlier in the day. Constance was distraught, humiliated beyond belief. At that moment, she vowed to never allow another man to seduce her. From then on, she would be in control.

Rebecca and Samuel Darby, Constance's parents, were also attending the dinner party at Whitfield Manor. Samuel ranked lower in the aristocracy than David Head, but he was still a wealthy landowner with profitable business ventures. The family divided their time between London and the country home they owned in Kent. As David and Catherine were blessed with boys, the Darbys were blessed with three girls. Constance was sandwiched in the middle, between her elder sister Miriam, and Gwyneth, the youngest. The governess was still schooling Gwyneth, and Miriam married her beau the year previous and moved to London. Constance's little sister didn't attend the dinner, as at age eleven she was too young for an evening affair.

Rebecca knew her children well and was keenly aware her daughter Constance was a determined girl. She pursued her quest unrelentingly until she made a conquest or tired of the pursuit. Right now her mind was set on Charles Head. Rebecca worried her daughter didn't really love Charles but loved what he owned and his position in society. She couldn't imagine Constance being satisfied living at Whitfield Manor, being a dedicated wife and raising children. Her daughter adored society life in London. Her friends traveled in social circles that went to parties, the theater, balls, and private soirees in aristocratic homes. Life in Kent was the polar opposite. Most parties occurred at Whitfield Manor; horseback riding, hunting, and rowing were the most popular pastimes of the landowners. Village life centered on family. The main source of entertainment was the local pub, church activities, and semiannual fairs. Naturally, Constance snubbed her nose at village entertainment. Rebecca wasn't oblivious to the fact Constance had a cunning streak, and at times she sensed a glimmer of dishonesty, but a mother squelches those thoughts and eagerly gives her child the benefit of the doubt.

When Samuel's colleague visited on business, she wondered why Constance retreated to her quarters for a few days after his departure and emerged with a cold resolve that unnerved Rebecca. Soon after, Constance set her sights on Charles. She knew her daughter would rather pursue Joseph, especially since he would be duke as the oldest male heir, but his duty to the Royal Navy called him away. The men of the village bet that Joseph Head would never marry since he was married to the sea. Constance rarely saw Joseph, so his younger brother became her target. They would procreate children who would inherit the title, the land, the manor, and the massive wealth. Rebecca wasn't at all surprised when Constance came home the previous night ranting and raving about Joseph drooling over some French tart he dragged home. Rebecca felt her daughter's keen displeasure. She wondered if this were a passing fling for Joseph or something more serious. It was certainly unusual for him to bring a female to Whitfield. She was curious to see the girl.

Rebecca and Samuel chatted with the Brodericks, who were down from London, when Joseph and Mademoiselle Emma Bouron were announced by the butler. Rebecca gazed at a very beautiful, very young girl. She wore a shimmering emerald designer gown. The fit was superb, probably from a fashion house in Paris. Samuel bent down and quietly spoke to his wife. "My, my, isn't Joseph a lucky man? His lady is young and gorgeous. I imagine Constance has ruffled feathers." Then he belly laughed. His determined daughter was an open book to him.

Rebecca turned and saw Constance glaring at the young girl. Joseph whisked Charles away and was talking intensely to his brother by the serving buffet. In three strides, Rebecca was by Constance's side. "Take that nasty look off your face. Do you want the guests to gossip about your jealousy?"

"Mother, don't be ridiculous. There is nothing I am jealous about." Her eyes threw daggers at her mother.

"Your face displays your disdain. I am no fool. After what you said last night and the way you look now, you are quite transparent. Listen to me, Constance; if Charles sees the way you look at his brother's guest, he will not feel kindly toward you."

Maybe her mother was right; she certainly didn't want to offend Charles, especially since she was making progress with him. He kissed her passionately last evening. "Of course, Mother, you are right. I am not jealous but genuinely perturbed Joseph brought a foreign woman to Whitfield." She smiled sweetly at Rebecca and kissed her cheek. Rebecca knew she was lying, but let it go. She simply did not want unpleasantness attributed to her family and blacken their name.

Charles was thrilled with Joseph's news. He thought Emma pretty and sweet, plus she immediately adapted to country life and seemed to honestly enjoy the land. It didn't matter to him that Joseph would most likely have children and his offspring would inherit Whitfield. The lineage was the law, and Charles had always known his place. He and Joseph were so close they forged a private understanding no one was privy to. He'd never seen Joseph so happy, and instead of being envious, he was glad. He imagined his brother as a father; he would be kind, loving, but strict like their parents. Charles thought it would be uplifting to have children at the manor, frolicking in the fields. He knew his mother and father longed for grandchildren. He hoped to marry one day and have a whole house full of children.

Emma was properly introduced to the guests she hadn't met. Each was captivated by her charm, wit, and beauty. Joseph was pleased. It still amazed and confused him how she was completely oblivious to the alluring aura she exuded. She extended her right hand for introductions, her left hand lost in the folds of her dress. He smiled as she carefully concealed her engagement ring.

Dinner was announced, and the guests found their way to the long banquet table. Emma felt nervous and anxious. She hoped Catherine and David's friends would welcome her into the village society, especially since she was French. The guests were formally seated. David was at the head of the table, still standing. Emma and Joseph flanked him on one side and Catherine and her older cousin Sarah were across from them. Years previous, Sarah's husband died from the sweating sickness. Catherine was always careful to make her feel comfortable and included. The guests were looking at David with curiosity. Catherine stifled a laugh; her husband beamed. The servants poured expensive French champagne. David waited until every glass was full. He cleared his throat.

"Dear friends, Catherine and I are grateful each of you accepted our invitation for dinner on such short notice. This is a special night for Catherine and me." He smiled at his wife. The faces around the table appeared puzzled. Emma's hands were slick with perspiration, and her heart felt like it would beat out of her chest. As usual, Joseph showed no hint of the impending announcement. He retained a calm demeanor, but it didn't settle her fears. "We are proud to announce the betrothal of our elder son, Joseph, to his future bride, Mademoiselle Emma Bouron."

Squeals and cheers of joy filled the dining room. Some guests felt disbelief and shock; no one thought Joseph would marry: he had waited so long and his love for the sea was legendary. Even so, happiness flooded the room. The duke and duchess would have heirs. David lifted his glass. "To Joseph and Emma, you have made us so very happy. May you have a long life of love and good health, as Catherine and I have." David's sincerity was palpable. Everyone clapped and drank champagne with one exception.

Constance fought to keep her composure. This news ruined her carefully laid plans, but she wouldn't give up; she would marry Charles and secure her place in the Whitfield household. If anything happened to keep Emma from having children, Constance would birth the "spare" as heir to the Kent family title and fortune. She conjured up her most alluring smile and tapped her spoon on her champagne glass. "To Emma, I speak for myself and the ladies in my family; you are a welcome addition to Kent." Her smile dripped honey.

"Thank you, Constance. I look forward to getting to know each of you and my new family." Her musical voice flitted through the air, and she blushed. Joseph took this as a cue to step in, but Charles spoke first.

"Emma, my sister-to-be, Father, Mother, and I are anxious for you to become a member of the family, but I'm sure not as anxious as Joseph." Charles laughed good-heartedly and winked at his brother.

Joseph stood. "We thank our friends and family for the well wishes. I know you will adore Emma as much as I do when you get to know her better." Emma looked up at him through her thick black lashes. She pushed back the tears of joy and smiled.

A jolly red-faced man Emma later learned was a neighboring landowner raised his glass. "I think I speak for all of us. Miss Emma has a magic spell on you. The whole village gave up on you taking a wife when you turned thirty." The whole room erupted in laughter. His wife pulled him to his seat and scolded him.

"It's quite all right, Pete." Joseph laughed. "I realize my friends and neighbors married me to the sea, and to be honest, so did I. Then one sparkling starlit night, Emma glided into my life, and I haven't been the same since. I am honored she agreed to marry me, and Monsieur and Madame Bouron have given their blessings." He looked at Emma with deep conviction. "Darling, you have made me the happiest man in France and England." Emma blushed crimson at Joseph's heartfelt words.

The evening flew by. The women fawned over Emma and admired her ring. A few of the older, less-reserved ladies gasped at the perfect emerald. Joseph got advice from the wise married men. The whole night was lighthearted. The only unpleasantness Emma experienced was with Constance. She oozed sweetness, but Emma saw that underneath her kind veneer lurked a deep-seated dislike. Her eyes betrayed her true feelings. Women had an innate way of reading each other if they observed astutely. Emma masked her own true feelings with people who didn't know her well ever since her breakup with Richard. Poor Charles, he was oblivious to Constance's insincerity. She gazed innocently into his eyes and hung on his every word. Emma believed Charles had no idea Constance was baiting the hook.

Joseph confided in Emma that his brother never paid much attention to women. His heart connected him to the land. Over the years he courted several girls, but they stopped seeing him when they got bored with his love of the countryside. His rugged good looks, combined with his gentle mannerisms, made him immensely attractive, which held a woman's attention for a while, but the romances fizzled out. Charles hadn't told a woman he loved her since he was a schoolboy with childish crushes. When he wanted his physical needs met, he went to London or Paris and visited high-class brothels for satisfaction. It suited him just fine; they expected nothing from him, which he liked. The biggest drawback of not having a wife was it meant not having children, which he wanted so he could pass on his love of the land.

Charles loved everything about Whitfield Manor and the village. Working the land gave him a deep sense of pride. The evolution from tilling to fertilizing to planting to growing, nurturing, and harvesting was a cycle that felt new every year since he was a boy tagging along with the men who worked his father's land. When the crops were harvested and the land dormant until the next season, Charles concentrated on the sheep. Reverently he facilitated the shearing process. The men who worked on the manor were taught to shear carefully so the animals would not suffer any burns or cuts. Charles instilled in the men the marvel of the raw wool that became blankets, coats, fine cardigans, and much, much more. He joined the fellows at the local pub, celebrated their marriages, births, and deaths, broke bread with them, and most importantly rewarded them for their dedicated service to the manor.

Charles was happy his brother was going to marry. It took the pressure from him. He thoroughly enjoyed the company of women, but he hadn't found one who loved the land like he did. Constance seemed very pleased to be in the countryside, but he also knew she ran with a fast crowd in London. He tried not to judge, because it was possible she indulged in the party lifestyle because she wasn't settled. He sensed she wanted to take their relationship to the next level, but something held him back. She possessed ripples of underlying insincerity that concerned him. Did she really love the land? He wasn't quite sure. She was a pretty girl who aroused his male instincts. He wasn't an accomplished suitor, but he realized if he continued to keep company with Constance, society and most probably her father would expect him to formally court her. He saw how Joseph had changed. The way he looked at Emma and treated her made it obvious he loved her deeply. Plus he saw right away that Emma liked Whitfield and would be a perfect duchess and heiress. She was beautiful, sweet, and intelligent. He knew why Joseph had fallen in love with her. Joseph's engagement caused Charles to contemplate his future. He wondered if he might cultivate those feelings about Constance.

By the time the last guest departed, Emma was spent. The night of her betrothal would be etched in her memory until she drew her last breath. From the moment Joseph put the ring on her finger, she felt a sense of belonging to the family and the land. Riding through the fields and pastures of the manor most of the day stirred an appreciation for the generations of Heads who defended and cared for the sprawling properties. Seeing the men and women who were descendents from serfs from centuries past enhanced the solid foundation of Whitfield. Their cozy stone cottages housed them now and their ancestors before them. Emma wanted to be part of it. She yearned for the relationship Joseph and Charles had with their parents. She could feel the love and respect between the boys and their mother and father. No nanny or chambermaid was a substitute for a dedicated mother. A father didn't ignore his children to care for a mentally distraught wife. Emma rubbed her temples. Openly recognizing the root of her insecurities was painful. At that moment she swore to herself she would never allow her children to attach themselves to servants for the love and nurturing she and Joseph would give freely. Her mind traversed the pattern of her life with Joseph and she smiled. She felt a small hand on her shoulder and turned her head. Catherine was smiling at her.

"Emma, you have a very serious gaze. I am sure you are overwhelmed from all the excitement of tonight and it's late; you must be tired."

"Sorry, Catherine, I was thinking about Joseph and his wonderful family. It's an honor to become a part of it, and I promise I will love and cherish all of you."

Catherine's girlish laugh filled the air. "Dear girl, David and I fell in love with you immediately, as did our son. Not for one minute did we doubt you are perfect for him and for Whitfield. We realize the engagement is sudden and I am sure you and Joseph haven't discussed your permanent living arrangements, but be assured we would be so pleased if you moved into Whitfield Manor. We could redecorate your rooms in the family living quarters to suit your taste and . . ."

Joseph and Charles interrupted the conversation with their boisterous laughter. "Mother, we are not yet married and already you have us moving, renovating, and settling in England."

Charles couldn't help himself from chiming in, "How do you know they won't settle in Calais by Emma's family? Maybe Mrs. Bouron would like the grandchildren right next door." His eyes were twinkling. He knew mention of the 'other grandmother' would ruffle his mother's feathers.

"So now you two have us married, moving, and producing legions of children for the grandparents," Joseph scolded, but his mother saw deep down he was pleased with the thoughts of a permanent home on land and having children.

"Well, Emma, how will we solve this dilemma?" Charles kept up the banter.

"I will put the whole burden of these decisions on my husband." Emma winked at Joseph, and they all erupted in laughter.

David came into the banquet hall from the main foyer. "What have I missed? I heard you laughing and joking from the foyer."

"You know Mother. She is planning our lives and the lives of our future children, and we have only been betrothed about six hours." Joseph's laugh was infectious.

"Father, travel to London to find an architect and draftsman to draw plans for the renovation of rooms in the family wing for Joseph and Emma. I am sure the minute the priest pronounces them husband and wife, Mother will hustle them to Whitfield. Don't forget to enlarge the nursery and new nanny quarters." Charles doubled over with laughter. The rest of the family joined in, including Emma.

Chapter 23

Realizations

The next morning Emma arose at first light. She roused Jenny to help her dress in riding clothes. Jenny grumbled about the time and where was Emma going and what about her breakfast. Finally Emma shushed her and out the door she went. Jenny went straight back to bed and thought how strange Emma had acted. Going riding at this hour—ridiculous.

Emma easily found the stableboy, who was barely awake when she opened the barn doors. She requested he saddle the horse she rode the previous day. The news of Joseph's engagement had spread like wildfire throughout the manor and the village, so the lad knew he was dealing with the future duchess and treated her as such. He shyly asked, "Shall I saddle Commodore Head's stead?"

Her sweet smile caused him to blush. "No need, sir, I am riding alone." The boy was surprised. The only other person who rode this early was Master Charles, but even he wasn't up yet.

The spring morning was brisk, but the early dense fog had lifted; just a light mist remained. The fields stretched out like thick green blankets. Emma easily found the trail the threesome traveled the day before; she started on her trek. She spent a restless night thinking about the conversation at the end of the evening. She looked at her left hand;

the huge emerald and surrounding diamonds sparkled in the sunlight, catching prisms of light. She reached the crest of the first hill and looked down at the serene pastures, the sheep grazing. She looked back at the manor house nestled in manicured lawns and terraced flower gardens looking like a natural part of the landscape, but at the same time fortified and stately. Emma knew at that very moment, Whitfield was destined to be her home. Inside, a feeling of belonging grew. Continuing down the opposite side of the hill, her thoughts raced as she drank in the beauty of the land. In the distance she noticed the stone cottages peeking through the tree line. The old church was a speck on the horizon. Emma searched to find answers why a manor in England with a tiny village attached stirred deep-seated convictions her life was meant to be here in this place.

The family unit inhabiting the manor was the key. In their company, her self-doubt dissipated. All the pain of childhood abandonment vanished. Here she was blameless. She allowed the thought to creep in that she wasn't responsible for the loss of her mother during those precious formative years. It was Maria's own mental state that plunged her into deep depression and ultimate seclusion from her living children while she mourned for her dead baby son. Emma dug deep to recognize she didn't cause Richard's rejection. It was his discontent, his immaturity, and his lack of commitment that caused him to flee from her and his life in Calais. Emma instinctively knew her drive and ambition at the Toy Depot served a specific purpose to fill the void in her life. Plus, if she were successful, somehow fulfillment and self-esteem would be the outcome.

Emma loved her parents in a removed way, but she adored Claudine. Thinking of her was the only tug from the other side of the Channel. She had lived in Calais in the same house her entire life but never felt oneness with the town, the house, even her family except for her sister. It amazed her that in such a short time Whitfield had won her heart and soul.

As she reached the church, she dismounted and entered the centuries-old building. The original stained glass window gleamed as the sunlight streamed through it. She sat in the family pew ornately carved of strong oak. Emma took a deep breath. Suddenly the tapestry of her life was very simple. Trade the complex past for a new beginning. Somewhere deep in the pit of her being, a voice clear and crisp said, "Marry in the old church." It would bind her to the family, the land, and the people of the village. Most of all, it would seal her allegiance to England, her native France becoming secondary. A curtain of darkness was raised from her soul. The quivering foundation of her childhood brought her these realizations. Whitfield was solid. Miraculously, it made her solid.

Opposition would barrage her from every angle. She knew her mother and father naturally wanted her to be wed in Calais, in the Catholic Church where she was baptized and confirmed. Strength welled up in her; this time she was determined to chart her own course. At last she would please herself. Wasn't God in every church, no matter what denomination? Edgar and Maria would just have to accept what she wanted, not what they wanted. Wasn't it her life?

Emma sat in the ancient wooden pew twisting her hair round and round her finger purely out of habit. She wasn't anxious. In fact, a new determination possessed her. Another realization hit her. The career she fought so hard to establish had served its purpose. It provided her with a sense of accomplishment. Yes, a woman succeeding in a man's work world was admirable. She received a promotion days ago, but it didn't matter now. She would leave it behind as well.

The quiet church wrapped her in peace with a new resolve. Suddenly she was ravenous. Emma had no idea how long she had been away from the house. She felt buoyant as she skipped from the church. A lightness enveloped her.

Chapter 24

Synchronicity

Charles heard her melodious song drifting through the misty morning air before he caught a glimpse of her. The rising sun and the mist outlined her figure in the distance. Once she was in his sight, he jolted straight in the saddle. It appeared as if a glow emanated from the small figure on horseback. He gaped at the apparition, and then she was directly in front of him on the pathway.

"Hello, Charles, you startled me. I thought I was quite alone so early in the morning."

He blushed crimson but didn't know why. He quickly composed himself and resorted to humor. "Early, it is almost ten o'clock. Just where have you been, Emma? Joseph was about to send out the guardsmen to find you."

She knew he was teasing. She laughed in a naughty way. "Why, Monsieur Head, I attended Mass at St. Peter's, as good Catholic girls are expected to do."

At first Charles missed the joke, then her slight laughter broke the silence.

"Why, Emma Bouron, you know that old church is Anglican."

She burst out laughing and he couldn't help but join in. Then a frown creased her brow. "Seriously, Charles, I didn't mean to upset or alarm anyone, especially Joseph, but some unexplainable pull drew me to the land. I wanted to get clarity about my future and my past. The answers were held on the hillside, in the village, and definitely in the church. I started out from the manor house with no direction in mind, but the wind whispered in my ear and led me to my destinations."

Charles shivered. *Oh dear Lord, she feels exactly as I do.* Then it dawned on him. This unnerving revelation explained why he felt so comfortable with her and, yes, attracted to her. She was to be his brother's wife, but she loved the land as he did. It was a paradox he could not deal with at present. He vowed to sort it out when he was alone with his thoughts.

"Charles, I am so very sorry; from your silence I see you truly are annoyed with me."

He looked away and covered up his feelings. "No, of course I am not angry, only hungry." He forced a laugh. "We have held breakfast for you."

Emma was mortified that the whole household waited because she carelessly took off without as much as leaving a message with one of the servants. She felt sick. How could she be so selfish? Who would believe she wanted, needed to be on the land? She admonished herself while waves of nausea nagged at her stomach.

God, she looks green. Charles thought. *I am a bumbling idiot for making her think time stopped because she was out. I'm no good with women. Damn it.* "Emma, I was teasing. Only Joseph and I haven't eaten. Mother and Father ate an early breakfast and must have gone into Dover as the landau is gone." He hoped this would reassure her and the pink would come back to her lovely cheeks.

Emma managed a weak smile, and they rode back to the house in a strange silence. Joseph paced outside the stables. "There you are, darling. I was about ready to look myself, but Charles decided he would ride out and I would wait here." Charles looked sullen, and Emma not much better. Joseph helped her down from the old mare.

"Joseph, I should have let someone know I was going riding. I am so very sorry. It was wrong of me to take leave without a word." Emma looked stricken. Joseph hugged her, telling her it was not important as long as she was safe.

The threesome breakfasted on the terrace with easy conversation returning. Joseph reiterated what Charles had relayed to Emma. His parents went to Dover for the day, Father on business and Mother shopping. Enough time passed, and Emma relaxed and enjoyed fruit and toast with a delicious cup of piping hot tea. Joseph broached the subject. "Did you enjoy your morning ride, darling?"

Emma had a faraway look. She looked through Joseph more than at him when she replied, "It was exhilarating riding through the green fields and over the hills in the early morning light." Her eyes glistened. "I went to old St. Peter's, which was so quiet and peaceful. The village was also quiet, and I imagined the families tucked in their beds sleeping."

Joseph lightly punched Charles's arm. "She sounds like you, ole chap. It is exactly something you would say." Charles laughed and punched his brother back, trying to act normal when in his heart things were amiss. "Honestly, Emma, I am being difficult with my brother. I want to hear all the details of your outing this morning."

"I made decisions I want to discuss with you after I bathe and dress for the day. May we take one of the carriages and ride into the village?"

"Absolutely. We are the talk of the town so let's go to the *Fox and Hounds* for a late lunch and chatter with the villagers." He turned to his brother, "Charles, are you coming along?"

"No, thank you, my work goes on as you languish around." He gave Joseph one last little punch, bowed to Emma, and strode from the terrace.

"Don't mind, Charles, darling. He is moody when the land tugs at him for one reason or another. Now never mind all that. I want a kiss from my gorgeous bride."

With the way Joseph looked at her, his loose blond hair framing his aristocratic face and those piercing eyes, all else melted away. She got up from the table, sat on his lap, and kissed him fervently. His lips covered her mouth, his tongue inside exploring. He felt her nipples getting hard under the thin blouse. She discarded the riding jacket earlier, which

made it easy for him to feel her responding to his kiss. Emma wound her fingers in his thick hair and pressed hard against his chest.

From the morning room window, Charles had a clear view of his brother and Emma kissing. He was wretched that a pang of jealousy reared its ugly head from a place unfamiliar to Charles. Rationally he told himself this was his brother, whom he loved and idolized, and his fiancée, whom Joseph waited for his whole life. Emotionally he battled his newfound feelings for Emma. He felt the rise in his riding britches and cursed himself. He must divert his attention to someone else immediately. As he backed away from the window, he thought of Constance. She aroused him, and he was almost sure she was in love with him. He would force himself to focus on her. In fact, he decided instantly he would ride over to her house and speak with her father. At this point, it was the only logical thing to do.

Emma's lighthearted mood was infectious. Joseph wondered what decisions she possibly made during her early morning jaunt. The intricacies of a woman's mind were something he hadn't bothered learning. Since previously he only manipulated a woman to get her into bed a time or two, his interest in a woman's psyche was nonexistent. He adored his mother, but took her easy ways and calm demeanor as natural to all genteel women, and now Emma. Her insecurities and imaginary inadequacies were a bit unsettling, but nothing his love and encouragement couldn't conquer. His interest was piqued, as she definitely appeared different than before. He waited for her in the great hall to embark on their trip to the village. He smiled to himself. He knew the people of Whitfield were abuzz with the news of his betrothal. He understood the significance of the direct heir to the barony getting married. Once children were a result of the union, the lineage was secured and the villagers guaranteed a continuation of their heritage passed from generation to generation.

The spring day was lovely, actually quite warm for May in England. Perfect for a carriage ride. The brougham was outfitted with blankets, wine, and a picnic basket for Commodore Head and his charming fiancée. Once on their way, Joseph observed Emma was brimming with anticipation. He decided it would be pleasant to enjoy a picnic instead of lunch in the village. They could go to the *Fox and Hounds* for a pint after some quiet time together. He was certain private conversation would be difficult in the pub with the town's people atwitter regarding his engagement.

Emma asked if they could stop at the top of the first hill. It was where she first tingled with Whitfield alive in her veins. Joseph spread the red plaid blanket, opened the wine, and then plopped down. Emma lay on her back, looking up at the clear sky with the innocent smile on her lips that Joseph loved.

"May I interest you in a glass of chardonnay, Emma? It was chilled in the ice closet and should be delicious."

She sat up, still smiling. "That would be lovely, Joseph." She looked at him through her thick dark lashes and saw the man she would spend her life with on this manor.

"Here, take the glass and I will toast my bride." Emma giggled. "To my beautiful Emma, the woman I am honored to soon call my wife and duchess." His throaty laugh filled the spring air.

The demure expression on Emma's face was alluring but not in a sexual way. He was a little confused. "I toast my husband and duke." She winked. "To my love." She glanced over the hill at the rolling pastures, then behind her at the manor house and added, "To my home and my new family." Joseph was wide-eyed as he thought he understood her implication. He began to speak, but Emma put her finger to his lips and continued, her eyes sparkling. "To the place we will wed. To the land where we will raise our children and grandchildren. To the foundation of my life." Tears of relief and joy poured down her face. Joseph grabbed her glass and threw it in the grass. He hugged her tightly, and she felt his sobs. His reaction erased any qualms she felt. They held each other for a long time before Joseph could speak.

"How did all this come about, Emma? You can see I am overjoyed, but I am still in shock. I naturally thought you would want to live in France close to your parents, the town you have called home since a baby."

"Joseph, I never imagined having this sense of belonging to the land, the people, your family. There has always been part of me missing, but I didn't know what it was or if everyone felt that way. It is a feeling I haven't discussed with Jenny, Claudine, and especially not my parents. I actually have struggled with my confidence ever since I was a very little girl. The relationship you have with your parents is different from the one I have with mine. Yours is a natural bond that I'm sure you and Charles take for granted. Your mother and father raised you on firm ground, continually reinforcing their love for you. My mother lost a son when Claudine and I were little girls. The loss threw her into a dark depression, so we were relegated to Jenny as a substitute mother. My father wasn't aware of my uncertainties; he was too busy working and tending to my mother when he was home. I don't blame them. It's circumstances of life. Each individual handles those types of life-altering experiences differently. Claudine wasn't impacted by Mother's detachment and isolation. For me, it was totally different. I thought I must have done something wrong to be rejected. Joseph, I hope you can understand how going from a solid, loving atmosphere to one of silence and walking on eggshells might affect a young child. It's followed me my whole life. Whether consciously or subconsciously, I am constantly waiting for my world to implode. At last, you have chased those demons away. You and Whitfield make me whole."

"I don't know what to say. I will dedicate every day to making you feel confident in my love for you. My mother and father will dance on air! You will make their dreams come true, never mind how you turned my life upside down." Joseph looked puzzled, as if he misunderstood one part in Emma's toast. "You said, 'to the place we will wed.' You can't mean you will marry me here at Whitfield," Joseph said incredulously.

"Oh yes I do. I sat in old St. Peter's this morning and envisioned us at the altar with the priest, our families, and the villagers. I saw the Heads from centuries past marrying their brides beneath those Saxon stained glass windows."

Joseph was reeling, trying to process all she was saying. Reality struck him. "Emma, my sweet, sweet girl, your parents will never agree to you marrying in England, and especially not in the Anglican Church." He didn't want to dampen her spirits, but he knew old Edgar wouldn't approve. It was going to be difficult enough telling them England would be their home.

Emma sat up rod-straight. Her clarity was profound. "How can I get married in the Catholic Church? I am not a virgin, and it would be hypocritical for me to take vows before God in my church. I'm not saying the Anglican Church condones impurity, but for some reason at St. Peter's, I still feel worthy of God's blessing on our marriage."

Joseph was so touched he couldn't speak. He was a cad to steal her virginity before marriage, but he wanted her so desperately he threw all caution to the wind. Maybe he allowed it to happen because in his subconscious, he thought she might one day be his wife, but he never thought it a violation of her religion. Joseph considered religion and sex two separate entities, but clearly the two were intertwined in Emma's mind.

He wasn't particularly attached to the church, although he was christened, confirmed, and raised an Anglican. Religion was part of life on the manor. He rarely attended services while away or at sea, but he did believe in God and in Jesus Christ. In a strange way, he hadn't dissected his religious convictions previously. He suddenly acknowledged it was at St. Peter's he felt closest to God. Emma, on the other hand, was a cradle Catholic deeply ensconced in the dogma and ideology of the church. Of course, engaging in sex before marriage was a sin to her. He blanched. "Am I a wretched man for wanting you, making love to you?"

"No, Joseph, I would do it all over again. What you have given me in those intimate moments is a sense of fulfillment physically and emotionally." She blushed and lowered her voice. "If I could, I would make love to you right now, right here." Joseph moved closer and stroked her hair, her face, and her back. He wanted her desperately, but this was not the time.

"Come on, let's eat some of the sandwiches and cakes the cook fixed for us, then go to the village. I want to show off my fiancée to all of Whitfield."

They finished their light lunch and jumped back in the carriage. The ride proved to be a glorious excursion. The weather was delightful. Their moods were as light as the warm spring air.

A slight wind caught Emma's hair in the breeze. Joseph thought how very young she looked. For nineteen she had both innocence and maturity, an enigma but a delicious combination. He attributed the maturity to her career. Suddenly Joseph pulled up on the horses. Her career, what about her career?

"Why are we stopping?" Emma asked.

"Sweetheart, what about your career? Days ago you were promoted and received accolades from management in Paris. How can you live at Whitfield and be employed at the Toy Depot?"

"Commodore Head, I choose to raise a family here at Whitfield. Puppets don't take the place of children." Emma giggled.

"Do you mean you will give up all of that for me?" Joseph was moved.

"I will give it up and more if I had it to give." Emma spoke seriously, with absolute conviction.

The couple arrived at the *Fox and Hounds* to cheers and well wishes. The villagers were exuberant, laughing with happiness. Emma shook hands with the men; some bowed and kissed her hand, and others smiled and nodded. She kissed each woman she met on both cheeks. The gesture warmed Emma to their hearts. Joseph bought pints of beer all around. The afternoon proved a huge success for the future duke and duchess. As the sun began to wane, Joseph and Emma said their goodbyes. When they were gone, the villagers agreed the French weren't so bad after all, especially Mademoiselle Bouron.

The sun had almost set when Joseph pulled the brougham up to the stables. The landau still wasn't back from Dover. Charles's horse wasn't in its stall, so he was also still out. Dinner wouldn't be served for a couple hours.

Joseph had a terrific idea. He had promised Emma to show her the turrets and hiding places where he and Charles played as children. Now was the most opportune time. He grabbed the blanket from the carriage. Joseph led Emma up the steep stone steps to the turrets. It was like a maze. Some old cannons were preserved, and several of the gun rooms restored. Emma was fascinated by the history and the vast number of passageways snaking around the perimeter of the castle. At the last turret station, Joseph explained this one was his favorite as a boy. He and Charles played there for hours until Nanny or Catherine discovered their absence and searched them out. They liked it best because they could lie down in the stone indentation hidden behind one of the old cannons.

Joseph spread out the blanket in his boyhood secret hiding place. He picked Emma up and laid her on the blanket. She looked questioningly in his eyes and saw the raw desire. It excited her he wanted her so much. He kissed her neck, ears, lips, and face. His hands roamed all over her body. Emma's breathing became erratic. She knew he was going to take her, and the thought thrilled her. He yanked down her pantaloons, but she didn't resist; instead, she guided his hand between her legs.

"Tell me what you want," Joseph whispered. "I'll do anything you want me to do, anything." In answer, she pushed his head down. He lifted her dress, and she pushed him down again. He let his tongue find the throbbing of her desire, and then the magic began. Joseph heard her panting with lust. He probed and probed until she burst with a scream. Emma's body shook, then went limp.

"Mon Dieu, Joseph, you are beyond belief." Emma's words came in short gasps.

"Lay back." He stroked her back gently and whispered in her ear words of love and desire. At first she was too spent to want him. He took his time, caressing her softly, then kissing her deeply. Slowly, very slowly, he pushed his hardness against her. Emma felt the pangs of desire igniting. She squirmed underneath him, spreading her legs. Joseph carefully entered her, moving slowly in and out until Emma wrapped her legs around his back and begged him to take her. Joseph drove in harder and harder, deeper and deeper. "Now," Emma screamed, "now!" They were crushed into each other's bodies and exploded together. Something new happened to Emma. She wanted him to push again! She could feel the pulsating all over. "Joseph, now go again, now." At first Joseph wasn't sure what she wanted, but she pushed him into her so deep and moved so quickly he knew she wasn't fully satisfied. She swiveled all around him. He pumped hard. She begged and begged for more. Emma clawed his back as her climax reached new heights. Joseph stifled her scream with his mouth. Emma dropped back, shaking and panting.

Chapter 25

An Impulsive Decision

CHARLES GALLOPED THROUGH THE COUNTRYSIDE to his destination, the Earl of Warwickshire's manor. When he arrived, Gwyneth and another little girl were playing croquet on the lawn.

"Hello, girls. Gwyn, is your father home?"

"Yes, Sir Charles, he is in his study. Come, Holly and I will take you to him." The girls skipped along to the great oak door of the manor. Once inside they took Charles to Samuel. "Papa, Sir Charles is here to see you, and we directed him to your study." Gwyneth glowed, as if she had performed an incredible feat. At eleven, she was quite precocious and had a girlish crush on Charles.

"Thank you, girls, you have been so helpful." Charles winked at Gwyneth. She blushed crimson. He turned his attention to Earl Darby. "Samuel, I do apologize for arriving without a set appointment, but my reason is of great importance."

"Girls, go back outside and play." Samuel gestured for them to leave the study. They were curious why Sir Charles would come without a set meeting. Gwyneth gave her father a downcast look but obeyed him. When both girls were gone and the door closed, Samuel turned to Charles. "Nosy little women." His jovial laugh made Charles smile.

"Oh, we laugh now, but it only gets worse with age." He chuckled again. "Sit down, Charles. What brings you here today?"

Charles's voice was low and nervous. "Samuel, our families have been close for many years. We have a wonderful relationship, and I want to . . ." His voice trailed off. Samuel couldn't fathom what was making the lad so uncomfortable. "I want to . . ."

"Spit it out, Charles. You're not usually tongue-tied!"

Charles cleared his throat. "I would be honored if you will allow me to formally court Constance. I think very highly of her, and we have a delightful time together . . ."

Samuel was thrilled. Binding the two aristocratic families would be ideal. More than he hoped for. He knew Constance was selfish and difficult, but he had seen her with Charles and she appeared totally enamored. He didn't want to sound overly anxious. "How does Constance feel about the matter?"

"Well, uh, sir, I have not revealed my intentions to her yet because I wanted your permission first."

Excellent breeding. Seeking my affirmation displays character and good judgment. "Charles, I give you my blessing. Let's have a brandy to officially acknowledge the courtship." The men drank and decided Charles would ask Constance after dinner at the family's country manor.

Plans made, Charles left to tend to daily business and dress for the evening. He rode back to Whitfield utterly miserable, but what else could he do? Coveting his brother's soon-to-be wife was abhorrent to him. He prayed that through courting Constance, he could fall in love with her and wipe Emma from his mind.

Samuel summoned one of the servants to get Constance from the sewing room, where she and her mother were working on new fair linens for St. Peter's Church. Constance was surprised her father wanted to see her late afternoon during his workday. Usually he stayed busy in his study working on one business aspect or another. She didn't know much about business nor did she care. As long as the money was available for new clothes, trips to London, and a large allowance, what her father did was irrelevant. Rebecca went along to the study to see what was on Samuel's mind.

"Hello, Papa, what is so vital that I am to interrupt your work?" Constance projected her sweetest smile.

Rebecca hugged her husband and plopped in a comfy chair by the fire.

"Ladies, I have news." The women looked at each other.

"Dearest daughter, I have been engaged in conversation with a gentleman caller who arrived without appointment or planned meeting." Constance stared at her father, a gnawing feeling in her stomach raging. "Sir Charles Head arrived on my doorstep with a question full of purpose." Constance wanted to grab her father and shake him. *What question?* "It seems, my dear, he has fallen in love with you, as he requested to formally court you." Samuel literally beamed.

Constance collapsed in the chair next to her mother. Her wildest dreams were coming true, but what triggered this sudden request? He hadn't said one word to her about love or courtship. All of Kent knew Joseph was engaged to the sugary-sweet French girl the night before. Did Joseph's betrothal spark a flame under his brother, or did Charles realize he loved her? Either way it didn't matter; she was going to say yes to his courtship and land him as a husband as soon as possible.

"My dear, are you so shocked you cannot express your feelings to your mother and me?"

"I'm sorry, Papa. It's so sudden, and he didn't discuss it with me although he's had many opportunities to do so." She didn't want her father to think her too anxious.

Samuel was a bit annoyed. The most eligible bachelor in Kent and the wealthiest next to his brother asked to court his daughter and she hesitated. Ridiculous! Plus he was so well-trained in proper etiquette he asked Samuel first. Samuel's annoyance changed to anger. "Listen to me, young lady, none of your coy teasing and jousting. I invited him for dinner, and I feel sure he will ask you afterward."

"Oh Father, don't be angry; I was merely surprised and am overjoyed." She donned her prettiest smile, which showed off her dimples. "I am in love with Charles but kept my feelings hidden away in case he did not reciprocate." She always won Samuel over with her sweet smile and reassuring words. Constance was sure she had placated her father.

Rebecca hugged her daughter and congratulated her, but something intangible made this whole episode unsettling. Why in the world had Charles Head procured his own courtship the day after his brother's engagement? Rebecca was suspicious of his motives.

David and Catherine returned early evening from Dover. They planned it that way so the family could have a quiet dinner together and discuss future plans concerning Joseph and Emma. David dropped Catherine at the front door, while he took the landau back to the stables. He made note Charles was still gone, probably working late with his sheep. He smiled. His boys were both so different, one tethered to the land, the other anchored to the sea. It didn't matter now because Joseph was going to marry and have children and the barony would pass through the hereditary peerage system without interruption. This had been the law of the land since 1387.

Dinner was to be very informal, so Emma chose a casual light pink dress to wear. She took a long bath hoping to revive herself. She was tired from the events of last night and her afternoon of lovemaking. She looked at her ring. Having it helped her feel less of a sinner and more a wife. She couldn't resist Joseph; his slightest touch excited her. He awakened an insatiable dormant lust. Combine the lust and love, and the result was an intoxicating mixture that transcended her virtuous upbringing. She wondered if David and Catherine ever felt the way she did. In her mind, she and Joseph held secret keys to true love. She believed without question that her bond with Joseph was everlasting.

Joseph, his parents, and Emma chatted casually over a glass of wine. Catherine was holding dinner until Charles came down. He was late, which was unusual for him. Finally she instructed one of the maids, Lucy, to go to his quarters and announce dinner was about to be served. The foursome discussed the Heads' day trip to Dover. Joseph explained his and Emma's excursion to the village. The conversation was natural, like any family. Lucy interrupted their talk. Charles did not answer her knock so she sent one of the chef's helpers to the stables, and the stableboy said Charles returned from work, changed into dinner clothing, and left in one of the carriages. Catherine knew how the servants gossiped. She was sure Lucy knew her son's destination. "Where was he off to, Lucy?" Catherine laughed.

Lucy stuttered, "Well, yes, madame, I did inquire where Master Charles was going in case you asked, and I wouldn't want you to worry."

Catherine laughed again. *Lucy may think I would buy that story, but I know she's just nosy.* "Do tell; what was his destination?" Catherine looked at Lucy.

"One of the stableboys said he was dining at the Darbys and would keep the carriage there until he was ready to return to Whitfield." Lucy looked as if she had just announced the signing of the Magna Carta. Catherine laughed and dismissed her.

How odd, Catherine thought. Why would Charles go off to the Darbys without telling her or David? Her mother's intuition kicked into gear. She shivered. This must have something to do with that conniving Constance, always ogling over Charles like he was the Messiah returned to earth. Also, Charles was never inconsiderate. Opting out of a family dinner with his newly betrothed brother was quite disconcerting. Catherine was acutely aware Joseph getting married and having children would on the surface change Charles's future, but the boys were so close, she couldn't imagine them not working out a situation that suited them both. She naturally assumed Joseph and Emma would reside in France, Joseph continuing his naval career and Emma as a military wife. Once, God willing, they had children, the Heads could visit them in Calais; also, the apartment in Paris was ample enough to accommodate a large family. Geographically, twenty-one miles separated Calais and Dover across the English Channel, definitely not a long trip for frequent visits. Legally, the manor lands would belong to Joseph, but she believed the boys would forge an arrangement regarding the manor. She tried to brush off the troubling thoughts.

"Never mind your brother, Joseph; he may have thought it appropriate for the four of us to share the evening meal to discuss your wedding plans." Catherine smiled broadly, despite her reservations. She forced herself to dismiss Charles's actions from her mind and concentrate on Joseph and Emma. The day outdoors certainly agreed with Emma. Why, the girl literally beamed!

"Speaking of your wedding plans," David inquired, "have the two of you set a date and place, or am I premature in asking?"

Emma squeezed Joseph's hand under the table. He put his arm around her shoulders. He laughed his throaty laugh, which resonated in the family dining room. "Funny you should ask, Father." He pulled Emma closer. "It appears my French gem experienced an epiphany this morning as she traipsed around the countryside on her own. She loves not only me, but our ancestral home and lands." Emma smiled her innocent, dazzling smile at David and Catherine. She leaned closer into Joseph's arm. "We would like to be wed at St. Peter's Church in late June. We haven't picked an exact date, as that must be coordinated with you and the Bourons. After an Italian honeymoon, we want your permission to reside at Whitfield."

David was thrilled. Both sons living on the manor! He was ecstatic. Joseph's choice of a wife was getting better and better. He looked at his wife. Catherine sat in stoned silence, her face devoid of all color. Emma noticed her demeanor immediately. Oh, dear God, she had misjudged everything. Catherine didn't want a foreigner getting married in her church, living in her home. Possibly she didn't even think she was right for Joseph. At that moment, Joseph could literally feel Emma withering like a day-old flower. He thought his mother would react the exact opposite.

Emma tried to fight back the tears, but they trickled down her face. The sight of Emma jarred Catherine back from where her mind had wandered . . . Charles. Was this why he had gone to the Darbys? Was he going to do something rash? She covered her true thoughts with blatant lies. "Dearest Emma, forgive me. I am happy and honored you and Joseph want to be married in our church and live at Whitfield. I was thinking of your mother, father, and sister. They will be so very disappointed the wedding will not be in Calais. I feel assured that your choice of Whitfield as your permanent home will upset your mother greatly. Of course, I want you here more than anything in this world, but I would understand her pain. It reminds me that when Joseph is away at sea, I long for him to be on homeland duty so I am able to see him as often as possible." She smiled sweetly. "I can't very well walk across water for a glimpse of him."

Emma breathed a sigh of relief and brushed away her tears. Catherine was so unselfish she didn't celebrate her joy, but anguished over Emma's own parents' disappointment. Her words tumbled out in torrents. "When I rode the hills and fields this morning, I felt part of the land. It was as though all the generations who have gone before you welcomed me home. When I went into the old church, I had the same experience. I could see you and David at the altar and the villagers rejoicing in the streets. I pictured Joseph and me making our vows before God and all those who stood in that very place throughout the centuries." She blushed. "I want our children to be born at Whitfield so they feel the tie to the land." Both Catherine and David nodded in total understanding. Emma giggled. "I almost ran Charles off the trail this morning I was so deep in thought! I had no idea I worried Joseph and him so much. Charles came looking for me as Joseph stood watch at the stables."

Catherine knew the answer to her question before she asked it. "Did you share with Charles your newfound revelations?"

"Yes, I wanted to share with him that I truly understood his attachment to Whitfield." Emma laughed happily. "I appreciate his land legs more than Joseph's sea legs." Joseph usually didn't miss much of his mother's insight, but he was so caught up by Emma's enthusiasm, it went right over his head. They started laughing and bantering about land legs, sea legs, and crab legs, all in good fun.

David joined in, but Catherine felt a cold premonition shatter her joy.

Chapter 26

An Evening at the Darbys

THE SPREAD THE DARBYS LAID out for dinner was divine: tender lamb chops with mint sauce, roasted potatoes rubbed with butter and herbs, tender young peas, fresh-baked bread, and scrumptious rhubarb tarts with fresh clotted cream. Charles ate the meal enthusiastically, although he wasn't hungry in the least, but he didn't want to insult Rebecca's cook or raise suspicions that he was out of sorts. He drank more wine than usual, Constance noticed, but she attributed it to his nerves concerning their impending courtship. After the meal, Gwyneth played the piano for the group, while Charles sipped a large snifter of brandy as he listened. The spirits gave him the courage he needed and a mask for his true feelings. When Gwyneth finished her piano selections, he asked Samuel if Constance could accompany him on a carriage ride to the cliffs. Samuel winked and gave his approval.

Once in the brougham, the couple talked about things in general—Joseph's engagement, the wedding, when would the marriage take place? When the carriage reached the turnaround at the edge of the cliffs, Charles suggested they go for a walk. Constance agreed, although she was desperately afraid of heights. Charles put his cape around her shoulders and his arm around her waist. Constance was actually moved by his romantic gesture. They reached one of the larger sandy beach areas and Charles suggested they sit down. Constance was more than willing to oblige; waiting for his declaration of love was irritating, but she kept smiling. The abundant stars and the bright moon made the night glorious. Charles began, "Constance, you know I am not much good with words or, uh, those sorts of things, but you and I have, well, been keeping company quite often and, uh, I have . . ."

Softly Constance encouraged him before the liquor wore off and he lost his nerve. "What, Charles?"

"I have realized, uh, I have known that, uh, I . . ."

She'd better fill in the blanks for him because he didn't have an iota of an idea how to say what he meant. She moved in close to him and whispered, "You have fallen in love with me, as I love you."

Relief flooded his brain. "Yes, I love you and want to officially court you, that is, of course, if you agree." It was as though he was listening to someone else say the words, not him. Saying I love you to a woman he didn't love was bizarre.

Constance threw her arms around his neck and kissed him wildly. She was convinced she had to get him physically committed to their relationship, now. "Here is my answer." She threw the soft wool cape from her body and lay back on it, pulling Charles down on top of her. Her kisses were probing and on fire. Charles was aroused instantly. He responded by kissing her neck, ears, and hair. Constance took his hand and moved it to her breast. He squeezed gently at first, but she wanted more. She pressed his hand hard against her breast and moved it in circles around her erect nipple. Then slowly guided it down her ribs to her stomach and then between her legs. Charles's breath was rapid, and Constance felt his hardness against her. His voice was raspy. "Oh dear God, Constance, if we don't stop now . . ." She answered by lifting her dress above her waist and putting his hand beneath her pantaloons. The liquor, the thoughts of Emma swimming through his head, made him lose complete control. He tugged open his knickers, pulled down her undergarments all the way to her knees, and thrust himself between her legs. Constance was in complete control, but Charles didn't know it. She slowed his pace, working him in carefully to be certain he was convinced this was her first time. In his alcohol-induced haze, he realized he might be hurting her. "Constance, I don't want to . . ."

"Shush, my darling Charles; I want this as much as you do." Her crooning voice and vibrating hips made it impossible to turn back. She took him in completely, thrusting against him until he exploded in one long moan. Now it was her turn to lose control. She had held herself in check until she satisfied his lust. It was her turn to feel satiated. She kept thrusting and rubbing against Charles until he responded to her passion. He turned over on his back, with her on top of him riding hard. He could tell she was getting close as her thrusts became more rapid and harder. He grabbed her hips and squashed her on his body, pushing so hard her orgasm was volcanic. She fell on him in a limp heap. His chest was heaving as he gasped for air. His eyes were closed, and he saw Emma with the glow emanating from her body as she rode toward him. He felt ill. He had fallen in love with his brother's fiancée. To cover his feelings, he dove headlong into courting Constance, then took her like she was a common whore, releasing his own pent-up frustrations. How stupid could one man be? He sighed with resignation. Constance interpreted it as a sigh of satisfaction. Now she must act coy and remorseful.

Constance learned to cry on the spot as a young child. If she wanted something she was denied, she would turn on the tears until Rebecca, Samuel, or Nanny gave in to her wants. Charles heard her soft sobbing against the distant crash of the waves on the rocks off the cliffs hundreds of feet below. Had he been so forceful he hurt her? Quietly, he asked, "Constance, have I injured you?"

"No, but what must you think of me? I have never had a liaison before, but your declaration of love and the feelings you awakened in me caused me to abandon all of my moral and spiritual upbringing." Constance lowered her head and sniffled.

Charles's gloom deepened. He felt like a cad. He asked to court her for all the wrong reasons, then declared his love for her. But the worst, he took her maidenhead, with no regard for the consequences. His misery was compounded as he realized he was trapped into a relationship he didn't want. If he hadn't acted on impulse after his encounter with Emma, he would be home lounging with his family by a roaring fire in the library enjoying a brandy. Instead, he was here with a woman he didn't love and a headache beginning to rage.

"Don't feel that way, Constance. I am guilty of seducing you. If you want to retract your decision to court me, I will completely understand, and not a soul will ever know what transpired here tonight." Charles was praying she would be so distraught over his actions she would gladly accept the offer. To his dismay, the polar opposite happened. She threw her arms around his neck, declaring her love for him, saying what a true gentleman he was to offer denial of his love because of an indiscretion, she adored him and would never leave him. Charles almost groaned because of his predicament, but he was in no position to negate the relationship. Instead, he put his arms around her and told her everything would be all right. In his mind, he didn't know how it would ever be right again. His life would be full of lies. He had to convince his mother that he was truly in love with Constance. He was so transparent to her it would prove difficult, but to obliterate his feelings for Emma, it was the only way out. Charles was resigned to his predicament.

Chapter 27

Revelations

Joseph and Emma were leaving Whitfield the following day. Quite naturally they wanted to make the most of their last day on the manor. After a light breakfast with Catherine and David, they went riding through the hills and valleys of the estate. The day was glorious, the English weather still cooperating with warm sunshine and no rain in sight. Joseph was hoping they would spot Charles working with the sheep as he wasn't at breakfast, and Joseph wanted to share his news of the nuptials and ask Charles to be his best man. He needed to talk to Charles alone as he was Joseph's closest confidant. He felt compelled to share with Charles his concerns over his deployment. Also, he wondered why Charles would dine at the Darbys while Joseph was home. Usually the boys were inseparable. Joseph smiled. He knew his brother well; he most likely wanted to give Joseph the time and opportunity to be with Emma without him tagging along.

Dinner was once again served in the family dining room. It was the first time Joseph had seen Charles since early morning the day before. Surprisingly Constance was supping with them. Joseph mentally noted her possessive grasp on Charles's arm. It wasn't his business who his brother kept company with, but Constance wasn't his type, whatever that may be. Joseph disliked her spoiled petulant attitude and hoped she was merely a passing fancy for his brother. He deserved a woman like Emma, unpretentious, sweet, and without airs.

Catherine's antennae were up as well. She was curious about her son's motives. He was at Earl Warwick's Manor House last night, and now tonight Constance was at Whitfield. She could read Charles easily and knew intuitively there was something he had not yet disclosed to the family. Conversation during the meal was easygoing and Catherine relaxed. Then the subject turned to Joseph and Emma's wedding plans.

"I know you are from Calais, Emma. What is the name of the Catholic Church where you will be married and when?" Constance showed great interest. *Probably planning to accompany Charles* was Emma's thought. *Wasn't she in for an unexpected surprise?*

Emma beamed at Charles, imagining how thrilled he would be that his brother would marry in the old church where his ancestors wed. "Actually, Joseph and I wanted to speak to Charles about this privately, but he has eluded us since we made our decisions." She squeezed Joseph's hand and giggled.

Here it is, Charles thought, *the perfect time to let the family know he was courting Constance.* The door of opportunity had opened, and he would walk through. "I don't have any secrets from Constance. I was waiting for the proper time to tell all of you, but now is as good as any." Constance had a look of pure victory. Her smile dripped with honey. "Earl of Warwick, Samuel Darby, kindly agreed to allow me to formally court Constance." He gave his family a halfhearted smile.

Oh my God, Catherine's heart plunged. *He sounds miserable. What a strange way to share with his loved ones his decision to court.* She gathered her wits, and polite breeding took over.

"Ah Charles, this is a surprise, I had no idea you and Constance had such deep feelings for one another." Catherine gave her son a quizzical look.

"Mother, you are embarrassing me." He wished he could bolt from the room.

Constance chimed in, "Lady Head, our feelings of love and affection have been growing for one another for a long time. I admire Charles so much because he waited to ask Father to court me until Joseph chose a wife." Catherine's shock was written all over her face. "Being the younger son, he didn't want to encroach on Joseph's territory, which is admirable. Don't you think so?" Her audacity was almost more than Catherine could bear. Charles wanted to crawl in a hole. He had to get the topic back to his brother.

Joseph and Emma were both dumbfounded. Joseph hoped he hadn't gawked at Constance like she was a two-headed freak in a carnival show. He cleared his throat to compose himself. He was a trained naval officer, who practiced diplomacy with foreign officers and government personnel. Falling into that mode was automatic when an ambush occurred, which is exactly what this was. "Yes, Constance, my brother is the kindest, most honorable man I know. I appreciate him sacrificing his own happiness for my welfare."

"We congratulate you both, don't we, Emma?" Joseph looked at his fiancée.

She followed Joseph's lead. "I am so happy for you both and look forward to us becoming fast friends, Constance." Emma exuded sincerity.

Charles squirmed uncomfortably and did not meet either his brother's or Emma's eyes. "Enough about us; let's discuss your upcoming wedding."

Catherine concentrated on not screaming because she saw that Charles was not happy. Somehow, someway the Darby girl cajoled him into this relationship, or he dove into it after his chance encounter and conversation with Emma. Either way, it was a disaster. David never said a word. He felt like he was watching a play at the theater, not a dinner conversation in his own home.

Joseph took command. "To answer your original question, Constance, the name of the church is St. Peter's, Whitfield." Like she didn't know the location of the old church, but he couldn't resist the sarcasm. Emma pinched his thigh and shot him a warning look. He softened and laughed. "We decided to wed here, as my parents did, and make Whitfield Manor our permanent home."

His words were like rapid blows to Constance's carefully manipulated plans. How could she mistress the manor if Emma were in residence?

She would think about this ghastly turn of events later. For now she must, at all costs, show enthusiasm.

"This is wonderful news. Mother and I are in the middle of sewing new fair linens for the altar, which I will be sure to have completed in time, and I want to help you in any way I can." She turned her insincere smile to Catherine and David. "I am certain Mother and Father will be pleased to open our home to any foreign or out-of-town guests who may need accommodation. Is the date set?" It wasn't lost on Catherine that Constance enunciated the word *foreign*. *God, she's downright spiteful.*

"No, I have to coordinate it with my parents, but sometime latter June. We don't want a large wedding, but something intimate for close friends and family." Emma smiled her brilliant smile.

David stood up. "Boys, shall we have a brandy in the library and let the women discuss plans for the wedding." It wasn't a question; he expected his sons to follow and they did.

Once the library doors were closed and drinks poured, David broke the silence with admonitions for Charles. He should have discussed a courtship with him; he was his father; it didn't matter Charles was in his early thirties. Charles looked so downcast, David stopped roaring. "Son, why did you make such a quick decision and act on it?"

Charles loathed lying to his father or brother, but he was backed in a corner. "I do apologize, Father, but I didn't want to spoil Joseph's engagement announcement, and I got caught up in the notion of a wife and children. I have truly admired Constance for quite a while, and I thought it a good match, especially with Earl of Warwick's place adjoining Whitfield."

"Is that what this is all about, land?" David was angry that Charles could compromise his feelings for material gain. He stepped in further. "Do you think because your brother has decided to take a wife that Whitfield is any less your home? I am appalled and disheartened to think my son would trade his honor for a slice of Warwick. Even with the peerage law, I have made provisions for you and your descendants. What kind of a father do you think I am?" David was shouting.

Joseph had never seen his father so angry with either of them, even when they were little and naughty. He needed to make this right. "Calm down, Father. You know Charles is a hopeless romantic and would never trade love for land. I am sure his haste was, as he explained, spurred by my betrothal. Come, let's not talk brashly and have regrets later. Let's celebrate mine and Charles's happiness."

David's anger dissipated. Joseph was right. He looked at Charles but saw sadness in his son that chilled his soul. What happened to change him? David shook his head and took a long pull of the brandy. He put his arm around Charles's shoulder. "Sorry, son, I shouldn't have said such hurtful things. You are a man of honor. I am proud of you." David thought it best to drop the subject. "Now on a different subject, your brother has something to ask you." David tried to sound lighthearted.

"Yes, I do, dear Charles. Will you do me the honor of being my best man?"

"Of course; it is my honor." Charles slapped Joseph on the back and the brothers laughed. In Charles's mind, alarm bells sounded. He would hand the wedding ring to his brother when in truth he wanted to put it on Emma's finger. God, why did he let her into his heart? Was his life to be a continuous masquerade when Joseph and Emma married, when they had children, when they lived under the same roof as him for God's sake? Was he to marry Constance vowing to love and cherish her when he loved and cherished someone else?

"Charles, are you listening?" Joseph sounded anxious; it jolted Charles from his quagmire of despair. "I was saying, I am being deployed within several days of my return to France. I'm not sure how long I will still be in Calais before shipping out. Admiral Smyth hasn't issued orders yet, but I can tell you both it's the damn Russians who have things stirred up. They want their hands on India, and the British army and navy will protect our jewel either by securing the Afghan border or blocking entry to the Suez Canal. This is pure speculation on my part. I don't know which place the admiral will want my services. I imagine when I return to France, the orders will be at the Embassy. I know I am to take four of my best lieutenants with me, and I won't go anywhere without Percy, so it will be the six of us deploying to my ship. The other sailors will be on board waiting."

"Dear Lord, son, this is a rotten time for these events."

Joseph chuckled. "I agree, Father, but the British Empire doesn't come to a grinding halt because I have fallen in love and plan to wed."

Charles stood transfixed. He was a louse, a traitor to his brother, who was a war hero. His jealousy and envy made him sick. What could he do to help Joseph, to ease his mind? His brother could ask him anything and he would do it for him.

Charles's voice was low and shaky. Joseph barely recognized it, his brother was so anguished. "Joseph, please, please tell me what I can do for you while you are at sea?"

"My dear brother, I am going to ask you to look after Emma. If she needs you in Calais, go there. If she needs you at Whitfield, be here for her. She worries and conjures up all sorts of dire straits. If our family and the Bourons can keep her occupied with the wedding plans and she stays busy at the Toy Depot, then she will get through this first deployment. Subsequent ones will become easier and easier. I have no doubt she'll be a marvelous military wife." Joseph laughed and added, "I thought the two of you would enjoy mucking about the manor since she shares your enthusiasm for the land."

Charles's situation worsened with his brother's request. He nodded in the affirmative. Inside he felt sick. It was her love of the land, innocence, and forthrightness he fell in love with, not to mention her remarkable beauty.

David added, "You realize, son, Mother and I already adore her and will do what we can to help. Don't forget we have the apartment in Paris she can use to get away and relax."

"Thanks for the offer. Her dearest friend, Annabelle, lives in Paris and visiting her might be a terrific diversion."

Joseph felt a need to cover his negative reaction to Charles's courtship. "I am sorry, Charles, I acted so rudely when you announced your courtship. I was being selfish because I needed your help. I wasn't considering your feelings and desires of the heart."

Charles blurted out, 'Damn it, Joseph, if I had known you were being deployed, I wouldn't have asked her father for the courtship. I could have waited. Now I am saddled with expectations of courting."

"Hold on, hold on. I don't want you to ignore Constance to entertain Emma. You can both be of help. I am sure Constance will be glad to pitch in. Ha, if she's going to be a member of the family in the future, we can start to include her now." Joseph gave Charles a light punch and laughed. In his own mind, he thought Constance a nuisance he could do without, but it was too late. Oh well, it would work itself out. He hoped his brother had chosen a woman who completed him in every way. Charles's happiness was paramount. It didn't matter what Joseph's opinions were regarding Constance Darby as long as Charles found true happiness. Somehow, though, he sincerely doubted he had.

Joseph, Emma, and Jenny set out on their journey back to Calais at first light. It was a teary good-bye. Joseph told Catherine about the deployment, and as his mother, it always left her uneasy. She hated to see Emma go as well. They had so much planning to do for the wedding. Catherine and David promised to come to Calais as soon as possible to join with her parents for the arrangements. Emma's tears flowed in silence. She didn't want to say adieu to Joseph's family or Whitfield. Jenny cried because Emma did. Joseph looked at the somber women and marveled he knew so little about the way their emotions worked.

Chapter 28

A Matter of Religion

THE TRIP BACK TO FRANCE was uneventful even though the sea was rough and Emma was sick until the ship docked. Seasickness was something she didn't usually suffer. She was fine once on dry land. It was dusk when the carriage pulled up to the Bouron residence. The house paled in comparison to the manor house in so many ways, not merely size. It was built on a busy street, not tucked into the lush countryside surrounded by trees and flowers of all varieties and colors. Emma had mixed emotions regarding her home. When she was very little, it was a place of sadness, a solemn shroud covering every inch of it. After her breakup with Richard, it served as a safe haven to heal her broken heart.

She felt instinctively the home lacked something that until now eluded her, unconditional love. Maria tried to be a good mother to the girls, but there was aloofness about her after the death of her baby son. Life went on, but she never truly recovered. Depression lurked in the background, an uninvited guest. Maria didn't understand how her mental breakdown profoundly affected Emma. It put a chink in her daughter's psychological landscape that was never totally repaired. She didn't possess the capacity to understand the different reactions of Claudine and Emma. Maria didn't comprehend the concept that each individual responds differently to circumstances during the formative years.

Emma looked out of the carriage at her home. She sighed, the weight of her unstable foundation on her shoulders.

Joseph had the luggage unloaded and taken in the house. He sensed Emma's deep melancholy, which he didn't understand. Maybe it was because they wouldn't be in the same house spending happy hours together. He walked her to the entryway door, trying to bolster her spirits. "Darling, are you excited to show your sister and parents your betrothal ring?"

She looked at her left hand and smiled. "Of course I am, Joseph. I know Claudine will be wild and have questions galore." She looked into the depth of his eyes, those blue pools she loved. "I apologize for my quiet mood, but coming back reinforces my resolve to live at Whitfield."

"You make me so very happy, Emma. I don't know how to express the joy I feel that you love Whitfield Manor, the village, the church, my family. It is more than I expected or deserve." He smiled sincerely. "Come on, enough serious talk. Kiss me good night and I will contact you tomorrow." Joseph brushed her lips with a light kiss, and then he was gone down the pathway.

Jenny waited in the foyer. She felt Emma's sadness and needed to give her words of encouragement. "Dear girl, put on a happy face for your family. It is going to take a firm stance to get them to agree on a wedding in England. You must be strong and not waver. It is time, Emma, for you to do what you want, not what anyone else wants. Show them the bubbly girl I was with in England, not a dour girl who is miserable."

Emma threw her arms around Jenny. "You always give me the best advice. I love you so much, and I will tell you this: when I settle in England, you will be with me. I can't be there without you." She kissed Jenny's cheeks.

The door opened. "I thought I heard you come in." Maria looked suspicious. Emma was always hanging on Jenny. It was annoying, but there wasn't much she could do about it. She spoke in a sweet tone. "We missed you very much and are anxious to hear all about your trip."

Maria had a conspirator's smile. "Do you have something you want to show me, Papa, and Claudine? They are in the lounge waiting for your arrival." Emma hugged her mother. Jenny winked at her girl, then they moved inside. Emma twirled into the lounge with her hands behind her back.

Claudine jumped up. "Oh no, you don't, Emma Bouron. Papa said Joseph was proposing. Let me see your betrothal ring." Emma held out her left hand. Claudine literally gasped. "Mon Dieu, Emma, it is breathtaking!"

"Let me see, child." Edgar motioned for Emma to come to his chair. He raised his eyebrows and smiled. As he speculated, the commodore must have a coffer of riches to bestow such an elegant expensive ring on his daughter. He hoped soon Joseph and his associates would become his clients at the bank. Life was certainly looking rosy. He concentrated on Emma. "Dear daughter, your mother and I, and of course your nosy little sister, want to hear all about Joseph's home, parents, and friends. Maria, call the maid to bring us champagne, cheese, and fresh bread to celebrate as we listen to Emma's adventures." Edgar squeezed Emma's hands and smiled broadly.

Emma took several sips of her champagne and nibbled on the cheese. Her stomach was still a bit unsettled. Possibly eating a little and drinking the bubbly wine might help. It would definitely help her nerves. She made up her mind during the train ride home that she would tell her parents right away she planned to marry at Whitfield. The news of her living there could wait until she was a married woman.

She centered her attention on her father, as he was the most logical one in the family, and she realized opportunistic. "Papa, you cannot in a million years imagine the shock I experienced when we arrived at Joseph's home. It is a sprawling manor house, a castle really, built in the most beautiful countryside I have ever seen. The rolling hills and valleys of the estate stretch for miles. A part of the land is a village, where the workers from the farm and their families live as they have for centuries." She paused to let that concept sink in. She assumed it wouldn't take Edgar long to realize the hierarchy of nobility Joseph fit into. "In the village is a quaint pub, where the people gather to chat, drink pints of beer, which is common to the English, and eat home-cooked pork pies, sausage rolls, and pudding." Emma paused and drank champagne. "In the center of the village is the most beautiful old church, dating from many centuries ago when the Saxons invaded England. It has stained glass windows that remind me of the smaller ones in Notre Dame. As far back as the records go in the parish, all of Joseph's ancestors were married there." Emma looked from her father to her mother and back to her father again. "The Duke and Duchess of Kent generously agreed we could wed in the old church and have the banquets at the manor."

Maria was utterly confused. "Who are the Duke and Duchess of Kent, and why would they allow you and Joseph to marry there?"

Emma paused. "They are Joseph's parents."

"What . . . His parents are upper nobility?" Maria was astounded. Edgar, on the other hand, experienced pure exultation. His position in French society was about to radically change. He would be related to the British upper crust. The business prospects soared.

Maria's eyes narrowed. "Emma Bouron, these people may be the aristocracy of England, but you are French, and if you have forgotten, a Catholic. Your wedding should be here in Calais at your own church."

Her mother had no idea that in a few short days, Whitfield had become her home. She wasn't rejecting allegiance to France but embracing the future in England. She was determined to have her way. In a quiet but firm voice she said, "I don't believe God will reject me because centuries ago Henry VIII wanted a divorce and formed his own church. The liturgy is the same as in the Catholic Church; the Mass is virtually identical. The only real difference is Anglicans have the Archbishop of Canterbury as religious head and Catholics have the Pope. Both are men. God does not dally in human politics but reigns supreme in all Christian churches. Our marriage will be just as blessed in the Anglican Church as it would be in the Catholic Church." Emma spoke with resolve.

"When did you become a theologian? Obviously, these people have put warped ideas in your head. Your father and I cannot agree to this type of union." Maria shot an incensed glare at Edgar.

Emma stood up. "It's your choice, Mother. You either choose to be part of the wedding ceremony and part of Joseph's family, or you don't." Emma turned and left the lounge without another word. Going up the stairs to her room, she began to shake. Never in her entire life had she outwardly defied her parents, but this was nonnegotiable.

Jenny was waiting for her on the top landing. "Well, Emma, how did it go?"

"Not well. Mother practically labeled me a heretic, but my guess is Father will bring her around. He sees the business potential in being related to the Heads. I have come over so tired, Jen. I want to get in my nightgown and get into bed; it's been a long, emotional day. Plus I bet Claudine bounces in here any minute!" They went into Emma's room.

"All right, my girl, let's get you tucked in. Are you hungry?"

"Actually I am famished." Emma laughed. "I believe the journey and the seasickness and now this confrontation have made me extremely hungry. Cheese, bread, and champagne just didn't quite fill me up!"

"I will have the cook make you a couple chicken sandwiches and a hot cup of tea. That should tide you over until breakfast." Jenny opened the bedroom door and Claudine bounced in.

Chapter 29

Deployment

Joseph didn't bother to stop at his hotel quarters. He directed the driver to take him directly to the British Embassy. He wanted to retrieve his orders if they had arrived. The ambassador was still in his office finishing up his business for the day. He greeted Joseph warmly, then in a more solemn tone, related that orders were delivered during his absence. The look on Cookson's face was unsettling. He must be fully informed regarding British operations to protect India from Russian encroachment. Queen Victoria as Empress wouldn't give up the territory without all-out warfare. Joseph borrowed the ambassador's letter opener to break the seal on the packet of documents. Moment of truth: a fleet of British battleships was already en route to the Suez to keep Russian imperialism in check. The fleet was under the leadership of Geoffrey Phipps Hornsby, a decorated naval officer. Joseph nodded silently; Geoffrey was a good choice for the mission, although he was surprised, as the admiral had intimated that Joseph would go to either the Suez or Afghanistan. In the short time he was away, the balance of power in the world required protection on another military front.

Ambassador Cookson saw the look of consternation on Joseph's face. He was apprised that the Russians were stirring trouble in Turkey, Afghanistan, the Balkans, and India, the main prize. The pundits called the power competition between Britain and Russia the "Great Game." The struggle centered on Central Asia, Russia trying to expand its dominance in the region and Britain countering the aggression. A dangerous game of cat and mouse was being played, with the stakes not only land, but also loss of human life. Queen Victoria and her chief advisor, Lord Melbourne, knew Central Asia was the gateway to Afghanistan, and Afghanistan the gateway to India via the Khyber Pass.

The Suez Canal wasn't the only vital waterway in the balance of world power. Two straits in Turkey, the Bosporus and the Dardanelles, had to be protected from Russian expansionism. The Bosporus forms part of the boundary between Europe and Asia and connects the Black Sea with the Sea of Marmara, which is connected by the Dardanelles to the Aegean Sea and spills into the Mediterranean. If Russia had the ability to utilize these waterways for warfare, Europe was extremely vulnerable. Uprisings in the Ottoman Empire that at one time consisted of twenty-nine provinces, with Constantinople as the capital, had a ripple effect in Europe, Africa, and Asia. For six centuries the Ottoman Empire was the center of interactions between the Eastern and Western worlds. Now different territories clamored for independence. The previous year, 1876, the Bulgarians instigated an uprising against the Ottoman Empire.

The first Russian offensive into Turkey began when Joseph met Emma in April. He lowered his head. He had been remiss in not keeping closer watch on the situation, but his focus was Emma. The damn Russians constantly maneuvered for more land and power. Joseph remembered being informed the first battle took place at Batum, a Turkish port on the Black Sea. He ignored the warning signs that a Russo-Turkish war was ready to erupt.

Ambassador Cookson broke through Joseph's silent self-admonitions. "Joseph, I have known you for a long time. Usually when you receive orders, you are eager to get started on the mission." He laughed. "Wild horses couldn't hold you back from your ship and the sea."

Joseph looked up. "Emma and I are to be married in June, sir." No smile graced his lips.

"That's wonderful news, my boy. I will pour us a glass of my finest Scotch." He opened a liquor cabinet and took out a bottle of Bush Mills. He gave Joseph a glass and they both drank. "Now, tell me your orders from the admiral that have shaken you."

"My men and I are to assess the true situation of impending warfare by going through the Bosporus to the Black Sea. Lord Melbourne, for the queen of course, wants to know how much havoc the Russians have caused in the area."

"Do you think this military assessment is one of grave danger?" The ambassador frowned and took a gulp of his Scotch.

"No, it shouldn't be. I dislike navigating through the Bosporus Strait because its S-shape makes it impossible at certain points to see if another vessel is coming from the other direction. There have been so many naval accidents there—too many to count really. I only trust my internal guidance system." Joseph laughed; he didn't want to sound boastful, but he was being candid.

The ambassador sighed. "This world is a topsy-turvy place. What with the collapse of the Spanish, Portuguese, Chinese, Mogul, and Holy Roman Empires and the rise of the British, German, and Japanese Empires, the world has changed drastically in my lifetime. We already control much of the world, and London is the world's largest city. But men are greedy creatures, Joseph, and those in power want more and more. Britain controls most of the key maritime trade routes and we have unchallenged sea power, but it seems we either want more or protect what we have already taken. Mark my words, Joseph, those blokes in America won't be held back long. I foresee them becoming a global influence. Did you know over 70 million people have left Europe for America or Australia? Incredible." Cookson chuckled. "Our queen, remember, even sent Sir Charles Wyville Thompson on an Antarctic expedition for four years. He just returned last year with all those photographs of icebergs." Cookson laughed and shook his head. "If I am not mistaken, your good friend Commodore Nares captained his ship *Challenger* on the voyage. Soon we will be colonizing icebergs and relocating people to live on them." Both Joseph and the ambassador laughed at government folly.

He filled Joseph's glass again. "Let's toast to the ever-expanding British Empire; may God have mercy upon us." Cookson's sarcasm was not lost on Joseph.

When he arrived at his quarters, Joseph was exhausted from the long journey and the stressful news regarding his deployment. The assignment would have meant months at sea before the invention of the compound steam engine. He was fortunate that under Admiral Smyth, he was awarded the helm of one of the fastest naval steamships in the fleet, *Mercury*. Conversion from sailing ships to steamships was the driving force behind the Industrial Revolution and the growth of British imperialism. Instead of a six-month journey around the Cape to reach the riches of the East, the time had been shortened to approximately three weeks. Commerce between East and West was flourishing, which made the East a place ripe for confrontation between expansionist governments and vulnerable countries. First, the East India Company from Britain controlled the trade routes. With the invention of the compound steam engine, the British Company, Peninsular and Oriental Steam Navigation Company, entered into a contract with the British government to run the trade routes from London to Bombay. Unfortunately, Russia wanted to pluck India from England for territorial expansion and the lucrative trade routes.

Joseph sat down at his desk at the Chateau Philippe to review maritime charts so he could calculate the approximate time required for the mission. He factored in the good weather, which meant calm waters resulting in improved travel time. His best estimation put him at sea for seven weeks as long as nothing impeded his voyage. He hoped to set the wedding for the end of June, but his orders changed everything. He would be deployed all of June and July; therefore, his best bet for the nuptials was mid-August. He would tell Emma tomorrow. He felt her disappointment before she even knew the wedding ceremony must be pushed back.

Chapter 30

Edgar and Maria Concede

EMMA HAD THE LUXURY OF one more day before returning to work. She was going to make good use of it. She wrote out her engagement announcement for the newspapers *Le Petit Parisian*, the *Daily Dover Press*, the *Illustrated London News,* and finally the *Kent Messenger.* She sent a telegram to Annabelle telling her of her betrothal and the date she and Claudine would arrive in Paris. The last task was sketching her wedding gown for the House of Worth. She wanted the father of haute couture, Charles Worth, to custom-make her gown. It was an extravagance she absolutely would not relinquish. Since she didn't need party clothes or really anything except personal items before she met Joseph, she had saved most of her earnings from the previous two years. She could afford a personally designed gown, no matter what the cost. Emma mused, *I want to be beautiful for Joseph and all of Whitfield.* Goose bumps covered her arms when she thought of the Heads and all the villagers so happy Joseph married. Emma marveled he chose her. God blessed her.

Edgar knocked on Emma's bedroom door. "Emma, I am home from the bank early. I want to speak with you. May I come in?"

"Of course, Papa."

"I talked with your mother at great length, and I am sure you understand her disappointment you will not marry at Sacred Heart in your hometown." Emma started to protest, but Edgar held up his hand to shush her. "After getting over the initial letdown, she supports your decision to wed in England." Edgar smiled.

Emma jumped from her chair, threw her arms around her father, and kissed his cheek. "Papa, you have made me so happy. Wait until you see Whitfield; it is lovely, and the church steeped in the Heads' tradition for centuries. Plus, your friends can attend. The Earl of Warwickshire has offered accommodations for our close family and friends at Whitehaven. Naturally, our immediate family, and I hope the Cousin-Montaubans, will stay at Whitfield Manor." Edgar felt a surge of joy ripple through his body. He could invite friends and associates to a royal wedding! It was unlikely they would travel such a distance to attend the wedding, but receiving a royal invitation was the impressive factor. His stature in Calais would soar. His business opportunities were boundless!

Edgar decided since he gave Emma reason to rejoice, he would question her about the Head family. "Your commodore certainly turned out to be a surprise."

"In what way?" Emma frowned.

"He didn't allude to the fact that he was the highest strata of royalty. Only the princes and princesses who are offspring of Queen Victoria and Prince Albert rank higher." Edgar raised his eyebrows questioningly.

"Joseph is not a braggart, Papa. He wanted my love to spring from purity of ignorance, not from greed of position in British society."

"Perfect answer, dear daughter, and you are right." Edgar smiled and left the room.

Joseph arrived for dinner looking dashing in his dress naval uniform. Maria had reconciled with the fact Emma would marry in England, and in a Protestant church of all things. Edgar convinced her the great wealth coming to the Bouron family would more than compensate for holding the wedding in England. Maria greeted Joseph warmly, complimenting him on his design and choice of Emma's engagement ring. The evening passed quickly. Claudine bubbled over about the wedding and going to Paris for training. Emma smiled, drinking in the happiness surrounding her.

After the meal, Joseph asked Edgar if he could take Emma on a carriage ride through the park. Edgar was more than willing to let the future Duke of Kent take a spin with the future duchess. He literally beamed as the couple left the house. The future duchess, his very own daughter!

Percy greeted Emma with a bow and a broad grin. It was obvious he was pleased Joseph had proposed to her. She smiled back, then disappeared into the carriage. Joseph said something to Percy, then got inside. "This was a lovely idea, Joseph. The spring air is quite pleasant tonight, and there are hundreds of stars twinkling above us." Emma relaxed and smiled.

"Come here, darling."

Emma questioned if something were wrong. Joseph's voice was gravelly, and he appeared somber, not the animated person he was at dinner. She moved next to him. The clop-clop of the horses' hooves on the cobblestones resounded in her ears. The sound was ominous for some reason. She shivered.

Joseph kissed her tenderly, then kissed her ring. "I received my deployment orders from the admiral last night." The clopping of the horses' hooves seemed to get louder and beat in unison with her heart. "I must report to South Hampton docks two days hence to meet my ship and men, and then we will depart for the straits in Turkey." Emma sat in stunned silence. "It won't be a long sea assignment. It will take three weeks to reach the Bosporus, then a week to assess what damage the Russians have done, and three weeks back."

"Joseph," Emma's voice was a whisper, "that will be all of June and July. We were to be married at the end of June."

Joseph tried to sound encouraging. "Yes, but we can plan for mid-August, when the weather will not be so fickle and we'll have a warm day."

"What will I do without you? I will be so lonely." Emma's voice spoke volumes of despair and misery.

"In fact, my darling, you will be so busy you will hardly notice I am gone." Joseph forced a light laugh. "You will have plenty of time to plan the wedding, go to Whitfield, go to Paris for your gown, and stay with Annabelle. Claudine should be there as well."

"What about my job?" Emma's head was swirling.

"I want you to formally request a sabbatical, which I am sure they will grant since your new puppet line was just approved. If they need help, you can do so by correspondence. It will be advantageous because you will assist in training Claudine while in Paris."

The tears poured down Emma's cheeks as she stared straight ahead. What would she do? Being with Joseph was like breathing. Joseph crushed her to his chest. "My precious girl, the first deployment is the worst for you, but I promise they get easier in time. Once we have children, you won't even miss me." He forced a laugh. "It hurts me that you feel so sad, but it is my duty to go."

Emma was miserable. She realized she should be supportive, but the thought of all those weeks without him was more than disheartening. Then it hit her like a lightning bolt. Was he going to be in danger? "Joseph, these Russians, will they bear arms against you?" Her voice was laced with panic.

"No, no, it is the Russians and the Turks fighting. I am only to see what, if anything, the Russians have gained. Politics and warfare, darling, are like a game of chess. I am sent to see if either has been checkmated." Joseph laughed.

Thank God. Emma felt better, and Joseph did have a point: she could keep busy with the hundreds of tasks ahead of her. She would request the leave of absence from work, and she would do the things he mentioned. By the time he returned, she would be waiting at Whitfield with every detail completed for their wedding. The first thing to be done was a night together at Chateau Philippe. "Joseph, ask my father for a late night tomorrow." Then Emma kissed him softly. "Dream about our last night together, for I will be imprinted on your memory."

Joseph and Emma's last night together, neither would easily forget. Any inhibitions that lingered totally vanished. She stood nude before him bathed in a soft light from the parlor fire. She put Joseph's hands all over her body, which worked her into a frenzy. She begged him to take her to new heights of passion. He maneuvered each sensitive place on her body, sometimes with a light touch, other times roughly, until she came over and over. Emma explored Joseph's body with the same fervor. His pleasure seemed endless. They made love until they were both exhausted and nothing was left to give. Joseph held Emma in his arms, both drenched in sweat.

They made love so long there was no time for sleep. He needed to get Emma dressed quickly and her disheveled hair back in place. He loved her more at that moment than he thought possible. They spoke very little; no words were necessary. When they went down to the carriage, they remained quiet and serene. On the ride to the Bourons, Joseph held her and they didn't speak. Finally he said, "I don't want you to come to the docks tomorrow. Please don't question me on this; just honor my request."

Emma could see in the dim carriage light the sincerity on his face. The carriage stopped. "Don't walk me to the door tonight, Joseph; I could not bear to let you leave."

Percy opened the door; Joseph got out, helped Emma down, and got back into the carriage. She went down the walkway with determined resolve. It took everything she had not to turn around and look at him. She fumbled with the key to open the foyer door; somewhere in the background, the clop-clop of the horses' hooves echoed on the cobblestones. She dropped the key and crumpled to the ground, sobbing uncontrollably.

The door opened; Jenny picked her up and led her to the stairs. Emma clung to her for support. Once in the bedroom, Jenny undressed her and put a nightgown over her head onto her body as if Emma were a child again. It was reminiscent of all those times Jenny cared for her when she was hurt, lonely, sad, longing for her mother's touch. The childhood routine flashed through Jenny's mind, but this was worse: she saw a hollow emptiness in Emma's eyes.

Chapter 31

Life at Sea and on Land

JOSEPH, HIS LIEUTENANTS, AND PERCY, of course, boarded the boat to South Hampton without any send-offs. Joseph slipped back into his military routine, blocking thoughts of Emma from his mind. Once at sea on his own ship, he embraced his duty as enthusiastically as a young sailor. Truly there were two loves in his life, Emma and the sea. It was time for the sea to resume precedence.

Emma walked to work the first morning Joseph departed. She thought she heard the ship's bell ringing from the harbor, but it was her imagination. Seven weeks! An eternity! She couldn't allow her emotions to run amuck. It would be crippling; instead, she chose logic to guide her through Joseph's first deployment of their relationship. She decided writing a plan would keep her focused. The first thing this morning, sort out work at the Toy Depot, compose the letter for a leave, and request a meeting with Ferra, and then write a calendar of weekly events. She felt a bit better after making decisions. If she operated without direction, she would crumble. She looked at her ring; it sparkled brilliantly in the sunlight. She smiled.

Maria was still disgruntled about Emma's decision to marry in England, but Edgar warned her she'd better approve and act as if she liked the idea. He felt assured he would reap huge rewards from the union of Emma and Joseph, not just from new avenues for wealthy clients but socially from being in the family of the duke and duchess.

Yes, Maria would do as her husband advised, but secretly the idea of Emma marrying outside the Catholic Church was repugnant. Also unsettling was Emma's newfound determination. Maria knew her elder daughter had a lack of confidence in all things but her work. Why, she couldn't fathom, but it was there during her childhood and especially as a young adult. Claudine was vibrant, with an effervescent personality. Emma was the more beautiful of her two daughters, but not self-assured. It puzzled Maria that Emma didn't even recognize her own good looks. Since Commodore Head entered their lives, Emma blossomed. The longer she was with Joseph, the more confidence she gained, enough in fact to defy her own mother. Maria sighed; what would come next?

When Emma arrived home for dinner, she carried her complete calendar plotted out for the seven weeks Joseph would be at sea. She asked her mother and father to join her in the parlor to go over her schedule. She sent Jenny to fetch Claudine, as it included her as well. Emma felt emboldened. Joseph's support, and the inner peace she experienced at Whitfield, gave her the courage to tell her parents what she was going to do, not ask for permission. It wasn't her nature to be assertive, but that changed so her plans could move forward. It was strange really: at home she projected a docile personality, but at work she was confident and assured.

"As you know, Joseph is deployed for seven weeks. We moved our wedding date to August 15, and without him here to help me with planning, I have many tasks to accomplish for our nuptials." Emma laughed to give the atmosphere some levity. "So with that in mind, today I worked out a calendar to help me complete my responsibilities." Edgar looked pleased with her organization; Maria was suspicious. Claudine felt true surprise at her sister's determination, but happy. The night before, she heard Emma's sobs from her open bedroom door, and it tore at Claudine's heart. Hopefully, a solid plan would occupy her in Joseph's absence. "Today I met with my manager and requested a sabbatical until after the wedding and he agreed." Claudine gasped; would that end her career with the company before it started?

Emma jumped up, sat next to Claudine on the settee, and took her hand. "Wait to hear what I have to say, dear sister." Emma gave Claud's hand a reassuring squeeze. "Monsieur Ferra and I devised a schedule that enables me to still work with Claudine's training in Paris, and with her help, funnel ideas for the new line. I won't be completely out of touch with work, yet I will have the freedom to achieve my personal tasks." Maria looked at Emma dumbfounded. Her quiet daughter was asserting her independence right before her eyes. "That being said, I will get everything organized at work this week, then go to Paris for two weeks. I sent a telegram to the Cousin-Montaubans telling them I would accompany Claudine, which was previously approved by the general. While in Paris, I'll work with Claudine, and at the same time plan the wedding. My gown will be designed by the House of Worth, and so will my attendants' gowns." Emma gave Claudine's hand another squeeze. Now her sister was beaming. "I will ask Catherine to meet us in Paris the end of the last week so she can have her gown commissioned." Emma looked at Maria; her mother was crestfallen. "Mother, please plan on coming to Paris that week to have your gown designed by House of Worth." Maria's whole demeanor changed.

"Where will I stay?" Maria stammered.

"The Cousin-Montauban mansion is huge, and Annabelle will welcome you there, or if you like, you may stay with Catherine at the Head's Paris apartment. Whatever makes you the most comfortable." Emma smiled sincerely at her bewildered mother.

"After those two busy weeks, we return to Calais. Catherine will accompany us so she can meet our whole family." She beamed at Edgar. "Papa, the duchess is most anxious to make your acquaintance." Emma batted her thick black lashes at her father. She loved calling Catherine the duchess to Edgar; every time, Emma thought he would literally jump out of his skin!

"I have organizational tasks to complete at the Toy Depot while you and Catherine shop, Mama. I am sure, Papa, you will arrange some evening activities for the duchess. At the end of the week, Catherine and I will travel to Whitfield." Maria noticed Emma's voice had a lilting sound with the mere mention of Whitfield. "We have three weeks for final preparations. Hopefully, our family will arrive the week before the wedding. Joseph is arriving about August 12 if the weather cooperates on the high seas." Emma felt emboldened by her firm resolve and smiled.

Claudine was bursting with excitement. Going to Paris, to England, staying in mansions, being in Emma's wedding, meeting nobles! What an adventure! She hugged Emma so tight they both burst out laughing.

Emma started twirling a lock of her hair round and round her index finger. She didn't want to, but she resigned herself to the fact she needed to tell her family Annabelle was courting Richard. It was a certainty they would cross paths at the Cousin-Montaubans and at her wedding, especially since she planned on Annabelle being an attendant. Having the wedding in England substantially reduced the chance of acquaintances from Calais making the connection that Richard was Emma's former fiancé. She wasn't inviting them. Emma didn't want a huge ostentatious wedding. If she arranged it in Calais, it would turn into a monumental production. The people from Papa's bank and his clientele, the people from Emma's job, Claudine's friends, Mama's friends, and the list would go on and on. These people wouldn't be expected to travel to England, nor would they. The wedding would be relatively small from her side. On the other hand, Catherine and David might have a long list of guests. Emma didn't really care as long as the Bourons, the Heads, the Cousin-Montaubans, and the Whitfield villagers attended. She was certain Richard would accompany Annabelle and the general.

Well, she might as well wade in; it had to be done. "By the way, I have some strange news that might surprise you," Emma said.

"All the news we've heard since your return from England has been strange," Maria said sarcastically.

"Be quiet, Maria. I won't tolerate you chastising Emma." Edgar raised his voice. "What is it, Emma? It can't be that untoward."

"Papa, when Joseph and I were in Paris, I learned Annabelle was courting Richard."

"Richard DeBarge?" Edgar was incredulous. Claudine whistled. Maria sulked after the reprimand from her husband.

"Yes, it seems when he left Calais, he enlisted in the French Army and serves under General Cousin-Montauban. That's how he met Annabelle. Very ironic—what are the odds?" Emma laughed. "Seriously, he is not the boy I was engaged to marry. He is mature, with a military career; and he advanced to lieutenant in two years, which is quite an accomplishment."

Edgar cleared his throat. "Emma, as long as your friend is happy, it doesn't impact you."

"I know, but that's not the crux of the matter." Emma looked away. "I haven't told her of our previous, um, situation."

For the second time in the conversation, Edgar raised his voice. "Emma, it is not like you to be deceitful. I am very disappointed."

Emma was on the brink of tears. Claudine and Maria sat riveted. "Papa, Joseph and I talked it over and decided why dig up the past from over two years ago? Annabelle has enjoyed so little social interaction with people her own age, as her father has been her first priority. Richard is a changed man, and we want Annabelle to be happy. He and I were so young when we courted, neither of us knew the meaning of true love. I can't spoil this for her. When the time is right, I promise I will divulge my former association with him."

Edgar nodded; if Joseph knows the truth and agrees, then Edgar would leave it alone. Good riddance anyway. Emma captured the heart of British royalty; let the Cousin-Montauban girl forge her own future path. Edgar's anger evaporated into thin air. "I am sorry, Emma dear. You caught me off guard, and I hastily drew negative conclusions. I trust you and Joseph to make the decision best for your friend."

Claudine saw a softer side to her father, whereas Maria sat in disbelief. Edgar was the master of the household; normally he would insist Emma be totally truthful immediately. Maria raised her eyebrows and gave Edgar a sideways look. This whole nobility thing affected him tremendously, and she wasn't pleased.

Emma decided to steer the conversation back to travel plans while her father contemplated the news. Throwing in the nobility aspect would help her.

"Oh, one thing I forgot to mention, Papa. I know I don't need a chaperone since a man isn't traveling with me, but I want Jenny to assist me with the heaps of small tasks that go into planning a wedding, especially since the wedding will be at Whitfield Manor, with who knows how many nobles attending." Emma moved in for Edgar's Achilles heel, "It wouldn't surprise me if one of the princes or princesses attended, especially if Queen Victoria has other engagements on August 15." Edgar's eyes were so wide, Emma thought they might pop out of his head. He sputtered and finally composed himself enough to say one word—yes.

Maria, on the other hand, resented Jenny going with Emma. The damn woman was too strong an influence in her own daughter's life. She didn't understand that Jenny filled a void created by her own nervous breakdown. Analyzing personal imperfections was not part of Maria's nature; it was easier to blame someone else. Right now, Jenny was the culprit diverting Emma's attention from her. Maybe she should make some changes to the household staff once Emma was married.

"Mama, I was saying, Joseph and I are going to Venice on our honeymoon." Emma blushed.

Claudine burst in the conversation. "How romantic, Em! How long is the trip?"

"I don't know. It depends on Joseph's orders." Emma's faraway look showed raw dread.

Joseph's voyage was invigorating. The salt air in his lungs, the fluttering of his flag in the breeze, and the routine of the sailors on board was a combination of perfection for a veteran commodore. He loved working the sea charts in his cabin at night, mapping the ship's course, deciding on how many knots to run depending on the weather, which had totally cooperated, checking the number of nautical miles traveled in one day. He was in his element. His onboard schedule was so busy, plus he was responsible for the lives of all men on the ship. He had little time to think about Emma and their upcoming wedding. Oh, the men teased and cajoled him mercilessly when first on board, but that passed quickly once the ship was underway.

The *Mercury* was one of the newest steamers in the British Navy. Its speed was unsurpassed. Joseph was honored this glorious vessel was entrusted to him. His last ship was a majestic clipper, but he needed the speed of the steamer to reach the Bosporus rapidly. Britain built a secure network of coal stations to fuel steamers, which made it possible to use them as warships. The *Mercury* had a crew of fifty-eight, not including Joseph and the lieutenants. The ship was outfitted with two cannons and seven machine guns. Although it was on a peaceful fact-finding mission, the ship was prepared for combat.

The seas remained calm throughout the twenty-three-day trip. What slowed the *Mercury* down slightly was loading the tons of coal at the refueling ports. At each port, Joseph sent Emma a quick telegram letting her know he was safe. The morning the *Mercury* sailed into the Bosporus Strait was bright and sunny. Joseph was surprised to see a squadron of Turkish ships anchored at various intervals in the narrow strait. He sent a small party ashore to gather information on exactly what the Russians were attempting. Under the leadership of Breton, the men launched the small tender and rowed to shore. It didn't take them long to learn the Russians were marching forward with the help of the Romanians and Bulgarians, with little resistance from the Ottoman forces. The Russians outsmarted the Turks by attacking and penetrating their territory by crossing the Danube River.

The Ottoman leadership expected the Russians to attack the garrisons along the coastline of the Black Sea. They were so certain, the Ottoman Navy had an ironclad squadron and a wooden-hulled squadron stationed in the Black Sea awaiting Russian attack. The Russians were under the leadership of Grand Duke Nicholas, a brilliant military strategist. The march to Constantinople was underway. The garrisons the Ottomans so vehemently guarded were not top priority to Nicholas; he felt the Turks' vulnerability was on unprotected land. His military prowess would prove exactly correct in the near future.

After several days of observing and gathering intelligence, Joseph decided to begin the voyage back to Britain to give Admiral Smyth the unsettling news. He could only relate cryptic information in telegrams, enough to let the admiral know the situation was adverse to Britain, but not enough to divulge the seriousness of the Russian military advance.

Emma was able to accomplish all of her goals while Joseph was at sea. She even managed to enjoy her visit with Annabelle in Paris. She adored working with Claudine, who was an enthusiastic avid learner. The pinnacle of her time in Paris was designing her wedding gown with Catherine's help.

Emma chose the renowned House of Worth founded by Charles Worth under the patronage of Empress Eugenie to design her wedding gown. The empress was the wife of Napoleon III, and having the royals as premier patrons ensured Worth's success. Eugenia was a French fashion icon, and all those who could afford haute couture clamored to become one of his customers. Charles Worth was a friend of Catherine's and was more than pleased to create Emma's gown. He was familiar with what complemented her petite figure since he designed the gold ball gown and some of the other gowns Joseph purchased. The Heads spent a fortune at his shop. Such lucrative, well-known clients further enhanced his business. He insisted his sons, Gasto-Lucien and Jean Phillippe, design the gowns for the attendants, Annabelle and Claudine, and for both mothers. Emma loved being with Catherine. She felt more natural with her than she did her own mother. It was thrilling choosing the silk, the beading, the tulle, and the brocading for the wedding gown.

It delighted Catherine to observe Emma and Monsieur Worth sketch the dress. They were both so talented. Emma truly contributed to the design of her gown. It was perfect.

Tears sprung to Catherine's eyes at the first fitting. She imagined her son seeing his bride walk down the aisle looking angelic in the yards and yards of beaded white silk and lace.

Things changed slightly when Maria arrived. Catherine thought her detached and a bit jealous of Emma's maid, Jenny. She was pleasant enough, but not someone Catherine would choose to befriend. For Emma's sake, she showed Maria some of the Paris museums and art galleries. At night they dined out and attended the theater. It was most enjoyable when Claudine, Annabelle, and Emma joined them for the outings.

The five women shopped at the houses of fashion situated around Rue du Faubourg Saint-Honore, and Catherine introduced Maria to the House of Jacques Doucet, where they had dresses designed for the wedding breakfast and wedding feast. It was a joyful time for Catherine. She had resigned herself to the fact that Joseph would never marry; now, here she was with his extraordinary fiancée, whom she adored.

Emma, Maria, and Catherine arrived in Calais at the end of the third week of Joseph's deployment. Emma received a telegram a few days before from him. The ship was still several days away from their destination. Every time Emma received a telegram, Catherine saw relief flood her face.

Catherine quite enjoyed her time with the Bourons. She found Edgar quite impressed with her position in society. Privately she chuckled; she and David were unpretentious people. It never ceased to surprise them when people were awestruck with their titles. Neither of them took any of it for granted. Their purpose in life was to sustain the manor so the villagers would always have a home, a place to work, and a lovely spot to raise their children. They appreciated all of their blessings.

The week in Calais passed quickly. Since Calais was the lace capital of France, Emma chose intricate lace to have made into purses for the women in the wedding party, and Catherine sent several bolts of lace home for the wedding decorations. The closer the time came for her and Emma to depart for Whitfield, the more animated Emma became. Her laughter was infectious. The whole household, including Maria, had a sense of gaiety.

The trip to Whitfield was quite uneventful. As before when she and Joseph arrived, the landau with the Head crest embossed on the door was awaiting their arrival. From the moment Emma took her seat in the carriage, her heart quickened. No wonder Kent was called the Garden of England. The wildflowers crisscrossed over the pastures in riotous patterns. There were gray creeping thistles, white and purple field bindweed, yellow gorse and celandines. Multicolors of iris, foxglove, and primrose covered the rolling hills. Emma took deep breaths of the sweet scents that filled the early summer air.

Catherine observed Emma's face and body language. *She feels alive here.* Catherine knew, because she felt exactly the same way from the moment David brought her here all those years ago. Now Joseph was bringing a new bride to Whitfield who loved the manor. As a mother, she was thrilled for Joseph, but she feared her other son harbored feelings for his brother's soon-to-be wife. Charles's strange reaction to Joseph's engagement, his hasty courting of Constance, it all pointed to a yes. Charles loved Joseph. As his mother, she was convinced he would wrestle with his feelings and in time put them away. Catherine sighed; it would all work out in the end.

Emma turned to Catherine. "What is it? Are you all right?"

Catherine took her hand and smiled.

"Yes, dear Emma, I am simply glad to be home."

Emma squeezed her hand. "Me too."

David waited for his wife and future daughter-in-law in the morning room. He read an article in the newspaper that referenced Russia's bold advancement into territories that were part of the declining Ottoman Empire. Russian diplomacy centered on allying themselves with disgruntled regions that craved independence. Even though David was a member of the House of Lords in Parliament, he disliked politics immensely. He just couldn't rectify loss of human life for expansion of the British Empire. It was especially disconcerting since Joseph was in the middle of a deployment. His thoughts were interrupted with the arrival of the women.

Jenny and Emma went upstairs to settle into their suite of rooms before tea. Emma opened the door to the suite, but their trunks hadn't been brought up. She peeked in the wardrobe, and unlike last time, her clothes were not inside. Phoebe suddenly opened the door. "Oh, so sorry, Miss Emma. I was instructed to show you to your rooms in the family wing, but before I could do my lady's bidding, you had gone up the stairs."

"Oh Phoebe, I assumed we would have the same accommodations."

Phoebe blushed. "Well, you're practically family now, and the duchess wants you and your chambermaid in family quarters."

Emma's happiness grew exponentially. She was already becoming entrenched at Whitfield even before the wedding. The rooms in the family wing weren't as opulent as those in the guest wing. Yes, they were well-decorated, but there was a cozy atmosphere about them. Emma felt right at home. Jenny was to occupy the nanny's quarters, which suited her perfectly. She was given a roomy bedroom with an adjoining sitting room. Jenny felt like royalty. The nursery kitchen was convenient as well. It was well-stocked with everything she could possibly need: tea, milk, biscuits, sugar, eggs, and bread and butter. Cooked meals were sent up from the main scullery and kitchen. The nursery kitchen wasn't completely stocked, as there were no children in residence.

Tea was served in the family dining room. Emma and Catherine chattered away, telling David all about their time in Paris and Calais. Many men were dismissive toward their wives' tales of city visits, but not David. He was thoroughly interested in whatever Catherine did and always attentive. Emma wondered why Charles hadn't joined them, but then she guessed he was busy on the manor and had no time for late afternoon tea. She made a note in her mind to ask Catherine about how his courting was progressing. She inadvertently shuddered when she thought of how wrong Constance was for Charles.

"Emma, I know you and Catherine are going to be very busy with the wedding arrangements, but are there other things you would like to do before Joseph arrives home?" David's question broke into her thoughts about Constance, which was a relief.

"Actually, there are some sights in Kent I long to see."

"How lovely, Emma." David smiled.

"If possible and schedules allow the time, I would like to take a few day trips to the borders of the county." David looked surprised, but was impressed. Emma continued, "I want to enjoy the banks of the Thames and the North Sea. I know they border Kent to the north. I haven't really had an opportunity to explore Dover and the Cliffs by the Channel. We disembarked there, but traveled straight to Whitfield. I believe Constance's family residence is close to the cliffs, and I would truly enjoy a visit to Whitehaven if possible. I don't want to intrude on her family, but they have been so kind, extending invitations to wedding guests who need accommodations." David literally beamed.

"I am sure, my dear, Charles will be more than happy to show off points of interest in Kent. He knows every inch of the county." David cleared his throat, "Um, since he is courting Constance, it should not be difficult to get an invitation for you to Whitehaven."

"Do you think I will have time to explore the countryside?" Emma asked.

"Of course," David said.

Catherine wished David hadn't been so quick to offer Charles's services, but it was difficult not to catch Emma's enthusiasm. Charles was a thirty-three-year-old man, not an age that lends itself to motherly advice. Emma was so naïve, she wouldn't suspect Charles had more than brotherly inclinations toward her. Catherine rubbed her temples; *why did life become so complicated?* Maybe she was wrong, but in her heart she knew she was right.

Every day was bustling with wedding preparations. First and foremost was sending out the wedding invitations. Maria was taking care of the few that were to go out on the French side. Catherine had many more to be hand-delivered throughout England. An invitation addressed to all Whitfield villagers was posted at the *Fox and Hounds*. Second, Catherine and Emma tackled the breakfast and evening feast menus. The family chef commissioned cooks from Dover and London to assist with both meals. Emma didn't have a preference for the main courses. She left that task up to Catherine and the chef.

Her wedding shoes from Gundry & Sons, designers of Queen Victoria's shoes, were scheduled for delivery the end of the week. The gown from Worth's would be delivered the end of the second week. The last thing to arrive would be a wreath of orange blossoms for her hair. Royalty had worn them for decades. They symbolized purity. Also, sprigs of myrtle, which stood for love and domestic happiness, would be incorporated into her bouquet. Emma smiled; the most important part of the wedding, Joseph, would arrive a couple of days before the nuptials.

Charles avoided keeping company with the family. Emma guessed he was spending his time with Constance at Whitehaven. She and Joseph were inseparable after their first meeting; now that Charles declared his love for Constance, he must want to be with her as frequently as possible. She hated to impose, but she longed to explore Kent.

Emma dressed in her riding clothes and went to the stables. She asked for her same mare, Molly, to be saddled up. One of the stable lads rode with her to find Charles. They didn't have to go too far; he and his fellow sheepherders were leading the sheep to the shearing stalls. It was time their thick winter coats came off for processing. Emma let the lad go back to his chores at the stables while she waited to catch Charles's attention. He looked very handsome in his rugged way, sitting tall on his steed. His hair was blond, like Joseph's, but not meticulously groomed; instead, wild curls went everywhere. He and Joseph were built alike: tall, slender, but muscular. Joseph's eyes hypnotized Emma, whereas Charles's smile was his winning feature. Emma thought how wonderful it was to gain a brother who could teach her every aspect of Whitfield.

He saw her from the corner of his eye sitting atop Molly by the far tree line. He didn't acknowledge he had spotted her. He needed a few minutes to compose himself. Since the time she arrived at Whitfield with his mother, Charles had barely seen her. He avoided family meals. It was easier to pop into the *Fox and Hounds* for a meal and friendly banter with some of the men of the village. They talked about the sheep and the manor; sometimes the wedding was brought up, but mainly the talk was work-oriented. The atmosphere allowed Charles to concentrate on the land he loved, not the woman he could never love. Ever since his conversation with Emma about Whitfield, he saw her in a different light. It infuriated him that he lusted after his brother's fiancée. He and Joseph were so close. He hated himself for his inner feelings, but vowed neither Joseph nor Emma would suspect his disloyalty. That's exactly what it was. Disloyalty. Disloyalty to his brother, to his future sister-in-law, and to his family.

Charles was relieved Constance had gone to London with her family to shop for wedding attire. It gave him at least a week to be free of courting obligations. He visited Whitehaven the previous week on two different occasions, once for dinner and once for a small party. He kissed Constance good night both times. He could feel she wanted him to make love to her, but he simply didn't want her. He was half-drunk the night he seduced her. It was hazy. The details of his cajoling her into sacrificing her maidenhead were sparse. He only sobered up really when he released his pent-up passion, and then she was on top of him getting her fill. He'd made up his mind he wouldn't have sex again with her until he married her or by some act of God voided the courtship.

He sighed. He couldn't put off acknowledging Emma any longer. She sat patiently for at least ten minutes.

Charles trotted to the tree line. He put on his mask. "Good morning, Emma, what brings you out on the manor this morning? I thought you and Mother would be busy on wedding preparations." His brilliant smile lit up his whole face.

Emma laughed. "I came to find you, Master Head, because you have avoided me."

For a moment Charles felt concern, but then he realized she was joking.

"Have you been living at Whitehaven?" Emma burst out laughing.

"No, no, Constance and the whole family went to London because of you." Charles's eyes twinkled.

Now Emma looked concerned. "Me, what have I done?"

"You and my brother have planned the biggest event of the year, maybe the decade, and all the dignitaries are off to London to buy new finery for the wedding and the feasts."

Emma breathed a huge sigh of relief. Her old friend self-doubt had caused her to think her actions led to evacuation of the county. *I am so ridiculous. He is joking with me, and of course I assume I have done some unmentionable act resulting in people leaving to avoid my wedding.* She looked at him from under her thick black lashes. "I am sorry, Charles. I get panicked at times not knowing if someone is teasing or serious."

Charles was puzzled by her candor regarding her feelings. "I'm truly sorry, Emma; I was pulling your leg. Enough of that. Back to my original question, what brings you out on the manor today?" He changed the subject to chase her despondency away.

Emma's face transformed from uncertainty to serenity. "Will you show me some of the sights in Kent? I am anxious to explore the whole county." She was animated, and all traces of her previous mood were erased.

Charles spent the remainder of the day showing Emma as much of the countryside as possible. She thrived on cantering through the woods, the pastures, and then reaching the sea. Watching the waves crash against the cliffs ignited her spirit. She chattered and laughed all day. They stopped for a quick pint of beer and sandwich at one of the pubs close to the Sussex boundary, then continued on their jaunt. Charles noticed her youthful exuberance and tried to recall her age. Wasn't it nineteen or twenty according to Joseph? It accentuated how truly lovely she was, her hair loose and blowing in the wind, her dainty figure on Molly's back, and her green eyes taking in all the sights. Charles was amazed at how comfortable she was riding after just a few outings. Kent was already part of her. He loved the manor and all the beauty Kent offered, but he never imagined a woman other than his mother would feel the same. Maybe that's why he hadn't married: because he had no intention of residing anywhere but Whitfield. Most of the young women in Kent wanted to leave the county to live in London, where the nightlife, the parties, the fashion shows were continuous, and their social position got them invitations to the most sought-after events. Here was Joseph's bride, the complete opposite. Charles pushed down his crazy thoughts about her.

After dinner that same evening, Emma strolled through the gardens alone. She was pleased Charles took the time to show her parts of the county; the rolling hills, the tiny villages, the sea all made her long to live right here on the manor. She pictured Joseph and her children frolicking in the garden, playing in the turrets as Joseph and Charles had done, and growing up appreciating the land that would be their birthright. She had been thinking about bearing children a lot lately. She would love all her children unconditionally and never abandon them emotionally or physically. A nanny raising her babies was out of the question. Oh, she knew she would need a nanny to help her, but not to replace her. Emma hugged herself. How in the world was she so blessed to find the perfect husband, who offered her the perfect life? She marveled at God's grace.

Chapter 32

Joseph Returns to Whitfield

THE WEDDING WAS FAST APPROACHING. Emma's parents and sister arrived, along with the Cousin-Montaubans and Richard DeBarge. *How ironic,* Emma mused; *the man who originally was to be her husband was attending her wedding to another man.* She observed that Annabelle and Richard had grown extremely close. It wouldn't surprise her if after her wedding, Annabelle would plan her own. Emma thought the general looked more tired and frail than the last time she saw him in Paris. Her family and the Cousin-Montauban party were staying at Whitfield. Guests of the Heads from London were at Whitehaven, and several of Emma's aunts, uncles, and cousins were staying there as well.

Commodore Joseph Head, looking splendid in his Navy blues, came home two days before the wedding. His face was tanned from the warm summer air, and his hair was bleached out from the bright sun. When he walked through the huge oak door at Whitfield Manor, Emma fell into his arms, laughing and crying all at once. The other members of the family waited to welcome him home until Emma let him go. Joseph's sense of humor lightened the mood. "Why, Mademoiselle Bouron, I think you have sorely missed me." Joseph's throaty laugh resonated in the huge hall. Emma was overjoyed, and the sound of the laugh she loved sent electric shocks through her body.

"Joseph, you were gone so long, and I have so much to tell you. I am so happy you are home. What was the mission like? How do you feel?" Jumbled questions kept pouring out. Then she stopped, realizing other members of the family hadn't had a chance to greet him, especially his mother. Emma felt selfish. She turned to his mother. "Catherine, I am so sorry I have dominated Joseph's homecoming. Please forgive me."

Catherine gave her son a tight hug and turned to Emma. "Nothing to forgive, dearest; he's soon to be your husband, so all this is natural." The rest of the family welcomed Joseph home. They went into the large family parlor, and David poured champagne all around to celebrate his son's return. Joseph was brought up to speed on what was happening on the manor and in the village. Then the conversation centered on the wedding preparations. Finally David turned the conversation to Joseph's voyage. Joseph answered briefly and did not elaborate on the deployment. David knew instinctively by his son's short cryptic answers that things were not good. He made a mental note to question Joseph as soon as they were alone. Catherine experienced the same feeling as her husband; something was amiss.

In the evening after the meal and brandy, Joseph and Emma escaped to the small parlor at the end of the wing where they became engaged. Joseph kissed her tenderly and stroked her face and hair. Emma looked deep in his blue eyes and saw a reflection of her love for him. Joseph's love was unconditional. She could literally see it in the way he looked at her.

The deployment was all-consuming and he'd had little time to think about Emma, but now, she was back in his arms again, and all the raw desire bubbled to the surface. His probing kisses ignited her desire immediately. She pulled him to the settee where they made love on the night of their betrothal. She straddled him and felt his hardness between her legs. Dear God, how she wanted him. Yet she forced herself away.

"Emma, what is it, darling?" Joseph was bewildered.

"While you were away, I decided I wanted us to wait until our wedding night to make love again." Emma appeared conflicted about her decision.

"I will respect your wish, of course. What brought this on, my little vixen?" She looked so serious Joseph hoped to lift her spirits with a little teasing.

"I've been going to St. Peter's quite often, and I realize I am not pure, Joseph, but I prayed if God brought you back safely, I wouldn't give myself to you until we were man and wife." Her eyes brimmed with tears.

"My darling, you are pure to me because I am the only man who has ever touched you. I understand your feelings, and I will wait as long as you like." He kissed her sweet lips gently. *I forget how young and impressionable she is, but that's one of the reasons I love her.* Then he tickled her and laughed. "I will be able to see you tomorrow, but not the day of the wedding. I think I can control myself that long."

"You won't see much of me tomorrow anyway. The dressmaker from House of Worth will be here for a final fitting, plus your mother and I plan to go over the last-minute preparations."

"I'll stay out of the way. Maybe Charles and I will hunt and leave you women alone. Temptation, temptation, oh it will be avoided." They both laughed.

Emma was relieved and disappointed all at the same time. She did miss him terribly, but being in the church before God, ordering the orange blossoms from the florist, and wearing a white gown made her determined to wait two more days. She hadn't seen him in over seven weeks; surely two more days wasn't the end of the earth.

The next day, Emma and Joseph saw each other briefly at breakfast. Emma's day was full. The cake arrived from the village. Emma didn't want a cake maker in Dover to bake the wedding cake. She learned the women in the village baked each other's cakes, so she asked them to bake hers. The request endeared her to them even more. They made a three-tiered fruitcake with white frosting embellished with pink marzipan roses. It wasn't professional, but Emma loved it because the Whitfield village women made it for her and Joseph. The servants buzzed around like bees, organizing the trip to the church, decorating the great dining room and ballroom at Whitfield Manor, and each doing specific tasks assigned by Catherine.

The dressmaker from Worth's, the younger son, Julien, arrived about noon. He had two assistants accompanying him and another woman who sewed any slight changes to the gown.

The fitting was in Emma's rooms in the family wing. The only other person she wanted with her was Jenny. She told Catherine and Maria she didn't want them to see her in the gown again until she walked down the aisle. Neither woman objected. One of the assistants would be doing their final fitting as well.

Julien unwrapped the gown from the thin tissue paper and shook it out. He hung it on the wardrobe door. Emma was so excited and nervous her hands perspired. Jenny danced around Emma, jumped up and down, and giggled constantly until Emma shushed her. The assistant brought in a wooden box for Emma to stand on like the one at the shop. Emma had stripped down to her corset and pantaloons. She felt shaky and exhilarated all at the same time. The gown was exquisite. She stepped into it slowly and Julien pulled it up. Emma put her arms through the lace sleeves, then Julien began to button the back with what seemed like a thousand small buttons. Emma didn't want a wedding dress popular at the time, much like Queen Victoria had worn to her wedding with Albert, a huge skirt with petticoats underneath and huge puffed sleeves. Emma was petite and felt the bulky style would swallow her. The gown she designed had a tight bodice with a modest décolletage, a flowing skirt with no petticoat, and tulip lace sleeves. The train was only six feet long, as St. Peter's wasn't a huge cathedral, but a small village church. Emma thought a long train would look ridiculously ostentatious in that setting.

Julien interrupted her thoughts. "Um, Mademoiselle Bouron, I cannot button these buttons at the waist."

Emma gave him a puzzled look. It fit fine four weeks earlier in Paris.

"I don't understand, monsieur."

"Well, um, since we designed and fit the gown, um, have you gained a little weight?" Julien was embarrassed. He knew how sensitive young women were regarding their weight.

Jenny stopped gliding around the room and looked directly at Emma. An unsettling feeling gripped her heart. "Miss Emma, step out of the gown, and I will check that I tightened the corset properly. Monsieur, may we have a moment of privacy? Phoebe will take you down for a cup of tea." Jenny smiled.

"Of course, madame; we will await your summons." Jenny ran from the room and burst into Phoebe's rooms. Phoebe was reclining on her bed napping.

"What in the world is it, Jenny?" Phoebe rubbed her eyes.

"I need your assistance. Would you mind taking the dressmakers down for tea and scones? I have put Miss Emma's corset on all wrong, and we need to get it adjusted."

Lord, the woman sounded like it was a major crisis, but Miss Emma's gown must be fit correctly. "I will be at Emma's rooms in a few moments, no worries, Jenny; Miss Emma must be perfect." Phoebe smiled sweetly.

The dressmaker and his assistant followed Phoebe to the morning room, where they were served tea, cucumber sandwiches, and scones. *Good break*, Julien thought.

When Jenny got back to the room, Emma was looking in the wardrobe mirror at her silhouette. She had shed the corset and pantaloons. She stood absolutely still, naked. Jenny saw instantly that Emma's eyes were riveted on a small but noticeable expansion of her waist. The air rushed from Jenny's lungs, making a whistling sound in the silent room. "Emma, dear child, when is the last time you had your monthly bleeding?"

"I don't know," Emma whispered.

"Try to think, my girl."

"It was before Joseph went to Turkey. I think it was about two weeks before he set sail."

"Now, Emma, you must be truthful with me. Did you have intimate liaisons with him after the one time?"

"Yes." Her answer was almost inaudible. The enormity of it hit her. Then she thought about her seasickness and other times she felt out of sorts, a bit nauseated but not ill.

"Dear God, Jenny, can this be happening?"

"Be calm." Jenny was figuring the weeks. Joseph was gone over seven, and Emma hadn't had her monthly time two weeks previous to his departure. Jenny sighed; she must be about nine weeks with child. There was just no other explanation. "Don't panic, dearest. I will pull the corset tighter, and Julien can let out the waist slightly."

"Won't he know? Won't it be obvious?" Emma sounded desperate.

"No. With all of the traveling, rich foods, and little time for exercise, some brides do gain a little weight. It is not unusual."

"Do you think any of the family or guests will notice?"

"Definitely not, Emma. You are still very tiny, and with the design of the dress, no one will be the wiser."

Emma still stood naked, stunned. "Oh, Jen, how will I tell Joseph?"

"Now you listen to me. You both want children, and I'm sure have discussed the matter. It is merely happening sooner than planned. I believe he'll be elated." Emma stared into space. Yes, Jenny was right: they wanted to start a family, but hadn't discussed when. She was so unworldly it never dawned on her that she was putting herself in a vulnerable position making love to Joseph over and over with no regard to any consequences. Birth control was not a topic of conversation in the Bouron household. She actually didn't know how pregnancy was prevented. She never thought about it. She followed her heart and her burning desire. "Emma, come to me." Jenny picked up the undergarments from the floor where Emma had thrown them. "Step into your pantaloons. Now pull on the corset, and I will pull the laces as tight as possible."

Emma whirled around to face Jenny and spoke the words for the first time. "Will it hurt the baby?" Jenny reassured her it would not. The baby, now spoken aloud, was real. She rubbed her hands over her stomach, the baby; Joseph's baby growing inside of her. Suddenly reality wrapped itself around her. She was going to have a baby!

"Listen to me, Emma; do not tell anyone until after the wedding." Jenny tugged on the laces and got the corset tighter. Emma felt like a trussed bird.

"Shouldn't I tell Joseph at least?"

"No, tell him after the wedding feast. It will be your wedding gift to him." *I am quite clever*, Jenny thought to herself. She hugged Emma to her. "You, my child, are going to be a mother, but be a bride first."

"Me, a mother." Emma was ecstatic. She would love this baby with her whole heart, and once she was married, she didn't care who knew she was expecting.

As if Jenny read her thoughts, she put her arm around Emma's shoulders and said quietly, "You and Joseph must keep this private until at least a month after the wedding."

"But why, Jen? I want to shout it from the rooftop now." Emma giggled.

"You don't want your parents and Joseph's parents to think you knew each other intimately before the marriage. Emma, you are still so naïve. Proper society would condemn you as a harlot." Jenny's stern tone brought Emma back to earth. Of course she was right. No one would understand the love she and Joseph shared. People would think her a tart, someone who trapped Joseph into marriage. She didn't want their child to have the slightest taint of scandal. Although she never thought about it before, many times an innocent baby is condemned for the sins of the parents. She wouldn't allow this to happen to her baby. Like an automatic mechanism, she brushed her hands across her belly. Jenny noticed the protective gesture and wondered what Emma was thinking.

"Another thing, Emma, you shouldn't drink alcohol while in this condition. Progressive doctors believe spirits may be harmful to an unborn babe." Oh God, the wedding. "Sip champagne when the toasts are given so no one notices, but avoid it as much as you can other than that."

Emma hugged Jenny tight. She thought how crafty and smart she was because she was right. She whispered to the woman she loved as a mother, "We are having a baby." Jenny laughed with joy.

Phoebe marched in with the dressmaker and assistant in tow. "Have you fixed that corset yet?" Rather a redundant question, as she could see Emma in her undergarments. She wondered what the two were laughing about when she came in the room, like there was a conspiracy brewing. Those two were inseparable, so close. Phoebe wondered why Mrs. Bouron wasn't with her daughter. Oh well, none of her business.

Phoebe was charmed by Emma's humility. She thanked Phoebe for her kindness and gave her a quick hug. Phoebe blushed. Most of the aristocratic ladies thought they were better than anyone else, especially servants. Catherine had never been like that; she would have a daughter-in-law with the same values. *Wonderful, just wonderful,* Phoebe mused. "It appears Jenny has the corset sorted out," Phoebe mumbled.

"Thank you for noticing. We laced it wrong before." Emma gave her a broad smile, then turned her charm on Julien. "I believe we are ready to resume the fitting; thank you so much for your patience." Once Emma was standing on the wooden box, she made small talk as Julien buttoned the gown. When his fingers approached her waist, she said offhandedly, "I am so annoyed. With all the traveling, bridal parties, and days full of wedding planning, I've eaten rich foods and haven't walked or rode Molly. Serves me right I've put on a bit of weight." She hoped she sounded casual and truthful.

"You would be surprised, mademoiselle, how many young women gain weight before the nuptials. We are accustomed to adjust either the waist or the hip areas of the gowns. It will be no problem at all to tailor the dress to look perfect." Julien smiled at Emma and winked at his assistant. What he didn't say was that most of the alterations occurred because the brides lost weight. *Oh well, the girl ate too many sweets or the commodore bedded her before marriage.* Either way, he didn't care. The Heads and other English aristocrats spent bundles of pounds sterling at the House of Worth. His father had a polished reputation for being discreet. If either of his sons or any of the assistants gossiped about the clients, they faced immediate dismissal, blood or not. He had an ironclad rule of never discussing the clientele. His policy was well-known in Paris and with the British aristocracy; it's what made them so comfortable in his shop and willing to pay not just for fine clothing, but also complete privacy. Many women told Charles Worth their deepest secrets. He was privy to tales of adultery, suicide, gambling, and financial plights—never to be repeated.

The morning of the wedding arrived. It was picture-perfect. The weather was sunny without a cloud in the sky and no rain in sight. The village was alive with anticipation. The men wore their best trousers and pressed linen shirts. The women were clad in their best Sunday dress, and many adorned their hair with flowers from the garden. As was the custom of mid-nineteenth century, the wedding took place in the morning, followed by a wedding breakfast. Then everyone rested, including the bride and groom, until the wedding celebration in the evening. The nighttime festivities were lively, with a banquet, musicians, and dancing. Bottles and bottles of champagne would be consumed, along with lager for those not keen on the sparkling wine.

Chapter 33

The Wedding

On her wedding day, Emma awoke early. Jenny brought them both a cup of tea and then began getting Emma ready for her special day. Both of the women were pleased Emma avoided any private time with Joseph for fear she would spill her joyful news. The next time she would see him would be at St. Peter's Church.

The church was full, from royalty to common village folks, from admirals to sailors, from French to English, a perfect eclectic mixture. Queen Victoria sent word to Catherine she wouldn't attend simply because her presence would detract from the bridal couple. She liked the Duke and Duchess of Kent very much and wouldn't upstage their son and his bride. Instead, young Princess Harriet arrived at the last minute to avoid any fuss, although the villagers stared in awe of a real princess.

Simple but elegant was the theme of Emma's wedding. A white carpet stretched down the middle aisle from the back of the church to the altar. The fair linens sewed by Constance and Rebecca covered the altar. Emma chose white lilies to decorate either side of the dais. No other flowers cluttered the stark old church. The sun glinted through the ancient stained glass windows, causing colors to dance across the stone floor by the kneeling bench. The pipe organ's melodic sounds filled the air. Joseph hadn't looked in the nave to see all the people waiting for him to wed; instead, he paced in the priest's robing room. Charles and General Cousin-Montauban, his attendants, teased him continuously, hoping to settle his nerves. Charles had always seen his brother calm and in complete control. This was out of character. He didn't blame him; if he'd been in his shoes, he'd do the same. He forced the corrupt thoughts away. This was his brother, whom he loved. He wanted him to be happy. For that matter, he wanted Emma to be happy. She was young and innocent and deserved to have the life of her dreams.

Father Payne stuck his head around the door. "Joseph, it's time to welcome your bride. Come along, gents; follow me."

Joseph and his attendants entered the main church through the sacristy. The organist played Handel's *Wedding March*. Joseph only vaguely saw the people in the pews, not even noting his father and mother. His eyes were glued to the rear church doors. It seemed like hours before the acolytes pulled the great doors open, and there she was arm in arm with her father. To say she looked angelic was an understatement. A tulle veil stationed in place with a wreath of orange blossoms covered her thick brunette hair. Joseph thought her gown was the most distinguished wedding dress he had ever seen. It wasn't huge with masses of petticoats underneath, but elegant, with a tight bodice and flowing skirt. The train was just the right length. Most captivating was the look on her face. Emma's cheeks were naturally rosy and her green eyes sparkled, but an air of peace about her mesmerized Joseph. When Edgar placed her hand in Joseph's and he looked in her eyes, he literally saw she was different. He wondered if it were that she would be his wife in a matter of minutes, but he didn't think so; it was something else entirely.

In a blur their vows were recited and the priest announced they were husband and wife. The cheers and applause rang out along with the church bells, but they sounded far away to Joseph. He couldn't take his eyes away from Emma. *She is the most beautiful bride God has ever created.* Joseph thanked God for bringing him the most perfect wife and partner he didn't imagine existed. The footmen flanked either side of the landau. It was decorated with white tulle and flowers, and the horses had floral blankets spread over their backs. The pungent scent floated through the air.

Joseph helped her into the carriage, and as they drove off, the villagers danced and cheered louder. Finally Joseph spoke. "My darling Emma, my wife, my love, you have made me the happiest man in the world." Joseph kissed Emma's wedding ring, and inexplicitly tears ran down his face. Emma was touched deeply. She took her lace hanky and patted his face. She wanted to pinch herself. Her marriage was real, her home was real, and her baby was real.

Emma was bathed in the morning sun smiling at her husband. "Joseph, you have made me a complete woman in every way. I never thought this kind of joy would be mine. I thank you for choosing me to be with you the rest of our lives." Emma looked at the fields still covered in the kaleidoscope of wildflowers. The manor house was getting larger as they approached. The air was fresh and clean. The cheers of the crowd faded in the distance, and the only sound was the clop-clop of the horses' hooves on the stones. She drank it all in and brushed her hand over her stomach. Soon, this would be the home for the three of them. She turned to Joseph and lightly kissed his lips. "I love you more than you'll ever know."

The wedding breakfast was a lovely affair. Catherine watched her son and his bride, Joseph so handsome in his dress naval uniform with all of his medals and pips, the gold epaulettes showing off his rank, and his gold and silver sword sheathed at his side. Emma, radiant in her couture gown, the orange blossoms complementing her porcelain complexion, and a look of total contentment on her face. After all the congratulations were said, the toasts given, and the food devoured, it was time for the rest before the evening festivities.

Joseph led Emma to his suite of rooms in the family wing. She hadn't been in them before her wedding day. Flowers were in vases everywhere, champagne was chilling in a silver ice bucket, and chocolates were in a large box on a table in front of his settee. Rose petals surrounded his huge bed. At the bottom of the bed on his blue satin coverlet was a white lace nightgown he bought for her in London. Joseph watched as Emma walked through the rooms touching everything. He was still mesmerized by her every movement. "Emma, come here." His voice was husky.

"Joseph, will you help me out of my gown?" She spoke just above a whisper.

"Darling, do you want me to call for Jenny to assist you?"

"No, I want my husband to help me." She smiled teasingly.

"All right; if I fumble with these buttons, no admonishments!" Emma hummed a little tune he thought was a child's song while he labored away undoing the damn buttons. He finally undid the last one. He was more than anxious to make love to her. "There you are, my sweet; now let me help you step out of it." She stood in front of him in her white silk pantaloons and matching corset.

"Will my husband unlace my corset, please?" She gave him a wicked little smile.

"I see. I am to be your chambermaid." Joseph laughed his throaty laugh that sent goose bumps up and down her arms. "I don't know how you women tolerate these things. They have to be terribly uncomfortable."

Emma giggled. "All for fashion, love." She let the corset drop to the floor. She slowly stepped out of her silk pantaloons.

He hadn't made love to her in so long her nakedness aroused him instantly. He tugged off his jacket, tie, and then shirt. He unbuttoned his trousers and let them fall in a heap as he kicked them off along with his shoes. Emma stood calmly facing him.

"Come to me, darling." His voice was husky.

She was in his arms holding him tight. "Joseph, remember in the landau on the way to Whitfield from the church, I thanked you for making me a complete woman."

"Yes, it was so sweet." He nuzzled her neck and stroked her hair.

She pushed him back and stared into his gorgeous blue eyes. "Today, my gift to you is I have made you a complete man."

"Emma, your becoming my wife made me a complete man. For that gift, I will be forever grateful."

She took both of his hands and placed them on her stomach. He was confused. He frowned from not understanding. Emma whispered in his ear, "Gently feel me where I guide your hands." He thought she would put them between her legs. God, he wanted her. Instead, she moved them over her belly, gently, lightly. He was hard; he was aroused, and thought maybe this was a new way of getting him to a fever point before he mounted her. Even though he hadn't made love to her for at least eight weeks, she felt different. He knew every inch of her body inside and out, and there was a slight fullness that wasn't there before. Emma whispered again, "Darling, my wedding present to you." She turned her head sideways and smiled.

He had literally been struck by lightning. He dropped his hands and stepped back. He stared at her stomach, then looked in her eyes. He knew! The gift was a child! Joseph dropped to his knees and kissed Emma's belly over and over. It tickled. Emma laughed with joy.

"How long have you known?"

"At my dress fitting yesterday, my dress wouldn't button. Oh, it's a long story." Emma giggled. "The only ones who know are me, Jenny, and now my husband."

"How far along are you?" Joseph was incredulous.

"Jenny and I calculated about nine weeks. I haven't had my monthly cycle since you've been at sea. Remember, I had it about two weeks before you deployed. I've counted, and we should have our baby in mid-March at the latest." Her excitement reverberated in the room.

It struck Joseph how bloody inconsiderate he'd been. He was so accustomed to using women for sex he took no precautions with Emma at all. Naturally he wanted children, but he hoped to take his bride abroad for a wedding trip. In addition, another deployment was on the horizon according to Admiral Smyth. After Joseph's exploratory expedition, the top naval brass sent a fleet to Turkey to help repel the Russian advancement. Joseph wasn't sure if his orders would send him back or if he'd take the_*Mercury* to the Afghan War for naval support in the Suez. He hadn't shared with anyone that a new mission was in the works, especially Emma. He wanted her to enjoy the wedding and the trip without worry. The admiral assured him he would have at least three weeks with his bride before the new deployment. It was the best he could promise. The Russians were causing havoc on two fronts, and Britain had to protect the imperial territories.

Emma stared at Joseph. She was crestfallen. She misinterpreted his silence for disappointment. She laid facedown on the bed trying to hide her tears. How could she have miscalculated his response to her news? Wasn't a baby, an heir, what they both wanted? Her sobs became audible in the quiet room.

The sound broke through Joseph's thoughts. *Dear God, she thinks I am upset.* He lay down next to her and rubbed her back. "Emma, my darling girl, I am thrilled we are having a baby. My surprise at the wonderful news startled me into silence." He kissed her ear and nuzzled her neck. "Don't cry. I love you so much, and now we will share our love and bond with a child." Joseph pulled her in his arms. He kissed her softly, but the feel of her body pricked his desire.

Emma pulled back. "Truly, Joseph, are you pleased? I thought you were when you kissed my belly, but you became so quiet and faraway."

"Your gift to me is the most wonderful present a man could receive." He took his thumb and wiped away her tears. She looked lovely. He understood her peaceful demeanor now. He kissed her again, only this time with unquenched passion. Her body responded to his touch, his kiss, and his whispers of love.

Once again she pulled back. "Is it safe for us to make love with our baby inside me?"

Joseph's voice was husky again, "Yes, darling; you are so innocent, not worldly in the least. You can make love to your husband close to the end of your term." With that reassurance, all of Emma's locked-up desire was unleashed. He was her husband, and they were free to do whatever they wanted to each other and as often as they wanted. She pulled him on top of her and wrapped her legs around his back. They began moving in unison. Joseph slowly entered her, but she needed more. Emma ground against him harder and harder and took him into her until her moans signaled fulfillment. Joseph lay still as she caught her breath. Her head was nestled in his shoulder. He stroked her hair and kissed her forehead. Emma sighed with contentment. Joseph knew exactly how to arouse her again, and this time he wouldn't contain himself. He rolled off her body so they were face–to-face. Staring in her eyes, he lightly traced the outline of her breasts, her hips, and her stomach. Slowly he traced round and round her nipples until they were hard and her breathing slightly quickened. He moved his hand between her legs and caressed her. Emma pushed against him, wanting him again. Joseph spread her legs and worked himself inside until her response drove him deeper and deeper until he lost control and filled her up. His whole body shuddered.

Emma wasn't finished. She demanded more. Her look and fervor excited him. He held her hips and moved her up and down. He felt her hard spot. He rubbed back and forth, gently, then with more pressure. Joseph looked in his wife's eyes and saw the look he knew so well. She was ready. He pumped her hard just a couple of times, and her scream rang out in his room. Emma fell back, totally satiated and exhausted. In a few minutes her breathing was even; she was asleep. Joseph watched her as she slept. He lightly touched her stomach; inside his baby was growing. God, she must be exhausted—the wedding preparations, the traveling, and all the while carrying his baby. Joseph drifted off to sleep thinking what a phenomenal woman he had married.

Catherine sent Phoebe to tell the bride and groom it was time for the evening festivities. She smiled thinking about the first time she and David made love between the wedding breakfast and the evening celebration. They were hungry for one another, but still awkward and shy. She laughed; that changed after a few weeks of practice. The thought crossed her mind that Joseph and Emma already knew each other's body well.

Phoebe listened at Master Joseph's door. No sounds came from within. They are probably sleeping after all the excitement of the wedding and the arduous task of greeting all the guests and well-wishers. She hated to knock, but they didn't have much time to get ready for the evening affair. Miss Emma would wear a different gown to the nighttime party. In fact, she didn't have a new dress made, but brought a gold and claret ball gown from her home. Phoebe hung the dress in Master Joseph's wardrobe along with some of her other garments and shoes. The rest of her belongings would be transferred to his rooms tomorrow. Phoebe knocked lightly at first, but when there was no answer, she knocked louder.

Mist rose from the sea in the dawn's morning light. The sound of cannons shooting balls toward the enemy broke the quiet calm of the day. Joseph stood on deck giving orders to fire. He heard the sound again and opened his eyes to see early evening shadows in his rooms at home. *I've been dreaming.* He rolled over; Emma slept peacefully on the huge bed. A knock came again. He got up, slipped into his dressing gown, and opened the door.

"Good evening, sir. Your mother sent me to tell you the evening wedding celebration will begin in an hour."

"Thank you, Phoebe. Have some tea and cake sent up, please. Oh, and tell Mother we will be down on time." Joseph laughed. *Mustn't breach decorum.* He closed the door and went back to the bed. He plopped down and Emma stirred. He licked her stomach with light little strokes until she awakened. Her laughter was the first sound he heard from his wife since her screams of ecstasy.

"Joseph, that tickles."

"I wanted to wake you with a smile on your face!" His throaty laugh echoed in the room.

"You are wicked, Joseph. You know I had a smile on my face when I fell asleep." She tweaked his arm.

"I thought you might. Just think, darling, I can put that smile on your face every day and every night." He covered her mouth with kisses, then probed with his tongue. Emma's reflex was immediate. She pulled his dressing gown open so their naked bodies touched.

Oh hell, getting ready would have to wait; he wanted her again. Her touch told him she wanted him as well. They worked themselves into a frenzy until both their sexual appetites were quenched.

The servant rapped on Master Joseph's door, but no one answered. He could hear muffled sounds from within and guessed they were having a tumble in the bed. He left the tray with tea and cake outside the door.

After their baths, Joseph remembered he'd ordered tea. He opened the door; the tray was there. The tea was cold, and it was too late to order more. "Darling, you must be famished. Let's dress quickly so we can go down and have tea and something to eat."

Emma giggled. "I am starving." She pointedly rubbed her hands across her belly.

Joseph smiled. "It won't do starving my child. Come on; let me help you into your gown." He watched his wife open the wardrobe and take out the gold ball gown. He had a lump in his throat. Emma was so unpretentious and sentimental she didn't buy a new gown, but chose to wear the one he designed for the Ambassador's Ball. It touched Joseph's heart.

Emma saw Joseph was pleased. She wanted to wear the gown again. It was special because he bought it for her. It was also that new style, with the corset built in the bodice. Bone stays were sown in the material, and the claret laces were on the outside of the gown. The cut accentuated her small waist. "Joseph, would you cinch up the laces?"

"I am not very good at this, my dear, but let me try." Joseph laughed.

Emma flipped her long tangled hair around. "This is your next project, to brush out this mess you have made of my hair." Joseph didn't laugh at her teasing. Her hair was the least of his problems; he couldn't cinch up the gown.

"I am only joking, Commodore Head; I can brush out my hair!" He was quiet. Emma did a half turn. "What's wrong, Joseph? I am only playing."

"Emma, I can't get the back of the gown to close properly." He winced.

"What do you mean? Are you lacing it properly?" His look told her volumes. "Oh, dear God, it's too small." She stammered, "I didn't think to try it on after I found out I was with child. It didn't cross my mind. What am I going to do, Joseph? Nothing I have will fit."

"What about the emerald gown you wore on the night of our betrothal?"

"No, it's as small as this gown." Emma was miserable, "We only have a short while before the party. Have one of the servants fetch Jenny; maybe she can think of something."

Joseph pulled the cord to the servants' level, and shortly the same boy that brought the tea tray arrived. He noticed it hadn't been touched. "Yes, commodore?"

"Vance, please go and find my wife's chambermaid and have her come hence. Oh, and send up another tea tray."

Jenny didn't expect Emma to summon her tonight. Something must be wrong. She scurried to Joseph's quarters. A lad with tea was arriving also. The door was open.

"Thank you, Vance; set the tea on the table," Joseph said.

"What's the matter, sir?" Jenny saw concern in Joseph's eyes.

"Your lady is in the bedroom, Jenny. We can't get her into her gown. I will bring in the tea and cake for you both. She needs to have a bite to eat, and for God's sake, find a solution to this problem." *So, she's told him about the baby, or why would he be so concerned about her eating?* She could see the champagne hadn't been opened either. Jenny opened the bedroom door. The huge bed was a rumpled mess, so Emma's condition hadn't dissuaded them from consummating the marriage. By the looks of the bed, it was consummated more than once. Emma was sitting in a chair staring at her.

"My dearest girl, you have been crying. Joseph is bringing in some tea and cake, which you are to eat while we sort out this problem with the gowns." Jenny's motherly tones made Emma feel better right away, and she was hungry. She did as she was told, like an obedient child. She watched Jenny lay out the gold gown on the mass of tangled sheets and coverlets. "I am going to your other room and get the emerald gown. I will be right back."

Joseph was sipping some brandy when Jenny left to get the other gown. He needed to get dressed himself. He wasn't wearing a uniform tonight; instead, he had a black evening suit made by Henry Poole & Company from Saville Row in London. They had a contract for all of the naval military dress uniforms. Their civilian clothes were exquisitely tailored, reflected by the hefty price tag. He wondered if it would make Emma feel better or worse if he got ready. He ended up just sitting sipping the brandy.

Jenny returned quickly. "You best get ready, sir, in your dressing room so as soon as I have your wife ready, you may go downstairs."

"I ate a piece of cake, Jen, and just about drank my tea," Emma said.

"There's a good girl." Jenny hugged her close. "We can't have you poorly, can we then? Let's see what can be done about these gowns. Step into the gold one, love." Jenny pulled it up, and as much as she tried, with the built-in corset, she couldn't get it closed. Next, they tried the emerald dress. Jenny cinched Emma in tight, but still the dress did not fit properly.

Emma looked utterly defeated. Jenny spotted Emma's wedding gown in a pile on the floor. She picked it up and shook it out. "Get back into your wedding gown."

"But, Jen . . ."

"No buts; I have an idea." Emma stepped back into the dress. Jenny sent Joseph off to get some pins and needle and thread. Once Joseph returned, Jenny worked her magic. She took the train and made it the same length as the gown by bustling the fabric in ruffles down the back. She sewed it into place with Joseph helping by holding the material in place. She twirled Emma around and made tiny slits in the fabric on the shoulders and pulled them down for an off-shoulder look. She shooed Joseph away while she groomed Emma's hair.

Jenny brushed Emma's hair until it shone. She sent one of the servants to bring all of Emma's belongings to her husband's rooms. Emma had a box for her hair ornaments, and Jenny found the diamond hairpins. She twisted Emma's long brunette hair into a loose chignon held in place by the sparkling diamond pins. With the hot iron she curled several ringlets down the back of her neck and let the tendrils naturally frame her face. Emma looked stunning. Her bridal gown was transformed. Joseph was amazed at Jenny's ingenuity, and he thought of a way to finish off the look perfectly.

Once again, Joseph rang for the servants. He told Vance to bring his mother to his rooms.

Catherine arrived with curiosity stamped across her face. "What is it, Joseph? If you and Emma don't hurry, you will miss being in the receiving line." Catherine looked around. "Where is Emma?"

"She's in the dressing room with Jenny. Mother, I have a request."

"You sound so serious, Joseph. What in the world is it?" Catherine was perplexed.

"I would be honored if you would allow Emma to wear Great Grandmother's diamond and emerald necklace. I think it fitting that the first night as the future Duchess of Kent, she wear one of the masterpieces of the Kent jewels."

"Son, you continue to amaze me. I will say it again. Who would have thought you to be such a hopeless romantic?" Catherine laughed out loud. "In all sincerity, I am the one who will be honored, and I know your father will be thrilled. I'll send for the necklace right away." Catherine stood and hugged her son. She had never seen him so happy, nor for that matter, so handsome. He looked dashing in the fine black evening suit with a white silk shirt. He was tanned from his voyage, and his loose blond hair framed his aristocratic face. He was a stately figure overflowing with happiness and joy. He had chosen a wonderful wife, mother someday, and future duchess.

Joseph knocked lightly on the dressing room door. "May I come in?"

"Yes, come in, come in," Jenny called.

His bride, his wife, his lover looked lovely. He turned her toward the mirror. Standing behind her, he put the heavy necklace around her neck and clasped the hasp. Emma and Jenny both gasped at the same time.

Joseph laughed. "My duchess, this is one piece of the Kent jewels that are worn on special or state occasions. This necklace belonged to my great grandmother. I believe tonight is a special, the most special occasion, and you should wear it. Plus, my darling, it looks lovely with your eyes and your wedding ring."

Emma was speechless, and for once so was Jenny. The necklace must have two hundred diamonds forming flowers, with three large teardrop emeralds in the middle. In the waning light, her neck glittered and her hair was alight. Emma spontaneously kissed Jenny's cheeks and Joseph's lips. "How can I thank you both? Together you have taken a disastrous situation and turned it into pure joy."

Jenny's eyes brimmed. "Go on now, the both of you. Make a memorable entrance."

All eyes were glued to the great staircase as Joseph and Emma descended. Catherine and David, along with Edgar and Maria, stepped forward. Edgar's pride was tangible. Seeing his daughter dressed so elegantly adorned by priceless jewels made him feel important. After all, he was her father and now linked with British royalty; it was more than he ever dreamed. Joseph bowed and kissed his mother-in-law's gloved hand. Maria, her eyes filled with tears, hugged her daughter. Emma looked like a princess. This insecure girl who moped around the house for two years was like a butterfly emerged from its cocoon. "Dearest Emma, you look magnificent."

Actually, Emma was surprised by her mother's emotion. Normally she was aloof or in control where her children were concerned. Emma smiled. Her sister was the exact opposite. She skipped around Whitfield without a care in the world. She openly showed Emma her deep affection toward her and how much she admired her new husband. Claudine enjoyed every minute to the fullest.

Catherine was so loving and warm; she hugged her son and kissed his bride. They looked like the perfect couple, clipped out of a magazine, Joseph so elegant in his evening attire and Emma gorgeous in her transformed wedding gown. The prisms of the jewels around her neck sparkled in the light from the chandeliers in the great hall. David welled up with joy and relief. His barony was now secure with his elder son married and sure to have a family. Emma would prove to be a perfect wife for Joseph. Just like Catherine was for him, never overshadowing the duke but always the correct partner.

"How clever you are, Emma, to revamp your wedding gown into the perfect evening apparel for tonight's festivities." Catherine gave her a huge smile. *It was quite ingenious*, Catherine thought. Little did she know it would become the fashion norm in the future.

Emma blushed. "The dress is so lovely we thought it a shame to wear it just in the morning. With a little adjustment, it became just what I wanted for our wedding feast."

The way she looked up at Joseph, showing they planned it together, gave Catherine a surge of joy. "I think it's brilliant, and I am sure you will start a new trend in fashion!" Catherine hugged Emma tight and whispered, "The necklace is the perfect accent for your gown."

Greeting the guests in the receiving line was fun for Joseph and Emma. There were so many oohs and ahs over Emma's gown, she silently thanked Jenny over and over. The only unpleasant moment was a veiled compliment from Constance as she smiled and spoke just loud enough for only Emma to hear. "Isn't it lovely that just hours after being wed, you are wearing the Kent jewels?" Her sugary smile unnerved Emma.

"What do you mean? It wasn't my idea, but my husband's." God, why was she explaining herself? She didn't have to explain or rectify her actions to Constance. It made her feel ridiculous. She wished she could take back what she'd said.

Charles wondered what Constance said to Emma because for an instant she looked bewildered. He didn't understand women and their interactions with one another. Constance had been hanging all over him all day except for the rest period. She did look splendid, but in an experienced way, not innocent like Emma, who radiated from within. He still hadn't touched Constance intimately since their first encounter, but Charles felt like she put a stamp of ownership on him. If he could just take it all back—the feelings for Emma, rushing into an unwanted courtship, deflowering Constance, and a promise to Joseph he would watch over Emma in his absence; everything was so damn complicated. A couple months ago, he was an easygoing farmer. He hated being embroiled in deceit and lies. It simply was not part of his nature.

The remainder of the wedding celebration went smoothly, and the bridal couple and all the guests thoroughly enjoyed the evening. Emma did get quite tired after the traditional waltzes with her father and her husband. It had been a long day with emotional highs and lows. She asked Joseph when it was socially acceptable for them to depart for their rooms. He was surprised, but when he looked at her carefully, he noticed she was exhausted and pale.

"Darling, you look tired. Do you feel all right?"

"Yes, just tired."

Joseph noticed she brushed her hand across her abdomen. It struck him her condition made her tired. He kissed her cheek, then held up his hand to the orchestra. They stopped playing. With his arm around Emma's waist, Joseph directed her to the center of the ballroom floor. "Dear family and friends, we have had a very long day beginning at sunup. My bride and I thank you all for sharing in our happiest occasion, but we are ready to say good night." Whistles and catcalls were heard throughout the ballroom, especially from some of the drunken villagers; Emma blushed with embarrassment. Joseph laughed. "We have a long journey tomorrow as we depart for Italy on the early train." With that he cupped Emma's elbow and led her through the raucous crowd. They stopped to kiss their parents and attendants good night, and then headed to Joseph's rooms. Halfway up the grand staircase, Emma could taste the fruitcake, which made her nauseous.

"Joseph, I think I am going to be sick." He took one look at her; her face had a green pallor and her hands had begun to perspire. He quickly picked her up and took the remaining stairs by twos. He literally ran down the family wing until he got her in the bathroom in his quarters. It was just in time. Emma vomited over and over. When he thought she couldn't have one thing left in her system, he laid her on the bed and put a cold cloth on her forehead. He strode to the bellpull to signal one of the servants to his room. Quickly he moved back to Emma. Her eyes were closed. She looked white as a ghost. *Oh God,* Joseph thought, *the morning sickness has come upon her, never mind that it's night.* He sent the lad who answered his call to get Jenny, who had already retired from the festivities.

When she arrived at Joseph's rooms, she saw Emma stretched out on the bed still in her gown and shoes and Joseph pacing back and forth. "What happened to Emma?" Jenny whispered.

Joseph cleared his throat. "I am aware that Emma has told you we are expecting a baby." Jenny cringed with embarrassment. These topics were just not discussed in proper society. Joseph took her hand gently. "I realize you are the true mother in Emma's life, so please put all things aside for her sake." Jenny nodded. "She has been violently ill, regurgitating all of the food in her stomach. She has fallen asleep from pure exhaustion. Will you help me get her undressed and into bed and render any remedies that helped her as a child from a bout with stomach sickness?"

"Yes, sir, let me go to her." Jenny carefully removed Emma's shoes before awakening her. "Emma, my girl, open your eyes; wake up."

Emma stirred. "Don't move quickly about. Your husband and I are going to undress you, put you into bed, and give you hot tea with honey to soothe your tummy." Emma nodded. Between the two of them, they were able to get her out of her clothes and into her silk nightgown. Joseph pulled back the blue coverlet, stacked four pillows, and then with Jenny's help got her comfortably into bed. He rang the bell lever again and sent the servant for tea and honey. Once Emma got down a few sips of the sweet hot liquid, the color began to come back to her cheeks.

"Oh, I am so sorry." She looked from one to the other. "The waves of sickness came over me so suddenly I almost didn't make it to the confines of our rooms." Emma looked directly at Joseph. "Dearest Joseph, what would I have done without you?" Her voice cracked with gratitude. "Jen, thank you for helping Joseph." Jenny squeezed her hand.

"I will leave you now, my girl; you are in good hands with your husband." Jenny had a much kinder opinion toward Joseph since she saw how he cared for Emma no matter what the circumstances, the debacle with the gown and now the childbearing sickness. Joseph walked her to the door, then impulsively hugged her. She blushed crimson and smiled.

Emma was propped up on the stack of pillows; she finished the soothing tea. Her thick hair was draped behind her, with the loose tendrils wet on her face. Joseph changed into his lounging pajamas and lay next to her on the bed. "Emma, darling, I don't want to upset you on our wedding night, but I don't think it wise for us to travel abroad with you suffering from morning sickness." Her reaction caught Joseph completely off guard. Emma threw her arms around him crying and laughing all at the same time.

"Oh, Joseph, I didn't want to leave Whitfield. It's not that I am unappreciative of having a wedding trip in Italy, but our baby is more important." Emma laughed. "Why, I would be vomiting all over the continent."

"You never cease to amaze me. Here I was worried I would disappoint my wife, but instead, you are glad." He held her tenderly. "How can one man be so lucky?"

Emma sat straight up in bed. "What excuse are we going to give everyone?"

Joseph considered her question for a moment, then answered, "I will blame it on myself. I'll say I'm worn out from the sea voyage to Turkey and then with the activities of our wedding. We talked it over and decided with the delightful weather and relaxed atmosphere at home, we would enjoy time here on the estate."

"What a brilliant idea." Emma threw back her head and laughed.

The color fully returned to her cheeks and her eyes were bright once again. Joseph couldn't help but laugh as well. They were like two conspirators in a devious plot. They snuggled under the coverlets and both fell into a contented sleep.

The revelry continued long after Joseph and Emma retired. The orchestra played on, champagne was drunk and beer guzzled, the dancing became more uninhibited, and flirtations were carried on between celebrants young and old.

Richard and Annabelle snuck away into the gardens with a blanket from his room and a bottle of fine French wine. Richard showered her with so many compliments it made her light-headed, like a schoolgirl with her first crush. They kissed and explored one another, but Annabelle never let it get too far out of control. Richard wanted her but didn't push the situation. He noticed that the old general had drastically slowed down in the last few months. His energy was depleted easily. In fact, Annabelle feared her father might not be able to make the trip to Kent, but in the end, he made a huge effort and came. Richard planned to ask for Annabelle's hand in marriage when they returned to Paris. He needed to marry her before the general's life was over if he wanted to inherit the estate. He wondered what Emma told her family, because they all acted as if they had never laid eyes on him before. Even skittish Claudine kept her mouth shut. It was working out perfectly.

Both sets of parents were worn out by the time the last guests departed. All agreed the wedding, the breakfast, and the evening feast and ball were successful. They bid one another good night and retired.

Charles returned from accompanying Constance home and sat in the morning room with a bottle of whiskey. He drank until he passed out cold on the settee.

Chapter 34

Change of Plans

When dawn broke, as directed by Joseph, Vance awakened the bride and groom. They were scheduled to depart for the train station at seven o'clock to catch the early train to London and on to Rome. Joseph opened the door bleary-eyed and still in his pajamas. Vance felt uncomfortable. "Um, sir, you asked to be awakened at daybreak for the wedding trip." He shuffled his feet back and forth.

"It's all right, Vance. Please send word to the conductor we shall not be going."

The boy was confused. "But it's your wedding trip, sir."

"I know, but we have decided to stay at Whitfield. Oh, and have Phoebe tell my mother as well when the Duchess gets up." Joseph closed the door, and Vance stood there wondering what in the world went wrong. He put his ear to the door thinking he might hear the master and his new wife having a go, but all he heard was muffled retching sounds.

Emma got out of bed to put her dressing gown on when Joseph went to answer the bedroom door. The minute her feet hit the floor, she was nauseous and sick all over again, only this time the only thing to throw up was the tea from last night. Joseph was at a loss. He didn't know what to do to help. He ran back to the door hoping to catch Vance before he went down the stairs. He was at the end of the corridor. "Vance, before you go down, will you get my wife's chambermaid, please."

"Yes, sir." *That's odd,* Vance thought; *he had me running after the maid last night. Well, something's in the works.*

Jenny saw the same sight as the night before when she got to Joseph's rooms. Emma, pale as a ghost, propped up on pillows with a cold cloth on her brow. "Sick again, my girl?"

Emma just nodded. She was miserable. This morning sickness was worse than a rough sea crossing from Calais to Dover. Here it was her first morning as Joseph's wife, and she was wretched. Jenny sat down on the side of the bed. "Did it hit you when you got out of bed?" Emma nodded again. "Some women eat dry toast before they get up to settle the stomach. I think you need to try it, Emma." She nodded yes. Jenny turned to Joseph. She looked at him very seriously. "You must mask this by ordering up a full breakfast each morning so as not to arouse suspicion. Just be sure to order plain toast and tea with honey. Let's give it a try."

"Thank you, Jen," Emma managed to respond weakly. "How long will this last?"

"Sometimes a few days, sometimes a few weeks, but you'll get through it." She didn't add that some women were sick the whole term.

Joseph ordered eggs, bacon, fruit, tea, and toast. He sent a note to his mother asking her to come by his rooms at her leisure. Of course, Catherine was surprised her son canceled their honeymoon trip. It was so unlike him, especially since Emma was so looking forward to the trip. The minute she finished breakfast, she was going to see Joseph. In the meantime, she had the butler and one of the other servants haul Charles up to his rooms. Apparently when he returned from Whitehaven, he'd gotten dead-drunk in the morning room, where Catherine found him this morning. The whole household was upside down, Joseph not going abroad, Charles in a stupor.

After eating the dry toast and drinking the hot tea, Emma felt better. "Joseph, I am going to bathe and dress in a light cotton day dress. My day dresses shouldn't be binding, because unlike evening dresses or gowns, there are no stays or laces. My condition won't show."

In some ways, Joseph thought, *she's like a child herself. She is shy and demure, not wanting to put a blot on their reputation, so concerned about social convention. Yet making love, she's wild and passionate, letting go with complete abandonment.* He thought about yesterday's lovemaking. He wondered if she felt well enough to . . .

"Joseph, what do you think about my dresses?"

"I wasn't thinking about your dresses, love, but about you being undressed." He laughed his throaty laugh. "Shall I help you get dressed?"

Emma felt the butterflies that Joseph released in her body. She lay back on the bed. "Would you help me out of my nightgown?" She looked up at him with pure innocence. Joseph laughed again. She raised her arms above her head. He pulled the nightgown off. She was naked.

"Are you sure you feel well enough to . . ."

"Shush." She put her finger to his lips. "Kiss me and let's see how I feel." As she was sinking into the black hole of desire, somewhere in the distance she wondered how she could be sick one minute and craving his body the next minute. She didn't want to analyze it now; she wanted to feel her Joseph, her husband, inside her body. Their lovemaking was at first slow and sensual, then harder and harder until they climaxed together. Emma pulled Joseph in deep over and over, letting her body override her mind. They were so totally enraptured neither one heard the knocking at the door.

When no answer came, Catherine knew they were making love. Only that would block out the sound of her firm knock at the door. She sighed. Well, that wasn't a problem, so maybe canceling the trip was for another reason, but she knew it wasn't exhaustion.

Emma felt much better after a bath. She and Joseph went down to the morning room hand in hand. Catherine was very predictable. She enjoyed having her midmorning tea in this particular room as it gave her a lovely view of the gardens. Joseph was certain they would find his mother there, and he was right. She greeted them with warmth and affection. It wasn't difficult to see the love between Joseph and Emma.

Catherine was not a woman who beat around the bush; hers was a straightforward approach to life. She got right to the point. "Why have you canceled your wedding trip, Joseph?"

"Actually, Mother, the thought of traveling after being gone for so long is not appealing. If you and Father approve, we would like to spend some quiet time at Whitfield. The weather is glorious this time of year. Also, it will give Emma and I an opportunity to meet with our architect. You know we will make some improvements to my quarters and redecorate so it's not so masculine." Joseph chuckled.

His mother looked questioningly at Emma. "Is this decision yours as well?"

"Yes, we started to pack last night, and neither one of us could get organized or enthused. Joseph has been gone, and I have been between Whitfield, Paris, and Calais and back to Whitfield, as you know because we traveled together. It seemed silly to travel for the sake of traveling when everything we both love is right here at Whitfield." *God, I have become such a good liar.*

There was a trace of insincerity in Emma's voice Catherine hadn't heard before. The girl was always so open. She didn't fully accept her son's explanation either. "You know Father and I will thoroughly enjoy having you here at home, especially since you have chosen Whitfield as your primary residence."

"Thank you, Mother."

"No thanks needed, Joseph. Whitfield is your home." She turned to Emma. "David and I will love having you reside here, dear girl.

"On another topic, the guests will be departing today. Do you two wish to bid them good-bye?"

Emma spoke adamantly. "Absolutely not. We said our adieus last night, and neither of us wants a string of questions regarding the canceled trip, or should I say, postponed wedding trip."

Catherine laughed. "Stay out of sight until after lunch or you'll be caught. Are you riding on this beautiful day?" She noticed a quick look dart between them.

"No, Mother, we are going to have a peaceful walkabout. The carriages will be in use taking the guests to their departure points. We don't want to take a chance saddling up at the stables." Joseph laughed. "A long walk in the fresh air will do us both good.

"Regarding another matter, Emma has not told her parents we have decided to live at Whitfield. It's not that we want to deceive them, but to avoid an argument, we both felt it would be better to inform them after we married." Catherine thought that a wise choice. She imagined the Bourons wanted Emma in France, where they might have greater influence over her. She couldn't exactly put her finger on it, but Emma's relationship with her mother was odd, distant.

"What about the chambermaid, Jenny?" In unison Joseph and Emma declared, "She's staying at Whitfield." They looked at each other and laughed.

"Already you two sound like a seasoned married couple!" Catherine saw the openness in their relationship. She was so happy for her son, who at thirty-five finally found his soul mate. Emma was a perfect match for her son. There wasn't one thing she disliked about her. Catherine took Emma's hands in hers. "I am so happy to have a daughter, my dear. I have had these bawdy sons for thirty-some years and am ready for some female camaraderie in the family. You are a Head now and part of this family."

Emma choked down her tears. It was difficult to absorb the unconditional love Joseph's parents gave freely. She didn't have to measure up to some invisible standard; they loved her for herself. It was the kind of love she craved as a child from her own mother. Since she didn't get it, she transferred those feelings to Jenny. She didn't blame her parents for abandoning her emotionally. Edgar was busy working and trying to cope with Maria's mental breakdown. The dark depression that secluded Maria from the world wasn't her fault either. The fact remained, it scarred Emma. Her vulnerability guided her to insecurity and to a life of personal self-doubt. Then Joseph magically appeared and changed everything. She looked at Catherine with gratitude. "No, I am the one who is happy."

Catherine kissed Emma's cheeks. "Since all is settled, off with you both. We will see you after tea or at dinner. Have a lovely day."

Joseph hugged his mother and whispered, "Thank you, Mother. All of this means so much to me."

The following weeks proved idyllic for Joseph and Emma. Between bouts of morning sickness, they took long walks on the estate, picnicked outdoors, read books to each other, planned the renovations of the five rooms that made up Joseph's part of the family wing and two rooms close by for Jenny, and made love day and night. Sometimes they dined with the family, but often they dined alone in their rooms in case Emma became ill after eating.

The only unpleasantness that occurred was between Emma and her parents once she told them she was staying in England and Jenny was staying with her. Maria wrote letters imploring her to come back to her birthplace and rightful home. Some of the letters tried to persuade her through cajoling and sweet persuasion; others were icy, pointing out Emma's selfishness to leave her family, especially her sister. These latter letters caused Emma pain and lured her into questioning her decision. Then letters of encouragement from Claudine, who was thriving at the Toy Depot and only wanted Emma to be happy, would lift her mood. Claudine's only regret was the loss of Jenny, but she always knew her sister needed the chambermaid more than she did.

Joseph was relaxed and happy. His deployment was postponed while the Great Powers watched as Serbia and Montenegro joined other Balkan rebels against the crumbling Ottoman Empire. Admiral Smyth sent word that the Russians enticed Austria into neutrality. The British government feared this shift gave the Russians another theater to rage war on the Turks. Joseph was commanded to sit tight while upper-echelon naval personnel decided where his expertise would be best utilized. Bosnia and Herzegovina were on the brink of declaring independence. When all the pieces fell in place, Joseph would be recalled to duty.

In the meantime, Joseph and Emma's bond became deeper and stronger. They reveled in each other's company, shutting out the world around them. As time passed, slowly Emma's sickness subsided. She was in her fourteenth week, and they couldn't hide it much longer. Joseph suspected his mother already knew. His brother left two days after the wedding to stay at the apartment in Paris, so he would be unaware. David was busy with the manor business and laws coming before Parliament in the fall session; consequently, unless Catherine mentioned her suspicions to him, he wouldn't notice subtle changes in his daughter-in-law's countenance.

Emma had fewer and fewer clothes to wear without her pregnancy showing. Jenny altered and restitched as many dresses as she could. When alone in their rooms, Emma could slip on a nightgown and be completely comfortable. Joseph marveled at the way his wife's body was changing. He loved to lie in bed with her after making love and stroke her stomach. Often he would daydream about the baby: Was it a boy or a girl, would the child look like him or Emma, would he or she have dark hair and green eyes or blond hair and blue eyes? He prayed he would be home for the baby's birth for many reasons. First and foremost, he did not want Emma to go though having the baby without his support, and he desperately wanted to see his child.

They bantered about girls' names back and forth, because if it were a boy, the name was Joseph without question. In fact, they settled on Joseph David Adolphus. For a girl, Emma liked Eugenie, named after Napoleon III's wife. Joseph liked Roselyn, after the flower. After much discussion and laughter, they settled on Eugenie Roselyn.

During the middle of September, the rains came. The sun went on holiday while the rain came for a long visit. The dreary weather kept everyone indoors except Charles. He had returned from Paris and worked outdoors, rain or shine. David was preparing to go to London to the House of Lords in Parliament. Catherine was always busy with one project or another. The architect was drawing up the final plans for the renovated rooms for Joseph and Emma. Life at Whitfield was perfect.

One evening after a quiet dinner Joseph, Emma, and Catherine shared in the family dining room, Catherine thought it an ideal opportunity to diplomatically broach the subject of her daughter-in-law's health. "Emma, you had such a poor appetite for several weeks after the wedding, but you appear to be enjoying your food again." Emma looked at Joseph, then lowered her eyes. Joseph didn't want to play a cat-and-mouse game; he decided to tell their news to his mother outright.

"Mother, Emma and I have been waiting until we were sure before we told anyone, but you will be the first." Joseph smiled so broadly Catherine thought his teeth would drop out of his mouth. "You are going to be a grandmother." He beamed and Emma literally glowed.

Catherine touched Joseph's hand and Emma's cheek, and then she burst out laughing. "Joseph Head, I have known for a long time. What with the servants gossiping, Emma's dresses being let out, her loss of appetite, then sequestering yourselves in your rooms. I suspected when you canceled your much-anticipated wedding trip." Her eyes sparkled. "Don't you know I can see right through you?" She shook her head and laughed some more. "At your own wedding, your bride took maybe two sips of champagne, and you left the ball early in the evening. Only a mother notices those types of things."

"You, Mother, are incorrigible." Joseph joined in her laughter. Emma sat silent, with a stricken look on her face.

Catherine didn't understand. "Emma, I am thrilled, and David will be over the moon; why so sad?" Joseph put his arm around her protectively.

"What must you think of me?" Emma's lips quivered.

"Dear girl, do you think I am so old I have forgotten the mind is taken over by the desires of the body and the heart? I realize you are young and swept off your feet by my mature handsome son. If anyone is to blame, it is Joseph, who is very familiar with the ways of the world." She took Emma's hand. "I cannot think of better news than this." Catherine spoke deliberately. "Babies are born prematurely all the time. When you give birth, we will simply say the babe came early."

"We have discussed that exact scenario. It's not unusual for women to be confined to the house before an impending birth. Actually, the only family members who will be aware are Father and Charles. The servants might gossip among themselves, but they wouldn't dream of being disloyal to our family. The village midwife's family has lived on the land for generations, so I doubt seriously she would divulge any information or gossip for that matter."

Joseph smiled at Emma, who appeared confused by the patchwork of deceit being created, but she realized it had to be done to protect the whole family. "Emma darling, it will all be all right because in the end, our child will arrive with no stain on his or her reputation." Joseph kissed her sincerely. Emma silently prayed all their plans would go as expected.

Chapter 35

Unwelcome News

The drizzling rain let up finally, and Joseph and Emma were able to get outdoors. They wandered through the pastures and meadows, which were bright green from all the rain. Life returned to perfection for Emma. David and Charles were both ecstatic about the baby. Catherine went into Dover and bought different yards of fabric so Jenny could make Emma some suitable clothes. The architect produced final drawings for approval. Life was blessed and full. Emma sketched toy prototypes and sent her sketches to Claudine, who made a smooth transition from Emma's position of chief designer to making it her own.

Emma loved Whitfield and at every opportunity explored the countryside with Joseph. On this beautiful late September day, they decided to take a ride in the landau to town. Emma enjoyed riding by the cliffs and listening to the waves against the rocks below. She was excited to get a chance to go to town. She chattered to Joseph about the upholstery fabric she had chosen with Catherine's help for the furniture in their bedroom parlor. He was listening closely when the footman pulled up the harnesses on the horses. Joseph saw another carriage from the corner of his eye. They hadn't yet gone through the gate. The carriage was on Whitfield land. "What is it, Joseph?"

"Another carriage is coming."

"I didn't know we were expecting guests."

"No, Mother didn't mention it." Joseph's heart beat faster the closer the carriage approached. His heart dropped when he saw the naval crest emblazoned on the brougham door.

He jumped down from the landau. Breton got out of the other carriage. "Hello, Commodore Head." Joseph knew from his tone the visit was serious.

"Good day, Breton. What brings you to Whitfield?"

Emma strained to hear what they were saying. She recognized the young lieutenant from when he was at the embassy in Calais. He and Joseph walked toward the other carriage out of earshot.

"Sir, I bring news and your deployment orders."

Joseph was attentive as Breton apprised him of the current situation with the Russian advancements. He related how they were marching through Austria, picking up soldiers from Ottoman territory for enlistment in the Russian cause. The fleet that was sent to the Bosporus after Joseph's first deployment, needed supplies and troop transport. Admiral Smyth was sending the *Mercury* with Joseph at the helm back to Turkey, along with other navy steamers. Joseph expressed surprise, as he calculated he would be sent to the Suez for support along the Afghan border. It would have been a safer assignment. Safety had not crossed his mind before he was married and expecting a child. He was usually exhilarated by the thought of being at sea doing what he loved. But his life had changed, and what he loved was sitting in the landau behind him. "Do you know when I depart?"

"Yes, sir, I am on deployment with you. We leave London in three days." Breton reached into the brougham, retrieved the packet of deployment documents, handed them to his superior, and saluted.

"Have the driver follow the lane and you will come to the house. Ask for the Duchess of Kent. Tell her you have spoken to me, and I asked that you and the driver be served lunch. Do not tell her what you have delivered. Thank you, Breton. I'll be there shortly."

Joseph hid his disappointment from Emma. He knew this meant he wouldn't be home for the birth of the baby. He must appear nonchalant about his assignment. He took a deep breath and blew it out slowly.

He glanced at Emma sitting in the landau. He saw instantly she was petrified.

"What is it, Joseph, what did he want? What are those papers?" Emma screeched with desperation.

"Emma, I want you to be calm. Think of our baby." He smiled and patted her growing stomach. "We knew I would be deployed again with the Russians causing trouble in Turkey and with other states in the Ottoman Empire. We discussed it. Remember, I wasn't sure how long I would have before my orders arrived." No matter how reassuring he sounded, tears streamed down her face. He took out his handkerchief and wiped her eyes. Emma was inconsolable. When they got back to the manor, Joseph took her straight to their rooms and fetched Jenny. Life was about to be anything but perfect.

Emma lay on the bed with her eyes closed. Jenny drew the curtains around the massive bed and the windows. Her sobs racked her body into exhaustion, but she couldn't sleep. Joseph would be leaving for London in two days, two days! The thought of his absence made her physically ill. *How can I give birth to our baby without him with me? I need him.* She felt the blue silk coverlet. *It will be unbearably lonely without him. What will fill my days? He is my breath, my love, my confidant, and my friend. He is everything to me.* The tears started again as she pictured life on the manor without him. Their rooms would be devoid of their laughter, their conversations, their private meals, their lovemaking. The emptiness gripped her soul.

The first thing Joseph did after he got Emma into bed was hunt for Charles. He rode the stallion hard up and down the hills and through the pastures until he found his brother with one of the herds of sheep. Charles looked surprised as his brother galloped toward him at full speed. It flashed across his mind that something had happened to Emma or the baby. As soon as Joseph's face was visible, he knew things were terribly wrong.

"What is it, Joseph? I can see you are distraught."

Joseph dismounted in a flash. "Charles, it is simple. I received orders to deploy for Turkey. I leave London in three days. I will leave

Whitfield day after tomorrow to meet up with my crew, then take the rail to Southampton, where my ship, *Mercury*, is docked."

"This is sudden." Charles was so surprised.

"Not really. I was aware the Russians riled up the Balkan states and forged alliances with promises of independence from the Ottoman Empire. Since I recently returned from the Bosporus, I surmised the admiral would send me to the Suez to appraise what havoc the Russians were waging on the Afghans. With that in mind, I convinced myself I would be here for the birth of my child." Joseph lowered his head.

"God, brother, I feel wretched for you. I don't know what to say."

"Say you will keep your promise to me."

"What promise?" Charles was confused.

"You promised if I left, you would watch over Emma for me." Joseph's eyes implored him.

"Of course I will. You don't even have to ask me that question. She carries the Head blood and the heir to the barony, but most importantly, she is part of our family." Charles draped his arm around his brother's shoulder and gave him a confident squeeze. "Isn't it possible you will be back before the baby comes?"

"I seriously doubt it. My mission is to replenish the fleet that is already there with supplies and troops. I won't be going alone. The *HMS Warrior* and other steamers will accompany me."

"Joseph, be candid with me." Uneasiness was creeping into Charles's body, "Are you going to be engaged in actual naval warfare?"

"I won't know until we get there. The Russians have been successfully gaining footholds along the Danube. The Turks have a couple garrisons on the Black Sea coast, but who knows how long those will hold? Rebels are volunteering to join with the Russian forces on a daily basis. Right now the Turks have 100,000 men battle-ready, whereas the Russians have 300,000 men. Our ships are stationed in the Black Sea, the Bosphorus, and Dardanelles. A battle between the Russians and us depends on their aggression. Their ultimate quest, Charles, is to steal India from us." Joseph laughed. "Our queen and Lord Melbourne will never let that happen; the country provides too much wealth to our economy."

"Don't make light of it, Joseph. The thought of you being in harm's way is disconcerting, to say the least." Charles's brow was furrowed with worry.

"Your concern for me is heartfelt, but I need you to take care of Emma. She cannot suspect I might be in battle or that you have misgivings about my assignment. Please, Charles, she and the baby are my first priority."

"I am honored you put your most treasured possessions in my hands. I won't let you down, Joseph; I promise."

Joseph wanted to lift the serious mood now that his brother had guaranteed his wife would be looked after. "I'll race you back to the stables." Joseph ran to his stead; Charles mounted his, and they were off just like when they were children.

The mood at the manor house was one of apprehension and solitude. Each family member was lost in his or her own thoughts. On Joseph's last night with Emma, he consoled her, made love to her, then consoled her again. Only when she slipped into the deep abyss of desire did she lose her forlorn face. She couldn't help it. If she weren't consumed with desire, she was consumed with dread. Her emotions ranged from one spectrum to another, joy to despair, fulfillment to loneliness. They finally fell asleep close to dawn wrapped in each other's arms. Joseph awoke after two hours of sleep. He watched Emma's even breathing. *How beautiful she is*, Joseph mused. He pulled back the coverlet and looked at her naked body. The baby was at least four months old, growing in the safety of her womb, not subjected to the upheaval of daily life. He sighed and rubbed his hand over Emma's stomach. He detected a fluttering of movement beneath his hand. For the first time, he felt the baby move. Dear God, it was a miracle of nature. It was real, and it was his. Flooded with emotion, Joseph wept. He wept for the love he felt for his unborn child. He wept for the anguish he felt leaving his wife. He wept for the loss of his love for the sea.

Emma awakened. Joseph was rubbing her stomach and crying. "What's wrong, Joseph?"

"It's the baby; I felt it move." His voice was soft. It virtually oozed with love for the baby. "I'm sorry, Emma, so sorry."

"Sorry about what, my darling?"

"Sorry that I'm called to duty and have to leave you."

Emma's face was stricken with dread. "Is there something you're not telling me about this mission?"

God, what an idiot. Joseph pulled himself together to ease her fears. He had to display a façade of strength. If he didn't, she would never get through it. "I am a sentimental sap." He forced himself to laugh. "I'm not hiding a thing from you except a weakness for my wife and child. Now, give me a morning kiss, and I will have our breakfast brought up."

Emma was flooded with relief. It would be unbearable if he were going into a dangerous situation, but he assured her once again it was an exploratory expedition. Anyway, she was glad her husband had deep feelings; that's one of his qualities she adored.

The family gathered in the great hall to say their good-byes to Joseph, all except Emma. They parted upstairs in the confines of their rooms. She couldn't bear to watch him walk out the huge oak door. It was too much. She heard the horses' hooves on the stone path, clop, clop, clop, a familiar sound, once joyful, now a sign that Joseph was going away. She shuddered.

Life changed at Whitfield with Joseph gone. Emma spent more time with Catherine and David, but most of the time when he wasn't working, she spent time with Charles. It was a particularly lovely autumn at Whitfield. The leaves on the trees changed into multitudes of colors—reds, oranges, and yellows. When it wasn't raining, Charles took her for carriage rides into the village and into Dover. Constance was in London for the opening of theater season and all the rounds of parties. Charles was rid of her until the Christmas season. She harped on him to come up, but he made excuse after excuse, always blaming work on the manor. If the truth were known, he was doing less work on the manor and more time keeping company with Emma.

Every day Emma wrote to Joseph. She was told the letters wouldn't be delivered because he was at sea. She didn't care. He would get them once in port. Writing the letters was a lifeline for her. She wrote about trivial events happening at Whitfield and in the village. She wrote about the baby growing and kicking her incessantly. She told him about the builders and masonry workers revamping their rooms. She had moved into the nursery rooms with Jenny while the builders worked on their wing. For Emma, it was cathartic being out of their rooms. Their quarters were a reminder Joseph was absent. In the nursery, she daydreamed about the baby, but most importantly, she shared the rooms and her dreams with Jenny.

Chapter 36

Military Mission

Once away from Whitfield, Joseph focused solely on the mission. As the highest-ranking commodore, he was responsible for seventy men on his ship and the lives of the men on all the other vessels in the fleet under his command. It was a huge responsibility, but he had been in similar positions on other deployments. The voyage to Turkey took longer than the previous one in June, as the seas were rougher and coordinating a flotilla was time-consuming. He didn't merely captain the *Mercury,* but strategized the configurations of ships. The convoy consisted of sixteen ships, all steamers, carrying men and supplies, but still armed with cannons, artillery, and long-range guns. When Joseph got close to his destination, he divided the ships into three pods: ten ships to guard the Black Sea garrisons, three to patrol the Dardanelles, and three to patrol the Bosporus. Since Joseph had charted and sailed the Bosporus, he was keenly aware of the dangers of its S-shaped channel. He led his ship and the two other steamers into the straits. He sent messages to the Ottoman's Bosporus Squadron, informing their commander the British ships were on a friendly mission carrying troops and supplies. They received a warm reception because the Turks needed the support of the great powers, especially the British Navy, which dominated the sea.

The first few weeks were uneventful. Supplies were ferried from the flotilla to the ships already in the Black Sea and the troops tendered to garrisons along the banks of the Golden Horn, an estuary off the Bosporus.

Joseph was able to go ashore once a week to telegraph Emma. Since the invention of the telegraph in 1837, much progress had occurred. In 1850, a cable was laid across the Channel, and then in 1866 messages were even sent across the Atlantic. Joseph smiled at how clever the inventor was to make communication a priority. Overland mail was so slow at times, the person away was back home before a letter arrived!

While Joseph was biding his time on board ship in the Bosporus, Russian aggression escalated in and around Pleven, a fort protecting the crossing of the Danube River in Ottoman-controlled Bulgaria. The Russians were involved in a bloody siege at Pleven while Joseph was on his fact-finding mission in early summer. Initially the Turks, under Field Marshal Osman Pasha, were able to thwart Russian advancement. The Turkish army had time to construct trenches and redoubts, receive repeating rifles from Winchester with huge amounts of ammunition, plus use their tactics to mark off anticipated battlefields. The method utilized marked off yardage by using sticks with ribbons attached from their vantage point to the perceived enemy point of engagement. During the first part of the siege from April to the beginning of September, the Russians suffered 2,800 casualties compared to 2,000 for the Ottomans. After the larger loss, they retreated until the Romanians joined forces with them to increase their numbers to attack again, and Austria claimed neutrality, which gave the Russians access to Bulgaria. Bolstered by fresh troops and supplies, the Russians launched a vicious attack against the Ottomans in Lovatz to the south and captured the area that virtually encircled Pleven. This event proved to be catastrophic for the Turks because it cut off supply caravans that carried fuel, food, ammunitions, medicine, blankets, uniforms, and shoes. With no supplies and disease ravishing the Turkish Ottoman army, Osman had only 40,000 men remaining to battle 150,000 fortified Russian, Bulgarian, and Romanian troops.

The maritime situation was stable in and around the Turkish territories along the Black Sea and the Sea of Marmar. Lord Melbourne, the queen's trusted advisor, was in contact with the Turkish sultan, who ruled the entire Ottoman Empire. The sultan felt grave concern regarding the siege at Pleven, as casualties were once again mounting and the Russians were gaining territory. He requested the queen send a group overland to assess the success of the enemies' offensive. He received word from Osman's top general that the situation was dire, and unless drastic change happened, Pleven would be in Russian hands by the end of November or the beginning of December. Since no British foot soldiers were stationed in the area, Lord Melbourne ordered Admiral Smyth to send a party of naval personnel. Queen Victoria wanted an eyewitness account of the true situation at Pleven. Because the entire fort and city were surrounded, only an overland party could view the battlefields, trenches, field hospitals, and supply bins at the sight. The admiral was convinced the only man qualified to lead the mission was Commodore Head.

Joseph received the telegram that same night ordering him to take a group of his sailors to Pleven. The ships Joseph led were assigned to ship captains and lieutenant commanders of his choice. Time was of the essence; Smyth expected Joseph and his men to leave the following day.

After choosing twenty of his best and most experienced men, he ordered the supplies and long-range guns and other artillery necessary for protection. Winter had descended on the area in a white cloud of snow and freezing temperatures. Gone were the hot dry days of summer Joseph enjoyed on his first trip, replaced by a ferocious winter of cold, snow, and farther inland, ice.

The blanket of snow made the trek difficult. The terrain was composed of plains, plateaus, hills, mountains, basins, gorges, and deep river valleys. The undulations of the land made the trip more daunting. Joseph was strong, whether at sea or on land. He chose men cut from the same cloth who could withstand the climate, the rugged geography, lack of sleep, and meager rations.

Joseph and his small band traversed the frozen countryside for several weeks before they spotted the first Russian stronghold, at least

100 kilometers from Pleven. Joseph sent out a scout to find a hilltop that would keep them out of sight, but at a vantage point to view the large, rambling campsite of the Russo-Romanian troops. The men climbed the hill, settled behind an ancient crumbling snow-covered stone wall, and encamped before nightfall. Unfortunately, Joseph could not allow the men to build a campfire, as the smoke would certainly draw attention to the intruders. It was a long night with only dry tack to eat and bedrolls that absorbed the wet snow.

At first morning light, all twenty-one men crawled to a spot from which they could observe the field camp. Joseph looked through long-range binoculars and panned the acres that served as the camp. He focused on each area. He calculated at least 10,000 soldiers occupied the area, guarding 5,000 frozen prisoners held in shackles. He could see the dead were mixed with the living and the living were starving. Joseph handed the binoculars to Breton, then rolled on his back. He closed his eyes. The situation was worse than he expected. He circled to the west to get a view of that front.

The western front wasn't much better. Russian soldiers appeared to be everywhere. Joseph had absolutely no way of telling how many thousands of soldiers were laying siege to Pleven, but he knew one thing for certain: the Turks were doomed. With the unyielding cold, rampant disease, lack of supplies, and the small number of troops compared to the enemy, defeat was inevitable.

Joseph decided he had gathered enough intelligence and his men had endured enough hardship. He was ready to make the trip back to Constantinople. Returning was even more difficult than going. The weather worsened, supplies were dwindling, but worst of all was dealing with Turkish deserters. Rogue bands of fleeing soldiers were scattered throughout the countryside. They weren't a threat to Joseph and his men, but an annoyance. They were hungry, many bloody, and some ravaged by disease. It was from one such small group Joseph heard the most disturbing news: the Turkish field marshal surrendered on December 10, 1877. The siege was over, the Russo-Romanians the victors.

What would stop the Russians from invading Constantinople? With the Ottoman Empire in a shambles and Turkish troops depleted by the thousands, assistance from Bulgaria, Romania, Austria, Montenegro, and Serbia surely emboldened the Russian tsar to move to the heart of the Ottoman Empire, Constantinople. Keeping this at the forefront of his mind, Joseph changed tactics and began moving at night to evade any confrontation. By Christmas, the British naval group was within fifty kilometers of Constantinople. Joseph allowed himself to think of Emma and his unborn baby. He looked forward to sending her a telegram wishing her a happy Christmas and assuring her he would be home soon.

Joseph and his men huddled under a grove of trees at morning light to rest after walking miles in the darkness. Even though they were cold and hungry, exhaustion brought sleep immediately. Joseph was dreaming of sitting beside the fire in his rooms at Whitfield, enjoying a cup of tea and biscuits with his wife. The gusting wind blowing snow across his blanket brought him back to reality. He heard a crunching noise like boots compacting snow. It was the last thing he remembered.

Chapter 37

Ambush

Aaron, one of Joseph's best sailors who had turned out to be among his best soldiers, had helped set up camp under the grove of trees, then ate a few rations, and settled in his bedroll to sleep. He had trouble sleeping during the day even though he was bone-tired. Commodore Head still didn't allow a campfire for fear the enemy was on the move and would find the small group. The consistent cold, the hunger, the pain from walking hundreds of kilometers weren't enough to induce deep sleep. Aaron squinted and looked through the blowing snow. He saw his mates were asleep. He envied their ability to rest under horrendous conditions.

He tossed around on the hard ground trying to get comfortable, but sleep eluded him. Finally he got up, squatted behind an ice-covered bush, and rubbed his hands and arms to encourage his circulation. He was about to put tobacco in his old pipe for a smoke, but ever so slightly the ground moved. He crouched lower behind the leafless bush. About thirty Russian soldiers surrounded the sleeping sailors. In an instant, the Russians jerked up the commodore and the other men. They were all bound and gagged. The snow whipped down the plain, limiting visibility to about a yard. Aaron couldn't see what was happening, but he heard the Russian leader screaming commands and yelling guttural obscenities at his mates. The sounds of men being dragged on the ground moaning from a barrage of kicks resonated in Aaron's ears. He was stiff from crouching, but he dared not move. He waited and waited until there was nothing but silence.

He lay down on his stomach. Using his elbows, he inched toward the camp. The snow was packed and dirty and in places bright red. Aaron's heart raced. The enemy had captured every sailor except him! The silence was deafening. He was completely alone. He quickly rooted through discarded bags. He found a few rations but most importantly a compass. He ripped off the British insignia on his coat and hat, then rubbed the dirty snow over where they previously were sown. Aaron removed them hoping if he were discovered, the enemy would think he was a Turkish deserter or a civilian. His training kicked into high gear. He had one mission: find his way back to Constantinople to report that his fellow sailors, including the commodore, were prisoners of war.

The following days were harrowing exploits of dodging, hiding, and escaping the grasp of advancing Russian soldiers. The formal surrender from Field Marshal Osman Pasha had not been delivered to General Ganetsky. The Russian general demanded Pasha present the white surrender flag to him. Because the Turkish leader was wounded and lying in a peasant cottage, lower-ranked officers attempted to present the surrender, but it was rejected. Eventually Ganetsky accepted the flag from the officer next in command under Pasha. The bloody siege ended with the Russians smashing the Ottoman Turkish resistance and gaining vast Balkan territory.

Communication avenues during the late nineteenth century were rudimentary at best. Aaron had no means to quickly alert naval officers anchored in the Bosporus that the Russians had captured the entire party except for himself. Although obstacles continued to hinder his travels, he persevered. Aaron was the scout Joseph had sent out to locate a redoubt, a protective barrier, so he could observe the Russian camp outside Pleven. It was Aaron who found the wall that served as the bastion for Joseph to assess the Russian camp. As a scout, Aaron was trained on land as well as at sea. He was adept at camouflaging himself to avoid detection and using zigzagging methods to cover his tracks. His scouting skills alerted him to the slight ground tremor as he squatted by the icy bush. In reality, of all the twenty-one men, Aaron was the most likely to make it back to headquarters.

Chapter 38

Sounding the Alarm

When Aaron scurried onto the dock at Constantinople, he was operating on pure adrenaline. Throughout the long march to Pleven and then back, he had lost at least twenty-five pounds. His hair was unkempt, his beard straggly, his clothes hanging from his body, and he was filthy from crawling though the trampled snow. The first sailor he encountered thought he was a street beggar. The British emblems gone from his clothing, he was unrecognizable as one of the Royal Navy's best.

His next encounter was with a young sailor from the *Warrior.* He dismissed Aaron as a pest. As the sailor was striding away, he heard two words: "Commodore Head." He abruptly twirled around and grabbed Aaron by his coat lapels—what was left of them. "What did you say?" The whole fleet was aware the secretive party led by Commodore Head had been missing for several weeks.

"I am Lieutenant Aaron Stamper. I was part of the party led by Commodore Head. I was the only one not captured." His goal of sounding the alarm accomplished, his adrenaline totally depleted, Aaron collapsed on the dock.

Aaron opened his eyes and tentatively looked around the officer's cabin. He had no idea where he was or how long he'd been there.

He tried to rise up on his elbows, but fell back onto the crisp clean bedsheets. Somewhere in the distance, he heard voices.

"Admiral, Admiral Smyth, he's awake. Lieutenant Stamper is awake." The medic was breathless.

The admiral moved like a gazelle; his tall thin frame rushed to the young man's bedside. He could see immediately that until the lad received some nourishment, questioning him would prove fruitless. "Ensign Bell, go to the galley and get broth, tea, honey, and bread."

While the medic was gone, Admiral Smyth pulled a chair next to the semiconscious young man. What must he have gone through to get back to port? He obviously was a dedicated dutiful young officer. Admiral Smyth had questioned the sailors on the *Mercury* once it became obvious Joseph and his men were missing. He wanted to know every detail about the men Joseph chose for the mission. What were their areas of expertise? What were their weaknesses, if any? Had they volunteered or were they handpicked? He learned Aaron Stamper was the party's scout, a chameleon really, who could blend into the landscape right under the enemies' nose. Joseph chose the twenty men wisely, each with his own special gifts. This bag-of-bones lad returned to port against all odds to fulfill his sworn duty of loyalty, honor, and integrity.

Ensign Bell lifted Aaron's head and slowly spoon-fed him broth and tea. He dipped fresh-baked bread into the honey and fed him tiny bit by tiny bit. Finally Aaron had the strength to speak. "How did I get here?" Then with a stricken voice, "How long have I been here?"

Admiral Smyth asked Ensign Bell to relinquish the chair. He sat down. Aaron's eyes widened. He had never seen the admiral of the fleet, the highest-ranking British officer, in the flesh. What he didn't know was that as soon as Commodore Head and the other sailors were reported missing, the admiral traveled to Constantinople immediately. It was his responsibility; he had personally given Joseph the orders. He spoke calmly to Aaron. "Son, you told a sailor from the *Warrior* your plight about a week ago. You were brought to my cabin on your commodore's ship to recuperate. I can see you have been through hell, but fortunately you were not badly injured, but terribly malnourished and exhausted. Ensign Bell here has been tending to you with medicine and wound care. You have some very nasty open sores, I would guess from crawling in the snow, and frostbite on your feet, but no broken bones." The admiral smiled warmly at Aaron.

"Lieutenant Stamper, are you able to tell me what exactly happened?"

Aaron's voice was almost inaudible. "Yes, sir." Smyth had him take a few more sips of tea. Very slowly, the young lieutenant recounted the trip to Pleven, the bloody battles, the Turkish prisoners dead and alive, the fall of Lovatz, and the Russian advancement into Pleven. He talked about Commodore Head's decision to move at night because of the Russian and Romanian troops forging on toward Constantinople. He described the onslaught of blinding snow, cutting visibility to virtually nothing. He shared how he was able to escape the Russians. He described the aftermath of silence and the picture of bloody snow. His mission became returning to port to inform the navy of the party's fate.

Armed with the information, Smyth shot off a telegram to Lord Melbourne. The government would have to deal with the release of the British men and inform the great powers of the outrageous Russian act. He requested that the public not be informed until he broke the news to Joseph's family. It was his duty to return to England and inform the Duke and Duchess of Kent and the commodore's new wife about Joseph's status. He refused to label the men *missing in action*, but instead, *prisoners of war*, a more daunting characterization.

Emma received no telegrams from Joseph for weeks and weeks; October turned to November, then December. Christmas came and went; still nothing. It was the end of February; Emma was close to term. She had been bedridden for the past month as the baby was so low in the birth canal it caused tremendous pressure and pain when she was on her feet. She was exhausted all the time. She suffered from sleep deprivation. If her active baby wasn't kicking her, she was imagining unbearable scenarios since there was no word from Joseph.

Catherine, David, and Charles knew something was terribly wrong. Joseph had never been out of contact for more than a month at the most. On each deployment he was sensitive to his mother's apprehension, so he kept in touch to relieve her anxiety. Three months and no word meant catastrophic news. Every night Catherine prayed he was alive and safe. The family shielded Emma from their fears by reassuring her it happened often when Joseph was at sea: he was unable to communicate. They threatened everyone in the household to keep quiet. Hearing idle talk might cause her to lose the baby. Speculation by servants or visitors would not be tolerated at Whitfield Manor.

Constance visited occasionally. She tired of Charles's excuses, plus she still didn't have a ring on her finger. He was distant and vague regarding their relationship. Other than the night he asked to court her, they hadn't made love. It irked Constance, so she sought pleasure elsewhere when she was in London. One of the young men in her social circle who was engaged and a bit of a cad seduced her frequently. She feigned surprise, but he knew she wanted it as much as he did. Once they got past the charade, Constance was an avid lover. She enjoyed being satisfied in every way. Her trips to London increased, and trips to Whitfield decreased. Emma's condition was also annoying. Because Joseph was deployed, Charles was expected to keep her occupied. Those two loved the countryside, whereas she couldn't care less about it. Who gets excited about wildflowers, sheared wool, and mixing with the villagers? Boring.

Emma had another fitful night's sleep. She tossed and turned for hours. At daybreak, she finally fell asleep. Joseph weaved his way in and out of her dreams. She dreamed of their wedding day, the discovery of the baby, the arrival of his deployment orders. Emma saw him so handsome in his evening clothes taking her to the theater in Paris. They were in the Embassy carriage in Calais kissing, touching each other, and feeling the pulse of desire. He was caressing her face, kissing her ears, and the only sound was their breathing and the clop-clop of the horses' hooves. She awakened hazy after her vivid dreams. She still heard the horses' hooves on the stone driveway. An icy chill climbed up and down her spine as she slipped out of bed and moved to the window overlooking the front entrance. Frozen in time and space, Emma could not make her feet move. The British Navy Seal stared at her from the door of the carriage. Her thoughts raced. Her fear turned to joy. *It's Joseph! He's home!* She didn't stop to put on her dressing gown;

she bounded down the staircase and into the drawing room, yelling, "Joseph, Joseph, Joseph."

Instead of Joseph, a tall slender man with gold braiding, epaulettes, and medals all over his uniform looked at her with a kind smile. She didn't understand. Devoid of all color in their faces, Catherine and David stared right through her. The decorated man spoke. "Mrs. Head, I am Admiral Smyth, your husband's commanding officer." His voice was slow and deliberate; Emma trembled. Realizing she was standing there in her nightgown, she put her arms across her bulging stomach.

"Where is Joseph? Where is my husband? I haven't heard from him in months." Emma's voice became shrill. She dropped her arms, stepped forward, and grasped the admiral's arms. "Please, please, sir, where is my husband?"

Admiral Smyth looked at Catherine. "Duchess, I need your assistance." His eyes pleaded with Joseph's mother.

Jolted back to reality, Catherine thought of Joseph's baby growing in Emma's belly. She put her arms around Emma and guided her to a lounge chair. Emma felt invisible gnarling fingers choking her throat. Before Catherine spoke, she knew. The reason the admiral was here was to deliver bad news.

"My dearest girl, Joseph is missing and believed to be a prisoner of war." Catherine's speech was direct. She didn't know any other way to tell her daughter-in-law this devastating news.

Uncontrollable tremors racked Emma's body; her scream was that of a wild animal ensnarled in a hunting trap. She slumped back in the chair gasping for breath.

Catherine yelled, "David, get Jenny and send one of the servants for Charles. Ring for Phoebe; I'll send her to the village to bring the midwife in case the baby comes."

"May I, Duchess?" Admiral Smyth sat next to Emma in the overstuffed chair. "Listen to me; you don't want anything to happen to your baby. You are hyperventilating. Breathe in through your nose and exhale through your mouth."

Torrents of tears flowed down Emma's cheeks. She felt ill. She didn't know what this man was talking about. Charles heard the admiral speaking to Emma; he burst in the room and knelt on the floor in front of her. He could see she was on the brink of passing out. He shook her shoulders.

"Emma, do as the admiral says. If you don't, you could lose the baby." He sounded stern, yet compassionate.

The words Charles said reminded her of when she was a little girl. She was in her house in Calais. The doctor told her father, "She's lost the baby, a little boy." Emma opened her eyes and began breathing as the admiral had instructed. Slowly, slowly she regained her composure. Then everything happened at once. Jenny put a cold rag on her forehead. Charles knelt in front of her, and the admiral was next to her holding her hand. She looked around the room. Catherine had collapsed on the settee. David was standing by the window drinking a brandy.

The initial shock past, Emma wanted details, details of her husband's whereabouts. Oh God, would she ever see her Joseph again? She learned what little the admiral knew. Scant details, but she was aware the Russians were holding him and the other men in custody, but where and why? Emma couldn't control her emotions. The thought of Joseph in the clutches of Russians doing God knows what to him made her start shivering all over again.

Rapidly Charles took total control of the situation. Phoebe and the midwife arrived. He instructed Phoebe to take his mother to her room, put her to bed, and give her a light sedative. He gave orders to have luncheon readied for Admiral Smyth and his assistants, plus guest quarters assigned to the coachman, the admiral, and his men. He told Jenny to get Emma's bed ready. He picked Emma up and took her shaking body up to the nursery. He had the midwife follow so she could examine Emma.

While the midwife checked Emma, Charles paced up and down the hallway in front of Emma's room. She had never moved back into the renovated rooms. She wanted to wait for Joseph. How quickly things changed. Charles shuddered to think what Joseph endured. He was keenly aware the Russians employed horrendous torture tactics on their captives. Although he harbored deep feelings for Emma, he would never act on them. He wanted his brother to be happy and enjoy the impending birth of his baby. Emma loved Joseph unconditionally. It was the type of love a man wanted. All of it was disintegrating with Joseph's capture. Charles vowed at that moment to do everything in his power to protect his brother's wife and child until Joseph's return. He dared not think of the alternative.

Chapter 39

A New Heir

Joseph David Adolphus Head was born the morning of February 27, 1878, the day after Admiral Smyth came to Whitfield and shattered Emma's world. In a way, the birth was anticlimactic for Emma. The baby was chubby, with rosy little cheeks and a loud healthy cry. For some complicated reason he reminded her of what she lost, not what she gained. Catherine, David, and Charles were falling all over themselves with joy. Whitfield had a male heir. A future Duke of Kent was born.

Jenny cajoled, rationalized, and tried to reason with Emma. Yes, it proved difficult that her husband was captured in war, but when he came home, a baby boy would be waiting for him. He would be disappointed in Emma if she weren't a good, loving mother. None of it touched Emma. The hole in her heart was a cavern. She was empty.

Although the baby slept in a basket by Emma's bed, his cries did nothing to move her. After the third day, Jenny was compelled to go to Catherine. She knocked on the morning room door.

"Come in." Catherine was trying to cope with the loss of her son and the birth of his child. The opposing emotions of despair and happiness collided. It was overwhelming.

"Excuse me, madame, may I have a word?" Jenny lowered her eyes. She felt she was betraying Emma.

"Yes, of course. I was just getting a telegram ready to announce little Joseph's birth and ask the Bourons if they would like to come over." Catherine smiled. "What is it, Jenny? You appear very concerned."

"Madame, Miss Emma's milk hasn't come in. I kept thinking it would. I've been giving the little tyke sugar water, but he's hungry." Jenny felt wretched.

Catherine was surprised but composed herself. "I will send Phoebe to the village for a wet nurse right away. I will also have a room readied for her and her own baby in the nursery." Catherine smiled and hugged Jenny. "You've done the right thing. Don't blame yourself and don't think you have betrayed Emma. I am afraid the shock of Joseph's capture caused her body to react this way." Catherine thought it quite unnatural, but she kept it to herself.

Emma convalesced in bed while all those around her cared for baby Joseph. She was bitter. All the joy of the baby was wrapped up with her and Joseph. With Joseph gone, she felt no bond with the baby. He served as a reminder of her loss. Just as she refused to return to her and Joseph's refurbished rooms, she refused to get motivated to decorate the nursery. Emma wasn't concerned the baby wasn't getting enough love as the weeks wore on. The grandparents adored him, and Charles literally doted on the baby. He would walk him up and down the hallway singing and crooning lullabies after his nighttime feeding. Little Joseph was thriving on the wet nurse's milk. He was a happy baby. Why wouldn't he be? He was showered with attention.

As the days became weeks and the weeks became months, there was still no news about Joseph. Every so often, Admiral Smyth sent a telegram giving an update, which amounted to nothing. Emma's parents came to England in late spring to see the baby. Inclement weather kept them from traveling when the baby was first born. Both Maria and Edgar thought little Joseph was an adorable baby. He had such a sweet nature, only crying when hungry or needing his nappies changed. They found Emma on the other hand to be detached and sullen. They both noticed right away she rarely acknowledged the baby's existence. Edgar saw his daughter was gaunt, with dark circles under her eyes. His mind flashed back to Maria's despondency and depression after they lost their son. The thoughts made him shudder. He decided to intervene.

If anyone knew Emma's true disposition, it would be Jenny. He summoned her to the guest quarters he and Maria occupied. "Jenny, I implore you to tell me what has happened to my dearest daughter. She ignores her baby boy, is as thin as a rail, and seems removed from the real world."

His words opened the floodgates. Jenny cried until no tears were left. Edgar handed her a handkerchief and led her to a comfortable settee. He encouraged her to speak, promising he did not blame her.

"Oh, Monsieur Bouron, it's been awful. The day the admiral from the British Navy came and told the shocking news of Joseph's capture, Emma shriveled before my very eyes. She went into labor that same night and gave birth without having time to absorb what happened to her husband. As you can see, her depression stopped her milk from coming in. We've had a wet nurse since the baby was three days old." Jenny cried some more. Edgar remained silent so she would continue. "She isn't interested in the baby. His care is in the hands of the Duke and Duchess, but mostly Master Charles loves and nurtures him. I have tried to talk to her, but she doesn't listen, she doesn't sleep, and she eats so little I don't know how she survives." Her tears poured again. "What are we to do?"

"Don't you worry yourself about that, Jenny. I will take matters in my own hands." Edgar's promise did not lift Jenny's spirits. All the people in the household had tried to reach her, especially Catherine, but no amount of coaxing brought her out of her self-imposed exile.

Edgar did not share what he knew with his wife. He feared it might bring back too many memories from the black period of their lives. He knocked on Emma's door.

"Come in, Papa," Emma responded in a flat tone with no affect at all.

"Good day, my sweet." Edgar kissed her hollow cheeks. "Where's my beautiful grandson?"

"Oh, the wet nurse is feeding him in her room."

"Well, good. I want to talk to you."

"What about?" Emma replied nonchalantly and uninterested.

"Sit down next to me, Emma." Edgar was sitting on the edge of the bed. She sat by him and stared across the room. "I am sure you remember when you were very little, Mama lost a baby boy. You lost a brother. I am not insensitive, Emma; I realize now, all these years later, it had a profound negative effect on you. I couldn't pinpoint why you felt such insecurities, but I understand now you didn't bond with your mama." Emma started to protest, "No, listen, you transferred your love and affection to Jenny, which I understand." Edgar cleared his throat. "I was so caught up in your mother's illness I neglected both you and Claudine. Your mother was in such a state she was unable to deal with two little girls. None of this is an excuse, but a fact. I have come to realize that the death of our baby instilled insecurities and lack of self-worth within your personality." He looked her directly in the eye, and with deep compassion said, "Is this what you want for your baby? Is this what Joseph would want for his son?" Emma began to cry softly. "Don't you want your son to develop into a man like his father? To be that man, he needs a solid foundation, not quicksand."

Emma lay back on the bed and covered her face with her hands. "Papa, I can't go on. I miss Joseph desperately, and I don't know how to live without him. I don't know if he is dead or alive. My heart aches with sorrow."

Edgar lifted her to an upright sitting position. "I realize the situation is deplorable. I know your heart is heavy, but look straight at me and tell me your and Joseph's baby should suffer his mother's neglect for a situation out of everyone's control, including Joseph's."

Emma laid her head on her father's shoulder and wept. She wept for her missing husband, her baby she ignored, and a life swept away by a Russian sword. Edgar comforted her until her sobs subsided, then he left her room so she could absorb what he told her. He silently prayed it would make a difference.

Emma got up and studied herself in the full-length mirror. God, she looked awful. She was reed-thin, with sunken eyes and a general unkempt look about her. She summoned Jenny to the room and asked her to draw a hot bath. After a steaming soak, she chose a pink day dress she hoped would mask her skeletal appearance. Jenny groomed her hair in a loose chignon that Joseph loved. For the first time, she applied face powder, rouge, and a dark pink lipstick. She never needed makeup before now. Emma looked at herself in the mirror again; at least she was presentable. "Please tell Catherine I will have lunch with the family, but first, bring my son to me." Emma saw surprise and delight in Jenny's face.

"Right away, my girl." With that Jenny whisked out of the door.

The wet nurse brought baby Joseph to Emma. It was like a veil was lifted from Emma's face. She held him in her arms and rocked him back and forth. His eyes were bright blue pools, like Joseph's. His chubby little cheeks were rosy. She unwrapped the blanket and marveled at his perfect tiny fingers and toes. His hair was quite thick, with curls and blond like his father's. Emma smiled, and at four months old, he smiled back. A thrill went through her body. He resembled Joseph in every way. How hadn't she noticed before? She swaddled him in the lace crocheted blanket, then walked him up and down the room singing a lilting lullaby. He fell asleep almost immediately.

It was as if the house breathed a sigh of relief once Emma fell in love with her baby. With the gloom of the winter gone, she pushed little Joseph in his pram around the grounds of Whitfield, talking to him incessantly. She explained to her baby about the wildflowers, the sheep, and the crops. The sound of her voice made him laugh or lulled him to sleep. The whole household revolved around the baby.

The telegrams from Admiral Smyth became more infrequent. Scraps of news about Commodore Head and his men never surfaced, even when the Russians entered into the Treaty of San Stefano in July 1878. The Russians were victorious over the Ottoman Turks. Once the treaty was signed, many prisoners of war were released, but not Joseph. The Russians claimed they had not captured the commodore and sailors. Lord Melbourne met personally with Tsar Alexander, who guaranteed they were not prisoners of war. He questioned all his top officers, and each related the same. Their troops had not taken the British sailors.

For a brief moment, a flicker of hope glimmered at Whitfield when news of the treaty reached them. Then as quickly as hope came, it vanished with the admiral's telegram stating Joseph was not among the prisoners. Emma had turned twenty-three, and she had lived longer without Joseph than she had with him. The day the telegram from Smyth arrived, she concluded her husband was dead. She grieved quietly, without the other family members aware of her solemn conclusion. It occurred to her that she should return to Calais with her toddler. Claudine and her parents came often to see little Joseph, but he wasn't attached to them like he was to the Heads. She tried to imagine raising her son in France, but leaving Whitfield would be leaving another part of herself. Little Joseph was like Emma in many ways, but especially in his love for the land. They spent glorious days picking flowers, romping in the pastures, visiting the villagers, and playing with the cats and dogs that inhabited Whitfield Manor.

Then there was Charles. He and the little lad adored each other. Charles didn't have to break up his relationship with Constance; she became sick of his being with the baby and Emma. She wasn't cut out for the domestic life, and she was tired of no physical intimacy with Charles. It was like he'd become a eunuch. Catherine heard through her London circle of friends that Constance was courting an Italian fellow who made millions of pounds sterling in textiles.

Charles was more than relieved that his courtship with Constance—or what was supposed to be a courtship—had fizzled out. Charles dedicated himself to little Joseph and was at Emma's beck and call. When the little boy began to talk, hearing "Unca, unca" throughout Whitfield was common. Charles played with him for endless hours, rocked him if he cried, read storybooks to him, actually doing all a loving father would do for his son.

Emma wasn't blind. She was very aware of Charles's devotion to her and little Joseph. She blamed herself for Constance leaving Charles, but he appeared more relieved than disappointed, so she didn't fret over it. Plus, she disliked the girl, and the thought of her living under the same roof was most unpleasant. In fact, the thought of anyone taking Charles's attention away from her and her son was distasteful. In the midst of her reverie, Charles and JD, as the family called him, blasted in the room laughing hysterically. "What on earth have you two been doing?"

"Unca Charles and me playing hide-go-seek in the turmits." JD giggled.

"You mean in the turrets." Emma laughed.

"Yes, Mummy. May I have a chocolate biscuit, please?"

"Well, it's getting close to dinner, but go tell the cook that Mummy said you may have one with a cup of tea. Have it in the scullery."

"Thank you, Mummy." With that JD bounded out of the morning room. Both Emma and Charles smiled.

"He doesn't need much encouragement where sweets are concerned. I guess for a lad of three that's normal," Charles said.

"The evenings are getting dark earlier and earlier," Emma mused. "Why, it's only four o'clock."

"It's that time of year again." Charles smiled.

"Actually, Charles, it seems impossible that another winter will be upon us. It's hard to believe how quickly JD is growing." Emma moved across the room to the big windows. The morning room was her favorite room in the manor besides the nursery. She hadn't returned to her and Joseph's rooms. After a year passed, David shut them off. Two years hence, the rooms remained closed off. Emma was happy in the nursery rooms. Soon she would think of hiring a governess. The wet nurse, Daphne, loved JD and stayed on as nanny. The rooms were a happy place, full of laughter and joy.

"You're daydreaming," Charles teased. He stood next to her at the windows.

"Yes, yes, I was."

"Happy thoughts, I hope."

"Yes, thinking about how much I adore this room and the nursery rooms. Both are cozy and full of love."

"There's a draft by the windows, Emma. You'll get chilled. Let me pull the draperies shut." Charles reached in front of her, and Emma turned around. In an instant she was in his arms, and he kissed her. She had been alone so very long. His muscular arms, his lips, his tongue all triggered desire that was buried with Joseph.

Charles pulled back. "God, Emma, I am sorry. I don't know what came over me." Emma didn't speak. She pulled him back to her and kissed him with unquenched passion. He pulled away again, his heart racing and his mind reeling. "Before . . . we can't go back to how we have been for over three years; you must be sure." He softly touched her face. "After JD is settled in for the night, come to my quarters and we'll discuss this."

Rejected, Emma smiled a small half smile. Had she read his signals all wrong? Did he love her only like a sister? She closed her eyes. *I've ruined everything. He won't be comfortable around me now. When together at family dinners, events, holidays, it will be awkward.*

He interrupted her thoughts. "Emma, I believe for a long time you have known my feelings for you. They never changed since at age nineteen you shared your love of Whitfield with me until now. But you must be sure." He kissed her cheek and walked out the door.

Emma sat in a chair as the room darkened around her. She wasn't a nineteen-year-old girl madly in love with the man of her dreams, but a woman and mother. The love she experienced with Joseph was a once-in-a-lifetime occurrence. That type of first love, first passion, wasn't possible to repeat. Charles was a good, solid man. He loved JD like his own son. He loved Whitfield as she did. It could be a good partnership. Her life didn't unfold the way she imagined with her and Joseph raising a family together at Whitfield, growing old together. The Russians snatched that life from her. Over the years she had begun to love Charles in a different way. She admired his work ethic, his kind nature, and most of all, his love for JD.

The door opened. It was Catherine. "Emma, why are you sitting in the dark?"

"Oh, just thinking."

Catherine turned on the gaslight and then touched Emma's cheek. "Dearest, you've been crying; what is it?"

Emma felt her cheeks. She wasn't aware tears rolled down her face. "I have resigned myself to the fact Joseph is never coming home. I buried him the day the telegram came notifying us he wasn't a Russian prisoner. We all act like he is going to come strolling through the front door like nothing has happened. Time hasn't stood still. His son is almost four, and I am a woman and mother, not the naïve girl he left behind. That's what I've been thinking, and the tears are for what's been lost." Emma sighed.

"You are Joseph's wife, Emma. Only you have the power to put him to rest. Don't you think it time we had him proclaimed dead? I am his mother and would have done it two years ago, but you held on to the hope he would return. For closure, for all the family, will you give your consent now?"

Emma grasped Catherine's hands. "I've been so inconsiderate thinking of my own feelings. Please forgive me." Catherine nodded. Emma noticed she was pale in the glow of the gas lamp. "Of course, I will file the papers in Kent County, but I can't do it alone. I need you or David or Charles with me." Emma sobbed uncontrollably. What she secretly knew for so long would become a legal reality. Commodore Joseph Head, heir to Whitfield, was dead. She and Catherine held each other tight. Catherine's son was dead, and it must be acknowledged. Emma's husband was dead and must have the honor of formal recognition.

Once JD was settled in his bed for the night, Emma bathed, brushed her hair, and pinched her cheeks. When she looked in the mirror, she didn't see the haggard wreck that looked back at her right after the baby was born. Instead, she saw a happy young woman who still had much to give, and she wanted more children. The newly installed electric lamps lit up the family wing. Emma thought how lovely the wood carvings on the hallway walls looked. She passed Joseph's rooms without glancing in their direction. She took a deep breath outside Charles's door, then knocked. He opened it immediately. Emma thought how ruggedly handsome he appeared in his red velvet smoking jacket and comfortable lounging trousers.

"Please come in, Emma." She heard the nervousness in his voice. "Sit down. Would you like a glass of wine or champagne?"

"Yes, a cabernet sauvignon, if you have it in your cabinet." She smiled.

Charles poured wine for both of them. Now that she was here, in his rooms, without JD, he felt slightly guilty. Even though his brother had been missing for almost four years, she was still his wife. Yes, he had promised to watch over her, and he had kept his promise to his brother. With Joseph's absence dragging on for years, he had grown to love Emma deeply. He knew when she first came to Whitfield, he felt deeply about her, but over the years the initial fascination and desire changed. Watching her with JD made his heart sing. After her initial depression, she took to motherhood naturally. She should have more children.

"I have something very important I want to discuss with you, Charles." Emma was very serious.

"Of course." *She's going to chastise me for kissing her and thinking there could be more to our relationship.* His heart sank.

"After you left the morning room, your mother found me sitting in the dark." Emma didn't mince words. "I was thinking about Joseph being gone all this time and how I mourned for him after he wasn't found among the war captives. It was then that I buried him, Charles. We all tiptoe around the subject, afraid we will upset one another. But it's done. Joseph is not coming back. Your mother confided in me that he should have been proclaimed dead two years ago, but wasn't because of me. It's time. We all must move on." Charles began to say something, but Emma stopped him. She wanted it all out in the open. "It's time you took your rightful place as heir of the barony and Whitfield. There is so much about English law I don't understand, but you do and you are keenly aware of what must be done." She took a breath and a sip of wine.

"Emma, I would never ask you to do this." Charles was dumbfounded.

She took another drink. "There's more. For a long time I have admired you and your caring spirit. In fact, over time, I have grown to love you." Emma smiled broadly. "If you'll have me, I am yours."

"Dear God, I fantasized about you, imagined you loved me, dreamed we would have a family together. This is much more than I expected. I gladly would have married you if you didn't love me in hopes someday you would." Emma knew he was telling the truth. With Charles, life would be stable here on the land. No deployments, no separations, no fears of what was lurking around the corner.

Charles kissed her gently, tenderly, but he couldn't hold himself back. She was in his arms responding to his touch, wanting him! God, she was beautiful. He took her hand and led her to the bed. She stood in front of him and removed every stitch of clothing. He kissed her all over her body. In moments they were tangled in each other's arms and legs. He planned on taking her slowly, but he felt her raw desire and couldn't contain himself. He was on top of her caressing her breasts, kissing her neck.

Emma whispered, "Take me, Charles. I want you."

The next two hours he made love to her in every way imaginable. It was the most erotic experience of his life. He released suppressed desire she'd shut off for years. Finally, exhausted, they fell asleep.

The light peeped through his curtains. Morning had arrived. Charles slipped out of bed to look at the clock. It was nine. Usually, he was up and in the fields by now. For once he didn't care. Emma slept, her breathing even. He got back in bed and kissed her lips. She smelled so sweet. He touched her breasts.

She stretched. "Good morning." Emma reached up and kissed Charles. "Did you sleep well?"

"Baby, it was the best night's sleep I've had in years." Charles laughed.

"What time is it?"

"It's nine." He fondled her when he spoke.

Emma sat up. "Nine? JD must be wondering where I am, along with the rest of the household."

"Don't worry; JD is with Nanny, I'm sure. As for the rest of the household, by now they have surmised exactly where you are." Charles laughed.

"Oh, don't say that. What will they think of me?" Emma frowned.

"They will think, *finally she has come to her senses*." Charles chuckled.

"You can't be serious!" He answered by covering her with kisses and arousing her all over again. "Charles, what about your mother and father?" She concentrated on not moving her hips. It didn't work. Her desire took control.

"My mother and father know me very well, and they have suspected my feelings for you from the beginning." His gleaming smile was sincere, "Now I am going to ravish you again." He laughed and tickled her side. "Come here."

At this point Emma didn't care; she wanted him to make love to her. She released her passion over and over after all these years. She let Charles explore every inch of her and come back for more. They stayed in bed all morning, then rang for tea, bread and butter, and jam. Charles ordered fried ham, fried tomatoes, and scrambled eggs. They were both ravenous. There wasn't a crumb left when they finished. For dessert, they had each other. Charles ran a bath they enjoyed together. He wrapped Emma in a huge cotton bath towel, then went to find Jenny.

When Jenny arose, Emma wasn't in her bed; she guessed she finally was with Master Charles. When lunchtime came and went, she was sure of it. She wasn't surprised when a knock came at her door. "Come in." It was Charles, literally beaming.

"Morning, or should I say afternoon, Jenny."

"Hello, Master Charles." Jenny grinned from ear to ear.

"Would you mind bringing your mistress some clean clothes for riding and her toiletries?"

JD skipped in the room. "Unca, Unca, where's Mummy?"

Charles tussled his hair, picked him up, and gave him a hug. "Your mummy is going riding. She said you could play trains with Nanny. Would you like that?" JD loved his trains, so Charles felt sure he would be happy. He was right; JD skipped out of the room calling for Nanny.

Jenny blushed. "I'll be right to your rooms, sir."

Chapter 40

New Beginnings

THE ENTIRE VILLAGE REJOICED WHEN Charles and Emma married. The barony would continue as it had for thousands of years. Naturally, the inhabitants of Whitehaven, mainly Constance, gossiped and whispered about the marriage, spitefully dubbing Charles second choice, Joseph's leftovers, and Charles Duke of Rebounders. The happy couple didn't care. Their family was thrilled and JD ecstatic. He slipped easily from calling Charles Unca to Papa.

Life at Whitfield was idyllic. Emma gave birth to Charles's son Fredrick in 1880 and the second son, Henry, in 1881. Emma was content. She loved Charles in a different way than she loved Joseph. Even though brothers, Charles was steady, bound to the land. Joseph was adventuresome, bound to the sea. Sometimes in her dreams she saw Joseph's face at the altar or his tears when she told him they were expecting a baby. Most of her dreams were nightmares of Joseph suffocating in avalanches of snow or huge Russian Cossacks torturing him with shiny golden sabers that dripped with blood, but the worst was Joseph starving to death because the enemy gave him no food or water. On those nights she whimpered in her sleep, and tears instinctively flowed freely. Charles held her and stroked her hair until the nightmare passed. He knew the dreams were about his brother, but he didn't ask her about them.

When they first married, he bought the Toy Depot for Emma as a wedding gift. At the time, Emma was surprised at her new husband's purchase. While the boys were still toddlers, Emma didn't have the time or the energy to get involved with the toy business, but as the boys grew and followed their father around Whitfield, Emma had free time to rekindle her career, even if on a part-time basis. It amazed her that Charles was so insightful early in their relationship. She could stay at home and still dabble in toy development. She elevated Claudine to vice president right after the transfer of ownership. Not one of Claudine's suitors captured her heart, so she hadn't married. Instead, what started as a job became a passion. Emma's sister was a true innovator, constantly creating new toys and finding ways to make them affordable to the middle class. Claudine adored Emma's boys and visited often. They loved her; JD and Frederick were old enough to travel with her to Calais. They enjoyed being with their Bouron grandparents, who spoiled the boys with sweets, toys, and trips to the circus and zoo.

Several times a year, the whole family stayed at the Paris apartment, which was very special to Emma because she spent time with Annabelle. General Cousin-Montauban died at Versailles in January 1878. Emma was unable to attend the funeral because she was close to term with baby Joseph. Annabelle wed Richard the month before her father's death, but because of an obscure French law that determined a marriage must have at least a sixty-day duration before the husband could inherit his wife's estate, the vast wealth stayed with Annabelle. Emma confided to Charles that it kept Richard a devoted husband with a divine lifestyle.

It came to light that Richard and Emma were briefly engaged while still in their teens. Cassandra, who still resented Emma for capturing Joseph's heart, spitefully delved into Emma's background to discover skeletons in her closet. The only thing she found was a former fiancé, who apparently disappeared and in the process dropped Emma from his life. As fate would have it, he reappeared as Emma's friend Annabelle's beau. Cassandra cultivated Claudine's friendship to get information about her sister's previous engagement. She rationalized Emma stole

Joseph from her, so at least she could ruin Emma's friendship with Annabelle Cousin-Montauban. Cassandra made a point of going to the opera in Paris and purposely "running into" the couple. She gushed about how she remembered Annabelle from the Ambassador's Ball in Calais. She innocently interjected she remembered Lieutenant DeBarge from seeing him with Mademoiselle Bouron at functions in Calais. She smiled at each of them sweetly, then scurried away to get a glass of champagne before the intermission ended. She looked back over her shoulder and saw the couple in a confrontational discussion. Cassandra smirked with satisfaction.

Annabelle was hurt. How could her best friend and her fiancé intentionally deceive her? Richard explained the engagement was brief; they were young and didn't really know the meaning of love. He left to avoid marrying a girl he didn't truly love. Annabelle felt betrayed. Richard perceived he needed to seal their engagement with more than a ring.

After the opera when they returned to the Cousin-Montauban mansion, the general had already retired for the night. Annabelle and Richard had the family parlor to themselves. Richard dismissed the servants and worked his magic on the woman he intended to marry.

"Annabelle, you must know I love you deeply, and the only reason neither Emma nor I said anything about our childhood romance was it paled in comparison to her love for Joseph and my love and devotion to you. We did not want to chance you might reject me for a relationship that actually wasn't much more than a friendship."

"I am so disappointed, Richard, that neither you nor Emma gave me a chance to form my own opinion. If you told me it was nothing important, I would have believed you." Annabelle looked completely crestfallen.

Richard detected her vulnerability and moved in to bind her to him. "Darling, don't you know from the first moment I saw you, I wanted you for the rest of my life?" Tears brimmed in his eyes. "I cannot bear it if you leave me now." He looked at her imploringly. She began to thaw. It was the right moment to take her. Richard grasped her shoulders. "I have never nor could ever love another woman. You are my everything."

Richard pulled Annabelle to him. "Can't you see the depth of my love?" He held her gaze for a few seconds, then kissed her mouth, her ears, her cheeks, and her throat. The bubbling of desire made Annabelle ache. Her anger wavered with every kiss and touch.

"Take me to your room." Richard's voice was commanding and strong. Annabelle led him up the grand staircase to her room. She locked her door. Her heart pounded. Richard wasted no time. Once on the bed, he took off each article of her clothing slowly. He whispered words of love and lust. Her response surprised him. She ripped at his jacket and shirt. He pulled off his clothes and pressed his hardness against her. He felt all of her. Annabelle arched her back and writhed against him. He made her wait until she begged for it.

"Please, Richard, I don't know what to do, but I know I want you to . . ." He covered her mouth and stifled her words. He spread her legs and probed with his fingers; she was ready. He rolled on top of her and entered her slowly. Annabelle felt a quick sharp pain, but the pleasure was so intense the pain mingled with it and intensified the feeling even more. Richard showed her what to do. They moved rhythmically, and all the while her breathing was becoming more rapid.

"Bella, my beautiful Bella, push harder until you explode." She came in waves of small explosions. "Wrap your legs around my back," Richard whispered. She did as he told her. The sensation was incredible. His circular movements made her moan and beg for more. Then she came in one huge climax. *Now she's mine completely*, Richard thought. He let himself go and filled her up. Afterward they lay in each other's arms and cuddled. Annabelle felt totally exhilarated. She loved Richard and didn't care a whit that he was previously engaged to Emma, but she was curious about one thing.

"Richard, did you and Emma . . ."

He laughed. "No, Bella, the closest I got to passion was a chaste kiss on the cheek." He pressed her close. "I have only made love like this to you alone. Don't you know both Emma and I love you completely?"

Annabelle laughed. "Yes, I do. Cassandra is a jealous prig." Her eyes sparkled. "Would you show me again how completely you love me?"

Thank God, Richard thought. At least my wife isn't going to be a prude. He took her again, only this time he aroused her with gentle caresses in all the right spots until she begged again.

Emma felt awful when Claudine told her Cassandra bragged around town how she told the rich heiress Annabelle Cousin-Montauban her fiancé was once engaged to Emma Bouron. The same Emma Bouron who married an Englishman and chose to live in England, not France. Gossip resurrected once again.

Emma wrote to her friend immediately, explaining why she chose not to tell her about Richard. Annabelle was blindly in love with Richard. Their lovemaking became a regular habit. She craved Richard's body. Throughout the day she longed for nightfall, when they shared unbridled passion. Richard was tender, demanding, passionate, unselfish, and a superb teacher. Each physical encounter took her to new heights of fulfillment. Annabelle wanted a lifetime to explore her newfound sexuality.

She forgave Emma without hesitation. The two women mended fences and remained as close as ever. It saddened Emma she wasn't part of Annabelle's wedding or with her during her bereavement after the general's death, but traveling during pregnancy was out of the question. A whole day in carriages, trains, and boats was too much. The two friends kept in close contact through their letters, and photography had progressed to the point where Annabelle had lovely wedding photos to share. Once Joseph became a prisoner of war, the letters stopped. Emma's deep depression was the cause. Annabelle was distraught over her friend's situation, but she couldn't travel as she and Richard were expecting a baby. Circumstances and miles got in the way of helping each other in times of need and times of joy.

After Charles and Emma married, the two couples visited often. The DeBarges came to Whitfield and the Heads went to Paris. By 1883, Emma had three boys, and Annabelle a boy and a girl. The children loved one another, which strengthened the friendship to a deeper level. Life was good. Emma was happy. She had a wonderful family, beautiful home, dear friends, and peace. She spent many hours at St. Peter's Church sitting in her favorite pew and praying. She believed God had a plan for her life, and she was fulfilling it. Ten years had passed since that day in 1877 that Joseph went on what he called a "routine" assignment. Enough time had passed that she was able to thank God for the time she spent with Joseph and thank God for the life she lived with Charles.

Charles officially became the heir of the barony after Joseph was pronounced dead. He would inherit the title and the lands, but JD was his heir. It was complicated, and Emma didn't really care as long as the barony stayed in the family and the villagers had security.

As the boys grew, they followed their father around Whitfield all day. He taught them about the crops and the sheep. He taught them to ride horses and milk cows. They went hunting and fishing. Their childhood was privileged and idyllic. Their mother taught them values of respecting others, having good manners, being loyal and trustworthy, and never taking for granted their station in life. Because of their wealth and social position, Emma taught them that giving back to their community and to charity was their duty. Three days a week, the governess taught them lessons in the schoolroom in the nursery. Those were the days they disliked most. They wanted to be outside with Charles.

Chapter 41

Expanding the Toy Business

Emma fostered a renewed interest in the toy business. Claudine had become president and remained unmarried. She said she didn't have time for marriage. She welcomed Emma's input into the business. Emma opened a branch office in England. The plan was to operate an office out of London and build a factory in Wales. Emma and Claudine hired a manger for the London office, plus Emma had a studio at home where she sketched and made prototypes of toys.

Wales was the perfect location for the new factory. Charles and Emma settled on Newport, a bustling growing city located on the River Usk and the sea. Three ports—Newport, Swansea, and Cardiff—proved viable ports for exporting the toys all over the world. The puppets Emma created before her marriage to Joseph were the most lucrative line for the Toy Depot. Puppet shows had been popular for centuries, entertaining children in the streets and markets of small and large towns. The fact a child could own his or her own puppets and play theater with other children was a huge selling point for the product. The interchangeable clothes made the toys even more appealing and affordable for families without a huge income. Opening a plant in Newport was much more cost-effective than having the manufacturing done in London. Workers in Newport were employed for lower wages. The town that had once been dirty and unsanitary, riddled with cholera and typhus, had been improved by a progressive town council. They built a network of sewers and incorporated piped water in the city. The wretched slums were torn down and council houses built in their place, affordable for the working class. An infirmary was erected and eventually became Gwent Hospital. St. Cadoc's Mental Hospital for the mentally insane opened its doors in the late nineteenth century. The horse-drawn trams gave way to electric trams, then to buses. An electric generating station was being built when Emma and Charles chose Newport as the place for the new factory. Alexandra Dock was already a booming port, filled with merchant ships exporting coal, iron, and other commodities. Three million tons of ore per annum went out from the three ports. The trade helped the town grow and prosper. To the Heads, Newport had all the components necessary for a successful business venture. It was easily accessible from Kent with the tangle of railway lines throughout England and Wales. The capitol of Wales, Cardiff, was located only fourteen miles away.

Wealthy aristocratic landowners found their power being eroded by a new population that supported entrepreneurs. The nouveau riche class amassed immense wealth from the mining and exporting of the minerals in the valley. The landowners like the Morgans, who owned Tredegar Park, which was about 40,000 acres, and the Duke of Beaufort barony, which was approximately the same in size, saw the agrarian society give way to the Industrial Revolution. Although the Head Estate in Kent still functioned as a prosperous venture, many of the old nobility saw their way of life crumbling. Emma and Charles had a foot in both worlds, land in Kent and industry in Newport.

Amenities sprang up in Newport for the privileged to enjoy. The Gaiety Theatre, the Victoria Hall, and Royal Albert Hall booked plays for patrons to enjoy. The Newport Rowing Club was established for high society to join, and rugby was becoming a popular sport. The populace could worship at the reconstructed St. Woolos Church or the stately St. Mary's Malpas Church. Lazy Sunday afternoons were enjoyed at Belle View Park or high tea at New Westgate Hotel. The poor, dirty, uncivilized town of the eighteenth century had been replaced by a city of wealth and culture by the latter part of the nineteenth century.

Charles purchased the land for the factory from the Jones family of Llanarth. They were an old established Welsh family, as were the Morgans. Both families were selling off parcels of land because they needed the money. The Welsh barony belonging to Lord Beaufort remained intact. Although his wealth was dwindling, he had enough in the coffers to keep his land and manor home.

Lord Beaufort had known David for many years and served with him in the House of Lords. When Emma and Charles traveled to Newport to sign deeds for the land and contracts for the builders, Lord Beaufort was kind enough to extend an invitation for all of them to stay at his manor. He thought David and his wife might enjoy the valley as well. David hesitated at first because William Beaufort had a salty reputation as a man who over-imbibed in strong spirits, which emboldened him with a loose tongue and a tendency for gossip. In the end, David decided a few days wouldn't be too difficult to endure William.

All four of the Heads went to Wales. Charles was pleased because he sought his father's input on final design and footprint of the factory. Emma was delighted, as it would give her and Catherine a chance to wander around Newport visiting the venues that were constructed for Queen Victoria's Golden Jubilee in 1887. Wales was of great importance to the queen, as the male heir was named Prince of Wales before ascending the throne. The bridge over the River Usk was constructed for the townspeople to watch for the queen's gold gilded vessel in a flotilla of boats of all sizes and shapes decorated with British and Welsh flags. The bridge, the gardens, the halls, and the specialty shops were all there for visitors' enjoyment.

After dinner the first night of the trip, the men went to the library for brandy. Both David and Charles saw William drink an extraordinary amount of wine before and during dinner. His wife, a cheery woman, encouraged him to taper off, but he ignored her. She gave up, as it was futile. She shrugged and began chatting with the women.

"I think it's brilliant that you are building here in Newport, old chap." William patted Charles on the back. "Gives the local economy another boost."

"Yes, we believe this is the perfect place for the new factory." Charles smiled.

William had downed a large snifter of brandy and was pouring another. He tried to fill Charles's and David's glasses, but both declined.

"I hate to bring up a touchy subject, David," he slurred, "but I always wondered: did you find out what those Russian bastards did with your other son?"

David bristled. "No, Lord Beaufort, he is still missing in action or a prisoner of war."

"Those Russians are a cold lot. I hear that rogue bands of their soldiers captured our boys and tortured 'em." He swigged the last drop of brandy in his glass and stumbled to the sideboard to pour another.

David and Charles were both incensed. Charles wondered if the old saying were true: where there's smoke, there's fire. He decided to probe the old drunk. "Did you hear where they took the captured sailors?"

"Well, some say they shipped 'em to Afghanistan to fight on their side." He belched loudly. "They were made to participate in the slaughter of Sir Pierre Cavagnari in Kabul and kill his guides."

Charles shuddered. It would take torturous deeds for a British military man to fight and kill one of his own.

William fell into an overstuffed chair and passed out.

Charles whispered, "Father, do you think there is any merit to what this man says in his drunken stupor?"

"I don't know, son, but I plan on delving into these allegations with the consulate to Afghanistan. The Treaty of the Second Anglo-Afghan War was signed in 1880, three years after Joseph's disappearance." David was confused.

"Let's leave the sot here and retire to our rooms. I am sure by now Emma and Mother have called it an evening." Charles nodded to his father.

David hesitated. He didn't want to intrude on Charles's married life, but he was compelled to encourage him not to tell Emma what Beaufort said. Why bring up something that might be lies? The two men walked toward the staircase that led to the guest quarters. "Charles, I am uncomfortable broaching this subject, but I feel I must."

"What is it, Father?" Charles frowned.

"Son, this Lord Beaufort is known as a drunk and a braggart. Until I have investigated his claims, I don't think you should share the conversation with Emma. Why dig up what transpired all those years ago unless it has merit?"

Charles knew his father was uncomfortable. How difficult it must be for him to lose his elder son and heir, then have his younger son marry the heir's widow. The whole concept would be absurd if it weren't true. He patted David's back. "Father, I won't say a word until we have a definitive answer, and quickly I hope."

They bid one another good night and went to their separate rooms. Charles took a deep breath before opening the door to the bedroom. Emma was sitting at the dressing table brushing her waist-length hair. *God she's beautiful,* Charles thought. *I have never deceived her since our marriage,* but was omission deception? He rubbed his temples. Emma saw his reflection in the mirror. She began to giggle.

Charles smiled. "What's so funny, my love?"

Emma jumped up and tottered around the room mimicking ole Beaufort's drunken antics. It was hilarious. Charles doubled over with laughter.

"You are very naughty imitating our kind host." He smiled again.

"Oh, Charles, I felt so bad for you and your father. The man was totally drunk before you went to the library." She copied Beaufort's slurring.

This gaiety helped lighten Charles's heavy heart. He pulled Emma to his chest. "Aren't you the saucy one, mocking a man's obvious addiction to the drink?" He laughed. Then he kissed his wife with the passion of an unrequited lover. Emma caught her breath.

"Charles Head, I think the smell of the old man's breath has made you drunk." Emma laughed lightheartedly. She threw her arms around Charles's neck and whispered, "Take me to bed."

Charles adored everything about Emma, but he loved her gusto for sex. They tumbled onto the four-poster bed. She was hungry for him, but he pushed her back and looked into her eyes.

Emma stopped fumbling with the buttons of his shirt. There was a sadness about him that sent a chill through her body. "What is it, Charles? I know you, and you can't hide your feelings from me. What has made you melancholy?"

Charles pushed his true thoughts into the crevices of his mind. He tickled Emma's waist.

"My darling, you have confused sadness with adoration." He ripped off his shirt, buttons flying everywhere, pulled off his trousers, and undressed Emma completely. He made love to her sweetly, then with desperation, then again with loving care. Emma didn't stop to analyze her husband's lovemaking techniques because she was lost in her own world of lust and fulfillment. Charles made love to her until the sun peeped through the early dawn mist. Finally, they both fell into an exhausted sleep. After a few hours, one of the servants knocked on their door to announce breakfast.

Emma stretched and kissed Charles lightly on his forehead. "I think I will parade you in front of drunken men who will immerse you in boring conversation until you desire only my company, which isn't boring." Emma giggled.

"The day is a busy one for me, and I'll have sunken eyes and walk with bowed legs." Charles tripped around the room laughing. "I'll tell the architects, builders, and lawyers my wife forced me to ride all night, which has left me in this condition." They both laughed uncontrollably.

"Unless you stop parading around naked, I will have you mount again." Emma winked.

Charles rushed to the bed and kissed her fervently.

"Emma, I love you desperately, and you have made me the happiest man in the world."

Emma was moved by his unabashed sincerity. "Charles, darling, I love you, and you rescued me from a life of pain and darkness. You have given me two beautiful sons and a life of peace and joy." She saw the tears in his eyes. What was wrong? This was so unlike him. "Is there something bothering you?" Emma asked quietly.

Charles turned away so she couldn't see the lies in his eyes. He bent over and picked up the discarded clothes from the night before. "No, my dear, I am just an old sap where you are concerned." He composed himself and turned back. "Now we better dress and have that breakfast before ole Beaufort comes up here with a morning toddy." Emma laughed and mocked his wobbly walk again.

David had already left the house when Charles and Emma went down for breakfast. Catherine was drinking her second cup of tea and chatting with Lady Beaufort. Her husband was obviously absent.

"Mother, I thought Father was going to the architect's office with me this morning. Is he upstairs?" Charles looked dismayed.

"No, Charles, he rushed out early, mumbling something about an appointment he forgot to tell us about. I thought it was quite odd, not like your father at all." Catherine frowned.

The hairs bristled on Charles's neck. His voice was solemn. "Did he say when he'd be back?"

"Oh, I don't think he's coming back. His meeting was in London, and he caught the early train." Catherine smiled at her son. "Charles, you are more than capable of dealing with the building of the factory."

Emma looked concerned; this wasn't like Charles either. "Is there a problem you perceive?" Emma had never known David to be impulsive or forgetful. She wondered what important meeting caused such an abrupt change of plans, especially if Charles needed him.

He saw his mother's questioning look and the concern in Emma's voice. He pulled out a chair from the table. "No, nothing like that. I was merely looking forward to Father's company and naturally his input." Charles smiled reassuringly. "There must be something at Parliament that was pressing."

Lady Beaufort summoned the servants to bring breakfast to her guests.

"I wonder if William should have gone," Catherine commented.

Lady Beaufort looked down and shook her head. William was still in bed sleeping off his drunken stupor from the night before. The women turned their attention to Lady Beaufort, striking up idle conversation to cover her embarrassment.

Thank God for the diversion, Charles thought. His father must already be on his way to the Afghan Embassy to find out the merit of

Beaufort's ramblings. Charles couldn't let the women find out about the disturbing gossip, especially from a drunk who most probably didn't know what he was talking about.

Charles was able to wrap up his business in two days. He was anxious to return to Whitfield. His mother received a telegram the day before informing her David was home at Whitfield Manor.

Chapter 42

Secrets Hidden in Newport

Emma and Catherine had thoroughly enjoyed their trip to Wales. They visited all the places on their list and found some lovely shops, where they bought trinkets for the boys. After that first embarrassing night, Lord Beaufort had gone out for dinner, which suited them all just fine, including his wife. The weather was lovely, the meals delicious, and the jubilee attractions well worth the trip. In fact, carefree joy for Emma was over; she just didn't know it yet.

Charles helped the ladies out of the carriage, summoned the footman to bring in the luggage, then went in search of his father. David was sitting in his study at his desk when Charles barged through the doorway. He looked up and his son stopped in his tracks. His father's face had aged a decade since he'd seen him in Newport a few days before. David didn't need to say a word. Charles knew from the depth of despair in his father's eyes, Lord Beaufort was right or at least partially right.

David spoke quietly in a broken voice. "Sit down, Charles."

"Father, it's true what Beaufort said. I see it in your eyes." Charles shook.

"Yes, much of what he said was true, but there's more."

"Is Joseph alive, Father, is he?" Charles's mind raced. He wanted his brother to be alive and home, but he was married to his widow or wife or whatever she was, and he couldn't give up her and their life together.

"Unbeknownst to the members of Parliament, these tales of British soldiers and sailors have been investigated off and on for the last ten years since the Russo-Turkish War ended. An elite committee of the highest-ranking military officials and intelligence personnel spent time and funds working with the Russian government to validate or repudiate rumors like the one Beaufort told us. Every time they have come up empty-handed, with no solid evidence to prove that British men were captured, tortured, and forced to fight as Russians until now."

Charles felt relief flood his body. The old drunk had been wrong. He pictured Emma and the three boys, his reasons for living, and Whitfield, the home he loved.

David interrupted his thoughts. "Charles, are you listening to me?"

"Yes, I'm relieved Joseph didn't endure suffering."

"Son, you didn't hear me say 'until now'?"

The color drained from Charles's face. "Until now what?" His voice was louder than normal.

"To gain favor with the great powers for trade-route purposes, several months ago the Russians turned over British soldiers and sailors. Our prime minister was outraged, but it didn't leak to the papers because he insisted the men be evaluated before being returned to their families. The POW Rescue Committee has kept this top secret."

Charles was outraged. "Months, Father, months?" he shouted.

"Keep your voice down before your wife or mother come running in to see what the problem is." David spoke sternly.

Charles took two long strides to the liquor cabinet, poured a large whiskey, and tossed it back. He felt the warmth of the drink all the way down his throat. He poured another, did the same again, and then turned to his father. "I apologize, Father. I am so shocked that this happened to the most powerful country in the world and to the families who have mourned their loved ones."

"Charles, sit down; there is more." David's voice was gentler than before. "These men have been evaluated in Scotland, Ireland, and Wales and kept out of England to lessen the chance of a breach of secrecy. Son, they are in terrible shape. I can't fathom what those bloody bastards did to our countrymen."

David paused and took a deep breath. "Here is the ironic part. Joseph and the few men who were captured with him are at St. Cadoc's Mental Hospital in Newport."

"Good God, Father—Joseph, alive in a mental hospital." Charles's whole body shook with sobs. What hell on earth had his brother endured while he was here at home married to Joseph's love, raising his son as his own and having two more boys? His life was full. His brother was in a mental hospital, a mental hospital! Then it crossed Charles's mind that maybe it wasn't Joseph. What was the proof?

"How can we be sure it is Joseph?" Charles asked.

"We can't until we see with our own eyes. That drunken fool Beaufort is a friend of the builder who is constructing St. Cadoc's. The place won't be fully functioning until 1906, but enough of it is built and equipped for secret military patients to receive proper care and treatment."

"This doesn't make sense, Father. Why would a builder tell Beaufort about a military patient treated there?"

David withered in his chair. "Because the staff and other patients call him Duke, Duke of Kent."

Charles doubled over in his chair. "This gets worse and worse."

David got up and put his hand on Charles's shoulder. "You must promise me on your honor you will not tell one word of this to Mother or Emma. We must be sure before we tear the family apart."

Charles stood and shook David's hand. Both men had tears streaming down their faces. David sent word to Catherine and Emma he and Charles would dine in the study, as they were deep into working on a glitch in the factory plans. The food was brought, but neither of them ate a bite. They sat in silence drinking whiskey until the sweet brown liquid helped them sleep, David on his leather settee and Charles sprawled on the floor. They arose early, dressed, ordered bread and butter wrapped in brown paper to take on their journey, called for the carriage, and left Whitfield for Newport. Both men turned and looked back at the manor house, where their loved ones slept peacefully.

Emma stirred when Charles came into his dressing room in the morning, but she went right back to sleep, thinking like any other morning he was getting ready to work on the land. Catherine heard David as well, but she knew when he was involved in a project like the Toy Depot, he was strictly focused. She assumed he freshened up and went back to the study to work. She hadn't heard him come to bed. She was in a deep sleep from a weary day's travel.

Emma was drifting in and out of sleep when she heard the clop-clop of horses' hooves on the cobblestones in front of the house. Did she imagine the noise at such an early hour? It was getting fainter. Fully awake, she scampered to her bedroom window. The carriage with the Whitfield Coat of Arms was becoming smaller and smaller in the distance. Emma shuddered. Why would anyone take out the family carriage so early in the morning? Maybe David had an early meeting in London; she turned to get back in bed. She glimpsed a folded sheet of paper propped up by her bureau mirror. She snapped it up. A shiver danced up and down her spine.

> *Darling, Father and I discovered a terrible design flaw for the manufacturing plant. The error needs rectifying before it's legally binding tomorrow. I will call you on that new contraption, the telephone, if we will be away more than one night. We'll stay at the Greyhound Hotel. Kiss the boys for me. I love you with all my heart. Charles.*

Emma's stomach twisted in knots; something was wrong. David departed Newport at the spur of the moment. Charles finished his business early. Then on return to Whitfield, neither of them dined with the family. Today they left for Newport at daybreak. The whole episode was totally out of character for both men. Emma threw on her dressing gown and ran down the hall. She knocked on Catherine's door.

"Come in. Good morning, Emma dear. Did you sleep well?" Catherine sat at her dressing table while Phoebe brushed her hair.

"Something is terribly wrong." Emma was pale. "I got this note from Charles saying he and David have gone back to Newport."

"Dear girl, I had a note from David also. It's nothing to be alarmed about." She smiled lovingly at her daughter-in-law.

"What did it say?"

"It's on my bureau; read it if you like." Emma clutched the note. It was like hers, but there was a subtle difference. David said the design error had to be corrected before construction started, not before the contract was legalized.

"They are lying," Emma shrieked. "The notes say two different things." She pushed Phoebe out of the way and turned Catherine around by her shoulders. "They never act like this. I am telling you, something is wrong, awfully, awfully wrong. I feel it, Catherine." Emma's eyes implored her mother-in-law.

"Emma, come sit down and let's see what has you so upset." Catherine read both notes. It was odd that they were slightly different, but there were many explanations for it. "Dear, it's just a difference in verbiage. They probably meant the same thing."

Emma jumped to her feet. She could see Catherine didn't understand her. She hadn't heard the ominous clop-clop of the horses' hooves. She shuddered again. "I'll have Nanny and Jenny watch the boys. I am going back to Wales. Catherine, there is something desperately wrong."

"Emma, you are overreacting. I am certain David and Charles meant the same thing, just expressed it in their own way." Catherine knew how emotional Emma was, but this was ridiculous, following them to Wales. "The boys have missed you, and I'm sure if you leave again, they'll be upset."

"The children will be absolutely fine with Jenny and Nanny." Emma had a cold resolve in her voice. Catherine knew trying to dissuade her would be fruitless. She sighed and nodded at Emma.

Emma packed a small case and left Whitfield within the hour. She didn't phone Charles. Instinctively she was convinced arriving unannounced was best, but she didn't know why. She knew Catherine wouldn't call the hotel. She hadn't mastered the use of the telephone.

During the entire train ride, an ominous feeling soaked Emma's brain. It caused her to revisit the depression and grief that consumed her when the Russians snatched Joseph from her life. It took time and the love of her family to drag her from the black chasm of heartbreak. Her overwhelming grief resulted in rejection of her own son. Charles's quiet devotion finally brought her back to the reality of everyday life. Together they endured ridicule by outsiders, especially the unflattering gossip Constance spread through the aristocratic social circles. Most royals ignored it, as for centuries a brother marrying the widow of his brother was common practice to guarantee the preservation of the royal line. The villagers of Whitfield loved Emma and were happy when she and Charles wed. With Joseph gone, a new duke made their lives secure.

The villagers rejoiced when Constance evaporated from their lives. She was arrogant and haughty. If Charles had married her, she would have treated them as inferiors. Once Emma and Charles married, peace and happiness spread throughout the village.

The rain sheeted down, which made it difficult to see the Greyhound Hotel. The doorman ran to Emma's carriage and helped her out. With an umbrella held over her head, the two made it inside the lobby without getting their clothes soaked. Emma thanked the doorman and proceeded to the front desk to get a key to Charles's room. Simon, the old gent checking guests in and out, looked slightly skeptical when Emma requested a key. The duke and his son had said nothing about other family members joining them. He didn't want to offend the lady, but she placed him in an awkward position.

"Well, uh, you see, madame, your husband and the duke left ages ago to visit a sick relative."

Emma's composure collapsed. "Where did they go?" Her voice was an icy whisper.

"Um, I don't know if I am at leisure to divulge the information." He perspired.

Emma stepped forward and grabbed the lapels of his uniform. "I demand you tell me, or when my husband returns, he will have you fired." Her tone was quiet and precise.

Simon could see the woman was adamant. What difference did it make to him anyway if he told her where the men went? He'd ordered the carriage, so surely it wasn't a secret. He wasn't about to lose his job over this. "Mrs. Head, the carriage was taking them to St. Cadoc's Hospital right here in Newport."

"St. Cadoc's? I am not familiar with it, sir. I thought Gwent Hospital was where the sick patients were referred."

"Well, uh, actually, uh . . ."

"Spit it out, man." Emma felt a sickness in the pit of her stomach. She wanted to vomit.

"Mrs. Head, it's the military mental hospital." Simon swallowed.

Emma slumped to the marble floor. It was cold beneath her arms and legs. The ceiling was ornate, with lovely carved friezes that spun round and round. She closed her eyes, and the sound of the horses' hooves echoed in her mind. She opened her eyes, and a lady in a white uniform was waving smelling salts under her nose.

"Are you all right now, missus?" the servant asked.

Her voice was deep. Possibly the deepest voice Emma had ever heard. It was like she was talking through a tunnel. The woman lightly shook her shoulders. "Can you sit up, me lady?"

Emma fought to concentrate on what the woman said. The man from the front desk was telling the woman about his conversation with Emma, how she became agitated, then fainted. Emma listened, but it seemed far away.

"Simon, fetch a cold cloth from the scullery, and I'll wipe her forehead."

Simon trotted off quickly. He didn't want any trouble from the aristocratic lady. Just hearing there was a mental hospital in town made her faint. *She must be quite weak*, Simon mused.

Emma looked at the servant. She was probably in her forties, and her hands were calloused from a life of hard work, but her eyes were kind. It was kindness Emma needed. She helped Emma up and into a chair. Simon returned with the cloth, and she gently put it on Emma's forehead. One of them put a glass of cool water in her hand. She took a sip. The room began to focus. The spinning stopped.

Emma whispered, "I am so sorry. I've had a long journey from Kent, and all of a sudden I fainted. I am so embarrassed."

The woman in white patted her hand. "Never mind. Me Lady, a long trip can do that to a girl as tiny as you." She smiled broadly. Emma noticed she had missing teeth. "I don't mean to be rude, mam, but where is your personal chambermaid?"

Everything came rushing back. The letters, the lies, leaving Whitfield, the journey, and the words burned in her brain: a military mental hospital. She took a deep breath and slowly let it out.

"I was called to Newport on short notice," she lied. "I left Jenny and Nanny at home with my three boys."

Emma changed the subject. "You have been so very kind. What is your name?"

"Beryl Jones. I work in the kitchen, and old Simon came running in to say a gentle lady fainted right in front of his eyes." She winked.

"I caused you both so much trouble. I am here to meet my husband. We have an ill relative who is in hospital." The lies poured out of Emma's mouth. "I am expected to meet my father-in-law and husband at the hospital." She turned to Simon. "Would you take my bag to my room and order a carriage for me, please?"

Beryl and Simon looked at each other. "Are you sure you are able to go? How 'bout some tea and biscuits first?" Beryl asked.

Emma stood up. "I am perfectly fine now, thanks to you both." She smiled her most dazzling smile.

"All right then." Simon nodded. "Beryl, when you go in the scullery, tell the footman to order a carriage to take her ladyship to St. Cadoc's."

Beryl's eyes widened. "Don't you mean Gwent Hospital?"

Simon's eyes stared into Beryl's with a warning look. "No, Mrs. Head's family member is in the military hospital." Beryl noticed immediately that Simon deleted the word mental. Why, everyone in town knew the men in the open wards at St. Cadoc's were crackers. Nuts, all of them. Some were released prisoners of war, some had been missing in action, and many were shell-shocked. Whatever the affliction, they were bonkers. She covered her error.

"Of course, since St. Cadoc's is so new and modern, I forget we have it in Newport. We are very fortunate." Beryl smiled. "Let me fetch the footman and you'll be off, mam."

The sheeting rain had turned to a chilly drizzle. The carriage struggled through the mud and puddles, which made the ten-minute journey seem like an eternity. Emma twisted her hair around her fingers over and over. An inner voice whispered that Joseph was in St. Cadoc's. What other explanation could there be for David and Charles to rush back to Newport to a military hospital? The carriage pulled up to the drab institutionalized building. Only a portion of it was completed. The largest part was still under construction, but today there were no workers because of the rain. As soon as the carriage stopped, Emma flung the door open and jumped down. Before the footman could assist her, she ran up the walk to the stone steps, her coat flying behind her, muddy and wet from the rain. She pulled on the doorknob, but it was locked. She balled her fists and beat on the door. It seemed like an eternity, but finally the door opened. A handsome man in a white smock with a stethoscope around his neck opened the door. He saw a bedraggled young woman in a soaking coat and wet ringlets hanging to her waist. Even in such a disheveled state, he saw a natural beauty.

"May I help you? Oh, how rude of me; please step into the hallway. I am Dr. Stewart." He looked at her questioningly.

Emma realized she was a frightful sight, but she didn't care. She could feel Joseph's aura in the building. She smoothed her hair down. "Hello, Dr. Stewart, I am Emma Head, and I believe the Duke of Kent and my husband, Lord Head, are visiting a patient in the hospital, and I want to see them now, please." Emma attempted a brave façade.

Dr. Stewart possessed zero bedside manner or gracious finesse. He was a medical man with one goal, to learn as much as he could about the human mind when under extreme duress. He looked the woman over, the wife, the widow, the wife, quite an intriguing situation. He wondered which Lord Head she referenced, her dead husband who was alive living in the ward or her present husband living with her in Kent. He hedged. "Madame, are the gentlemen expecting you?"

Emma's patience evaporated. "I don't give a damn if the queen herself is expecting me. Take me to them. Now." Her voice had a sternness that sounded foreign to Emma, but she was desperate.

Dr. Stewart stood full height and rod-straight. He was more than annoyed. "Do you understand, Lady Head, that this is a mental hospital, with men suffering from all sorts of psychological ailments, some worse than others?"

"I do." Emma's eyes narrowed. "I have reason to believe my husband, who was taken prisoner of war and declared dead, is in this building. Do you refute that claim?"

Dr. Stewart softened. What a horrible predicament. Commodore Joseph Head was legally alive and married to this woman. His Lordship Charles Head was definitely alive and also married to this woman; two brothers, one woman, equaled one enormous tragedy.

"Please, come to my office." His voice had tenderness to it that wasn't there before. Emma wondered why. "May I get you a cup of tea or some water?"

"A glass of water. Please." Emma's initial toughness and determination waned. She pictured her boys, her life at Whitfield, and Charles. He rescued her from the bowels of hell. She loved him so very much, but differently than she loved Joseph. How could one woman be in love with two men at the same time? She buried Joseph long ago, but the old feelings she stuffed down welled up to the surface. The first time she laid eyes on Joseph, she knew she loved him; their courtship, lovemaking, and wedding were all perfect. He instilled in her self-confidence that she had lacked from childhood. He made her feel beautiful in every way. All of her inhibitions and self-consciousness were erased by his love. She closed her eyes, and pictures of him danced through her mind. She saw him at the theater in his evening attire, his masculine physique in his decorated uniform, his chiseled body nude lying next to her, his anticipation as she walked down the aisle, his tears when he realized she carried his child, and the sadness he tried to hide when he was deployed the last time. She could almost feel his hands tenderly caressing her body, and then his urgency when he wanted her. How could their dreams have become a nightmare? The doctor's voice broke her reverie.

"Lady Head, are you all right?"

Emma sighed; would she ever be all right again? But she answered what he wanted to hear. "Yes, Dr. Stewart, I am fine and ready to see my . . ."

Dr. Stewart took her cold hand in his and smiled with sadness in his eyes. "Lady Head."

"Call me Emma, please."

"Yes, well, Emma, I have been apprised of your, uh, situation by the duke after he visited his older son."

Emma felt icy needles piercing her heart. She was right. Joseph was here at St. Cadoc's, alive. She wondered what emotions his father and brother were experiencing. After all these years, it was mind-boggling. The doctor's voice droned on.

"Your husband," Dr. Stewart quickly clarified his words, "Commodore Head, has only recently been brought to this hospital. I am afraid the years of torture, deprivation, and mind control have altered him a great deal." God, how could he make this less painful?

Emma asked quietly, "Exactly what do you mean?"

"I honestly don't know what to tell you. There may be glimpses of his former self, but radical changes have transpired as well." Dr. Stewart sighed. His evaluation of Joseph had revealed a chronic progressive condition that was spiraling out of control on a daily basis.

"May I see him now?"

"Yes, of course, but prepare yourself, Emma. Mental illness ravages the mind and the soul."

Emma drew in her breath sharply. She didn't know what to expect. She was frightened. Dr. Stewart led her down a bleak hallway painted a stark white, with no paintings or embellishments of any kind on the walls. She noticed the doors had no knobs, just exterior latches locked from the outside. At the end of the hall, they took a right turn; Charles and David were standing in front of a door that was partially open. They heard Emma and the doctor coming toward them. As Emma got closer, she stopped. David looked wretched. Charles had a pained expression on his face, the polar opposite to his usual merry demeanor. She knew instantly they were devastated.

Charles stepped forward and held Emma by her shoulders. He wished they had never come to St. Cadoc's. Sometimes the unknown is more kind than reality. He didn't know what to say. No words of comfort would suffice. He wanted to prepare her as best he could. "Darling, if I could spare you . . ." His words trailed off as Emma moved past him to the door that was ajar. She closed her eyes and begged God for strength. She pushed on the door and it swung inward. In one swift glance, she saw the contents of the room: a bed, a cheap bureau with no mirror, and a stand-alone sink. He was standing at a small window covered with bars. Emma saw immediately he was thin to the point of being emaciated. He didn't hear her enter the room. How was it possible he didn't hear the thumping of her heart beating against her chest?

Dr. Stewart came up behind her. "Emma, he most probably will not know you, and at times he can be violent."

Emma whirled around and faced the doctor. "You, sir, are mistaken. He will know me, and would never lay a hand on me." She turned her back on the doctor. He looked at David and Charles and shrugged.

Joseph turned away from the window. Emma began to shake uncontrollably. His blond hair had turned gray and dull. He hadn't shaved and appeared unkempt. His green cotton hospital pants and shirt hung loosely from his bony frame. The worst part for Emma was his eyes. The beautiful blue pools that mesmerized her so long ago were vacant. He didn't recognize her.

Charles walked in closer and put his arm around her waist. "Darling, he didn't know Father and me either. You must accept our Joseph is gone and will never come back." Emma looked at him in disbelief. She still hadn't spoken one word to Charles or David.

She took two steps and was directly in front of Joseph. She took his hand. It was limp in hers. He examined her fingernails intently. She fought back her tears. She lifted his chin with her other hand and stared into his eyes. "Joseph, Joseph, you know me." He looked at her blankly. She touched his cheek. "Please try to remember." Her plea ripped at Charles's heart. David shook his head in pure agony. Somewhere his son was in this shell of a man.

Emma led Joseph to the bed and pulled him to a sitting position. "I am your wife. You brought me from Calais to be married and live at Whitfield, your ancestral home. We have a son. His name is Joseph David Adolphus after you, your grandfather, and your father. We call him JD. He was born after, um, after you went away. We still live there, and he loves to play in the fields, ride the horses, and hunt game." Joseph stared past her.

Dr. Stewart thought now was as good a time as any to explain Joseph's mental state. Waiting wouldn't make it any easier on the family. He looked at David and Charles, and then spoke directly to Emma. "Lady Head, Commodore Head is suffering from a condition known as general paralysis of the insane."

Emma spoke softly, but the raw pain in her voice was tangible. "Is it caused from being tortured?"

"Well, no," Dr. Stewart said.

"From lack of food, sleep, or medical attention?" Emma frowned.

"No, it is a deteriorating condition caused from syphilis." Dr. Stewart had decided glossing it over with medical jargon wasn't fair to this family, who believed their loved one had been dead for over ten years.

"Syphilis!" Emma squawked. "You must be the one insane, doctor." Emma was indignant. Joseph wouldn't dally with prostitutes or streetwalkers. It wasn't in his nature.

Dr. Stewart was losing his patience. "Lady Head, I don't want to be rude or out of line, but what this man has been through, he may have sought comfort from anyone. He has laceration scars all over his back and legs. I don't like being so graphic, but it seems I must to help you understand. I have used the new X-ray technology, and both legs and arms previously were broken in several places. The bones in his left arm healed improperly; consequently, his arm hangs quite limp." Emma silently began to cry. "He has burn marks all over his torso, and ligature scars where he was bound."

"Enough, enough," Charles said. "We understand the magnitude of my brother's suffering. What we don't know is how he got here, to St. Cadoc's."

"Commodore Head and a fellow named Percy were brought here by two, uh, concerned women from London." Dr. Stewart cleared his throat. "If it weren't for their kindness, both men would be dead by now."

Emma was reeling. Her most vivid nightmares were never as diabolical as what Joseph actually suffered: torture, prostitutes, venereal disease, starvation. She quivered. She wiped her tears and choked back the bile that threatened to spew out of her mouth. She looked at Charles and David. "What are we to do?"

David spoke firmly. "Dear girl, there is nothing to do. Our Joseph is gone, buried, never to return. We must leave what's left with Dr. Stewart to care for him while we go back to our lives at Whitfield. You have a husband, three children, a home, and a business." David's voice became compassionate. "You know our Joseph would not want or expect you or any of the family to relinquish the lives we have built." David turned to Dr. Stewart. "Sir, what is my son's prognosis?"

"Duke, all I can tell you is he has an incurable disease and its outcome is fatal. How long he has, only God knows. From my experience, I feel confident in saying he is close to the last stages, especially with no memory of the past."

"Thank you for being candid. It is always best to be told the truth."

Joseph was still touching Emma's hand and studying her fingers. He rubbed the ring finger of her left hand. Tears streaming down her face, she leaned over and kissed his cheek, then out of reflex from long, long ago, she tweaked his arm and forced a smile. She stood up and began walking away. It took every ounce of courage in her body to leave him.

"Emmmma." Joseph's eyes rapidly fluttered.

In a flash she knelt in front of him, "Joseph, you know me!" A hint of the blue pools sparkled.

He touched her hair. "Emma?"

"Yes, Joseph, yes, it is me, Emma." She threw her arms around his neck and hugged him.

Joseph reached around and brought her wrists down from his neck. She looked in his eyes. They were blank. He had receded back into his own world.

Chapter 43

Plundered Lives

The three of them rode back to the hotel in silence, each trying to absorb what they saw and heard at the hospital. None of them wanted dinner, but settled for a cup of tea with bread and butter. David phoned Catherine to heap on more lies. Their business was going to take a few more days. Emma arrived safely and decided to stay to shop. Nothing out of the ordinary, business as usual, but nice that Emma could come to share some time with Charles.

For the first time in their married life, Emma didn't make love to Charles. Instead, she made love to Joseph. She felt his blond hair wrapped around her fingers as she pushed his head down lower and lower. After being satisfied, she pulled him up and into her. Their synchronized thrusts ended in a perfect climax. She smiled as she felt him trace the outline of her breasts and buttocks. His touch aroused her again. Emma pushed him onto his back, then straddled him and rode him hard, harder than ever before; tonight she wanted to be crushed into him. She needed to feel him deep inside, throbbing in ecstasy. He lay back panting, physically spent, but Emma demanded more. She took his hand and put it between her legs and began pushing. She laughed with joy as the sensations became more and more intense. At the last minute, Emma slowed him down until he wanted her desperately and took her all over again. She opened her eyes and looked for the blue pools that captivated her. The heavy curtains at the window cloaked the room in darkness, and she couldn't see his eyes. It didn't matter; what mattered was he was back and in her arms. Emma nuzzled his neck and drank in his scent.

He was thrilled she hungered for his body. He didn't know what to expect after the heartbreaking scene at the hospital. She fell asleep in his arms. Charles kissed her ear, ran his fingers from her throat to her belly, then down further. He couldn't help touching the places he knew aroused her. He felt her stir beneath him and begin to move. He kissed her cheeks, ears, and lips lovingly, softly. She responded with a low moan. He could feel she was ready for him. He entered her slowly; her reaction was to pull him in deeply and grind against him. Dear God, it was so sensual he couldn't contain himself.

She took it all, then started letting herself go completely. "Joseph, oh Joseph." Then Emma released a deep moan. Charles froze on top of her. "Don't stop; I need it now." He couldn't move. He was paralyzed. "Please, please," Emma begged.

Charles rolled off her aching body. He realized with horror the whole night she was making love to Joseph, not him. It was over.

Emma didn't understand why Joseph stopped. She propped herself up on one elbow. He got out of bed and lit a small gas lamp on the bedside table. He turned around. Charles stood before her. She saw the sorrow in his eyes and on his face. Oh God, what had she done? She was so completely consumed by the past rising from the ashes of her grief, the reality of her life slipped from her grasp. She truly believed she was making love to Joseph. Seeing him after believing he was dead brought back the feelings of her youth. The young girl that made love all night was buried along with Joseph, but like him was alive again.

"Charles, I don't know what to say. Today was such a shock it threw me back into the past." Emma's voice reeked with desperation, but Charles couldn't comfort her. He felt betrayed. His wife had been unfaithful.

"Emma, I can't talk about this now." Charles was putting on his clothes. "I am going out for some air." His frosty tone was foreign to her.

"Please, Charles, don't do this. We have to work through this."

He opened the door and looked back. "I don't know if I can." The door slammed shut.

Emma was stunned. She realized she was naked and cold. She covered herself with the down duvet, but still shivered. Had she lost everything? A husband who was ravaged with disease returned from a long-forgotten war devoid of his brilliant mind. A husband who adored her and gave her beautiful sons, a privileged life, and unconditional love. Who was she married to? Emma's mind kept reeling, looking for answers, but no answers came.

She stared at the ceiling the remainder of the night. Charles didn't return. At first light she got up, dressed, and went downstairs to the restaurant. David was sitting at a table drinking a cup of tea. One look at Emma, and David thought, *evidently Emma didn't sleep much*; dark circles surrounded her eyes. He stood up and pulled out a chair for her.

"Where's Charles?" David looked puzzled.

"I don't know. He went out in the middle of the night and hasn't returned."

David nodded slowly. The whole situation must be unbearable for his younger son and his daughter-in-law. He gave Emma a weak smile and ordered her tea. She refused any food.

"David, what are we going to do?" Emma pleaded for his wisdom.

"After absorbing the shock of seeing Joseph in this state, I decided to return to the hospital and discuss options with Dr. Stewart."

David's despair was palpable. They sat in silence, staring at nothing.

Finally Emma broke the silence. "May I go back to the hospital with you?"

"Are you sure that is wise, Emma?"

"Yes, I want to hear what the doctor recommends."

"Of course, my dear, forgive me, I am so consumed by my own confusion; I have not considered your feelings." David patted her hand. "Also, I am sure Charles is having a difficult time grasping the enormity of his brother's malady." Emma looked away.

David couldn't imagine what had transpired between Charles and Emma, but it was not good, he knew. It was so unlike Charles to leave her alone after the brutal reality of the day. His younger son was not adventurous like Joseph. He loved Whitfield, pure and simple. He was married to the land before Emma came into their lives. He speculated that his brief courtship with Constance was a result of some feelings for his brother's fiancée he fought to control by getting involved with another woman. Once Joseph was captured, Charles dedicated himself to helping Emma through the grief and depression. Out of their friendship, a love developed that survived through ups and downs of married life, but could it survive now? David didn't have a clue. Oh, how their lives had changed in forty-eight hours. The rest of the family at Whitfield continued with their day-to-day activities oblivious to the fact that soon life as they knew it would never be the same. David took a deep breath. *I can't think of any of that at this moment. Decisions must be made regarding Joseph, and they must be made with a clear head not driven by tangled emotions.*

David and Emma rode to the hospital in silence. Both were locked into their own thoughts and fears. An orderly opened the main door and ushered them to Dr. Stewart's office. He was busy pouring over some medical journals. When Emma shook his hand, she saw a book was opened to a chapter titled *"Last Stages of Syphilis."* She felt sick.

Dr. Stewart saw Emma's stricken look and closed the journal. "Good morning to you both. I expected your arrival. Commodore Head's brother got here very early, so I thought you would be along a little later. He's been with Joseph for several hours."

Emma's misery deepened and her stomach knotted. She wanted to double over to ease the pain, but she fought to keep her composure. "May we see Joseph now?" Dr. Stewart led them down the same corridor with the same locked doors to the same small room. The door was closed. He opened it quietly.

The scene would be a picture burned in Emma's mind until she took her last breath. The brothers were sitting on the small bed in the barren room. Charles had draped his cloak around Joseph's shoulders and his arm was around him. Joseph huddled against Charles humming a sailor's song. He looked so small against Charles's muscular chest and arms. Years of working in the fields and shearing the sheep kept him fit and strong. Years of torture and starvation made Joseph gaunt and withered. Emma cringed at the pitiful sight.

Charles looked at his father and his wife resolutely. He directed his statement to Dr. Stewart. "I am taking my brother home."

"Lord Head, Charles, you can't be serious!" Dr. Stewart was incredulous.

"I am dead serious, sir." Charles spoke quietly, his eyes narrowed.

"He needs proper medical attention and twenty-four-hour nursing care." *My God,* Stewart thought, *this man must be as mad as his brother.*

Charles's voice had the same icy tone Emma heard the night before when he left her. "Dr. Stewart, my father and I have the means to provide my brother with the best medical care money can buy, and I intend to do just that."

"But his disease is progressing daily. You don't understand what it will be like at the end."

Charles jumped up and stood a few inches from the doctor's face. "He deserves to be at home with the family who loves him. You of all people should know he has suffered enough."

"I agree that if he were lucid, being at home would be beneficial for a time, but sir, he is not." Dr. Stewart dropped any shred of kind bedside manner. "This man is mad."

Emma saw Charles clench his fists. "Hold your tongue. My mind is made up."

Dr. Stewart tried one more time. "This is a military facility. The navy will never release him."

Charles smirked. "The navy declared him dead. He no longer exists." He turned to David. "Father, I want you to go home and prepare Mother and the rest of the household for Joseph's arrival. Take Emma with you. Once I have all the arrangements made, I will telephone when to expect us."

"Charles, are you sure this is wise?" It was a rhetorical question. David was in a complete quandary between what was right or wrong for Joseph, but he didn't have the strength to fight Charles. His son's mind was made up.

"It is not only wise, Father; it is the morally right thing to do. If we leave him in this hospital waiting to die, lost in his own world, we could not live with ourselves. Such a decision would haunt us for the remainder of our lives."

For the first time Charles turned to Emma. "I want you to have his rooms opened up and outfitted with the medical supplies he needs that kind Dr. Stewart will list for us." Charles's voice dripped with sarcasm. Then his eyes softened. "Tell the boys as little as you can until I get home with Joseph." Emma's heart fluttered. The ice was melting! His tone had the tenderness in it she loved. Then she realized it was not meant for her. "You can move into his rooms or I will." He turned back to Joseph.

Emma's voice was just above a whisper. "Charles, may I have a word outside for just a moment?"

He didn't look at her. He began to gather the few belongings Joseph possessed in his hospital room. "Not now, Emma, not in the presence of Father, Dr. Stewart, and Joseph. It can wait."

She was humiliated. Charles completely rejected her in front of her father-in-law and the doctor. What was she going to do? She lost Joseph a very long time ago. Her conjuring him up as he was and imagining making love to him was a fantasy destroying her marriage to Charles. What warped crevice of her mind made an apparition seem real when all along it was Charles she loved and had made a life with for the last ten years?

Every time Emma returned to Whitfield after a trip, she felt the same exhilaration she experienced the first time as a nineteen-year-old girl. This time was different. The rolling hills, the thickets of trees, the village in the distance, the steeple of St. Peter's were the same, but she was different, gutted, empty, and completely alone. Where did she belong? In rooms that were shut off by death or rooms that were snatched away by life?

She and David remained silent; the clop-clop of the horses' hooves were the only sounds. Emma despised those sounds. At first, when she was young and naïve, the sounds meant happiness was arriving, but since Joseph's deployment, it was a foreboding of tragedy and sadness waiting to engulf her very soul.

Catherine waited for them at the main door. She knew something was drastically wrong by the sound of David's voice on the telephone. The contraption crackled and hummed, but the despondency in his voice wasn't masked by the poor reception. She had the foresight to have Jenny and Nanny take the boys to Dover for the day so whatever happened, they wouldn't be exposed to bad news until she could process it. Emma had the same look she had the day the officers came to report Joseph's abduction by the Russians. David looked just as bad. *Dear God, what happened?*

The three of them went into the family parlor. David poured each of them a brandy. He took a long drink. The household staff surmised something was amiss by the way Catherine acted before the family returned home. Phoebe and Harvey, David's valet, listened outside the parlor door. They could only hear muffled voices until Catherine screamed, a guttural sound that made Phoebe's skin crawl. She wondered if Charles was killed in an accident, as he hadn't come home with the duke and Emma. Then the wailing started. It unnerved them both so much they retreated to the kitchen, where the other servants waited to hear a snippet of news. Hours passed. When the mistress rang for Phoebe, she was outwardly composed, but her face was ravaged with deep pain.

"Gather all the staff in the great hall, even the stable workers. I will meet you there in ten minutes." Phoebe nodded, squeezed Catherine's hand, and trotted off immediately. She dreaded whatever was coming. The last time the staff gathered in the great hall, they were told Commodore Head was a prisoner of war.

True to her word, the duchess came into the great hall to meet with the staff. Her face was grave, but her natural grace held her together. Neither the duke nor Emma were with her. Phoebe knew it was bad. Something terrible must have happened to Master Charles, as he still had not returned from Wales.

"Commodore Head, Joseph, was found in a hospital in Newport." Catherine paused as an audible gasp bounced off the walls. The staff was shocked. "Charles will be bringing him home, possibly as soon as tomorrow. I want Joseph's rooms opened, aired, and thoroughly cleaned." Catherine exhaled slowly. "Joseph is very ill." She omitted the nature of his disease. "As a prisoner he endured years of torture, sleep deprivation, and starvation, horrible acts that are unimaginable to me." Catherine brushed a tear from her eye. She willed herself to stay strong. "When Charles arrives, we will have the regimen of care from his brother's doctor. As you all can imagine, his father and Emma are exhausted and emotionally drained." Catherine intuitively felt the servants' curiosity regarding Emma's role. She didn't know the answer, so how could she tell them what was going to happen? She rubbed her temples.

Harvey stepped forward. "Mam, I speak for all of us." Harvey was solemn. "For generations our families have lived in Whitfield, either in the village or at the manor. We are dedicated to your family and will do whatever you need us to do. You and all the family have always been good to our families; you can count on our loyalty." Catherine heard mumbles of "yes," "of course," "naturally." She was overwhelmed with their kindness.

The main door opened wide, and the boys tumbled in with Jenny and Nanny. Their laughter broke the eerie atmosphere in the great hall. Jenny felt a hot flush rush up her body. The unusual gathering meant there was trouble. "Nanny, take the boys up to the nursery for their tea." Jenny's voice was sharp. The boys stopped laughing and followed Nanny up the stairs.

"Thank you all." Catherine smiled. "Go back to your work, and we'll get through this twist of fate together." Some of the older servants hugged her, others squeezed her hand, and the younger servants curtsied or bowed reverently. Jenny was still rooted to her spot, her face void of color.

"Where is Emma?" Her voice trembled.

Catherine knew Jenny thought of Emma as her own daughter. This situation would affect her greatly. *Everyone will be affected,* Catherine sighed, *even her innocent grandsons.* "Come sit in the parlor with me, Jenny. I'll order tea."

Jenny followed Catherine. She was desperate to know what happened and terrified at the same time. Tea was served. Jenny noticed the serious look on Minnie's face when she placed the tea tray on the table in front of the two women.

"Jenny, I am just going to tell you outright. Joseph is coming home." Jenny stared at Catherine in disbelief. "His father and brother found him in a hospital in Newport when they went back to Wales. The details are complicated and not important. He's very ill." Catherine stared out of the window, then continued, "So ill he won't recognize us."

"What about Emma? Does he know Emma?" Jenny screeched.

"David said he recognized her for a split second, then slipped back into his own world."

Jenny wrung her hands. "What are we to do?"

"Emma hasn't eaten or spoken to me. She sat in complete silence when David told me about Joseph. She's up in her rooms. You must go to her, Jenny. I cannot fathom what she is feeling. She is going to need you more now than she ever has in her life." Catherine rose. "Go now; I will placate the boys."

"When will he be home?" Jenny asked.

"I don't know. As soon as Charles has all his medical needs sorted out, he will bring Joseph home to Whitfield, where he belongs."

Jenny opened the door to Charles and Emma's rooms. Emma was sitting in her lounge chair staring out the window. Even looking at her profile, Jenny saw the defeated child she cared for after Maria's nervous breakdown. "Emma, Catherine told me the news." She spoke softly. Emma didn't respond or turn around. *God, what am I going to do to help her?* Jenny watched as Emma twirled her hair round and round her finger. She tried again. "Em, dear girl, we must talk about this incredulous situation." Jenny stepped behind Emma's chair and massaged her shoulders. "Catherine and Nanny are occupying the boys. For their sake, we must discuss Joseph's return."

Hearing Jenny speak of the boys deepened Emma's self-persecution. She loathed herself. In God's eyes, she must be the epitome of sinners. She violated his commandments. She engaged in premarital sex with Joseph and even conceived his child out of wedlock. After his disappearance, instead of being celibate and chaste, she fornicated with his brother, then married him with no proof of Joseph's death. She herself had declared him dead. She made vows to Charles that God could not bless, as it in truth was adultery. To make everything worse, she reverted to her carnal nature with Charles, believing it was Joseph; it destroyed Charles's faith in her. She didn't deserve to be a mother or a wife. In the eyes of God, she was Joseph's wife. In the eyes of the law, she was Charles's wife. Who was she? The loss of her identity clawed at her mind.

Jenny decided to try a tough approach. She sat on the end of the chaise lounge and made Emma look at her. "Listen to me. You cannot sit in this room and wallow in your own self-pity. You have three sons who need you. They haven't seen you in several days, and they miss their mother. Put your own despair aside and deal with the children. Have you decided what you are going to tell them about Joseph?"

Emma crumpled in Jenny's arms, sobs wracking her body.

"What have I done, what have I done?" Emma sobbed.

"You have done nothing wrong. Do you understand me?" Jenny's voice was firm.

"Oh Jenny, I have lost Joseph all over again, and I have lost Charles." Emma wept openly.

"What do you mean you have lost Charles? He adores you and has dedicated his life to you and the boys." Jenny was bewildered. Master Charles was loving and kind. He wouldn't reject Emma.

Emma choked out the bare truth. "It was such a shock to see Joseph alive and so ill with no memory. He knew me for a second, then slipped back into the place of darkness where his mind dwells. Jenny, that night, so many conflicting emotions . . . such confusion within me, I made a terrible mistake." Emma shivered like someone walked across her grave.

"What was so horrible that you have lost Charles?"

Emma's head dropped. She couldn't look Jenny in the eye. "When we went to bed, I was so physically tired and mentally drained, I responded to Charles's, um, affection, but imagined he was Joseph."

"Mon Dieu!" Jenny paused. "I am sure Charles is not a mind reader."

"He didn't have to be. At the most intimate moment, I called out Joseph's name."

The human mind could play such tricks. She had no words of comfort for Emma. *Charles's very soul must have been cut to ribbons.*

"He left our hotel totally heartbroken. Yesterday he told me to either move into Joseph's rooms or stay here and he would move in with Joseph." Emma held her head in her hands. "What am I to do?"

Jenny paced around the room. *God, so much had changed in the blink of an eye.* She had to think of something. She didn't want the staff gossiping, although she knew they were completely loyal; it would be difficult not to speculate about Emma's position, especially if she or Charles changed rooms. There was one plausible solution. "We will move you back to the nursery." Jenny saw the first glint of hope in Emma's eyes. "It will make sense to everyone that you want to be with the boys during this confusing time. Simply, they have an uncle, and he has returned." It was true in part. The boys were inquisitive little tykes and would need answers, especially if Joseph's state were as bad as Catherine and Emma said. "You don't want them to be afraid, so it's natural their mother would stay with them to dispel any qualms they might have." Jenny cleared her throat. "Emma, I must be direct. Is Joseph harmful to himself or others?"

Emma's face twisted into a grief-stricken grimace. "The doctor thinks so, but Jenny, I don't believe it."

"Dear God, help us all." Jenny hugged Emma. She needed to act fast, as Charles could arrive with Joseph anytime, and she wanted Emma safely ensconced in the nursery before that happened.

"Emma, bathe, comb your hair, and apply face makeup. I'll fetch Minnie, Phoebe, and some of the others to move your things and set up your old room in the nursery."

"But how can I do that and see the boys? What will I tell them?"

Jenny's voice was steady and even. "You will tell the boys you are staying with them because their father needs privacy to help his brother. All they have ever been told is their uncle was killed in a long-ago war. They are too young to understand, so anything you say will satisfy their curiosity, plus they will be thrilled to have you in the nursery." Jenny sighed. "Now do what I say before anyone questions your move, and for God's sake, mend the breach between you and Charles."

Chapter 44

Preparations

Charles didn't know what to expect from his brother. There was so little known about the prognosis of syphilis. He knew there was no cure, but it affected different people in different ways. Historical documents recorded deaths of royals from the disease for centuries. The most famous royal to die from it was Henry VIII. His notorious womanizing, multiple marriages, and unsanitary personal hygiene resulted in contracting syphilis and dying from it.

Charles spent hours picking Dr. Stewart's brain; Dr. Stewart finally cooperated regarding Joseph's release into his brother's care. The doctor relayed the stages of deterioration and what to anticipate. He allowed Charles to visit Percy, whose case was in a more advanced stage than Joseph's. He observed the lieutenant, Joseph's companion of many years, curled in a fetal position on a bed that was soiled with excrement. His mind was completely gone. Unlike Joseph's world of silence, Percy babbled nonsense incessantly. It was from him the staff heard mumbling about the Duke of Kent, pointing at Joseph, and jabbering utter nonsense. Dr. Stewart shared that he didn't believe Percy had long to live. He refused all nourishment; consequently, he was starving to death.

Dr. Stewart contacted the medical university's research department in London to inquire if there were a young doctor who would be willing to move into Whitfield Manor to tend to Joseph's needs, and subsequently publish an individual case study, of course with anonymity of the patient. The perfect candidate, Dr. Alexander Blain, recently graduated from the Doctor's School of Medicine and was fascinated with the spectrum of venereal diseases that plagued England, and for that matter, much of Europe. He loved research, and the opportunity to care for one patient suffering from the most vicious form of sexual diseases piqued his interest.

Alex, as his friends called him, wasn't married but rather on the socially awkward side, which made it difficult to cultivate female relationships. He went on a few dates in his life, but nothing serious developed. He was an intellect married to his work. His dedication and brilliant medical mind caught the eye of his professors at the Doctor's School, the outcome being a fellowship in the research department of Oxford University Medical School. He was only twenty-nine years old, with a brilliant career ahead of him. It was an easy decision to accept the post at Whitfield Manor caring for Commodore Head and simultaneously studying his disease. The university issued him an indefinite sabbatical from his fellowship. No time constraints applied because the life expectancy of Joseph Head was unknown.

Alex packed his personal belongings from the flat supplied by the university, gathered several different drugs he anticipated the patient would need, and shipped his medical books to Whitfield. He felt as if he were embarking on a great adventure. He had never been to Kent except for boarding ship in Dover to cross the Channel to the European mainland. He lived in London all of his life and traveled abroad infrequently. He attended several medical conventions in Paris and Lisbon, but that was the extent of his travels outside the British Isles.

As an only child born to older parents, he learned life lessons early. His mother was thirty-eight when he was born. She doted on her son, read to him incessantly, and taught him kindness and empathy toward others. His father, on the other hand, wanted Alex to hunt and engage in sports as he grew up, but his son wasn't interested at all. He much preferred going to the London library and museums, and reading. His books were the windows to the outside world. His family wasn't wealthy, but they had the means to send him to university and then to the medical school in London. Both parents were proud of their son's accomplishments. Alex explained the opportunity to study a patient at Whitfield without divulging the patient's illness, and they supported him completely. In fact, his father was fascinated Alex would be living in a royal household and looked forward to chatting about the lives of a royal family.

Alex was tall and thin, with a kind face. He wasn't particularly handsome, but his empathetic nature drew people to him. He was the type of person others confided in with their secrets, their fears, their aspirations, their dreams, and their desires of the heart. His mother could be credited for this quality in her son. She cultivated his attitude toward mankind and continually assured him he had much to contribute to the betterment of the human condition. Alex attributed his desire to be a doctor to his mother. She instilled in him that through his talent, he had much to give to the world. His research, she assured him, would help the world. If horrible diseases such as venereal diseases were cured and eventually eradicated and his contributions in research were part of that end, her son would be a success. Matilda Blain looked at Alex's opportunity to take care of Commodore Head much differently than her husband, Theodore. The lives of the royals didn't interest her much, but for Alex to have a living, breathing subject to study thrilled her. Matilda felt sure it would be a step toward helping many people, not just one.

Charles had spoken to Alex on the telephone from St. Cadoc's regarding his brother. Just from the long conversation on the telephone, Charles felt comfortable with the young doctor and offered him the position without meeting him personally. Charles was a realist, understanding not many young doctors would leave their practices or studies to care for one man in a little village in Kent. He felt fortunate Dr. Blain was willing. He read his dossier, which was brought by courier to Newport. His credentials matched exactly what Charles needed for Joseph. He told Dr. Blain he would be treated as part of the family, but paid in pound sterling for his employment. The men entered into a verbal agreement. Charles made arrangements for Dr. Blain's traveling expenses and called his father to have him meet the doctor at the train station. The plan was in place for Joseph's return home.

Charles talked to Joseph as if nothing were the matter with him. He treated him with the same respect that was always between them. Although there was no recognition since the day Joseph spoke Emma's name, Charles carried on as if nothing had changed. His heart was still in turmoil over Emma's unfaithfulness. He loved her, but he didn't know if she loved him or if their whole marriage had been a sham.

He knew one thing for certain; he could not, would not, leave his brother in the hospital to die. What despicable nightmares Joseph endured, no one would ever know. He deserved to die on the land where he was born and was rightful heir. The entire situation was convoluted and a quagmire of uncertainty. He had to get Joseph home.

Emma's transition back to the nursery was smooth. The staff accepted it as it appeared on the surface. The boys were delighted their mummy would be with them much more. At first they didn't ask too much about their Uncle Joseph, but after the first couple days of relishing their mother's constant presence in the nursery, they became curious. They knew Papa had a brother who was lost in the war, but that was about all. No one at Whitfield seemed to talk about him much, and their little minds were occupied with frolicking in the fields, riding horses, playing games, and schoolwork. Now that he was coming home, they asked their grandmother and mother many questions. Emma avoided their quizzing, so it was left to Catherine to answer questions.

Catherine went to the nursery to have tea with the boys, Emma, Nanny, and Jenny. Once they were seated at the table and tea served, she began, "JD, I know you and your brothers have bothered everyone in the house about Uncle Joseph."

"No, Grannie, we haven't bothered anyone. We just want to know about him." JD gave a big grin. Catherine took a deep breath. He was the spitting image of Joseph. She hadn't seen it since he was a baby in her arms, or maybe she simply ignored it.

"I know you boys meant no harm. Your mummy and I are not angry." She gave Emma a quick look. "I am going to tell you about his life while we have our tea." A lump was in Catherine's throat. "Would you like that?"

The boys were rambunctious, jumping up and down in their chairs, chanting, yes, yes, yes. It gave Catherine a moment to compose herself. "Your Uncle Joseph, as you know from his portrait, was a decorated officer in the British Navy. He fought in two wars, one as a young man in China and then one in Turkey. He traveled all over the world and loved being at sea commanding his ships. He is two years older than your father, but they were very close brothers, like you three." The boys giggled. "They grew up together right here at Whitfield, then Uncle Joseph went in the navy and Papa stayed here on the manor working the farm. A very terrible thing happened to Uncle Joseph many years ago, before you were born. While on a mission in Turkey, he and his men were captured by Russian soldiers and never heard from again."

JD interrupted, "Where did they go, Grannie?"

"We don't know exactly, but we do know that they were treated very badly. In fact, we were told they were all dead." Catherine stretched the truth. Going into detail had no purpose; they were too young to understand the death declaration. "By accident, or by the grace of God, when Grandfather and Papa were in Wales, they were told by a friend that British sailors were in the hospital right there in Newport."

The boys were all talking at the same time. "Blimey, how did that happen? What a coincidence. Wasn't God good like the Bible says? Was Uncle Joseph happy to see Papa? How soon would he be home?"

Catherine held up her hand to shush them and cleared her throat again. "I have a very sad part to tell you, children. Uncle Joseph was treated so poorly, he became very sick. The Russian captors didn't give him any medical attention, and he got worse and worse. He is very ill. So ill that he doesn't recognize Grandfather or Papa." All three of the boys were wide-eyed and stared at her. "Now, don't be worried or afraid. We have a nice doctor coming to live with us to help take care of your uncle." Catherine smiled. "Maybe with the doctor's care and our love, he will remember."

Emma jumped up and ran for the bathroom. She vomited until nothing was left in her system. Jenny waited for her outside the door.

"Emma, you must put on a calm face for your children." Jenny was stern.

Emma slid down the wall and buried her face in her hands. "I can't do this, Jenny. I can't. I am going to be living under the same roof with my first husband's shell and with my second husband's disdain. How am I supposed to put on a happy face when I am dying inside?" Emma sobbed. "My wickedness has come back to haunt me."

Jenny sat on the floor by Emma. "You have no choice. Those three children in the other room need you and must be protected. If they see you fall apart, their world will be torn more asunder than it is now. Most of all, JD must be shielded. He doesn't know Charles is not his biological father. What will his reaction be if he finds out his sick uncle is his real father?"

Emma's voice was hollow and empty. "You are right as always. I'll do my best." She looked Jenny straight in her eyes. "I have lost Charles. I can't lose my boys. Why, what would they think of me if they knew the truth?" She stood up, smoothed her dress, pinched her pale cheeks, and walked back to the nursery kitchen.

Emma smiled at the children. "Sorry, sons, Mummy choked on a cucumber."

JD, ever sensitive, asked, "Did you cough it up? Are you all right?" His little brow was furrowed with concern.

Emma hugged him. "Yes, son, I did and am fine." She changed the subject. "Now that Grannie has told you nosy little boys what you wanted to know, let's play outside while the sun is shining." All three were grabbing their coats and finding shoes strewn around the room. Emma mouthed to Catherine, thank you. They both smiled, but pain dripped from their eyes.

Chapter 45

Doctor Alexander Blain

EMMA WAS COMFORTABLE IN HER old bed in the nursery wing, but she slept fitfully, up and down, up and down. After breakfast she ordered the landau brought round; she thought an open-air ride to the village might break her melancholy mood. One of the footmen came back to tell her David took the landau to the station to pick up a houseguest. They all knew it was the doctor Charles hired, but no one spoke openly about it.

She went back inside and wandered to the family wing. Joseph's rooms were opened. She hadn't stepped foot inside since his deployment, not even after they were refurbished. They were sealed until several days ago. She slowly turned the brass knob on the entry door. It opened without a creak; obviously staff thought of everything, oiling the hinges so there would be no reminder the door was closed for over ten years. Emma walked through each room. The parlor, the main bedchamber, the servant room that was converted to the doctor's room, the modernized bathroom, and a small anteroom converted into what looked like a doctor's examining room. The rooms were beautiful, exactly how she and Joseph planned. The fine furniture, the silk coverlet on their bed with matching fabric at the huge floor-to-ceiling windows, everything done to perfection, to her and Joseph's specifications. She sat in an easy chair by the window, then leaned back and closed her eyes. It was surreal. She was catapulted back in time. They planned the rooms together. It was fun; she could hear their laughter as they chose pieces they both liked. Their taste was perfectly suited, just as they were perfect. She drifted off to sleep. The image of Joseph skipped through her slumber.

The butler lightly tapped her shoulder. She opened her eyes. "Mam, the doctor is here."

Oh dear God, here she was in Joseph's rooms, and the butler found her. She quickly covered up her indiscretion. "Thank you. I was awaiting his arrival and drifted off to sleep."

"I present Dr. Alexander Blain," the butler announced.

Emma's first observance of him was spot-on. He was kind. He looked very young, but wise. His hair was dark and wavy, his eyes a chocolate brown, and his smile inviting. She also noticed he was quite thin, not gaunt but thin, as if he forgot to eat.

"You must be Emma. I have looked forward to meeting you." Her discomfort was obvious. He didn't want to call her Mrs. Head, too confusing, so he took the liberty of using her first name. He hoped he hadn't offended her. "It was so very kind of you to wait for me here."

Emma blushed crimson. "Oh, uh, no trouble at all."

"Since I am sure we will be seeing quite a lot of each other, I hope you will call me Alex. That's what my friends call me, and I am certain we'll become good friends."

Emma's embarrassment evaporated into thin air. "Of course, Alex, and please call me Emma." Her smile was genuine. "Let me show you to your room and you can get settled. Dinner will be in a couple hours. You may want to rest beforehand after your journey from London."

"Thanks, Emma. I had a box sent. Did it arrive?"

"I don't know. Let's look in your room." They went into Alex's new bedroom, but the box wasn't there. "Oh, a, um, a clinic-type room was set up in your wing; maybe it's there." The box of medical books and journals was placed in the examining room. Alex felt relieved the crate had arrived, as he also had some of his research manuals packed. They would be invaluable while treating Commodore Head.

He smiled. "Now I can rest, then freshen up for dinner."

"Of course. One question, Alex. When will Charles and Joseph arrive home?" Emma's voice quavered.

His eyes oozed with empathy, as if he could read her mind, which was a jumble with the overload of events from the last week. He took her hand in a comforting gesture. "I don't know," he said softly. She didn't pull away; his kind gesture brought tears to her eyes.

Emma left his room wondering about his background and how Charles found such a congenial doctor. At least one thing went right.

Two more days crawled by. The weather had been cold, and drizzling rain added to the bleak mood that permeated the house. The boys were stuck indoors, which proved exasperating. They wrestled and picked on each other until Emma thought she would scream. They never acted like this when Charles was home. He was a strict disciplinarian who kept them in line. He never caned them, but sent the naughty one to a quiet room without toys. This method was effective. Emma just threatened and didn't follow through.

Dr. Blain was busy setting up his room and his clinic. The name stuck: the clinic. Although the rain had been steady, Alex left for Dover early each morning to order the medical supplies he needed for the clinic. The family provided the rudimentary items, but specific medical equipment was needed. David emphasized the cost was inconsequential. He wanted his son to have the best money could buy. Alex visited the apothecary shop and ordered the medicines he deemed necessary for Joseph's comfort. Because of the opiates he purchased, he bought a medicine cabinet with a lock and key. When Alex returned that evening, David told him privately his sons would arrive the next day. He didn't inform the women because he hoped they might have a good night's rest, for who knew what lay in store for the family? Alex worked late into the evening setting up the clinic so it would be ready to receive his patient.

For years Emma had had a recurring dream. She was always about seven years old, living in Calais. She would run and run and run through the mist to reach her mother, who was waving her in, but she couldn't get to her no matter how hard she tried, and then the mist would lift. She was alone in the street, unfamiliar buildings on each side, but her mother was gone, vanished. It was always the same; she would jolt upright in bed gasping for air, covered in sweat. Sometimes Claudine would hear her cry out and come to her room to comfort her. She usually had the dream when she was under tremendous stress, and then it would leave her. In fact, she had gone for years without it invading her sleep, but recently it had stealthily weaved its way in and out of her much-needed rest.

The waiting for Joseph's arrival was excruciating, not knowing what to expect. Emma was praying Charles forgave her, but she didn't know what to expect from him either. The stress intensified. The dream came to her that night. She tried so hard to get to her mother. The mist swirled around her body all the way up to the waist. She fought to get to Maria, then Maria disappeared into the thick mist that hung like a gray curtain in the distance. Emma lurched up, sweat slathered over her body. She blinked and recognized the haunting dream that had plagued her mind since childhood.

She heard a sound that was real, the clop-clop of the horses' hooves on the stones. She ran to the window. She saw Alex waiting for the carriage door to open. The Kent Barony Crest seemed to shrivel and expand, shrivel, expand. Emma felt weak and sick. It was like she was outside herself, watching a play at the theater. Charles jumped down from the carriage and quickly shook Alex's hand. Emma remembered they hadn't met in person. Her heart pounded. David joined Charles. Father and son reached into the carriage. The figure that was lifted out was even more pathetic than when she saw him at St. Cadoc's. From her window, Emma saw his terror. Fear was emblazoned on his face. Catherine emerged into the scene. Emma saw her tears flowing freely. She couldn't hear what she said, but she touched her son's cheek for the first time in over a decade. His overcoat hung from his shoulders. His gray hair blew in the breeze. Emma held onto the windowsill so she wouldn't fall. She saw he didn't recognize his mother. Suddenly, he looked up and smiled. Catherine, David, and Alex followed Joseph's gaze. They all stared at her. Charles didn't turn around. Then in an instant, the terror returned to Joseph's eyes.

Emma crawled back into bed and wept. She didn't leave her room all day and ate nothing. Charles never came. He hadn't forgiven her.

In the early evening, Alex knocked on her door. "Emma, it's Alex. May I come in?"

She didn't answer. He opened the door and entered anyway. He sat on the end of the bed. "I have sedated Joseph. The trip was very hard on him. Tomorrow I will give him a thorough physical examination. Emma, even though his disease has progressed, he may have moments of clarity. He knew you today. Possibly because you were the most important person in his life and the one he loved more than anyone or anything else. When he glimpses into our world, you are the conduit."

Emma wept again. She thought no tears were left. Her eyes were so swollen they hurt, but the tears came anyway. Alex sat next to her and held her hand. "Deep breath, Emma. Breathe in through your nose; blow out through your mouth. I can't have you hyperventilating and fainting." Emma did as she was told, just like she had when Admiral Smyth gave her the same instructions. Alex waited for her crying to subside.

She had only known him for a few days, but Emma trusted Alex. She had to talk to someone. "Alex, I am in a vise, an impossible situation. The husband I mentally buried years ago has reappeared. The husband I am married to now has rejected me. What am I to do?"

"Time is quite a healer, Emma. I don't know what happened between you and Charles, but you both need time. Finding Joseph was a shock to you both, but in different ways. I want you to understand this household dynamic has changed for now. Joseph has a terminal disease. When he dies, this household will go on. You have three vibrant boys who are accustomed to living in a loving, nurturing environment. You don't believe it now, but that will return after everyone has adjusted to Joseph's return."

"Do you really believe that, Alex?"

"Yes, I do." Alex paused. "I need your help, Emma."

"Me, how can I help you?" Emma's voice screeched.

"So far, Joseph has experienced two moments of clarity. Both have been recognition of you. Will you help me understand his mental condition?" Alex almost pleaded.

"How could you ask me that question? You know I can't refuse to help Joseph."

"I am asking for a daily commitment, so once in a routine, his anxiety will abate, and he may have more frequent and longer times of being lucid."

"Yes, whatever you need." Emma was miserable. Patching her relationship with Charles was impossible if she spent each day with Joseph. But how could she say no? Joseph was a victim of circumstance. He didn't leave her on purpose. It was totally out of his control. He had assured her the deployment was routine, and then he was snatched from their lives. Charles picked up the pieces and filled her life with love and joy. Alex was talking.

"I apologize; what did you say?"

"The boys have lessons in the mornings three days a week, and Charles will occupy them the other days. If you have breakfast with the children, then come to me, spend the morning, we'll have an established routine that will help Joseph be comfortable."

Emma agreed. Alex ordered them a light supper, and then he convinced Emma to take a sedative to help her sleep. She looked haggard, which was understandable, but Alex needed her to be focused.

Emma and Alex followed the same routine every day, seven days a week. Joseph had fleeting moments when he brightened up, but mainly he lived in his own mind. Alex was right. Following a routine, after a few weeks, calmed Joseph. The few times Emma was late, Joseph became agitated. From his observations and research, Alex found that repeating daily functions was a comfort to his patient.

Charles came often in the afternoon, when he could leave his work on the manor. He also had a positive effect on his brother. Alex kept hoping that Emma and Charles would reconcile, but so far there was no progress. They were like strangers living under the same roof sharing the same children. They made an agreement to keep their adult problems away from the boys. Joseph had no interest at all in the children; the few times he saw them when Alex took him out for fresh air and sunshine, he showed no reaction. The novelty of having an uncle in the house wore off quickly. They mainly stayed away from Joseph's rooms. The one time JD wandered in to see what his uncle was doing, Joseph cried uncontrollably. It spooked him and he didn't go back.

Emma was lonely in her marriage and life. The boys were attached to Charles and enjoyed traipsing around the manor with him. She knew they loved her and liked it when she read stories to them or showed them how to sketch, but it wasn't the full life she lived before Joseph came home. She decided to send Claudine a telegram asking her to come to Whitfield for a visit. Emma told her parents about Joseph, but they hadn't traveled over from Calais yet. Edgar was swamped at the bank thanks to all the business connections Joseph had arranged for him. Maria spent her time cultivating her social standing. Being related to the Duke and Duchess of Kent opened many doors.

Claudine was still the lighthearted fun-loving sister Emma adored. Her excitement regarding the factory in Wales bubbled over. Emma hoped a visit from her sister would lift the gloom and depression from her daily life. She wanted to confide in her sister the misery she endured and get advice. Although Claudine wasn't married, she understood Emma and was with her the night she met Joseph.

Emma's personal life was such a tangled mess she longed to be with Claudine. She would love to travel to Calais or go to the apartment in Paris, but she couldn't break the routine Alex had developed for Joseph. The routine was working. Joseph gained weight and was definitely much less agitated. He became accustomed to all the family members and the staff.

Emma was tethered to the manor, and it stifled her. Having Claudine visit would break the tedious pattern the whole house had adopted. Charles continued to shut her out as if she were disposable. She tried a few times to make amends but to no avail. Her self-esteem was crushed; she resigned herself to the fact her marriage was ruined by her own stupidity. Charles could not forgive her.

When Claudine arrived, her presence uplifted the entire family. She rattled on and on about the new factory and shop in Newport.

She became extremely successful in the toy industry and developed a prototype of little iron cars that could be manufactured cheaply in Newport, where iron was mined.

Emma was elated to have her sister at Whitfield. The night after she arrived, Emma took her to Joseph's rooms in the morning, as she couldn't break her normal routine. Claudine expressed her apprehension about seeing Joseph. She loved her brother-in-law so much, and to see him ravaged with disease distressed her greatly. Emma told her to act naturally and talk to Joseph as if he knew her.

"Hello, Alex, I would like you to meet my sister, Claudine."

Alex smiled broadly. "Good morning, mademoiselle. I am pleased to meet you."

Claudine blushed. Emma thought that was an odd reaction.

"Claudine. would you like to visit with Joseph?" Alex asked her gently.

"Yes, doctor, but I am so afraid to see him in this condition."

"It's all right. Simply make general conversation. He had a very good night and is well-rested." Alex's voice was quiet and lyrical. He reached out and took Claudine's hand. She felt a calmness come over her. He led her into the parlor.

"Joseph, you have a visitor all the way from Calais. It is your lovely sister-in-law, Claudine."

The dashing commodore that swept her sister off her feet was a wreck. She fought to keep her composure. She squeezed Alex's hand hard. Joseph showed no sign of recognition.

"Speak to him," Alex whispered.

Chapter 46

Lucid Moments

CLAUDINE SAT ON THE SETTEE next to Joseph. She rattled on and on about the Toy Depot. Then she switched topics to the past. She talked about La Mansion Dance Hall. How Joseph and Emma met and how her sister fell in love with him at first sight. Claudine described the excitement in the Bouron home the day Joseph had a designer gown delivered for Emma to wear to the Ambassador's Ball. Reminiscing about the past made Emma giggle. Suddenly Joseph jerked his head around and stared at Emma.

"You," Joseph cleared his throat, "you looked beautiful in that gold gown, the most gorgeous woman at the ball."

Emma fell on her knees right in front of Joseph's face. "You remember?" She was flabbergasted.

"Of course, I remember, darling." He spoke to her like it was yesterday.

Emma looked at Alex. She saw he was baffled as well. Claudine was riveted to the settee barely breathing.

"It was such a special night. Emma, that's when the Cousin-Montaubans became our close friends. We have enjoyed so many happy times with them over the years." Joseph reached out and pulled Emma to her feet. "Darling, should you be resting?" He rubbed her stomach. "Claudine, are you excited to become an aunt?" His eyes twinkled.

He had slipped back in time. It was astounding. He looked at Alex. "Who are you, sir?" Joseph frowned.

Alex smiled. "I am your doctor, Joseph. You have had a rare malaise, so the family thought it best if I stay here with you until your condition improves." Alex lied smoothly. He had no idea how long Joseph would be lucid. He was treating him with a new sulfur drug as part of his research. Was that what caused the breakthrough? He didn't have any idea.

Joseph laughed. "What's wrong with me? I don't recall feeling ill."

Emma's face was stricken with grief. Joseph turned to her. "What is it, darling?"

"I, I, don't know."

Joseph touched her face. "Doctor, I think you upset my wife. What illness is it? Obviously nothing contagious, since my sister and wife are with me."

"No, you are not contagious. You had plague-like symptoms, but it's not the plague. Your family wants to be sure you have the best care." Alex's voice was soothing.

"You see, Emma, I don't have the plague. I must have contracted scurvy on the ship or influenza. The doctor should be here for you, my love. You don't look well, and it is important we protect the baby." Joseph took Emma's hand. "Where is your wedding ring? What ring are you wearing?" Joseph looked puzzled.

"My hands have been swelling from the pregnancy, so I am wearing a ring from the Kent jewels." Emma hoped Joseph couldn't see through her lies.

"What a smart girl you are." Joseph kissed her lightly on the lips. "I am starving. Doctor, will you dine with us?"

"Yes, I would enjoy that immensely. I'll go down and order up the lunch from the cook. Emma, a word please."

"Go on, darling, the good doctor wants to know what you will eat."

Emma practically stumbled across the floor. Joseph chatted easily with Claudine and didn't notice. "My God, Alex, he has reverted to the past. It's as though time stood still for a decade."

"I know, I know. What I don't know is how long it will last, and if he sees the changes in the manor, he may spiral into complete madness."

"What are we to do, damn it? Don't you know what utter torture this is for me?"

"I can't imagine, Emma. I am going to alert Catherine. We just have to play along until I can figure this out." Alex left the room.

Emma slowly walked back to her past, but he was gone. The blank stare stole the twinkle from his beautiful eyes.

Claudine was weeping uncontrollably. Emma handed her a hanky and rubbed her shoulders. "My God, Emma, how do you endure this?"

"This is the first time he was this aware, but it's awareness of the past before he went to war. My heart bleeds with sorrow for what he endured at the hands of those barbarians." Emma cried silent tears. She wiped them away with the back of her hand. "Claudine, I am riddled with fear, guilt, despair. What am I to do?" Emma's tears flowed again. "My first love, whom I married and bore a son, has no knowledge of these past ten years. Charles, who rescued me from pain and grief, is my husband now, who. I have bore two sons, and I love him. I am only able to tell you this, Claudine." Emma shuddered.

"What is it, Emma?"

"I don't understand, but I love two different men. I love the Joseph that was and the Charles that is. It's pathetic, because in reality I have lost them both. Most of the time, Joseph is trapped in a world that exists in his mind. Charles despises me for my betrayal. I am totally alone."

"What betrayal, sister?" Claudine's voice was a whisper.

"The very first night we saw Joseph in the hospital, we were in shock. David was distraught. Charles was destroyed, and I, I was thrust into the past Joseph and I had shared. I was angry and irrational. Charles and I were bone weary, but when we returned to the hotel, we sought comfort in each other. Claudine, what came over me I don't know, but when I closed my eyes, I was in Joseph's arms and making love to him. At the most intimate of moments, I called out Joseph's name."

"Mon Dieu, Emma."

Emma laughed; it was a bitter sound, riddled with guilt and self-loathing. "Ah, Jenny's exact words when I told her of my betrayal.

"The apparition was so real I got lost in it. Charles's heart was broken. He loved me unconditionally, and he is convinced I broke our wedding vows because in essence Joseph was my lover. I have tried and tried to reconcile, but he is finished. Oh, he is polite around the boys, but he mostly avoids me. He gave me the choice in the beginning to move to Joseph's rooms or he would. Jenny is the one who suggested I move back to the nursery to save face and dispel chatter among the staff. But everyone in the household knows we are separated although under the same roof. He stayed in our rooms. It's obvious he's erased me from his life. All my things have been moved or packed up and put in the storage bins."

"Emma, dearest, I am so sorry; I don't know what to say." Claudine looked into her sister's pitiful eyes.

"There is nothing to say. I don't know if I am legally married to Joseph or Charles. Is JD the rightful heir and the other two boys bastards? Can't you see, Claudine, I am being sucked under by quicksand? My family foundation was shattered by circumstance and my own wicked nature." Emma was resolute.

"How can I help you?" Claudine asked.

"You can't, but I need your love and support now more than ever."

The sisters hugged one another. There was so much pain and agony in Emma's dilemma, Claudine literally hurt. The tender moment was broken as Alex barged in through the door with Catherine and Charles following.

Emma looked at them and shook her head. "He's gone again. I am so sorry."

Alex frowned. "What happened?"

"When I came back in from speaking with you, the light had left his eyes and the blank stare returned. He's been sitting on the settee in the same state ever since."

Alex looked at Charles and Catherine. "I apologize. He was completely lucid except for understanding the year and his, uh, circumstances."

Charles shot a look at Emma. "Just exactly what do you mean?"

Alex was a man of science; he didn't mince words when it came to his patient. "Commodore Head's mind has wiped out what happened to him in the Russo-Turkish War. It's a defense mechanism. Whatever the Russians put him through is too painful to comprehend, so he reverted to a safe haven where he was happy and most of all safe." Alex shook his head. "I have been treating him with innovative drugs that have triggered a type of reality, no matter how briefly."

"How often will this occur?" Catherine asked Alex.

"Unfortunately, that's entirely unpredictable. He could come back now or days from now. I just don't have an answer."

Charles tried to be delicate since his mother and sister-in-law were present. "Exactly at what point in his life is he stuck?"

Again, Alex was direct. "He thinks he is still married to Emma and expecting a baby."

"Thank you, doctor," Charles said stiffly, then turned and left the room.

You could cut the air with a knife. Catherine saw the way Emma and Charles had severed their relationship. Her life of joy as a mother was torn asunder. Whatever happened in Wales brought one son back from the dead and threw the other into an emotional turmoil. The charismatic girl who played in the garden with her children and enjoyed her husband was gone also. A cloud of darkness cast its shadow throughout Whitfield.

Claudine extended her stay, and with the convenience of the telephone, she continued to conduct business for the Toy Depots. She worked while Emma spent her mornings with Joseph. Two weeks passed, and there was no change in Joseph's demeanor, no spark of light from the dark corners of his mind. One aspect of life changed; Claudine and Alex were growing very fond of one another and spent a great deal of time in each other's company. The Bourons were planning a visit in the spring, and the dreary weather was lifting. Emma, on the other hand, became more withdrawn and isolated. Claudine was worried. Emma didn't exactly shut her out, but the open conversations of the first days disappeared. The boys were thoroughly enjoyable. Their little lives continued on without a ripple of instability. David returned to London for a session at Parliament. Catherine kept busy with her volunteer work in the village. On the surface, Whitfield Manor seemed to be operating as it had for centuries.

Chapter 47

Life at Whitfield Becomes More Complex

Just when Emma thought life could not be any more complicated or miserable, she discovered she was pregnant. She was nauseated occasionally, and at first attributed it to eating rich foods or not eating at all, but when she missed her third monthly bleeding, she knew instinctively she was carrying a baby. The irony of the matter was the only time she could have conceived a child was the night at the Greyhound, the night that changed her life. She hadn't told anyone, but she wouldn't be able to conceal it much longer. She had an inkling Jenny was suspicious by her not-so-discreet, probing questions. Questions a mother would ask her daughter.

The days clicked by, with the monotonous routine consuming each hour. It was comforting having Claudine at Whitfield, even though she didn't visit with her much. Emma stayed cloistered in the nursery for days except for visiting Joseph. She was reading a book when a knock at her door broke the silence. "Who is it?"

"Emma, it's Alex, may I come in?"

Emma jumped to her feet and yanked the door open. "Has something happened to Joseph?"

"No, no, sorry if I alarmed you. Joseph is asleep." Alex paused. "It's not Joseph that has me concerned; it's you."

Emma blushed. "Where are my manners? Come in, Alex, please. Don't worry about me. I promise I am fine, just stressed from the constant drama in the house." Emma laughed.

Broaching this subject with Emma would be delicate, and he needed to use proper decorum yet be pointed. "Emma, is there anything you want to discuss with me regarding your health?"

For the second time, Emma blushed. She turned away and began to twirl her hair round and round her index finger. She gestured for Alex to sit down. She wondered what brought this on. "Why, no, I don't think so," she lied.

"Think of me right now as a doctor, not a friend or companion to Joseph, but purely a doctor." Alex was very serious, which made him more direct. Emma didn't respond, but shrugged. "Emma, this is the point. Since I arrived at Whitfield Manor, I have noticed subtle changes in you. Sometimes you eat. Sometimes you don't. Some days you have an upset stomach; others, you don't. Your mood swings have traveled the gauntlet, especially since Claudine arrived. She has interacted much more with the children than you have and most days goes with Nanny on excursions with the lads if Charles doesn't have them tagging along. It's as if since she got here, you shifted your mother's duties to her. Also, Nanny is with them far more than their own mother."

Emma felt defensive. "You don't understand how my life completely changed since Joseph came home. I am as alone in this house as he is in his secret world."

Alex spoke softly. "Do you have a secret in your world, Emma?"

"No, no, I do not." Her voice was elevated.

"Ah, but I think you do. I see you every day, and it is part of my profession to be observant. These last few weeks, you haven't worn dresses that require a corset."

"Aren't you being very rude?" Emma tried to sound indignant.

"No, Emma, I could never be rude to you, but what I can be and will be is truthful. I am certain you are with child." Alex looked directly into her eyes. "If you are, changes must be made."

Emma looked like a deflated balloon. She sighed. What difference did it make if Alex knew she was expecting? It would be all too obvious soon enough. She might as well admit it. "You're very astute, Alex." She tried to sound indignant.

"Emma, please don't be flip with me. I only want to help and be sure you get proper care." Alex smiled kindly.

Emma didn't cry, but she was broken. "Alex, don't you see, I am having a baby with Charles? He doesn't want me, and he won't want this baby, especially the way it was conceived. When Joseph has flashes of his previous life, I am carrying his child. The whole situation is crazy."

"Have you told Charles?"

"No, I have told no one."

"Emma, you have to tell him; he's your husband."

"Is he, is he? Or is Joseph my husband? I imagined I was making love to Joseph the night I conceived this baby, so is the baby Joseph's?" Her voice was shrill and bitter. "I can't be a wife, but I can be a rotten mother. I have abandoned my children, just as my mother abandoned me. I have given their care into the hands of their father, Nanny, Jenny, Catherine, and now Claudine. I can't deal with my own flesh and blood, and now I am going to bring another baby into this twisted world at Whitfield. I'd rather be dead."

Alex grasped her by the shoulders. "Emma, don't ever let me hear you say those words. Your children would be lost without you, and once Charles has enough time to process Joseph's return and the impact it has on all your lives, you especially, things will go back to happier times."

Emma drew in her breath. She didn't want to hear his lecture anymore. "I am tired, Alex. I appreciate your concern. I will tell Charles and the others my news at the opportune time. Thank you for your concern." Emma ushered him to the door. "Good night, Alex." She shut the door behind him. During her days of solitude, she had resigned herself to the fact that her life was finished. She'd paid the ultimate price for her sins, loss of both Joseph and Charles.

Two more weeks passed with Emma sequestered in the nursery except for visiting Joseph. Claudine stayed on, and in fact was given a small office on the first floor that was perfect. All of the contracts were signed and executed for the plant in Newport, and construction started. Claudine left her sister alone to decipher how to cope with her situation. She attempted over and over to reach Emma, but it was pointless. She shut Claudine out like she did the other members of the household.

Alex and Claudine spent more and more time together as the weeks passed by. Claudine enjoyed his company more than suitors from the past. He wasn't as handsome or as rich as many who pursued her, but his caring nature made him more appealing. He was the type of person who was innately trustworthy. He didn't play silly games, but was direct. Claudine admired his qualities, especially his dedication as a doctor. He was brilliant and had a bright future ahead.

Emma wrote Charles a note. Jenny delivered it for her. The note asked if he could possibly find a few minutes after dinner to speak to her in the nursery. Her normally flowing script was shaky and smudged.

"Tell your mistress I'll be in to see her shortly after dinner, about half past eight." *How odd*, Charles mused. He thought he'd made it clear their marriage was over. He loved Emma deeply, but he couldn't tolerate disloyalty, unfaithfulness. That night in Newport, he wandered the city streets until dawn, her voice screaming Joseph's name ringing in his ears. The day had been so heart-wrenching, discovering Joseph in such a dreadful state, he expected Emma to have deep feelings of sorrow and loss. What he hadn't expected was her unbridled lust. It was the most erotic feeling he had ever experienced. She demanded satisfaction, and he gave it to her over and over. The last time, when they were both drenched in sweat, she ground into him with a force so fierce he exploded like gunpowder touched by a match. He wanted her to feel every nerve ending in her body pop and crack like fireworks in the night sky. She was on the brink when two words shattered his world . . . "Joseph, Joseph." Those two words cut like a knife through his heart and soul. He could never trust her again. Had she fooled him so thoroughly that in ten years of marriage, she didn't make love to him but imagined he was his brother?

Walking in the damp mist, he shivered. He pulled his overcoat collar up around his neck. He was cold inside and out. Before he reached St. Cadoc's, he made two firm decisions. He was taking Joseph home to Whitfield with or without the doctor's permission. That was the easy decision. More difficult was what to do about his relationship with Emma. He thought about it over and over, but kept coming back to the same conclusion. No matter how much he loved her, he could never trust her again. It was over.

He fought to keep his resolve since that night four months previous. He almost wavered when she crept to his room in the middle of the night and begged him to give her a second chance, but he held firm. The next time she came to him was her last. She pleaded with him to put himself in her position, to imagine the emotional upheaval she felt. She tried to sway him by undressing and trying to kiss him, but again he held firm. The depth of her humiliation was a bottomless hole. She shrunk before his eyes. He wanted her. He wanted to make it right, but his pride won and obliterated the thoughts of reconciliation. Emma left his room shattered in a million pieces. Any shard of self-worth lay on his bedroom floor. She was gutted.

Thinking about the incidents hurt him, but why should he feel guilty? She was the one who cheated in spirit. Now, was it to be another emotional showdown? He didn't think he could bear it. His emotions were already shredded. What with dealing with Joseph, the boys, the farm, he had nothing left to give. He ate dinner alone. Catherine dined in the village, his father was in London, and the good doctor had escorted Claudine to a fine Italian restaurant on the outskirts of Dover. The family dining hall was quiet. The boys still ate their dinner in the nursery kitchen except for special occasions. Once they reached twelve, they would start to take evening meals with the family. While they were little, they ate with Nanny and Jenny.

Charles drank two glasses of white wine with his fish, so unusual for him. He didn't indulge much in spirits, but he wanted to be relaxed, especially if there were a confrontation with Emma. He decided to linger and drink a third glass of wine. He put off the inevitable meeting as long as possible.

Emma awaited Charles's arrival by nervously pacing the floor and twisting her hair. She didn't eat any dinner, fearing she'd be sick. Both Jenny and Nanny encouraged her to partake of the meal, but she was adamant. The last thing she wanted was to be ill in front of Charles. She looked in the mirror for the hundredth time. She had bathed in lavender water, and the scent wasn't too pungent but just enough. Her hair was held back loosely with a pink ribbon, the wild tendrils she'd been twirling framing her face. She applied face powder and a small amount of rouge, hoping it would hide her pallor. Her lips were colored a light pink. She wore her pink silk dressing gown, with nothing underneath. She didn't anticipate a sexual encounter with Charles, but if he doubted her word about the baby, she would show him her body. Her protruding abdomen wouldn't be concealed after tonight. She stopped in front of the mirror once more. Emma looked intently at herself. She was turning thirty years old, but her body looked much like it had as a girl of nineteen. After three children, she had no stretch marks and her weight remained the same. She wondered why she was so undesirable. Obviously some flaw only men could see.

The rap came at the door. Emma's heart pounded.

"Emma, it's Charles, may I come in?"

Of course it was Charles. Who did he think she was expecting, the Prince of Wales? "Yes, the door is open." She stayed seated on the settee, twisting her hair round and round. She felt awkward, like they were courting, going on a first outing together.

Charles was succinct. He didn't smile. She looked so beautiful, he feared he would melt in her presence. He vowed to keep a strong resolve. "Your note said you wanted to speak to me."

Emma's heart dropped. Any hope of light conversation was dashed. She tried again. "Will you sit down?"

"Uh, no thank you. Say whatever it is, and I'll go to the boys' room and read them a fairy tale."

Emma sighed. *My fairy tale turned into a horror story.* She received no inclination of kindness from him. She shrugged her shoulders in defeat. "Charles, I am going to have a baby."

He raised his voice. "Impossible." He was incredulous.

Emma stood up from the settee, untied her pink dressing gown, and dropped it to the floor. "See for yourself." She turned sideways. The bulge was obvious.

Charles grabbed her wrists and turned her to face him. "How could you do this to me? We are still married, if in name only."

Emma pulled her wrists free and slapped him across the face as hard as she could. Charles took a half step backward. "How dare you insinuate this baby is not yours?" Emma shouted. "Look at me; I am over four months along. No other man but you has touched me since I was nineteen." Emma lost all control. She beat her fists against his chest. She screamed, "Stop punishing me for meeting Joseph first, falling in love with him, and marrying him. You selfish bigot, I gave him the love of an immature girl. A woman fell in love with you, but you are too stubborn to see it."

Charles pulled her into his chest, then his hands were all over her, feeling her growing breasts, her silky hair, her protruding stomach. He kissed her lips and ears and throat. Emma fought not to give in, but her willpower disintegrated. Charles picked her up. Emma wrapped her bare legs around his waist. They fell onto the bed. In one movement Charles ripped off all of his clothes. He easily penetrated her. It had been so long, her wetness and warmth sent him over the edge. He came in a rush. He had been rough, but she responded to his every touch. He kissed her neck and throat. Neither of them uttered a word, but he knew his wife so well and she wanted more. "Emma, make love to me, only me, like you did at the Greyhound. It's how I got you pregnant." His voice was deep and anguished.

She didn't give a damn about decorum or seduction. She had a hunger that hadn't been nourished in months. She pushed him off her and onto his back. Emma straddled Charles and ground him into her aching body. She trembled from within and exploded like a volcano gushing lava. Emma rolled off and lay on her back, gasping for air. Charles was gently rubbing her quivering body. He brushed his hands across her belly, then stroked her forehead. Emma's breathing finally slowed. She rolled on her side and faced Charles, tears streaming down her face. In a tortured cry she croaked, "I love you, Charles, and only you, and I have for a very, very long time." She felt as if the lump in her throat would choke her.

He felt the truth in her every word. He completely lost sight of the life they built together because of pride and jealousy. "Emma, I closed you out from fear you still loved Joseph."

"Charles, the girl who wed your brother is dead. Her innocence and youth were buried with Joseph." Emma touched his cheek. "Don't you remember my dark depression and rejection of my own child? You were my lifeline back to peace and acceptance of the twists and turns in life. I fell in love with you. Our marriage and the birth of our children have made me a woman. You have made me a woman. You have to know this. Seeing Joseph at St. Cadoc's was so unnerving. He looked so beaten, so alone. I was literally emotionally spent when we returned to the hotel. I actually think I was in shock. My mind played cruel tricks on me, and I am so sorry but I can't change it. If you can't truly forgive me, then you can't truly love me."

Charles swallowed. "I built a wall around myself because I was very hurt. You know me better than anyone, and you know loyalty is paramount with me. I questioned your loyalty, but I understand the paradox you faced. I do forgive, and I do love you." The timbre of Charles's voice accentuated his truth. The callous shell he worked so hard to build cracked and broke.

He tried to put himself in Emma's place. How awful it must have been to see the wreckage of a man who was so vibrant and alive when he left for his second deployment. His brother was her first love and the father of her firstborn. Charles acknowledged to himself how his envy clouded his judgment. Yes, it was true; the night at the Greyhound made him question their life together. His hurt ego consumed him. If he thought with his mind instead of his heart, he knew she loved him, but shock and exhaustion threw her back in time. He wasted precious months with her because of pride. He let it go. He wanted her back.

Charles cradled Emma in his arms. "Dearest Emma, you are giving me another baby. I am so very happy. Maybe this time we'll add a little girl to the Head brood." Charles laughed.

"You may be right. I feel different this time. My sickness is worse. My eating habits are atrocious." Emma smiled.

"What do you mean?" Charles stroked her back.

"I am either ravenous or can't eat a thing."

Charles frowned. "Have you shared this with Alex?"

"No, he has so much on his plate managing Joseph's illness. He's trying experimental drugs that have worked in some respects, but he has to be careful of the side effects. With all of that, I don't want to bother him with silly pregnancy issues." Emma cuddled closer. It was indescribable feeling Charles hold her. She felt safe again. Then the invisible curtain dropped between them. Emma sat up. "Charles, you know I have to go back in the morning for my regular routine with Joseph."

"I am the one who brought Joseph home. I promise I'll become more involved with his health management. I have stayed away because every time I saw you, my heart broke a bit more."

"Our family must be the most complicated mess in all of Britain." Emma's eyes brimmed with tears.

"Be assured, Emma, war scars different families in different ways, but all are scarred. I'm a peaceful person, so the fighting over territories, minerals, and power seems pointless to me. The result is death, destruction, and devastation. Think of all the families that suffered when their loved ones were killed, maimed, or kidnapped like Joseph. Why can't we all live in harmony with each other and the land? I don't understand it." Charles shook his head. "Because of war, my brother's mind was relegated to a place where he dwells alone. His body is breaking down on a daily basis. Pointless." Charles kissed Emma tenderly. "A baby will breathe new life into our house, which is desperately needed."

Emma was physically and emotionally exhausted. She couldn't keep her eyes open one more minute. "Charles, my love . . ." She drifted off before finishing her thought. Charles stared at her for a long time. She was more beautiful at thirty than she was at nineteen, if that were possible. He believed her love for him was real, and she was giving him another child to bring laughter into their solemn house. Charles kissed her brow, turned over, and fell into a deep sleep.

Jenny and Nanny danced around the kitchen when it got to be past midnight and Charles didn't emerge from Emma's room. They both knew she was pregnant, but kept it a secret between them. She hid it very well with the clothing she chose, but they both heard her regurgitating at different times of the day. Since they ate most meals with her, it didn't go unnoticed that she either didn't eat or ate like a famished waif. Both of the women loved Emma and wanted her to be happy. Hopefully, Charles's long visit would end her misery and exile from his life. For the first time since Joseph's return, the women went to bed with hope for the future.

Emma awoke drenched in perspiration; she was lost in the mist again, only this time Charles was out of reach, not her mother. She looked at him sleeping in her bed. Could it be true that he really did love her and their lives would return to some sort of normalcy? What was normal? Living with two husbands in the same house? She was sure he did forgive her for now, but would his doubt resurface once he became more involved with Joseph? She questioned herself over and over. One thing was an absolute certainty: she would give birth to a new baby in about five months. She patted her belly and smiled. She lay back down next to Charles and curled around his body. He was warm and felt good against her nakedness. Emma draped her arm over his waist and kissed the back of his neck. Suddenly she felt the queasiness in her stomach. She bolted out of bed just in time to reach the bathroom. She vomited over and over until everything, even the bile, was out of her system.

"Emma." Charles knocked on the door. "Are you all right?"

She managed a weak yes, then opened the door.

God, Charles thought, she looks white as a ghost. "Come back to bed. I'm getting you a cup of tea and some dry toast." He tucked her in, then went to find Jenny.

Nanny fed the boys breakfast, and they were in the schoolroom doing their lessons. Jenny was sitting on the settee sewing a baby dress. She looked up and grinned from ear to ear. "Morning, sir."

Charles didn't exchange pleasantries but got right to the point. "Jenny, please get Emma a strong cup of tea and some dry toast. She's been vomiting, and I fear is quite faint."

A frown crossed Jenny's brow. "I don't know what she could have puked, sir. She refused her evening meal last night."

Dear Lord, Charles reprimanded himself, *I've caused her to be extremely ill with this pregnancy.* "Well, hopefully, Jenny, I can rectify her eating habits and offer her comfort. Now be a good girl and get the tea." Jenny went straight into the kitchen.

Charles sat on the bed next to Emma. She wasn't asleep. He spoke in a low soothing voice. "My darling, Jenny is brewing you some tea and a bit of toast. I want you to try to get it down." Emma started to protest, but Charles held up his hand. He read her mind. "You are not well enough to assist with Joseph's routine this morning, and I refuse to put you or the baby in any more jeopardy. I'll be with Joseph, and when he lies down to rest, I'll send Alex to look in on you." Emma didn't have the strength to argue. She felt really rotten, and resting sounded so inviting. She attempted a joke.

"Maybe the baby is sick this morning from the bumpy ride last night." She smiled at Charles.

He laughed. "You little vixen." He looked at Emma intently. She actually looked very poorly. "Listen, darling, I think we should remain in the nursery rooms until the baby comes. You are comfortable here, and moving all your things back to our rooms is just too much commotion. I can sleep here with you every night and simply dress in our rooms. Plus, I'll have more quality time with our three boys."

Emma didn't argue. She really couldn't move and rearrange during the pregnancy, but knowing Charles would be here with her and the children and sleep with her at night chased away her loneliness. "That would be perfect."

Charles entered Joseph's room, and as usual, his brother sat in a comfy chair staring into space. Alex looked surprised to see Charles. "I'm here in Emma's place today. She has wretched morning sickness that has left her weak and shaken. Tell me what your routine is with my brother, and I'll step in. Also, Alex, have a look in on Emma when Joseph lays down for his rest, please."

"Of course I will check on Emma, and it is kind of you to come, although it will disturb Joseph's routine. Hopefully his reaction won't be too severe." Alex explained the morning routine of grooming, conversation, and midmorning tea. "Conversation is of the utmost importance, but I'm afraid the conversation is locked in time. We speak as though the last decade didn't exist."

How odd, Charles thought. "Why is that, Alex?"

"It's simple; he has erased the time of his departure from Whitfield and his captivity. Somehow his brain cannot deal with the horrific deeds done by his captors. He has compartmentalized his life as a preservation mechanism. If he loses that ability, Charles, I fear he will descend into total madness."

Alex pushed his wire-rimmed spectacles up the bridge of his nose. They continually slipped down, which annoyed him greatly. "Changing the subject, I am worried about Emma. She's experienced such immense pressure, the stress has been debilitating. From my medical training, I learned carrying a child under such duress may have adverse affects throughout the pregnancy and birth." Alex looked concerned. "I am the one who insisted Emma be here every day so Joseph has a routine with the one person with whom he possesses such closeness. Then the few breakthroughs we've had with your brother are always directed at Emma. She is my medical partner really."

Charles silently chastised himself for being so oblivious to the everyday turmoil Emma endured. "Yes, it makes the situation so very difficult," Charles said. "Honestly, Alex, I think at least for a few days Emma needs a break, and I will take her place."

"Agreed. Thank you, Charles."

The first morning progressed without incident, as did the second, third, and fourth. Emma remained in the nursery resting and getting her appetite restored. Charles left for Joseph's rooms on the fifth day as usual. Emma felt rejuvenated but bored. "Jenny, I think I'll wander down to see Joseph for a little while."

"Do you think that wise without consulting Charles?" Jenny didn't want anything to bring on another breach between Emma and Charles.

"I think he'll be pleased, as it will give him a chance to check on the farm. He misses being out in the fields and with the sheep very much." Emma kissed Jenny on the cheek and left the nursery.

Emma opened the main door to Joseph's rooms. She heard Charles and Alex chatting about Whitfield. She smiled to herself. Alex was such a dedicated doctor. He helped Joseph and conducted research at the same time. He experimented with drugs she couldn't even pronounce. What neither she nor anyone knew was that his work would contribute to the discovery of penicillin in 1928.

His kindness toward Emma was genuine. He had examined her carefully and assured both her and Charles that the baby was fine. Every pregnancy was different, and this one was a particularly trying one.

"Good morning, Alex. Hello, Charles. I was bored and wanted to come for a little while. I thought you might like to check on the farm?" she asked sweetly.

Charles stood up. "Darling, do you think you should be up and about?"

"Yes, our dear doctor said I was just fine." She giggled and patted her tummy.

Chapter 48

Damages, Desire, Destruction

Emma turned her attention to Joseph. It was only four days since she'd seen him, but he looked more haggard. "Joseph, you are looking well today," she lied. "Would you like to have tea, bread and butter, and jam with me?"

He made eye contact, squeezed his eyes shut, then blinked several times. "What did you ask, Emma?"

The room swayed under her feet. She looked at Alex and Charles. They nodded.

"I asked if we should order midmorning tea." Emma's voice cracked.

Joseph laughed. "Yes, we should. I am particularly famished." He looked at Charles. "Well, little brother, do you and your friend have time for tea with Emma and me?"

It was a replica of the day he became alert when Claudine was with her. He wanted to eat and drink. Somewhere deep in his subconscious, hunger lurked. Emma tried to imagine what starvation was like. She could ring for food anytime night or day. It heightened her awareness of the perils in the world and the despicable aspects of war.

Charles's eyes were wide; he tried to hide his amazement. "Of course, that would be great. I'll order it for us." He stepped out into the hallway to compose himself, then rang for tea.

"Come here, Emma, and sit by me. I want to give our baby a pat." Joseph winked.

Emma moved across the room in a trance. His voice sounded strong. He pulled her on his lap. He felt like a skeleton through the material of her dress. Joseph smiled and rubbed his hand over her belly. He whispered in her ear, "I'd like to rub my hand between your legs, but we have guests." His throaty laughter filled the room.

Charles felt physically ill, repulsed, and heartbroken all in the same instant when he walked back in the room and saw Emma sitting on Joseph's lap with his one arm around her waist and the other on her stomach. His chest hurt; he could hardly breathe. Emma's eyes looked imploringly at Charles. He felt awful for her. Joseph noticed none of the unspoken despair between his brother and Emma.

Joseph kissed the back of her neck. "My sweet wife gets heavier and heavier as the baby grows, but she is still the most beautiful girl in the world." Joseph laughed.

Emma jumped up. "We don't want to crush you." She managed a weak smile.

"Are you all right, darling? I'm joking." Joseph was concerned. Emma usually wasn't so sensitive. He attributed her mood to the pregnancy. He wouldn't hurt her feelings for all the gold in America.

"Yes, yes, I'm fine, Joseph."

"Why don't you get in our bed, and when the tea arrives, I'll bring you a cup?" Joseph's concern was real. Emma was pale, he'd noticed.

Emma didn't know how much more of this living hell she could take. She felt sick. Joseph thought she was carrying his baby, the baby she gave birth to in 1878, not the baby she carried in 1889. Fate played cruel tricks; this baby was his brother's. She fought to keep the tears back, but they came against her will.

Joseph stood up. "Charles, why don't you and your friend have tea in the morning room? As you can see, Emma is unwell."

Charles hesitated; what in the hell was he supposed to do now? Leave his wife here with his crazy brother? Play along with the charade? He looked to Alex for guidance.

Alex stepped in. "Sir, I am a doctor. We have met before, but regrettably you have forgotten. I'll stay in case, uh, your wife, um, needs medical attention."

Cool, calm, rational Commodore Head answered him. "I apologize for my memory, but my concern is for my wife. I will be most grateful if you will stay, Dr., Dr. . . . ?"

"It's Dr. Blain, sir, but please call me Alex. Shall I help you get her to bed?" Alex silently prayed the answer was yes.

"Absolutely not," Joseph said in his most decisive voice. "As a physician, you know how delicate the ladies are in this condition. I'll return shortly." Joseph cupped Emma's elbow; she shuddered, just like the first night at La Mansion. He guided her to the bedroom.

He shut the door and gave her such a tender look it ripped her broken heart, which broke all over again. "Come, my love, let's get you undressed and into bed."

Oh, my God, I have no nightgown in here. If he goes to the bureau drawer to get one and all my clothes are gone, he'll know something's wrong. It could be the thing that pushes him over the edge. She hurriedly spoke. "Joseph, I don't feel like changing. This is a light cotton dress. I am going to slip into bed as I am." She held her breath, hoping he would agree.

He pulled back the coverlet and helped her to the bed. She lay down and he covered her up. He sat on the edge of the bed. "Emma, are you sure you are all right? You are so pale, and I feel your body shaking." He brushed the tendrils back from her face. "Move over, darling; let me hold you."

Before she could protest or feign illness, he was in bed next to her. She shivered. He interpreted it as a yes. Joseph pulled her to him and stroked her hair, all the while crooning comforting words in her ear. He traced the outline of her breasts with his finger, just like he had always done. He put his hand underneath the bodice of her dress and rubbed her nipples. Emma silently begged God to keep her from responding. Her husband, the father of the baby growing inside her womb, was in the next room! "Joseph, I really don't feel well."

"Shush, Emma, I hold the power to make you feel better." He smiled his sensual smile that never failed to arouse her. He locked eyes with hers, then kissed her like a starved animal. He remembered all the right things to do. His tongue was in her ear, then he kissed the hollow of her throat. Her body betrayed her while her mind struggled. She closed her eyes, and his hand was between her legs. He pulled her pantaloons down and felt the wetness that told him she wanted him right now. Joseph didn't understand why, but he wasn't hard. This had never happened to him before. He thought subconsciously her condition was too delicate, and that made him stay soft. He knew every inch of her body and how to bring her to cosmic orgasm. This time he didn't want his needs met. His desire was to fulfill his wife.

Joseph whispered in her ear, "Just lay there, my darling, I am going to make you so happy you and the baby will be lost in contented slumber." He rubbed the spot that ached for him.

Emma fought a battle in her mind. Her intellect was slipping away as her lust escalated. She should stop the way he manipulated her body, but she was weak. She started to move against him, and he rubbed her harder. He stopped to tantalize her. He didn't want her to climax too soon. Joseph kissed her rounded belly and spoke words of love to the baby. He spread her legs and kissed the inside of her thighs. She couldn't stop him, didn't want to stop him. His tongue found its way inside her. At that moment, time stopped. Emma moved her hips up and down. Joseph's tongue was in and out, licking her, probing her inside. He felt she was ready to let go. He flicked his tongue until the last moment, then plunged his fingers inside her and led her over the brink. She came in a hot rush. Her beautiful, brilliant commodore was alive.

She started crying and couldn't stop. She was choking on her sobs. Her mind was ablaze with condemnation. "Joseph, Joseph." He didn't respond. His hand rested on her left thigh, but it was still. She lifted up on one elbow. His head was on the pillow, his mouth slack, his breathing even, his eyes closed. Emma shook him by the shoulder, "Joseph, say something; you're frightening me." He turned his head and looked at her with a blank stare.

"For God's sake, man, what can they be doing in there? It's been almost an hour." Charles was ready to jump out of his skin.

"Charles, don't worry about your brother molesting, I mean taking advantage of Emma. His illness has made him impotent." Alex spoke with authority.

"I'm not concerned about that. My brother would never force a woman." Charles was indignant. "I'm worried about Emma. She clearly wasn't well and has vomited for days. My poor wife must be placating him in some way to keep him lucid, but I swear, Alex, if that door does not open in the next ten minutes, I am going in."

Emma lay very still. Joseph, or what was left of him, still aroused her and satisfied her lustful nature. She was ashamed of her betrayal once again. The desire that bubbled up throughout her whole body took on a life of its own. She tried not to respond, but she was powerless. She had no control at all. The nineteen-year-old girl was exhilarated by his magic touch, like that first night in the alleyway. Emma pictured clearly making love at Chateau Philippe. In his private quarters, he taught her the seductive nuances of sexuality. Any shyness or inhibitions she harbored, Joseph erased. She was completely natural with him, as she was today.

His muddled mind still knew the ways to arouse and satisfy her. She had to hide her infidelity, or Charles would leave her forever. She pulled up her undergarments and arranged her dress bodice. She inched her way over to the other side of the huge bed so as not to disturb Joseph. He was asleep. She lay perfectly still. Charles was an open book to her, and she bet he would enter the room shortly. She had no idea how long Joseph made love to her or how long they were in bed. She turned on her side facing away from Joseph; she inched closer to the edge of the massive bed, closing her eyes on the past again. Emotionally and physically she was drained; she drifted off into a light sleep.

Emma heard the door opening, but it seemed a long way away. Her eyes wouldn't open; she was exhausted. Charles gently shook her shoulder. It was difficult, but she opened her eyes. Her husband was kneeling by the side of the bed.

His voice was pained. "Emma, my darling, are you all right? I should never have allowed Joseph to bring you in here."

Emma's lies flowed from a deep well of deceit and shame. "I'm fine, Charles, honestly." She spoke quietly. "Joseph told me to undress, but because my clothes are not here, I said I was too tired and wanted to sleep in my dress. I'm afraid it's all rumpled now." *God, what am I rattling about?*

"Sweetheart, don't worry about the dress as long as you are all right."

"He pulled down the coverlet, and I got into bed. I felt so lousy, Charles, I must have fallen asleep immediately." More lies; she could not let her marriage be destroyed.

"Joseph got in bed with you," Charles said. His eyes were full of pain.

"Oh, I didn't know." She rolled to her right. "He must have slipped in after I fell asleep." One lie tumbled out after another. Emma sighed. "Charles, may we go back to the nursery kitchen and eat a meal, please?" She didn't have the strength to keep up the façade much longer.

"Of course we can." Charles wanted her out of his brother's bed and back at the nursery as quickly as possible.

"Then I want a long hot bath, clean nightgown, and into bed." Emma let out a sigh of resignation.

"You deserve it after being put through all of this." Charles gestured around the room.

Emma bolted upright. "Dear Jesus, is his disease contagious? What about my baby?" She was shrieking.

Alex ran in the bedroom around to her side of the bed and coaxed her out and into the parlor.

"Joseph is what we researchers call in the tertiary phase of syphilis. When it reaches this point, it is not contagious or dangerous to others, but fatal for the victim of the scourge. A patient can be in this stage from one to five years. It depends on the individual."

Charles stared at Alex for a long time. "One to five years; I had no idea. I thought my brother was close to death."

Emma was hysterical. "One to five years. Are you in your right mind? I can't come to these rooms day after day for years. I have a baby coming, and soon. My routine will be centered around the baby, don't you understand?" She screamed at Alex and Charles.

"Calm down, Emma," Alex said. "No one expects you to dedicate your life to Joseph. What you've done to get him comfortable and into a routine is more than anyone could expect. He's been fine with Charles every morning. As he gets more and more accustomed to the family members, he will become more and more adaptable."

"What about these moments of living in the past? I have agreed to the charade because you, Dr. Blain, have said it helps him. Do you know it helps him, or are you guessing?" Emma was direct with her questions for Alex.

"Charles, Emma, please sit down and let me explain the details of Joseph's condition. It is extremely complicated, but I will tell you in laymen's terms." Alex decided he should put all the information on the table since the situation had come to a head. "Joseph actually suffers from a primary illness that presents itself as syphilis that is transmitted sexually. The disease progresses through stages. Usually, during the primary phase, a lesion or chancre erupts, but it's not painful and it goes away in three to six weeks. Most patients I have studied thought the lesion was a boil. The second phase is very unpleasant. The patient develops sores in various places—the hands, trunk, or private parts. It abates and goes away as well. The patient attributes this phase to allergic reaction to something as innocuous as poison ivy or food allergy. Then the disease can lay dormant. We just don't know. The last and most vicious occurrence is the tertiary phase. Dr. Stewart and his colleagues hypothesized Joseph is in this stage, which means he is no longer contagious. Since Joseph's neurological centers have obviously been under attack, the most logical diagnosis was final stage of syphilis. Unfortunately there are no medical tests I can employ to give me definitive answers." Alex paused. "Do you have any questions thus far?" He looked at both Charles and Emma. Each shook their heads no.

"Charles, when you and I agreed I would come on as your brother's personal doctor, we also made another agreement: I could study the progression of his disease."

"That's exactly true." Charles wondered where this was going. He wouldn't go back on his word if that worried Alex.

"I have several journals full of my observations and drug experimentation. I am sure Dr. Stewart was incorrect in his diagnosis." Alex paused again.

"What in the hell are you talking about, man? Spit it out." Charles was getting annoyed. For God's sake, he needed to tend to Emma.

"Uh, this is complicated, and I don't have a name for it, but I am sure Joseph is suffering from prolonged exposure to trauma because of his entrapment, or captivity if you will. I am convinced he has amnesia." Alex drew in a breath.

"What is that, Alex, something even worse?" Emma didn't understand any of this.

"It's not worse, but complicated. His mind is so damaged from torture or injury, there are alterations in his consciousness. He has repressed the memory of the horror through a psychological defense mechanism. His long-term memory has been obliterated; that is why when he has moments of clarity, they are from a decade ago. The psyche enlists whatever is necessary to protect the mind."

Charles interrupted Alex's stunning revelation. "Why in the hell would Dr. Stewart diagnose Joseph with a sexually transmitted disease as wretched as syphilis?"

"Charles, I am sure Dr. Stewart examined Joseph and drew conclusions from several sources. He was brought in with his friend Percy, who definitely has the disease, as you saw with your own eyes. Prostitutes brought both men into St. Cadoc's. Human nature leads men to draw certain conclusions from the company they keep." Alex paused and pushed his glasses back up his nose.

"His physical examination exhibited scars on his trunk the doctors surmised came from sores, along with torture tactics. The most specific indication was his mental state, which presented itself exactly like general paralysis of the insane. Until the day Joseph saw Emma in the hospital, he never focused or spoke. This is why my research is so important. As a profession, we are in the infancy of proper diagnosis and treatment. More research is needed. I give you my word, when I came to Whitfield, I was certain Joseph suffered from syphilis, but his breakthroughs are just not consistent with the disease. It's taken me hours of poring over medical journals and observing Joseph to reach this conclusion."

"Are you sure?" Charles asked.

"I am not sure of anything. I am learning and studying as I treat your brother." Alex massaged his temples.

Charles asked the most difficult question. "Is he dying?"

"From his physical condition, although it has improved, all indications are yes. Malnutrition damages vital organs beyond repair. How long it takes for them to become nonfunctioning can't be determined. It varies from person to person." Alex was frustrated he couldn't give Charles definitive answers. He shook his head.

Chapter 49

Illness Invades Whitfield

Emma sat in stunned silence. What was she to do if Alex's findings were correct? She had totally succumbed to the Joseph of old. His physical power over her was still intact. The husband she sat next to, she loved but deceived. She carried a baby both men claimed as their own. This purgatory could not go on year after year or she would go insane.

Was she being punished for her sins? She wantonly lost her maidenhead to Joseph before marriage, engaging in carnal pleasure over and over. She gave birth to Joseph's son and allowed the child to believe Charles was his father. She had sex regularly with Charles before their marriage. She had Joseph declared dead, for God's sake. There was no atonement for her. No one gave in to the devil that much and lived unscathed. Now she was having another baby conceived on a night she lusted after Joseph but had sex with Charles. Her actions were despicable. She wanted to scream for forgiveness, but no screams came because she feared her next sin, and the next and the next. Charles and Alex were talking, but she didn't listen. What they said made no difference. She was like Joseph, trapped.

A new routine was carved out for Joseph in the months that followed Dr. Alex Blain's new diagnosis. Far, far in the future, it would be called posttraumatic stress syndrome, but for those living at Whitfield, it had no name, though it lived in Joseph. Catherine, Charles, and David divided up the morning routine.

Emma was too ill and aloof to help Joseph. She hadn't returned to his rooms since the day he made love to her. Joseph's mind did not allow him to resurface either. They were both locked away in their own personal torment. Emma despised everything about herself, and her depression darkened the closer she got to term.

Emma stopped making love to Charles as well. After she betrayed him with Joseph, she rebuffed his attempts by saying she was sick. Literally she was sick. Her appetite fluctuated between nonexistent and gluttonous. When she gorged herself with sweets, cakes, puddings, and biscuits, she regurgitated every mouthful of food that passed her lips. When she starved herself, she vomited acidic green bile. Everything in her life was out of balance.

Alex got on her nerves. He and Claudine were openly courting. Her sister moved into Whitfield on a permanent basis. Emma couldn't confide in her because she was afraid Claudine would tell Alex. She hated it when he tried to tell her what to eat and how much. Edgar and Maria came over for a long visit, but they found their daughter to be sullen and unsociable. They attributed her behavior to the difficult pregnancy. They took the boys back to Calais, which gave Emma some relief from her guilt. She didn't have the patience to deal with the lads. Mostly they avoided her so they wouldn't be reprimanded for every little thing. At age eleven, JD was beyond his years, and he corralled his younger brothers when they got rambunctious around their mummy, but it wasn't enough for Emma.

Her self-imposed exile was a breeding ground for her inadequacies to multiply. The family noticed the drastic change in her countenance, but didn't have solutions to draw her out of the mire. Jenny tried to reach her precious Emma through kindness; when that failed, she would scold her like a child. None of it worked. Emma was totally removed and indifferent.

In the last month of her pregnancy, Emma's immune system was so depleted she caught a cold. Her body didn't have enough sustenance to fight it off. One moment she was shivering cold, and Charles piled blankets on her. The next she was burning up, and he wiped her down with cool cloths. Emma's fever got so high she was delirious. Whitfield stood still. The only soul oblivious to the drama unfolding in the nursery was Joseph.

Alex went to the apothecary in Dover and bought every elixir and medicinal compound used for colds and fever. Nothing helped. He examined her daily, but there was no improvement; instead, she got worse. He was the one who told the family she had developed pneumonia and the outcome looked bleak. He experimented with new poultices and remedies, but it was futile.

Annabelle and Richard came over from Paris. Edgar, Maria, and the children returned from Calais. Charles did not leave Emma's side. Day and night he stood watch over her. When he couldn't go any longer, he lay on the floor next to the bed and slept a few hours.

Chapter 50

When the Mist Lifts

Emma saw figures through the mist, but wasn't sure who they were. She was finally happy again. The mist swirled around her, the figures indiscernible. She tried so hard to reach them. They were just beyond her grasp. Her lovely smile lit up the room, but her breathing was so shallow it wasn't reaching her lungs.

Charles shouted at Jenny, "Get Dr. Blain now. Hurry before it's too late."

Jenny ran down the long hallway screaming, "Dr. Blain, Dr. Blain, come quick, come quick." Jenny panted. He bolted after her, leaving the main door to Joseph's wing open wide.

Emma didn't hear any of the commotion. She was light and airy, full of joy. The wildflowers were in bloom at Whitfield; their kaleidoscope of colors amazed her every year. She meandered through the fields to the village, waving at the people whose roots grew from centuries past. She walked into old St. Peter's Church. It was chilly; she shivered. She sat down in her favorite pew. The sun sparkled through the thirteenth-century stained glass windows, throwing prisms of light throughout the little church. How could she be so cold when the sun shone through? It didn't matter; she felt safe.

Alex barged into Emma's room. Tears streamed down Charles's face. His voice was panic-stricken. "I'm losing her; she's slipping away. I beg you, Alex, save her. I will never ask for another thing, as God is my witness, if you will just save her."

Nanny bounded down the great staircase yelling at the top of her lungs, "It's Emma, it's Emma, hurry, hurry, hurry." The word spread through the huge manor like a rolling tide. Claudine ran from her office. Catherine and David dashed out of the family parlor. The servants roused Edgar and Maria from the guest wing. The boys were in the nursery schoolroom frozen to their chairs, afraid of the commotion they heard.

Emma wondered for a moment why so many people were in the church. Was it Sunday? She thought she saw Jenny, which was odd. Jenny usually sat at the back of the church so she could leave after communion before the closing prayer. Emma couldn't help but laugh.

The boys looked so sweet in their little coats and trousers. She loved them so much. They were such good little lads. She told JD to straighten his tie. He reminded her so much of his father.

Charles had his ear to Emma's lips, but he couldn't understand what she was saying. Her voice was a soft whisper.

"God, Alex, do something," Charles pleaded.

Emma heard the clop-clop of the horses' hooves outside the church. The sound was not ominous as in recent years, but beckoning. The carriage was here to take her home. She smiled. She pushed open the massive oak door. She stepped outside the church. The sun crept behind a blanket of clouds. The mist spun around her ankles and drifted up to her waist. The carriage waited in the distance. Joseph stood with the door open. He wore his dress uniform decorated with all his medals. His blond hair blew in the spring air. It brought another smile to her lips. Charles was there with his brother, so ruggedly handsome and tenderhearted. She felt an overwhelming love for both of them. Suddenly, the sun peeked through the floating clouds and the mist dissolved. The carriage wasn't so far away. She wanted to let them know she was coming. She whispered, "Joseph, Charles . . ."

Alex pushed Charles out of the way. He saw immediately she wasn't breathing. He put his head to her chest, but no beating heart responded. He pumped her chest over and over, but the effort was futile. He hung his head. "I am so sorry; she's gone."

A booming voice from the doorway called out, "What is wrong with Emma?" Joseph appeared, paralyzed with fear. Catherine went to him. "Joseph, she is ill." Catherine cleared her throat nervously. Joseph's eyes bulged; he knew his wife was dead.

He threw himself across the bottom of the bed. "Take me with you. I can't live without you, please, Emma, please." He choked on his tears. What, in the name of God, had they done to his wife?

The whole scene was unreal. Charles couldn't believe it—his wife and his baby. Gone, gone in an instant. A wild notion infiltrated his mind. Was there a chance for the baby? His eyes widened with horror. "Alex, could the baby be alive?"

"I don't know, Charles." Alex was familiar with a Caesarean operation that was performed on dying or dead pregnant women, but the success rate was minimal.

"There's an operation; I've heard of it." Charles was frantic. "I want you to do it now; the baby could still be alive." Charles shouted at Alex with a desperate edge to his voice that sent chills through everyone in the room.

Charles took charge. "Nanny, go into the nursery kitchen and boil as many pots of water as you can. Mother, tell Phoebe to have the staff boil water in the main scullery. Have one of the maids bring up bundles of fresh linens. Father, go to Joseph's rooms and get Alex's surgical tools and medical bag; they're in the clinic. Jenny, you can weep afterward; right now help Dr. Blain with whatever he needs. Claudine, go to the stable and have one of the lads take the carriage and fetch the priest." Charles's adrenaline motivated his every move.

Alex scrubbed his hands and arms in the bathroom with antiseptic soap kept in the cupboard for the children's cuts and scrapes. He was keenly aware from his studies that many women died from infection during the operation because the surgeon passed on bacteria from unclean hands. He didn't have that concern because the mother was dead, but the baby could contract sepsis from the placenta. He looked at the clock on the nursery wall. It seemed like hours had passed since Emma's last breath, but in fact, it was mere minutes. There was hope, although slim. He heard clanging in the kitchen. Charles threw every surgical instrument into a large pot of boiling water. Time was of the essence.

A guttural howling came from the bottom of Emma's bed. Joseph gathered all his strength and yelped, "What have you done to my wife?" His eyes were wild, and his nostrils flared. His entire body was shaking, on the verge of convulsions.

"Alex, we cannot deal with Joseph now. Do you understand me? No matter what the consequence to him, I want the chance to save my baby." Charles was firm and deliberate.

"Father, you and the male servants take Joseph to his room and restrain him." David was distraught. "Do you hear me? Now. Move now." David listened to his son. David, Edgar, Harvey and Vance carried Joseph from the nursery. It was terrible. Joseph bellowed and screamed incessantly; finally the doors of his wing closed behind him, and they could no longer hear his cries of anguish.

Alex cleared the room except for himself, Charles, and Nanny. She was a practical woman who lived with the family since wet-nursing JD. She was the most suitable assistant available. Charles gently lifted his lifeless wife from the bed. He kissed her forehead and whispered in her ear while Nanny pulled off the sweat-ridden coverlet and threw down clean linens. Charles carefully laid Emma back on the bed. He groaned; she was still so warm. Nanny silently removed her wet clothes.

Alex went to work quickly. He made a low incision on the abdomen above the pelvic bone. He cut through the thin layer of skin, fat, and muscle. He and Charles pulled back the flesh. Alex made a swift incision in the uterus. He pulled out the baby. Nanny wiped it down with warm cloths while Alex cut the umbilical cord and cauterized it. Alex suctioned the baby's mouth. The tiny little infant was blue. Alex held its body upside down and patted its tiny bottom. Each moment crawled by. Charles felt hope slipping away. A cry filled the room! The baby lived!

Alex was crying uncontrollably. His hands shook like leaves. Nanny took the baby, swaddled it with clean linen, and handed it to Charles.

"Take your daughter, Sir Charles." Nanny placed the baby in his arms.

Charles looked at his baby girl with wonder, grief, heartache, and joy, the emotions tangled, intertwined together, but he loved her the minute she was in his arms. He looked at Alex, the doctor, the surgeon, the brilliant innovator and medical pioneer. Charles swallowed his words. Tears streamed down his face. He was finally able to say, "I will call her Alexandria Emma."

Alex was overwhelmed with the honor, but he was physically exhausted. Emma was dead. He tried to save her to no avail. The pneumonia invaded her body and suppressed her breath until no oxygen could reach her lungs. He delivered a baby from the womb of her dead body, and in this great manor, his first-priority patient was tethered, restrained. Alex wondered if Joseph had retreated back to his world.

"Charles, I am honored. I think I should get your mother to sit with you until the priest arrives. I must return to Joseph."

Charles smiled weakly. "You are an amazing doctor, Alex. I don't understand how you were able to do all you have done this evening, losing Emma, then bringing a new life into this world. How will I ever thank you?"

"You can thank me, Charles, by agreeing I can go to Joseph." Alex's voice cracked.

God, Charles thought, *the man has to be drained.* "Of course, Alex, is there anything I should know about caring for the baby?"

For the first time, Alex laughed. "I think Nanny and Jenny have that mastered."

Alex was leaving the nursery when the priest from St. Peter's arrived. "Father, I ask that you bless Emma's body and bless the new baby girl." He was heavy with emotion, which almost got out of his control. Alex took a breath. "Father, I ask for your prayers as I deal with Joseph." The priest nodded and made the sign of the cross on Alex's forehead.

Alex opened the main door to Joseph's rooms. His patient was in his bedroom, restrained with strips of linen to the bedposts. Joseph was fully present. Alex dismissed the servants but encouraged David to stay, as Alex had no idea what to expect.

Joseph's eyes blazed with hatred when he looked at Alex. "I do not know who you are, but you must be some demonic spirit who has taken over my house, my parents, and my wife." Joseph's demeanor was combative.

"Joseph, I am your personal doctor, who has lived with you for a year as you are extremely ill." Alex felt sick. He just took a living baby from a dead body, endured complicated family dynamics, and treated a patient who teetered between sanity and madness.

"I see." Joseph's voice dripped with sarcasm. "Now, please release me from these restraints."

"Yes, Joseph, of course." Alex cut the restraints from the bedposts. Joseph rubbed his wrists. It took all his energy, but he stood up. The brilliant commodore emerged. "May I ask, what has befallen my wife that I was not privy to knowing?"

"There is much to tell." Alex was hedging.

He grabbed Alex's arms. "Damn it, man, have you no honor, no pity? I saw my wife dead, or am I dreaming?"

David stepped in. "Son, so much has happened in the last ten years."

Oh, God, Alex was sabotaged. He had no intention of telling Joseph ten years had passed. His gut knotted.

"Father, what are you talking about, the last ten years? I am confused. Emma and I are expecting a baby, are well and happy here at Whitfield, but Father, it's only been less than a year, not ten." Joseph wondered if his father were experiencing early senility.

David plunged in. "Joseph, you were captured by the Russians over ten years ago and only recently returned to us."

"I don't mean to be rude, Father, but didn't you see my Emma and I are expecting a child?" What the hell was his father talking about? *Maybe I am delusional; didn't I see minutes ago Emma dead, yet with child?*

"Joseph, Joseph, so much has happened." David cringed, trying to explain.

The conversation sent Joseph slipping back and forth between reality and his world. He was agitated. Alex knew a sedative would make him sleep, and if he were present the next day, truth would prevail. "Joseph, may I get you a brandy?"

"Yes, that would be helpful." Sarcasm spewed from his lips. Alex handed him the brandy, and Joseph downed it in two gulps. Alex and David were able to get him to bed with no objection. The drug Alex put in the brandy was strong; hopefully Joseph would sleep for at least eight hours.

Whitfield, the happy manor and manor house, were encased in black darkness. All in the village were told Emma Bouron Head was dead, but her baby girl lived. Alexandria Head remarkably was a healthy baby girl, fighting for life. Some in the village thought it was magic; others attributed her life to God's will. But all were thrilled the baby lived. Yet all mourned the death of the vibrant future duchess who loved them and loved life. Again, life handed out the unexpected.

The puzzle of life, pieces fit together without intention or direction, that was the story of Joseph, Emma, and Charles.

Emma was finally free of her self-loathing for sins both real and imagined. Joseph was released from his tortured mind and ravaged body by jumping from the top turret where he and Charles played as children and he and Emma made love as adults. Charles doted on his baby daughter to fill the void left by his dead wife.

The one most affected by the deaths of Joseph and Emma was their son, Joseph David Adolphus Head. Jenny was so distraught she didn't see JD creep out from his nursery schoolroom the day of his mother's death. He hid behind the heavy curtains of the windows in her bedroom. He trembled as he witnessed his father grieve for his mother and his mentally ill uncle bellow gibberish. He watched Dr. Blain cut his baby sister out of his dead mother. He experienced tragedy no child should know. At age eleven, he was changed forever. The events cast his fate without his knowledge or awareness.

Epilogue

If I sit very still, I am able to hear the lilting musical notes of a funeral dirge. Emma is laid to rest in the earth of my ancestors. Her great-granddaughter mourns her death. She was young, beautiful, and vibrant, yet flawed. Her childhood was obliterated by inadvertent neglect, which led to a lifetime of uncertainty and instability. A mother suffering from depression mottled Emma's core.

The legacy left by Joseph and Emma would infiltrate the lives and permeate the souls of future generations.

As I look back at their lives, the parallels of this generation are reflections from a nineteenth-century mirror. Emma longed for a solid foundation, as do I. Unfortunately; quicksand has a stronger composition than any foundation in this family.

A son, Joseph David, deceived by his parents, is driven by greed and self-gratification. His son, Joseph Royston, crosses the Atlantic Ocean to America with his young family, but the burdens of ancestry cling like barnacles to a ship's bottom.

All of their stories are as poignant as Joseph and Emma's; they simply happen at a different time and place. Centuries change, people change, but the one constant—quicksand—never changes; it continues to pull and tug at each of us, generation after generation.

About the Author

THE AUTHOR, VICTORIA THOMAS, HAS a bachelor of science in education degree from Northeast Missouri State University, Kirksville, Missouri, and a master's degree in educational leadership from Texas A & M, Corpus Christi, Texas. She furthered her education by receiving a principal certification and a superintendent certification, both from Texas A & M, Corpus Christi. She has taught English, history, philosophy, and economics to high school students in both Missouri and Texas. After leaving the classroom in 1993, she held positions as director of curriculum and the last fifteen years as assistant superintendent of schools. Victoria has written articles for the Texas Education Agency, the Texas State Historical Commission, and the Texas State Board of Education.

Victoria emigrated to the United States with her parents and two sisters from Newport, Wales. She became an American citizen in 1977. The story she tells through a trilogy is loosely based on actual events and individuals from her own family.

Today, Victoria lives at the Lake of the Ozarks, Missouri. She also divides time between Austin and Rockport, Texas, to visit her three daughters and granddaughter.

About the Book

Quicksand: A Family Foundation begins a family saga in the early 1800s that stretches across France, England, Wales, and eventually America. Deceit, lies, secrets, and character flaws weave their way into the lives of each family member and corrupt the quest for a solid foundation.

Joseph and Emma experience love at first sight. He awakens in her dormant lust and unquenchable desire, but their love story is besieged by powerful circumstances beyond her control and his dedication to England and the British Royal Navy. What starts as a romantic journey ends in tragedy.

Fate deals the couple a disastrous blow, and the irony that follows is so twisted that the next generations suffer the consequences.

Lightning Source UK Ltd.
Milton Keynes UK
UKOW03n0733300514

232587UK00002B/12/P